THE THIRD REALM

Also by Karl Ove Knausgaard

A Time for Everything

MY STRUGGLE
A Death in the Family
A Man in Love
Boyhood Island
Dancing in the Dark
Some Rain Must Fall
The End

Home and Away: Writing the Beautiful Game (with Fredrik Ekelund)

SEASONS QUARTET
Autumn (with illustrations by Vanessa Baird)
Winter (with illustrations by Lars Lerin)
Spring (with illustrations by Anna Bjerger)
Summer (with illustrations by Anselm Kiefer)

So Much Longing in So Little Space: The Art of Edvard Munch
In the Land of the Cyclops: Essays

MORNING STAR
The Morning Star
The Wolves of Eternity

THE THIRD REALM

KARL OVE KNAUSGAARD

Translated from the Norwegian by Martin Aitken

Harvill *Secker*

LONDON

1 3 5 7 9 10 8 6 4 2

Harvill Secker, an imprint of Vintage, is part of the Penguin Random House group of companies whose addresses can be found at global.penguinrandomhouse.com

First published by Harvill Secker in 2024
First published with the title *Det tredje riket*
by Forlaget Oktober, Oslo in 2022

This translation has been published with the financial support of NORLA

penguin.co.uk/vintage

Typeset in 10/15 pt Swift LT Std by Jouve (UK), Milton Keynes
Printed and bound in Great Britain by Clays Ltd, Elcograf S.p.A.

The authorised representative in the EEA is Penguin Random House Ireland, Morrison Chambers, 32 Nassau Street, Dublin D02 YH68

A CIP catalogue record for this book is available from the British Library

HB ISBN 9781787304185
TPB ISBN 9781787304192

Penguin Random House is committed to a sustainable future for our business, our readers and our planet. This book is made from Forest Stewardship Council® certified paper.

To Michal

There is no God where I am.

TOVE

They say that depression is congealed anger. I think of it as a petrified troll. A creature of darkness and the incomplete – irate, dangerous – transformed by daylight into something unmoving and lifeless.

I think of mania as similar to forgetting yourself, the way you might forget a saucepan on a hot stove.

The psychosis occurs when the mania exhausts itself, when the encounter with reality is the only thing left for it (and mania fears reality more than anything else). The psychosis is like one of the three doors in the folk tales, the one that must never be opened no matter what. It mustn't be opened. Everyone knows. And yet it always gets opened in the end. When faced with nothing and something, you choose something first.

The folk tales.

The trolls, the three doors, the forest. The one where the animals can talk, and people turn into animals. The one with witches, crofters, kings, underground halls, tree stumps, princesses no one can spellbind, stepmothers and poor women, mountain pastures and rugged blue peaks.

Even as a small girl I sensed that the folk tales were concealing something. And that their secrets were significant. Later I would read Jung and his theory of archetypes and the collective unconscious, but *that* wasn't what I'd sensed was present in the tales, it was something else. What I took from Jung was that I was the Magician and Arne the Orphan (even though his relationship with his father, right until his father died, had been a happy one, and even though he continued to enjoy a happy relationship with his mother), as well as an understanding of the universality and power of symbols. Apart from that, nothing.

The Magician is the one who transforms. The Magician is a revolutionary. The Orphan is the one who needs. The Orphan is a manipulator.

Hell isn't the psychosis. Hell is leaving the psychosis. Hell on earth is what that is. Nothing of what you've thought, seen or felt has been true. And you've thought, seen and felt with your entire being. But that's not all. Now suddenly they're staring at you, your husband and kids. Imploringly or angrily, I'm not sure which is worse.

That's when the tears come. The bottomless grief.

Over what?

My self, my inadequacy.

Nobody wants a mad mother. Nobody wants to be one either.

'Are you normal now?' Heming once asked when they came to visit me.

What could I do but nod and cry and hold his reluctant body tightly to my own?

We arrived at the summer house late in the evening, having driven all day. Heming, Asle and Ingvild on the back seat, more or less paralysed by the monotony. Arne, whose excitement had risen during the last part of the journey, the landscape becoming more and more familiar to him, switched off the engine and turned beaming to the kids.

'Eight hours and two minutes,' he said. 'Thirteen minutes up on last year!'

'Well done,' said Ingvild, smiling back.

The twins didn't react.

'Everyone take their own things inside with them,' Arne said. 'And do it now so it's done. Ingvild, you bring the cat in, will you?'

'The child lock's on,' said Heming.

'Yes, yes, all right,' said Arne. 'There, it's off now.'

I looked at Ingvild and our eyes came together. She smiled at me the same way she'd smiled at Arne, lifted the cat carrier from her lap, put it down on the seat next to her and undid her seat belt, as the boys clambered out the other side.

She was too obliging.

'It's all right to get annoyed, you know,' I said.

'Yes,' she said, and smiled again. But this time there was a flicker of something darker in her eyes. She had it in her, a lot of it.

Did she even realise?

I got my cigarettes and lighter from the glove compartment and lit one while still standing beside the car. The others disappeared round the corner of the house lugging their rucksacks and suitcases.

The air smelled of the sea. It rushed in the bay. Cautious and consistent, as if someone lay sleeping down there.

Shhhh – shh. Shhhh – shh.

The sky grey-white. The grass grey-black. The trees and bushes black.

The outside light came on and coloured the grass unnaturally green.

'Nice to have a smoke, I imagine,' Arne said, coming back out to fetch some more things from the car.

'It is, yes,' I said. 'Do you want one?'

'Ha ha,' he said, wriggling into a heavy rucksack before picking up the carrier bags of food we'd bought at the supermarket below the bridge and going off round the corner again.

The neighbours with the Rottweilers were here – the lights were on in their house behind me.

No doubt everyone was here, now that the summer holidays had started.

I dropped my cigarette end onto the gravel and grabbed a suitcase to take in with me, and met Arne on his way back. He bobbed his head a couple of times, the way he did when listening to music he liked.

'Are you dancing for me?' I said.

He leaned forward and gave me a peck.

'It's good to be here,' he said. 'Don't you think?'

'Yes, of course.'

'I'll open a bottle of wine.'

'Have we got any?'

'Yes, we've plenty left over from last year. Unless Egil's drunk it all. I don't suppose he will have though. The plonk we drink won't be good enough for him!'

Inside, Heming and Asle went from room to room. We'd been away from the place just long enough for it to be exciting again. Ingvild was nowhere to be seen, in her room with the cat probably. I lugged the suitcase upstairs to the bedroom and then went back out into the garden and stood at the edge of the steep bank leading down to the bay. I lit another cigarette as I tried to feel my way into the surroundings, to become concurrent with them. To be here.

The summer evening. The greyish light, a slight tinge of blue. The glow of the house lights in it all.

'Shall we sit out?' Arne called from the open door behind me. 'I can just as well get the table and chairs out now as later.'

Without waiting for an answer he crossed in front of the house and unlocked the door of the annexe, emerging again a moment later with a chair in each hand, putting them down on the grass underneath the apple tree.

'Do you need some help with the table?'

'No, I can manage. You could fetch the wine and two glasses though?'

I was standing with the wine bottle between my knees, trying to remove the recalcitrant cork when Asle came into the kitchen.

'We're hungry,' he said. 'Is there any dinner?'

'What would you like?'

'Tacos.'

'That sounds all right,' I said. 'They're easy to make and won't take long.'

'Can't Dad make them?'

'Yes, I should think so,' I said, focusing on opening the wine again, the cork now releasing at last, sliding slowly up through the neck. 'Why do you want Dad to make them?' I called out after Asle as he made for the living room.

He turned towards me and gave a shrug.

'The meat's juicier when he does it.'

'Oh, I see,' I said and picked up the glasses in one hand, gripped the bottle in the other and went outside. Arne wasn't there. I sat down and lit a cigarette, noticing that I only had three left.

I'd go to bed early, it wouldn't be a problem then.

Behind me, the door of the annexe closed and Arne came walking across the grass with a lantern dangling from his hand.

'Give me your lighter a second,' he said.

The yellow light seeped out into the grey as if filling an invisible bowl that enclosed the lantern he then placed on top of the table. He poured wine into our glasses and lifted his towards me.

'*Skål*, Tove. A toast.'

'To what?'

'To us. To the summer. To being here.'

'*Skål*.'

'Come on, a bit of enthusiasm wouldn't hurt, surely?'

'I'm tired. It was a long journey.'

'I was the one driving, not you.'

'True.'

He sighed and we fell silent. The whisper of the sea was the only sound.

'I like the light here,' I said after a while.

'Of course you do, you're a painter.'

'I've always liked the light from a lantern when it's not quite dark. At the end of the day, at dusk.'

'Like I said, you're a painter.'

'I liked it before I started painting. I remember thinking just that when I was little.'

'That's romanticism, that is. Or rather, neo-romanticism. They loved painting summer nights, the gloaming. It was the mysteriousness they were after. Oda Krohg's best-known picture is of a lantern on a summer night. And then there's Richard Bergh's *Nordic Summer Evening*. It sounds like the same fascination.'

'Perhaps.'

'Not that you're a romantic exactly.'

'Oh? What am I then?'

'A neo-symbolist, maybe? A post-mythologist?'

'That's the big difference between us. You categorise. I decategorise.'

'As you often point out.'

'Not that there's anything wrong with categorising.'

He smiled wryly as he looked out at the sea.

'It's what pays our bills, at any rate,' he said.

'Dad?' one of the boys called out from the house.

It was Asle.

'Yes?' said Arne.

'Can you make us some tacos now?'

'In a minute.'

'We're starving.'

'Daddy's coming in a minute,' I said. 'Go back inside and he'll be right there.'

He did as I said. Arne filled his glass again.

'Let's have a nice holiday this year, shall we?' he said.

'Yes, of course.'

'Perhaps we both can make an effort.'

'Yes.'

I woke up in the middle of the night having dreamt. Although I lay quite still and focused, I couldn't remember what it was about. All that was left of it was the mood. Reluctance, unease. And that Mamma had been involved in some way or another.

Arne lay on his back snoring, as he always did when he'd been drinking.

Outside, the night was almost light.

I tried to sleep again, though I knew it was no use. And wasn't it that very sense of knowing you couldn't that made it impossible?

I thought so.

I got up, went downstairs into the passage and put my boots and jacket on, thinking I'd have a cigarette in the garden. Only when I sat down at the table did it occur to me that I didn't have any left.

I couldn't just sit there and not smoke, I'd only think about it then. So I got to my feet and crossed the grass, then followed the path down the bank to the bay. The grass, long and wet on either side, the sea still and gleaming, the sky grey-blue.

What time was it?

It didn't matter. I wasn't in the slightest bit tired, and I had the whole world to myself.

Three black slugs stood out in the yellow grass at the side of the path. I crouched down beside them. Their black was the black of car tyres. And with the creases that ran side by side along the length of their bodies, like tread patterns, they looked like they'd been made in a tyre factory too.

Small, waving tentacles. Their will, slow and resolute.

I stroked the tip of my forefinger over the head of the one that was closest. It shrank back with aversion. Unlike a man's cock that swelled to its full length at the same touch.

Slugs liked what was soft and moist. Slugs liked slime. They came from the mushy forest floor.

I stood up. They were probably no more than a couple of months old. Yet when I studied them it felt like they were ancient. As if they came from the depths of time.

That was how it was with everything. Everything we could see was about as old as us. But their forms, yes, it was their forms, were ancient.

Imagine.

I came to the smooth flat rocks at the shore and gazed out across the shiny surface of the sea, wanting my thoughts to open out the same way the sea and the sky opened out, not to be squishy and slimy, black and slow.

When I was little I loved animals more than anything else, without distinguishing between them. I gathered snails and slugs and put them in my coat pocket, beetles and worms and spiders too. I made small homes for them in shoeboxes lined with soil and grass and leaves, and hid them under the bed. Mamma hated it and went mad at me whenever she happened to find them.

But she would never be as angry as when she'd washed the floors down and I came in with dirty shoes on. She must have thought I did so on purpose, to provoke her. And provoke her it did, at any rate. You little bugger, she would often yell, and could dish out a slap in the face too, if she was in the mood for it. After which she'd be overcome with remorse, she'd be completely in bits about it. There'd be no end to the kisses and cuddles then, the pats and caresses, and I'd be allowed to sleep beside her, as close as could be, she'd give me all the love and concern she had in her then. And it was a lot.

Just a shame it was so unevenly distributed.

Why was I thinking about her?

The dream. She rose up in me when I slept, like a dead body rising up from the bottom of a pond.

Not that my prayers had been answered. After all, she was still in the land of the living. Though not as far as I was concerned. As far as I was concerned she was a dead body that occasionally rose to the surface.

I went all the way out on one of the rocks and crouched down again. The sea lapped gently, as if contained in an enormous vessel someone was carrying, the seaweed lapping gently back and forth, yellow-brown in the gleaming, black, cold element.

The woods behind me were still. Everything was motionless apart from the sea's careful movements.

It was the most splendid hour of all, was it not? The hour before sunrise.

Was the difference between us simply that I liked dirt, mud, mould, soil, loam, all that crept and crawled, whereas Mamma was just the opposite, everything having to be clinically clean, completely disinfected?

Of course not.

If only I had a cigarette.

I went round the point and crossed the band of stony beach, climbed up onto the bare rock above and started walking along as the sky to the east blushed red, then, only seconds later, became gilded by the first rays of the sun, which for a moment remained unseen before pouring out over the edge of the world and throwing their light across the expanse of the sea.

Aurora.

It was no big deal: it had been going on every morning for four billion years.

I laughed out loud.

Perhaps the holiday would be all right in spite of everything, I thought as I carried on walking. If the weather stayed the way it was, this was a good place to be. Especially for the kids.

Happy, but not *that* happy.

As the rock sloped away towards another stony beach, I realised it wasn't far to Egil's place. As the crow flies, there was barely a couple of kilometres between our two houses. And Egil smoked. Egil would have cigarettes!

He probably wouldn't be pleased to be woken up at this hour of the morning. But then again, had I been put into the world to please him?

No, I had not.

Happiness is easy, I sang.

Funny how songs so often came to mind like comments on what I was thinking or feeling.

This one was quite ironic. My subconscious just didn't realise.

The fresh smell of the sea merged with something rotten. Seaweed or seagrass washed ashore by a storm or something.

The winter I met Arne I'd often go to the toilet immediately after he'd used it, just so I could smell him. If I'd told him, he'd have been aghast. He might even have lost interest.

Or no, he wouldn't have. But he'd certainly have frowned at the thought.

I just wanted to know all about him.

The sky was bright blue now, and rays of light flooded the world. A fishing boat lay bobbing off the shore of an islet, no doubt the fisherman was checking his nets. The world was full of people who were good at something, who knew what they were doing. They didn't care for those who could do nothing. What was the point of being a human if there was nothing you were good at? they surely thought, harsh in their minds. But helplessness could be a friend too. Only a person who had no idea what something was supposed to be like was able to create.

The gulls were on the wing. Although I saw nothing but trees in the woods behind me, it felt as if life there had woken too.

Emerging onto the smooth rocks of the shore once more, I took off my boots and walked barefoot, a boot dangling from each hand. Egil's house was just beyond the next inlet, no more than five minutes away now.

What time did the sun rise in July exactly? Four o'clock? Five?

It felt more like five now than four.

There in the distance his red-painted shed came into view. I sensed I was looking forward to seeing him again. Perhaps I would sneak into his bedroom and ruffle his hair. It would scare the life out of him!

Standing on the veranda in front of the house I settled for knocking on the big sliding glass door, which when I tried to open it turned out to be locked anyway.

There was no response. I shielded my eyes from the sun and peered through the pane.

The place was a tip. Books and newspapers everywhere. Clothes too, dumped here and there.

I knocked again.

A door inside opened and Egil appeared with messed-up hair and a towel wrapped around his waist.

He looked at me in surprise, then came over, unlocked the glass door and pulled it aside.

'Tove? Is everything all right?'

'Ran out of cigs. Have you got any?'

His eyes appraised me briefly before he nodded. No more than a second or two, but enough for me to notice.

He was trying to gauge what state I was in.

'Sure,' he said. 'Just a minute.'

He went over to the table, returning with a packet of cigarettes and a lighter in one hand, the other gripping his silly towel in order to keep it from falling down.

'You're a good man,' I said, lighting a smoke immediately. 'My saviour.'

'I didn't know you were here. When did you arrive?'

'Yesterday evening.'

'Aha.'

'I couldn't sleep, as usual.'

'I thought it might be something like that. If you'll excuse me a second, I'll put some clothes on. Do you want a coffee?'

'Yes, if you're offering!'

'I'll have to make it first,' he mumbled, turning towards the bedroom. I pulled a chair out and sat down, leaned back and put my feet up on the rail.

Not a cloud in the sky. Not a ripple on the sea.

He returned wearing a pair of baggy cotton trousers and a white T-shirt, barefoot like a sailor, and put two cups down on the table.

'Coffee will be ready in a minute,' he said, then disappeared again.

He wasn't the talkative sort, more the bashful, introverted type, so I wondered if hanging around for coffee had been a good idea.

Proper cups. Fine china, the thinnest, with a blue-and-white floral pattern. The shipowner's heirlooms.

He reappeared carrying in one hand the coffee pot, which was shiny from wear, in places blackened, in the other a metal trivet to stand it on.

'Does Arne know you're here?' he said after pouring for us both and sitting down on the other side of the table.

'Arne's asleep.'

He nodded and lifted his cup to his lips, sipped his coffee and then offered me another cigarette from the packet. I took one, he likewise.

'So, how's things?' he said. 'Haven't seen you in a while.'

'Do you want the polite answer or the honest one?'

He smiled.

'The polite one, I think.'

'In that case, everything's fine.'

'Glad to hear it!'

He laughed, more of a giggle really.

'How about you?' I said, and blew a smoke ring.

The Magician.

'Same as ever.'

'Doesn't it get a bit boring? In the winter, I mean, with no one around?'

'I'm never bored. Are you?'

'Sometimes. If I can't work.'

He nodded and sipped his coffee again. He was sitting with his legs crossed. His trousers weren't long enough and most of his lower leg was exposed, hairless but for the lightest down that seemed almost luminous in the sunlight. Did it mean he didn't produce enough testosterone?

His cheeks showed no stubble, though he couldn't possibly have shaved yet.

'What are you working on at the moment?'

I shrugged and stared out at the sea. The sun was already burning my shoulders.

'I've been drawing all winter and spring.'

He didn't follow up on the information, the way I thought he would. I'd thought he was the inquisitive type.

But he was cautious too. Yes, wary, like an animal.

Why was that?

'Aren't you going to ask what I've been drawing?' I said, tapping the ash of my cigarette onto the decking.

'What *have* you been drawing?'

Was he being sarcastic now? If he was, I wasn't going to stay.

I stubbed the cigarette out in the ashtray.

'No, I'd better be getting back before they all start waking up over there. Thanks for the smoke.'

'Take a packet back with you,' he said, getting to his feet.

'Are you sure?'

'Of course, I've got two cartons.'

It was just gone six by the time I got back. The house was completely silent. The neighbouring houses were all quiet too. No cars, no boats, just the gulls in the bay and a squirrel darting about in a corner of the garden before scampering up a tree.

Whenever I was up early I could never fathom how it was possible to sleep until nine, or even worse, until eleven or twelve o'clock, the way Ingvild often would.

An ocean of virgin time stretched out ahead of me. I could just as well spend it doing something useful.

I went into the annexe and looked around. There was such a wonderful smell in there. Terps and oils, albeit their particular odours were faint in view of the fact that I hadn't used the place for some time. But there was something raw and damp too, the brick walls most probably. And then the woodwork, the floor and the ceiling, a drier, dustier tang.

Everything seemed to become open in the sunlight that flooded in through the windows, onto the floorboards, onto the desk with all its brushes and boxes and palettes, and onto all the canvases too, which stood leaned up against the opposite wall, facing away from the light.

What should I do?

The drawings I'd been working on that winter and spring, which Egil hadn't asked me about, were drawings based on the Norwegian folk tales. I'd grown up with the ones done by Werenskiold, Gude, Peterssen and Kittelsen, that crowd. I loved them, they'd stimulated my imagination immensely and were just as much a part of my childhood as the house I'd grown up in. But they were illustrations, and as such superficial. They had nothing of the depth the tales themselves possessed, nothing of their wildness, their grotesqueness. Which was what I wanted to delve into. The mountain man who wrenches off the girl's head and hurls it into the cellar along with her body. The old hag who sleeps with the troll and tries to talk him into killing her son so they can be on their own and spend more time shagging. The girl on whom the three giant heads of the lake cast a spell, causing her mouth to fill with ash whenever she speaks. Animals and humans mingling and merging. Wolves that devour small children. The blood and the body. Rape and killings. The freakish deformities, the want, the banquets, the secret room it is forbidden to enter, always the third or the seventh.

Those were the hallowed numbers. The hallowed was thereby associated with temptation, something they were warned against. Open all others, but never that door! Did they believe hallowedness to be a peril?

The folk tales were about all that moved under the surface of the culture. Everything that was sensed, though never thought about or shared, became creatures and tales.

How could it be drawn?

I wanted my drawings to smell, to stink, to seep and bleed, writhe and squirm. But I hadn't succeeded. I told myself it was the fault of drawing itself, the very form of expression. The pen stroke served only to encase and bring under control, rationalising everything and thereby rendering it tame. But these were just excuses. All I had to do was look at Goya and see what he'd done in *his* drawings.

I'd shown some of my own to Arne, thinking I owed it to him.

'These are very good,' he said, and put them down again.

'Is that all you can say?'

'These are good, anyone can see that.'

'Why do you keep saying *these* about them?'

'It's a way of referring, that's all. I can't keep saying *your drawings* all the time!'

There was more to come, later the same day.

'Why is it you persist with the sexual theme exactly? Is that how you see the world?'

'So I'm *persisting* now, am I?'

'All right, *pursuing*. But why that theme in particular? Why are they so sexualised, your drawings?'

'I don't know. They just are.'

He was afraid of sexuality, my husband. He would never admit to it or even realise it was the case, so I left it alone.

The energy of the folk tales is pure sexual energy. It's where they come from. Sex is the force to which the tales give shape. It's the same with everything, in fact. The body's desire for other bodies is extreme. But we pretend it isn't the case. If we didn't, everything would be ripped apart.

So yes, my drawings were sexualised.

But not enough.

I liked that a cunt was sometimes called a *mouse*. It was apt, sometimes it really did look like you had a mouse between your legs. The analogy was probably very old too, one that had been in use in the language for thousands of years. And there was the transformative aspect too, the cunt becoming an animal.

So I'd drawn a mouse between a pair of wide-open female legs, and another two scuttling about alongside.

But the picture was laughable. It was like one of those cartoons in the *New Yorker*.

Then I'd drawn a wolf with its tongue hanging out between a pair of legs.

That one was better, though not much, if only because it illustrated something rather than trying to *be* that something – nothing came from the picture but the picture itself, the girl-wolf juxtaposition.

I'd left them all at home. This wasn't the place to continue working on them anyway.

I lay down on the sofa and smoked while staring at the ceiling.

What was hidden in the depths would often appear so flat when brought to the surface. The meaning would be squashed if the symbols were too familiar.

If I'd used colour, the problem would have been solved. Colours are deep, colours are bottomless. Colours merge. They seep and bleed.

But I didn't want to use colour. The whole point of doing the folk tales was the desire the old illustrations provoked. Those of Munthe, for instance, with their suggestion of ancient Norse culture.

I stood up and went over to the shelves where I kept my art books and cuttings. I took out a volume about Gustave Moreau's watercolours of La Fontaine's fables. Most of the pictures were straightforward illustrations, but a couple seemed to veer off in another direction and I sat down again to study them. The first was of a monkey riding on the back of a dolphin. The monkey's mouth was open in a scream or cry. A pink tongue in the dark cavity of the mouth, two rows of teeth catching the light. It looked human, as if it was a man crying out. But the eyes. There was the key. The eyes were undeviating. They were completely true to nature in the way they were painted, and could easily have belonged to a human. But they were undeviating. The eyes of the animal, the cry of the human.

I leafed through the pages to the second picture I remembered.

It was extraordinary. A snake's head with its venomous fangs bared, blood dripping from its jaws in the foreground. A fall of colours, dark browns, yellows, rust-reds, pouring into a pool. And above the pool, at the edge of the painting, naked, writhing bodies, human beings bereft.

In La Fontaine's fable the tail of the snake had complained about never being allowed to lead. Always, the head would decide. Why couldn't they be treated the same? As equals? So the gods allowed the tail to decide. And away it slithered, straight into the hellish Styx, river of the underworld. Being the tail, it couldn't see where it was going.

The snake possessed something of what was also in the eyes of the monkey, only more so.

Distracted by a movement outside, I turned and looked out of the window. Arne. He was on his way over the grass with a mug in his hand.

I put the book down and went outside to meet him.

'I thought you said you weren't going to work during the holiday?' he said, then sipped a mouthful of coffee and gazed out.

'I wasn't working. I was looking at some books, that's all.'

'Couldn't you sleep?'

I shook my head.

'Have you taken your medicine?'

'Of course,' I said, though I hadn't.

'You know how important it is for you to sleep.'

He was making me angry. But I didn't want to argue.

'It's always hard for me to sleep after a change of place,' I said. 'It's no more than that.'

'Let's hope so,' he said. 'There's some coffee in the pot, if you want some.'

We went out to the lighthouse in the boat that morning. It was an old lighthouse, rising up where the open sea began. Ingvild didn't want to come, but Arne insisted, so she sat next to me on the thwart, the twins kneeling in the bow, while Arne sat at the stern and steered.

She wasn't in a mood, but she wasn't happy either. Resigned, I suppose was the word. There was nothing else for it but to endure, I imagined her thinking.

I was thinking the same thing.

But it was wrong to think that way. I was out in the boat, a nice excursion with my kids and husband.

My precious little family.

She was so different from me. Another creature altogether. Mild and tolerant. Did what was asked of her at school and at home, and very often more. It was what they call nice girl syndrome. Her friends were the same.

But I liked her a lot. She could have been my sensible best mate.

I stroked her arm and gave her a smile. She smiled back, her hair dancing in the wind.

'What are you thinking about?' I said.

She shook her head, almost imperceptibly.

'Nothing.'

'Nothing important or nothing at all?'

'Nothing important.'

'What would that be then, that isn't important?'

'Mum . . .'

'I'm wondering what's going on in my daughter's mind, that's all.'

She turned her head to the side and gazed at the land. Pulled her hair away from her face as the wind tossed it.

Arne thrust the tiller from side to side. Heming and Asle laughed. Arne grinned and ran his hand through his hair, wet with spray.

The pills made me bloated. And I didn't want to be bloated. As long as I kept an eye on myself, I'd be all right. As long as I didn't ignore the signs when they appeared.

Besides, I felt safe with my family. It was all the other stuff that made me ill.

Like what?

It had been there long before they came along. It was something inside me. Not out there. But it changed everything that *was* out there.

Or rather no, that wasn't quite it.

It was like something inside me opened itself towards something *outside* me. Then dragged it in. Cautiously at first, then more and more greedily. And it changed me.

The fact that it changed me was what set me apart from others. From Arne, for instance. He stood firm in what he was. He could be sad about a thing, or he could be happy, he could become eager and excited, but he wouldn't be changed by it, he stood firm. He was Arne.

People weren't meant to change.

The monkey and the dolphin looked like they were a kind of biological machine.

Next to me Ingvild took a hair tie from her wrist, held it for a moment between her lips, gathered her hair, took the tie again and wound it a couple of times around the root of the ponytail she'd made.

There was something foreboding about the sea.

We weren't the only ones out. The strait that separated the main island from the smaller islets was busy, pleasure boats and dinghies were moored at every shore and jetty and the flat rocks carpeted with bathing towels and picnic rugs. People dived from the outcrops and swam in the dark blue waters.

We approached the lighthouse. Arne slowed the outboard and narrowed his eyes against the sun. He liked himself now, in this role of father and seaman, instructing others in what to do.

'Hand me the grapnel, will you, Ingvild?' he said. And then louder: 'Are you ready at the front?'

He threw the outboard into reverse, got to his feet and took the grapnel from Ingvild's hands. It looked like a folded-up octopus. He tossed it into the water, the line running as it descended.

Asle and Heming jumped ashore with the rope, positioned themselves, one in front of the other, as they took hold. Their flaxen hair, bronzed boy bodies, gleaming white teeth.

When they were still very small, sitting in their double buggy one day, an elderly man approached me as we stood waiting at the bus stop and told me he had twins too. They were grown up by then, of course. I'll give you a piece of advice, he said. When they start school you must separate them. Each in their own class. If you don't, the weaker twin will follow the stronger one and you'll never be able to separate them. You'll never be able to come between.

He told me that, and then went away. I never saw him again.

We laughed about it when I told Arne. The notion of the weaker twin and the stronger twin seemed so incredibly archaic, from a time more primitive than our own. It was almost as if he'd been talking about animals.

But I'd never been able to eliminate the thought, it was there always. Which twin was the weaker and which the stronger? I refused to even consider what the answer might be and would put it from my mind the moment it came back to me.

They were in the same class at school and they were inseparable. It was no use doing something with one and not the other, talking to one without the other either being there too or being told everything that had been said as soon as possible.

But was it a bad thing?

No, it wasn't a bad thing. It was natural, it was the way they were. That was what it was like being a twin.

'Are you coming ashore, then?' said Arne.

The rocks were smooth and slippery with sea water and I kept tight hold of the swaying rope as I stepped out, not feeling entirely secure until standing on the dry rock a few metres further up the shore.

Arne handed the things to Ingvild and we all then clambered up the slope in search of a spot on the other side. The lighthouse rose up in front of us, towering towards the sky, white with a red band around its midriff. Although it was no longer in use, it was in no way derelict. Someone was obviously looking after it.

Arne led the way with a childlike spring in his step. He put an arm around Heming's shoulder, and Heming looked up at him and smiled. And there, Asle too slipped into place under Arne's other arm.

It was only a small islet and we reached the other side within a couple of minutes. There were quite a lot of people there, but the boys found a spot where the rock was sufficiently flat and so we spread our towels there. The sea was rather more agitated this far out. Not that the waves were big, but they swelled against the rock and withdrew with a rush, their foam swirled, and now and then they could be heard to give a faint rumble.

Arne and the boys changed into their trunks. Ingvild and I sat on our towels.

'Aren't you going to swim?' I said.

'Later, maybe.'

'Do you want something? Crisps or cola? An apple?'

'No, thanks.'

Arne balanced his way out onto an outcrop a man's height above the water, brought his hands together above his head and dived in. Heming and Asle watched with admiration before clambering down to the water's edge and gliding out.

'It's lovely!' shouted Arne – or Arne's head, the only part of him I could see.

After swimming around for a while they all came back up and sat down, panting and dripping water everywhere. Arne got the biscuits out and a soft drink for each of them.

'It's not at all cold,' he said to me. 'You did bring your bathing costume, didn't you?'

I nodded and smiled.

The boys crunched their biscuits. Ingvild lay on her back with her eyes closed to the sun.

'Shall we go and explore, boys?' Arne said. He looked at me as he got to his feet. 'Do you want to come with us?'

'I think I'll stay here and sunbathe.'

'OK.'

After they'd gone I lay back, rolled up a towel and placed it under my head, unfolded another I then spread out on top of me so as not to get sunburnt, closed my eyes and listened to all the sounds. It was how I normally went to sleep, and sleep was what I wanted now for a while, I could feel a tiredness beginning to get the better of me.

I woke up and shuddered with cold. I realised I was on my own, and glanced around to see where the others might be. All four were in the water. A wind had picked up. The sea breeze. I must have slept a few hours.

Why hadn't they woken me up?

I rummaged for the biscuits in the bag, my blood sugar was low, my body was crying out. They must have finished the biscuits, but there were still some crisps left.

Arne waved and shouted something.

I stuffed a handful of crisps into my mouth before getting up and going towards them.

'Last chance!' he shouted.

'I'm a bit cold,' I said.

'What?'

'I'm cold!'

'OK.'

The water was dark blue and chilly-looking. It was a puzzle that creatures could live in it. But my creatures looked like they were having fun. Asle and Heming had their diving masks on and were swimming around with their heads under the surface and only their snorkels sticking up. Ingvild lay floating on her back, while Arne swam further out.

He'd been writing a novel for years. He'd never shown it to me. It was saved on his computer, protected by a password. It had taken me about ten minutes to work it out. He wouldn't have used the kids' names or mine, I was sure about that. His own name was too obvious, as were those of his parents. But what about his hero, Bowie? The problem then was that the password had to include numbers too. I cracked it after two guesses. It was the date of his death: Bowie10012016.

The novel began with two brothers diving in darkness in a fjord. I supposed that was the reason it came to mind now.

Arne thought the manuscript contained the truth about him. That was why he wouldn't show it to anyone, and why it would never be finished.

But it was the other way round. There was nothing of him at all in the manuscript. That made it a bad novel. But it didn't make him a bad person.

Quite the opposite.

He'd never understood that it was precisely because he was so ordinary that I'd fallen in love with him. He would take it as an insult if I ever told him. But I loved ordinariness. Arne was a bit of everything. A bit vain, a bit petty, a bit funny, a bit considerate, a bit loving, a bit ambitious. A bit handy, a bit clumsy. A bit alcoholic, a bit everyman, a bit intellectual. A bit son, a bit father, a bit husband.

Together, these uncomplicated parts made something complex. But nothing extreme. I hated, genuinely hated, extremes.

In life, that is. Not in art.

Ingvild was coming in now. A swell lifted her up, she gripped the edge of a rock and was just about to wriggle onto it when she slipped, at the same moment as the water drew back. It could have been nasty, but she seemed all right and swam a few strokes before finding a place where it was easier to get out.

A moment later she was standing in front of me, bending down to pick up a towel. Blood was trickling down her thigh.

'Did you hurt yourself?'

She shook her head and began to dry her hair.

'But you took a proper scrape there.'

'What?'

'There, on your thigh.'

She looked down at herself.

'Oh my goodness. I didn't feel anything.'

She dabbed the wound with her towel, then wiped away the blood.

'It's just a scratch.'

A sailing boat backed out a bit further along the shore. A family of four, perhaps moving to the leeside. The waves were heavier now as they broke onto the shore. I went down to Asle and Heming and said it was time for them to come out now.

'We'll come when Dad does,' Heming said.

Arne was perhaps a hundred metres out. I waved at him, but he didn't see me.

'Can't you do it now?' I said. 'You've been in for ages.'

'When Dad comes,' said Asle.

'OK,' I said, and returned to Ingvild who had now put on her skirt and top and was sitting with the towel pressed to her thigh.

'What's your father doing so far out?' I said.

'Playing the action man for you,' she said, and smiled as she tied her hair again, her face to the sky.

Halfway between the islet and the main island where our house was, Arne stopped the outboard and got the fishing tackle out. The boat began to pitch on the swell. He could have asked me first, but didn't. Now we were going to fish.

'Trolling or handline?' said Asle.

'It'd be nice to get some mackerel,' said Arne. 'How about trolling at the same time as we head home?'

He looked at me.

'It won't take much longer than it normally would.'

'All right by me, I suppose,' I said.

'We'll need to spread out a bit then,' said Arne. 'So we don't get tangled up.'

He dug out a rig for each of us. Ingvild didn't want one. I put mine down on the floor between my feet.

'How's that scratch doing?' I said. 'Is it still bleeding?'

She shook her head.

'Does it hurt?'

'It stings a bit.'

'Poor you.'

'Mum, it's just a scratch!'

The boys loosened the weights and hooks from their winders and dropped them into the water. Their movements were almost synchronous.

Arne started the motor again and we set off slowly.

'I've got one!' Heming shouted out after only a couple of minutes, and began to bring in his line.

'Easy does it,' said Arne.

'I've got one as well!' Asle shouted, he too then bringing in his line as quickly as he could.

'Mind what you're doing, try not to get in a tangle now.'

He glanced at me, shaking his head as if in despair, as if to say, with a rolling of eyes, *These boys of ours, eh?*

'I think I've got more than one!' shouted Heming.

'Me too!' shouted Asle.

I crossed my arms and rubbed my shoulders a few times as I looked across at the island, green woods framed by yellow-brown rock. The dark blue of the sea. I turned the other way and looked towards the horizon. So much water. It could hardly be comprehended. How deep was it here? Probably about fifty metres to the bottom. If not a hundred.

A litre of water was a lot in the kitchen. Here it was nothing.

I wasn't exactly scared, but I wasn't far off.

Do you know what they think about you exactly? Your family?

Oh no, no.

Arne stood up and with his upper body almost at a right angle to his legs stepped over the thwart where Ingvild and I were sitting.

'What have you got?'

'I don't know yet,' said Heming, Arne now leaning over his shoulder.

'There, look!'

'Yes!' said Heming. 'There's three!'

My heart pounded. I bent forward and put my head in my hands.

Perhaps it would stop at that.

Arne's hoping you'll soon be ill so he can get rid of you for a few months.

I don't like you.

I think you do.

I'm not listening. You can say what you want. I'm not going to listen.

Laughter.

Heming pulled the first of the fish over the side. It hung motionless and glistening in the sunlight, then dropped with a thud to the floor of the boat, where it began to flap its tail.

The twins are glad too when you're not here.

'Are you all right, Mum?' said Ingvild. 'Are you feeling seasick?'

I straightened up and smiled at her.

Now it was Asle's turn to bring his fish over the side. Arne crouched down and released Heming's first from the hook. Once it was free, he dashed its head hard against the gunwale a couple of times, a soft thump of a sound. He dropped it into the bucket and turned to the next one. The boat, unsteered, dabbed at the swell. The wind swept past us on its way towards the land.

'I'm fine,' I said. 'A bit tired, that's all. I didn't sleep very well last night.'

'But you have to sleep,' she said. 'It's important that you do.'

'I know. But I can't just do it on command. Besides, I always find it hard to sleep in a different place at first.'

She nodded while looking at me. Scrutinising me, it felt like.

'Are you sure you're all right?'

'Yes, I'm fine. Don't worry about me.'

More laughter.

Remember, you can't keep anything secret from me.

Go away.

I will. But I'll be back.

There were five fish in the bucket now. Blue, with shimmering black spines, white bellies.

'Well done, lads,' said Arne. 'I think that'll do for now.'

'But we've only just started!' said Heming.

'It's going to take ten minutes just to untangle your lines,' said Arne. 'And we don't need any more fish. We can go fishing again tomorrow.'

'OK,' said Heming.

'Are you going to sort your lines out on the way home then?' said Arne.

They nodded earnestly, both of them at once.

When we came back up to the house, the cat was lying on the doorstep in the sunshine. She was heavily pregnant, the kittens were due any time now and she was quite lethargic.

Ingvild crouched down and ruffled her fur, then looked up at me.

'We've hardly any cat food left,' she said. 'Will you be going to the shop today?'

'There's fish for dinner now.'

'You're right, I forgot,' she said, then turned to the cat again. 'Do you want fish too, puss? It'll be good for you.'

I put the cooler bag down on the worktop in the kitchen, went to the bathroom and decided to run myself a bath, still feeling the cold from before. As I turned the tap on, I heard Arne and the boys coming up the bank.

Why couldn't I get close to them now that we were all together?

I undressed and lowered myself into the bath, even though there was barely enough in it to cover the bottom yet. I cupped my hands and scooped hot water onto my thighs and stomach, spread my legs, knees against the sides, and saw my cunt reflected in the shiny metal tap.

Now *there* was a subject for a painting.

Woman having a bath.

But not a very good subject.

You're right about that.

A cunt is nothing on its own.

I agree.

I don't think you do. You just think I'll go away if you agree with everything I say. You think I'm actually you, a part of you. Don't you?

That's it exactly.

Well, that's where you're wrong. I'm not you. I'm not even a part of you.

You don't say. Who are you then?

I have no name to give you.

I closed my eyes and slid down into the water, deep enough now to cover my head.

Blub, blub.

I sat up, smoothed back my hair and turned off the tap.

What do you want with me?

I picked up the soap from the side of the bath and started to wash while waiting for more. But nothing more came.

Hello?

Nothing.

I leaned my head back against the edge of the bath and closed my eyes. Tried to savour the feeling of my body being immersed in hot water. To be present only with my body. Without thought. The voice belonged to thought. I hadn't even to think about what it felt like. I just had to feel it.

Float.

Be present.

Everything was dark and warm. I was dark and warm. Darkness and warmth were all I was now.

Something soft and viscous ran over my lips. I wiped it with my finger, held my finger up in front of me. Blood.

A nosebleed?

I hadn't had a nosebleed since I was a little girl.

What did we do about them then?

I drew myself up a bit more and tipped my head back as far as I could. I felt my nostrils fill.

Urgh.

But it stopped. I washed the blood away, watched it disperse like a veil in the silvery water, twisted a small piece of toilet paper into each nostril, dried myself, wrapped a towel around me and went upstairs to the bedroom. It was empty. The window was open to the road outside, it too empty. Carefully I removed the toilet paper from my nose, dropped it into the wastepaper basket, and took a clean pair of knickers from the suitcase.

The sun was still quite high in the sky by the time I went downstairs again. It looked like it was bathing in blue. But in reality it was completely black where it was.

A car came up the road and pulled up outside the house next door. The two Rottweilers started barking, thrashing up and down on the other side of the fence.

Where was everyone?

I went into the living room. The boys were sitting beside each other on the sofa with their iPads.

'Where's your dad?'

'He went to the shop,' said Asle.

'We're having a barbecue,' said Heming.

'I see,' I said.

Was he deciding things just to annoy me?

No information.

What if I didn't want a barbecue?

'What are you up to, anyway?'

'Playing,' said Heming without looking up.

I sat down next to him. He moved over with a sigh of irritation.

'What are you playing? Anything I know?'

'FIFA.'

'Is it football?'

He nodded.

'What are you playing, Asle?'

'FIFA.'

'It looks fun.'

I sat and watched them for a minute before getting up again.

'Don't play for too long, now. It's not good for you, all that screen time.'

'We know,' said Heming.

'We're going to help Dad with the barbecue when he gets back,' said Asle.

They were enjoying themselves and doing fine on their own, so I went over to the studio in the annexe, only I couldn't think of what to do there and went back out after a few minutes into the garden, sat down and lit a cigarette.

Just as restless there.

The only thing to do about it was go for a walk.

I borrowed Ingvild's trainers and went the same way as I'd gone that morning.

It was still quiet, but the quietness was different now. It was the light. Thin and delicate in the morning, thick and dense in the evening.

The waxing and the waning.

Conception thin and delicate. Death thick and dense.

Yes! The life to come slips cautiously through the membrane to flourish, and then, when it dies, it pushes back, thick and dense, until the membrane bursts!

We live within membranes. Reality is a bubble.

Should I go over to Egil's again?

He'd only think I fancied him.

Did I?

Straddle him and lean forward. Does he crane to reach my breast and suck my nipple? Making my every muscle tingle, right down to my cunt. Smooth and wet. His hands on my buttocks. The grunting and groaning. Noises beyond control, like animals.

It wouldn't be bad.

And not beyond the bounds of possibility either. He'd often eyed me up.

Egil fantasises about you. But he's afraid of Arne.

Tell me something I don't know.

His favourite fantasy is you standing at the railing on the veranda and he comes up to you and pulls his trousers down and licks your arsehole and you're groaning and are so horny you almost erupt when he takes you from behind.

I could do something about it sometime.

But he hasn't got the guts.

No, I don't suppose he has.

In the shadow of the rock I was standing on, the water in the bay was black. The trees behind the pebble beach shone green, it was almost as if they were about to let go of the green and lift themselves up into the colour above. Which was? Yellow, gold, white. Other way: white, gold, yellow, orange, red, brown, black. Back up again: black, brown, purple, blue, green, yellow.

You must paint earth. Shit. Night. Blood. Brown and black and red. They should be your colours.

Are they your colours?

You're not stupid, are you? They're my colours.

Are you here? Nearby?

Silence.

I turned round and screwed up my eyes against the glare. I could see the roof of the neighbours' house, though not ours, ours was hidden behind the bank.

Happiness is easy, I sang, and started walking again.

Happiness is easy.

The first time I was really ill, I was so confused I didn't know what was happening. I'd been accepted into art school, it was my dream, the only thing I really wanted. But it was as if I was funnelled there into something that just got smaller and smaller. By the time spring came I was sitting on the floor in the corner of my rented room, surrounded by all sorts of little male and female figures I'd made. I'd constructed a whole little dolls' world for them too. There was a castle in it, and a forest, a street with buildings and cars. Only it wasn't small enough for me yet, so as I sat there in my miniature world I started making tiny drawings, sheet after sheet covered with microscopic figures and landscapes. I wasn't eating, I don't think I was sleeping either, everything had to be in such small amounts. I still don't know why everything had to be so small, what it was all about. Because it was only on the outside things had to be small. While the outside world shrunk, my inside world grew. In my mind, everything was big. In my mind, the paper castle was a real castle, the male and female figures real men and women. That was where the real world was. It was called Anara and I lived my life there.

Everything else was shadowlike, insubstantial, meaningless. Anara was thrilling. Life there rich.

Some of my fellow students were concerned about me never turning up any more. They found me sitting on the floor playing with my little dolls. I was unreachable. But in Anara things were coming to a head. *It's got nothing to do with them*, said the Maintainers. *They want to harm you*, said the Bringers of Joy. *They want to destroy you*, said the Redeemers.

'Cunts,' I said to my classmates. 'Get out of here, you fucking cunts.'

I found myself sitting in the back of a police car, wedged between two policemen. Even the Thunder King, who I hadn't seen or heard in such a very long time and yet pined for, manifested himself. *Don't give in*, he said. *Never give in*. I tried to make a run for it as soon as we got out. They caught me, of course, after only a few metres. I kicked and thrashed, spat and seethed.

Three weeks in the closed psychiatric department. Then the open one for the rest of the spring.

But that was it. No more attacks, no more stays in hospital. I finished art school. Didn't tell anyone the voices were still there. I didn't want to go back, and I could control them. I knew what ill was, and what well was, what were voices and what was me. That was the important thing. As long as I could tell the difference, I could live with it.

I included some of the little dolls and microdrawings in my first exhibition. I papered the walls with pictures, hundreds of works. I was the talk of the town and making a living, and I met Arne, a well-defined, no-nonsense sort, a man full of self-confidence and ambition, secure in the person he was, and together we brought Ingvild into the world.

I read about inner voices. Most of those writing about it seemed to agree that the voices came from parts of the personality that were either repressed or repressive. Normally the personality, for all its conflicting elements, makes up a whole, or at least feels that way. That was what they wrote. In the case of personality disorders, the part of the person that keeps the whole together loses its grip as it were. So the single voice by which we think becomes several.

You can learn to live with your voices, I read. The man who said so had treated numerous patients who did. And Jung heard voices all his life. I hadn't heard of Jung and so I read about him and about his archetypes.

I was the Magician. Arne the Orphan, the manipulator.

The voice I'd heard today was different. It didn't come from any other world. It was all on its own. Like a person from this world. But it was in my head. It could only be a product of my mind. Three days without medication, that was the reason.

There was only one thing to do about it. Start taking the pills again. This evening.

Why not now?

I halted. The sea blue. The sun red. The rock yellow.

An aversion. Not towards the pills. I had to take them.

Towards the house? The kids?

I carried on walking, quickly now, as quick as I could without breaking into a run. It was as if they were living behind a glass wall. But they were my children. I'd given birth to them. I was their mother.

No glass wall between them and Arne, though. I knew he rejoiced in it, having that connection with them when I couldn't. He never missed a chance to strengthen the glass. Barbecuing with them without asking me, for instance, a chance of them doing something together, just him and them. Going fishing with them, swimming with them. If I said anything about it, he'd just say I could join them if I wanted. Nothing was stopping me, he least of all.

Egil's house came into view at the edge of the woods, the jagged spruce like hair, the roof a forehead, the windows were eyes and the flat rocks below a bib that ran down to a great blue belly.

He was sitting at the table in the middle of the living room, tapping away on that old typewriter of his. He jumped when I knocked on the pane. I don't suppose he got many visitors.

'Tove,' he said as he slid the door aside. 'Run out of cigarettes again?'

I held the packet up in front of him.

'A light, then?' he said, then smiled.

'Felt like a bit of company, that's all,' I said. 'Have you got anything to drink?'

'Sure. Coffee? Beer? Something stronger?'

'Something stronger. I won't stay long. We're having a barbecue.'

He wants to shag you.

So what.

Why don't you do something about it? Have a bit of fun.

No.

Tove, go on.

'Vodka and tonic do you?' said Egil. I nodded, he went back inside, and I sat down on the same chair as before, lit a cigarette and stared for some time at the sea, which seemed not to want all that sunlight, casting it back as glitter.

'Who are you?' I said out loud, allowing a wisp of cigarette smoke to issue thinly into the air in front of me where it swirled a moment before dissipating.

No answer came.

My eyes followed a gull. It flapped its wings a couple of times, then sailed low over the flat rock at the shore. Such vast spaces. And so empty.

I was well aware that the voices were me. But this one was so different.

Through the window, which looked to be aflame in the sunlight, I saw Egil's figure come from the kitchen. He narrowed his eyes against the bright light as he stepped out, a drink in each hand. Ice cubes and lemon, the works. He knew about such things.

'What are you writing?' I said as he handed me my glass.

He shrugged.

'Nothing in particular,' he said. 'Just bits and pieces, really.'

'Arne's writing a novel in secret. Did you know? He's been at it for years.'

'Do you think he'd like you telling people?'

I blew out my smoke.

'It's hardly a revelation. Show me a professor of literature or a critic who hasn't worked on a novel at some point. Is it a novel *you're* writing?'

He shook his head. I drained half my drink, felt the burn of the alcohol in my mouth and had to pause and take a breath before knocking the rest of it back.

He glanced at me now and again, as if his gaze simply brushed me in passing.

I stubbed my cigarette out in the ashtray and lit another.

'If you could be a hundred per cent certain no one would ever know,' I said, and fixed my eyes on him, 'would you fuck me here on the veranda now?'

The astonishment in his eyes. And the fright.

'A hypothetical question, I hope?'

'It's what you want it to be.'

'Nevertheless, I'd have to say I wouldn't.'

'Don't you like me, Egil?'

He got up and stepped over to the railing with his drink in his hand, his shadow long and narrow on the decking.

'It *was* hypothetical,' I said with a laugh. 'I was looking for a reaction, that's all.'

'You managed that all right.'

'I'm bored, you see.'

'So I gather.'

'Anyway,' I said, and got to my feet. 'There's a barbecue I'm meant to attend. No hard feelings, I hope. It was only a joke.'

He smiled faintly.

'Will you bring Arne with you next time? It'd be nice to see him.'

I didn't reply, just left.

The barbecue had been brought out onto the middle of the lawn, its flames were almost transparent. Arne was sitting on the chair he'd pulled back to the wall, a bottle of white wine on the table in front of him, holiday mode, aviators and a straw hat. Asle and Heming were stretched out on the grass a bit further away. It looked like they were bickering about something. I went towards Arne and sat down on the other side of the table.

'Long walk?' he said.

'Fairly,' I said. 'It's such a lovely evening. So still.'

'Yes.'

When it appeared no more would be said, I got to my feet again.

'Leaving already?'

'I'm going to the kitchen.'

I took a biscuit from the cupboard and ate it as I went to Ingvild's room. She was lying on her bed reading. The cat was lying next to her, her belly with all her kittens inside so swollen it didn't seem to belong to her, it looked more like a bag of some sort she was lying beside.

Ingvild marked her page with a forefinger and looked up. I sat down on the edge of the bed.

'How's it going?' I said.

'Fine.'

'Are you enjoying being here?'

'Yes, of course.'

Pause.

'Did you want anything in particular, Mum?' she said.

'No,' I said. 'Just wanted a talk, that's all. But it's like there's a glass wall between us. Don't you think so?'

'A glass wall?'

'Yes. We never talk any more. It hurts sometimes. It's the same with the twins.'

She looked at me.

Beautiful, compliant Ingvild.

'There isn't always that much to talk about,' she said.

'Isn't there?'

'No.'

'But we used to talk all the time when you were a child. About everything. Do you remember?'

'I'm not a child any more.'

'No,' I said, and smiled at her.

A door opened somewhere. I looked out of the window. The boys were still stretched out on the lawn, so it was Arne coming back in.

'The twins are still children,' I persisted. 'But they're behind the glass wall too. They shouldn't be though, should they? Or what?'

'I don't know, Mum.'

She looked at me again. I stood up.

'Is everything all right with you?' she said.

'Me? Yes! It feels good to be here. You are joining us for the barbecue, aren't you? We'll be eating in half an hour, I think. You will, won't you?'

She nodded and returned to her book.

Outside, Arne had moved the table to the barbecue and was now busy fetching meat and vegetables, plates and bowls. I sat down and poured some wine into the glass I'd brought out with me. I needed to sort through my thoughts. It was as if I no longer knew what was important. I needed to decide what was and what wasn't. To get a clear handle on that. But I couldn't sort through anything with Arne and the twins in the background.

I picked up my glass and went into the annexe. Sat down on the sofa, balanced the glass on the arm as I lit a cigarette.

Asle and Heming and Ingvild were important.

But how was I to approach this situation? What tactics was I to employ?

Arne, was he important now?

No sooner had I asked myself the question than he was standing in the room in front of me.

'Won't you come and join us?' he said. 'Help with the barbecue?'

'Yes!'

Not that there was much to help with, not exactly. Heming and Asle put the chops on, Arne cut the vegetables for the salad, Heming and Asle put the sausages on, Arne set the table and brought steaming potatoes from the kitchen, while I sat on the chair against the wall, smoking and drinking wine. At least she's here with us, that's something, I imagined Arne to be thinking.

He didn't look at me, not once did he look at me, he just let me sit there.

He wants rid of you.

You've said that.

When you're ill, he's the superman taking care of everything.

Is that what he thinks?

He's looking for signs now, hoping you'll deteriorate.

I don't believe you.

Believe what you want. I know.

The sun disappeared behind the roof as we sat eating. It didn't seem to be going anywhere in particular though, darkness did not follow, not even when the final rays had retreated beyond the fields – the sky remained boundless and bright. Only at ground level did darkness seem to find root.

In the kitchen, as Arne put down a stack of plates on the worktop, I put my arms around him. He tensed.

'Are we friends?' I said softly.

'Of course we're friends,' he said, turning and giving me a quick peck before going out to fetch some more.

He wanted an early night, it had been late yesterday, he said. It was fine by me.

'You're not on your way up, are you?' he said when I wriggled up close to him, naked. He put his book down.

'No, it's not that,' I said. 'I feel glad tonight, that's all. Naturally glad, that is.'

He folded his arms behind his head.

'I don't feel up to anything tonight,' he said. 'I ate too much, one too many chops and too many potatoes. Not to mention all that ice cream afterwards.'

'I understand,' I said, and smoothed my hand over his chest. 'I'm glad we're here, anyway.'

We switched the bedside lamps off. A few minutes later he was already breathing heavily, steadily. I lay with my eyes open, gazing out into the dim light with not a shred of fatigue in my body.

It was true what I'd said. I felt glad, naturally glad. Something had let go of me as we'd sat there eating. I had all of this! The kids, Arne, the house here. We were on holiday like a proper family. We lived a proper life. Our kids were fantastic kids. So when we switched the lights off, Arne on his side and I on mine, and said goodnight to each other, it filled me with gladness. We were husband and wife, we lay in the same bed, were together in life and living it to the full.

Somewhere in the roof structure, the timberwork made a clicking noise at regular intervals. It was the sun having gone down. The heat leaving the house.

I didn't need my pills any more. It had all evened itself out on its own. So that was good.

That too was good!

A sudden noise, mournful and yet aggressive, came from outside. I sat up. It sounded like someone howling, but not exactly. A response came, from somewhere further away. It wasn't human.

The Rottweilers next door began to bark. Through the window I saw them on their hind legs, straining, front paws against the fence.

Arne slept on.

It'll be foxes.

You again? I'd almost started missing you.

They'll be mating.

I'm sure!

It's the only thing they're interested in now.

You don't say.

I put on a T-shirt and a pair of shorts and crept out from the bedroom. Looked in on the boys to see if they'd been woken by the noise and perhaps lay there frightened. But they were sleeping like two angels. They *were* two angels. Fair and fine.

Ingvild too was fast asleep, lying heavily on her stomach. I couldn't see her face but stood for some time in the doorway to make sure she wasn't pretending.

The foxes had stopped. The dogs too had quietened down.

I went outside. The trees stood motionless in the summer night. The only sound was the faint rush of the sea. Breathing gently in and out. Crossing the grass to the studio, I heard the foxes again. From the woods now. I turned and went in their direction. Between the tall trunks of the pines, onto the path that led to the house where that old man lived on his own. What was his name again? Kristian?

No, Kristen, that was it. Arne held him in high regard, though I didn't know why, even if he had built his own house and his own boat – *and* his own wheelbarrow, Arne told me once, full of admiration, as if it topped everything.

The house lay darkly among the trees. Its yellow walls put out their sorrowful song. I carried on walking. The old man and his house didn't interest me in the slightest.

IIIIIIIHHH IIIIHHHH

There it was again.

I stopped and tried to gauge where it was coming from. The woods, in the direction of the sea. Perhaps right down on the rocks at the shore.

I followed the narrow track that went down from Kristen's place to his boathouse. The landscape was becalmed, my feet were the only thing moving. Between the treetops, stars shone.

It was a magical night. And it was mine.

I was the Magician.

IIIIIIIHHH IIIIHHHH

So close now! But where?

IIIIIIIHHH IIIIHHHH IIIIIIIHHH IIIIHHHH

I emerged onto the rocks and glanced around.

There they were, perhaps fifteen metres away. Two foxes. One mounting the other. The male thrusting its hips, the female screeching, twisting, trying to bite him.

'Don't mind me,' I said quietly and crouched down. An image from a party I'd been to once flashed in my mind as the female suddenly extricated herself and tore away. The male, left to stand, turned its head and looked at me.

'What are you waiting for? Run after her, take her.'

He tossed his head with a growl before making off as if to follow my suggestion. I stood up again. From the veranda at that party I'd been to I'd seen a man take a woman from behind, she was standing, bent forward with her hands flat against a car, her moans echoing between the buildings. He fucked her hard with his hands gripping her buttocks, his trousers round his ankles. It had made me so horny. The only thing I wanted was for someone to come and take me just like that, up against a parked car with a crowd of partygoers watching us from a veranda.

Another howl.

The foxes are having fun tonight.

What do you want with me? And who are you? You're not from Anara, are you?

I'm whoever you want me to be.

So you're a joker. But what do you want with me?

I need you for something.

Like what?

You'll see.

And then he was gone. I sensed it, that all of a sudden there was no one else there but me. It was strange, because I hadn't really felt he was there in the first place. But if I could sense that he wasn't there now, then surely I must have done?

Where are you?

Empty, still, only my thoughts and their echo.

I didn't want to lie awake in bed for hours on end. I didn't want to go back and work, Arne hated me working at night. I didn't like it much either, it so easily turned me into someone else.

Should I go and see Egil?

I could at least walk in that direction!

The sea dark and still on one side, the woods dark and still on the other. But the sea was dead. The woods were simply asleep and would wake up again.

Ten minutes later I stood on Egil's veranda and peered in through his window. I knew what would happen if I knocked. The whole sequence of events played out in my mind, so I carried on into the trees, following the path that ran off behind the house. The air was warm and smelled of salt and pine needles. The light, weird. The darkness, white. I walked and walked. Sweaty thighs rubbed against each other. An enormous longing inside me. For anything at all, really.

Like something in the folk tales, the stone church was there in front of me as I emerged from the woods. Low, whitewashed, towerless. Probably a thousand years old.

I'd forgotten it even existed.

Weren't churches always open? Or was that just in the old days?

I lifted the heavy, rust-covered bar and pushed the door. Empty and still inside. The stained-glass windows shimmered in the mild light of night. Nets and rowing boats. Jesus, fisher of men. The fishermen called to be his disciples.

Suspended from the ceiling was a sailing ship. White clouds, as if it were sailing in heaven.

A religion of blocks and tackle, ropes and sails.

I went back out. So unimaginably quiet. Long grass grew up between the gravestones, many lopsided, some mottled with lichen, those nearest the boundary wall with moss.

Below, the night sea stretched away in all its might.

Perhaps God was aquatic. An underwater god, his son sent up to the surface.

Washing another person's feet is an erotic act. The one who washes subordinates themselves to the one who is washed. But only apparently so. For the hand passes over the bare skin, made sleek by tears and ointment, it presses and rubs and smooths, and such intimacy carries a promise of more. She looks up at him as she strokes his foot, does not look down but up, looks at him with solemnity and warmth. His blood begins to course. Although she cannot see his cock as it begins to rise underneath his robe, she knows that it does. She knows all about the minds of men. She places his foot in her lap, presses it to her crotch, looks up at him, smooths his foot firmly with both her hands, first one foot, then the other. He swallows and wants more of her, wants to penetrate her. She knows that this is so, for no gaze can keep such a thing concealed.

At once I felt so tired. I sat down on the low stone wall. Looked out across the woods, which were low and windswept here so close to the sea. I imagined the disciples in a little boat, tipping the body into the water. It was weighted with a heavy stone. Mary Magdalene was there too. She was a disciple as well. The most cherished. A series of pictures focusing on her. Like the ones in the churches. Stained glass, perhaps? Jesus casting the seven demons out of her. The washing of his feet. The two of them fucking. Mary watching him die on the cross. The disciples committing his body to the sea.

I looked at the church, the woods stretching away from it. It was a long walk back. Did I have the energy?

There was a grave marker, set flat in the ground. There was a verse on it.

How sweet now rest when life itself is wear
When age but sickness' name doth bear
How now the soil the noble soul doth please
Whose wistful longing but Heaven may appease

To vanish blissfully into the soil, there to long for heaven?

Or is heaven down there?

Heaven in earth.

The verse was flanked on one side by a relief showing a skull with a worm crawling through an eye socket, on the other by an hourglass.

I clambered over the wall and set off down the slope. I was so tired I could hardly see straight. Low, stunted pines, thicket and scrub. My T-shirt was soaked through under the arms. My hair too was damp. Sweaty, fat and ugly I was. And so tired, so tired. The night was magical no more. My steps were heavy, my thoughts were grey. Perhaps I could find a nice little spot here and sleep for a while. Arne and the kids wouldn't be waking up for hours yet. I wouldn't be able to sleep for long here anyway, it wouldn't be possible. An hour's rest. And then home.

A bit further on I came upon a dip in the rock. Dry, yellow grass grew in it. Small trees and bushes gave shelter. I lay down on my back. The chances of anyone coming past were less than zero. I was quite safe.

I closed my eyes, and sleep came.

I was woken by a cry. An unfamiliar child stood looking at me. The sun was behind him and his figure was haloed by its bright light. I sat up without meeting his gaze.

'She's awake now!' he shouted.

'Come here immediately!' a man's voice shouted back. 'This instant!'

The boy, who in his hand held a carrier bag, stared at me inquisitively for a few seconds before turning and running away.

I got to my feet and brushed myself down. My first thought had been that it was Asle or Heming who had shouted out and that I was at home in bed.

If only.

What time was it?

Nine, perhaps. Ten, even.

They were probably out looking for me now.

I rejoined the path and saw the father and son stepping across the flat rocks of the shore below. I paused, waiting for them to reach the water's edge before I set off myself, over the rocks and the stony beach, the rocks beyond. The sun burned my neck, the sea was unmoving, not a breath of wind in the air.

Suddenly, the dream I'd been having came back to me. Not just a fragment as was usually the case with the dreams I had, which dissolved almost instantly. This one was still vivid, and so powerful that it stopped me in my tracks.

I'd gone through the woods and into the church. But I hadn't *experienced* it. I'd seen it from the outside. And the person seeing had not been me. It was as if there was someone else inside me who watched me go through the woods and into the church. Or rather not *someone* else, but *something* else. Something hard, cold and disturbing.

It had to be him. It couldn't be anything else. His voice had been inside me. Now his eyes had been inside me too.

Tove, get a grip. It was a dream! He wasn't real.

He was a figment of the unconscious mind. And my unconscious mind did as it wanted. Especially when I was asleep.

Nevertheless, it was unsettling. It had been so real.

As if I hadn't enough to worry about as it was, I thought to myself and walked on, hastening over the bare rock into the woods at the back of Egil's place, down to the shore again.

Why couldn't I be together and in control of myself the way other people were? I wanted to be good with the children, a mother who made them feel secure, but then I had to go and do things like this. Things I didn't want to do. They just happened.

I tried to think up an explanation as I climbed the steep bank leading to the house. If I said I'd gone for an early-morning walk, it wouldn't be that far from the truth.

They were sitting outside having breakfast at the table, all four of them.

Why weren't they out looking for me?

Didn't they care?

They looked up as I came over the lawn.

'You've been away for a while,' said Arne.

'Yes,' I said. 'I woke up early and decided to go for a walk. The weather's glorious!'

I ruffled the twins' hair. They ducked, without taking their eyes from their breakfast.

'Did you sleep well, love?' I said as I sat down next to Ingvild.

'Mmm,' she said with a nod.

She's embarrassed about you. She doesn't want a mother who sleeps rough. All she wants is to get away from here.

I looked at her as she sat there so fair and fine, in her hand one half of a bread roll topped delicately with salami and two slices of cucumber. Even her breakfast had to be done properly.

'What would you like to do today, Ingvild?' I said, picking up the bread knife and parting a roll for myself. Ingvild shrugged.

'Don't know.'

'Go for a swim?'

'Maybe. Or go into town.'

'It'll be far too hot in town,' said Arne. 'Anyway, what would we do there? We're on holiday. We can shop when we go home.'

'OK,' said Ingvild.

'We could go for an ice cream in town,' said Asle.

'We're not going into town, that's final,' said Arne.

Why was he in such a bad mood? Why couldn't he think about what the kids wanted?

All he thought about was himself.

'How about if Ingvild and I go into town and you three go swimming?' I said.

'No, Mum, we don't need to. I'm fine. It was only a suggestion.'

You see?

She's a teenager. It's normal for a tenager to be embarrassed about her parents.

I looked at Arne, who looked back at me. He didn't seem best pleased with me. I shifted my gaze to the doorstep where the cat lay motionless in the sun.

'Is there any coffee?' I said.

'In the pot in the kitchen.'

I stood up and went inside, poured myself a cup.

'Leave me alone,' I said out loud. 'I want you to leave me alone now. OK?'

No answer.

I took my coffee back out with me, stepping carefully over the cat at the same time as I squinted under the sudden deluge of sunlight. I knew the voice was mine, it just didn't feel that way. And that dream . . .

Was he watching us now?

I sat down. The mood wasn't good.

'Don't mind me,' I said. 'I'll just sit here with my coffee and have a smoke.'

'Don't you want your bread?' said Asle.

'Oh, I forgot about that.' I picked up one of the two halves and took a bite, put it down again and then lit a cigarette. 'Let's have a nice day today, shall we?'

They were having a nice day until you turned up.

Oh, for God's sake. Enough's enough.

I stubbed the cigarette out on my plate and got to my feet.

'I'll have a shower before we get the day under way,' I said. 'Decide what you want to do. I'm easy.'

GAUTE

It's amazing what a summer can do. Some of the boys who had started the school holidays in June thin-limbed and slight, with the high-pitched voices of children, returned to the classrooms in August tall and gangly, with whopping great hands and feet and voices like rust. There was a lethargy about them now as well, something you don't see in young children but which throws a shroud over many teenagers. The girls had shot up a year or two before, so the imbalance that had characterised years six and seven, when the boys had been children and the girls young women, often a whole head taller, now evened itself out.

'Lovely to see you all!' I said. 'Did you have a nice holiday?'

A few mumbled in the affirmative, some nodded, others sat doodling in their own world.

'Did you?' Sindre said, and let out an unmotivated laugh.

'I did indeed. We were in Crete. Interesting place. Have you ever heard about the man from Crete who said that all men from Crete were liars?'

'Why did he say that?' said Sindre. 'Are they?'

'The man who said that was called Epimenides. He lived two and a half thousand years ago. Why do we still remember what he said? Because it's what we call a logical paradox. If what he said is true, then he's a liar, which means it's false. In which case it's true! Do you follow? And, if it's true, then it's false! And on it goes into infinity.'

They gawped at me. I smiled and went over to my desk, sat down and took out the register.

'OK,' I said. 'That was just a digression. And I promise not to ask you what a digression is.'

'It's when you lose the thread,' said Astrid. Her name always made me think of Princess Astrid, Mrs Ferner, as she was officially called, so in my mind she was never anything but Mrs Ferner. She was as sharp as a knife, but overly sensible too, which was a shame.

'That's right,' I said. 'Anyway, as you've no doubt realised by now, I'm your form teacher again this year. Besides that, I'll be taking you in maths and science – *and* social studies! I'm even looking forward to it. No newcomers this year either, and no leavers. Are we all here?'

'Gudrun isn't.'

'Anyone know if she's ill?'

There was a shaking of heads. Gudrun was a bit special, she kept herself to herself, and barely spoke. Hardly a word to anybody. I'd been told about her when I'd taken over as form teacher the year before, but I'd assumed it was just shyness. I'd pushed her a bit the first few days, cautiously, only for some of the others to turn against me in one of those typically exaggerated displays of solicitude that groups of young girls so often put on. It makes them feel like they're responsible and doing the right thing, it boosts their self-awareness.

I'd had a lot of trouble with Gudrun. She was clearly a case for the schools services' mental health counsellor but couldn't be referred without the consent of her parents, which they wouldn't give. It was the mother I'd spoken to. I'd found it striking how little she resembled her daughter. The daughter's face was lean, the mother's fleshy, and while the daughter avoided all eye contact, the mother seemed to seek it as often as she could. Her eyes were fixed on me when she explained to me that Gudrun was talkative enough at home, there was nothing special about her in that or any other way, she was just a normal child of that age. But she won't say anything at school, I said. She won't talk to anyone. Not even to me. In which case, perhaps it's the school that's the problem, she said, not Gudrun. Did that occur to you?

Mothers. Some of them will defend their children to the last drop of blood.

I compromised and arranged for the counsellor to sit in on one of our lessons so as to observe her. Afterwards she told me Gudrun was indeed communicative and had been shaking and nodding her head and smiling too, so she wasn't shutting the world out in any way. And she was writing as well, wasn't she? Yes, I said, she hands in all the written assignments. So she's just decided not to speak, the counsellor said. That's it, yes, I said. And that's not normal. No, it isn't, she said. It's a sign something's not quite right, I went on. Very likely, she said. But if neither Gudrun herself nor her parents want to talk to me, there's nothing I can do.

Gudrun stuck out from the other girls, always in the same old clothes, presumably hand-me-downs, things no other teenager would be seen dead in. She looked special too, with her pallid face and jutting chin, her deep-set eyes and the bluish skin of her sockets.

'The poor girl,' said Kathrine when I told her about her. 'Nothing's worse than not fitting in when you're that age.'

'I know,' I said. 'Sometimes she looks like she's from the nineteenth century. You know, those old photos of consumptive children?'

'What's she like at home?'

'No idea. The mother seemed all right, though. I think they're quite poor, not that it means anything necessarily.'

'It means they're poor,' said Kathrine.

As I noted her absence in the register I decided to ring the mother at home if Gudrun wasn't at school the next day either. They could have moved away for all I knew, it wasn't unknown for parents not to inform the school, they thought it happened automatically.

That afternoon the kids and I ran Kathrine down to the airport shuttle bus. I'd offered to take her all the way to the airport, but she said it was a waste of resources, so instead we said goodbye at the side of the main road in the rain.

She crouched down and kissed the kids on the cheek, drew herself up again and gave me a peck on the mouth, a couple of brief little pats on the back.

'Have a nice time,' she said.

'You too,' I said. 'Enjoy your freedom!'

'What freedom?' she said with a laugh. 'I'll be working!'

When we got home again, Marie wanted to text her and sent her a whole load of emojis. In reply she received a single heart. I imagined

Kathrine thought all her love was contained in it, but that was a bit too advanced for Marie, who wondered why her mum had only sent one emoji when she'd sent so many.

I put them to bed early, then sat in the basement with my guitar and the Moog. I never used the word compositions for what I did down there, preferring instead to think in terms of ambient soundscapes or sound collages. Kathrine liked it, at least. And Martin too, when I'd allowed him to listen. The thought of putting it out in some way had occurred to me, but I didn't know of any suitable forum. I could have sent something to one of the radio stations, but nearly all of them played purely commercial music, while the ones that didn't, like P2, hadn't the kind of programme that aired music by unsigned artists. Spotify or SoundCloud might have been options, but my thinking was that my stuff would only drown there. Besides, how much fun would it be to have eight or nine followers, knowing that every time I logged on I'd be confronted with how few listens I'd got. The work I did in the basement would take on a different slant then, it would seem like I had ambitions, and was failing. All of which meant I was better off as I was, making music on my own down there, pretending it wasn't important.

The piece I was working on at the moment was entitled 'Nature. A Sermon'. It began with a kind of electronic murmur over which I'd laid a simple guitar part.

Di-da-da-doo
di-da-da-doo
di-da-da-dii
di-da-da-diiii

The synth provided a warm background, and the idea was that the guitar part was a living creature. A bird over a whsipering sea, perhaps, or a fox cub on a windy day in the woods. After it had looped a few times I started building it up. The Moog could distort the input from the guitar, making it almost unrecognisable, and it was so easy to get something good out of it that sometimes it felt like I was cheating. You hardly needed to be able to play anything. A little sequence of chords could be manipulated until it sounded like an entire orchestra of synthesised sound. In the case of this particular composition, this sound collage or whatever it was, I laid down various guitar patterns one after another, then manipulated them to produce a storm of sound. Or a storm of life, as I was alluding to in the title. On top of that I put in a good old-fashioned guitar solo with a lot of distortion. I played it back to myself, then went upstairs into the living room to watch the television news and to come down to earth again. It wasn't that I missed Kathrine, that would have been absurd, she'd only been away a few hours, but the house did feel strangely empty nonetheless. Emptier still when I climbed into the double bed on my own. But it was a good feeling too in a way, to know that I wasn't taking her for granted. I picked up my phone from the bedside table and typed her a text about the bed being empty without her, only to delete it before I'd sent it. She didn't care much for sentimentality, and besides, it might make her think I didn't want her to go anywhere. Which wasn't the case at all. On the contrary, it had been good to spend a whole evening on my own in the basement, it had been ages since I'd had the chance.

Gudrun was still absent the next day. I called her home number after first lesson, but there was no answer. It was Friday, my timetable gave me an early finish and so I decided I could just as easily stop by on my way home. I entered the address into the satnav and submissively followed the directions intoned by the dispassionate female voice. A few kilometres along the main road, then away from the main valley into a side valley where smallholdings were still dotted about between residential houses belonging to a newer estate. I'd never been there before and glanced around with idle curiosity as I followed the road. Half the valley lay in the shadow of the fells, and although the vegetation was green and lush, there was still something desolate about the area. It could only be the looming fellsides that gave the impression, I thought, for they sloped so darkly, in places almost black, and the road glistened with their moisture.

The house they lived in was set back against the rock, on a ridge slightly above the road, next to two others. Block Watne homes from the eighties with a garage underneath the veranda. I drove up and parked outside. The doorbell I pushed made no sound, so I knocked on the glass with my knuckles and stepped back a bit, my eyes darting around casually as I waited. None of the houses had a garden and all three had something forbidding about them, as if their purpose was not to provide a place to live but to keep something out, or keep it in.

The mother came to the door. She looked worn out. Drooping, dog-like jowls, long reddish-brown hair with broad stripes of grey in it.

'Hello,' I said. 'I was just wondering if everything's all right with Gudrun. I tried to call earlier, she hasn't been to school and –'

'She's a bit under the weather, that's all,' the woman said, her eyes as staring as I remembered. 'We thought she'd be going in this morning, but then she felt a bit poorly again, so I thought it best she stayed off another day. I forgot to let you know. I've been busy, you see.'

She smiled apologetically. I hadn't seen it in her before.

'Good to know it's nothing serious!' I said. 'Do you think she'll be there on Monday?'

She nodded.

'I should think so.'

'OK,' I said. 'Tell her I was asking after her and I hope she's well again soon!'

'I will,' she said, and smiled again before closing the door. I felt a bit stupid as I got back in the car. Would I have checked on any of the other students like that if they'd been off for two days? Probably not.

I started the engine and fastened my seat belt. It was profiling that had brought me here. They were obviously poor and so I'd naturally thought . . . well, what? That she was neglected. That there was . . . alcohol involved, domestic violence perhaps.

At the next house along, the front door opened. The man who came out waved his arms and came hurrying towards me.

I flicked the switch in the door and the window slid down.

'Are you going into town?' the man said, leaning forward. He was in his sixties, with a face that was unusually round, soft and kind-looking.

'Yes, I am,' I said. 'Do you need a lift?'

'If you don't mind, that would be *very* handy. The buses are few and far between out here and my car's at the garage, so when I saw you there, well . . .'

'Hop in.'

He opened the door and got into the passenger seat. I pulled away slowly down the hill and indicated before turning onto the road. He sighed with satisfaction. White T-shirt underneath a dark blazer. Blue jeans, white trainers. Balding. Bit of a pot belly. Sunglasses parked in the neck of his T-shirt. He looked like someone who worked in arts administration. With the jazz festival perhaps. Or at the university.

'Not seen you out here before,' he said.

'No, you won't have,' I said. 'Never been here before.'

'But you know Antonsen?'

'Not exactly.'

'You had some business there, though. You're not a doctor. You're not selling anything. And you're not a tradesman.'

What do you know? I felt like asking, but said nothing. The man was right.

'There's only one thing left,' he said. 'The dependable old schoolteacher. Gudrun's been off school and you came out here to check up on her.'

He flipped the sun shield down in front of him before looking at me with a smile.

'You've voted Socialist Left all your life. Now you're thinking Liberal Party. No, wait, how silly of me! You've become *more* radical as you've got older. You're voting Red Party now.'

I gave him my frostiest look.

'Where do you want to go?' I said. 'Town centre all right?'

'That'll be grand. It's true though, isn't it? Teacher, Red Party? Oh, and you're married with two kids.'

'What if I'm divorced?'

'You wouldn't be wearing your wedding ring, would you?'

'And if we couldn't have children?'

'Try again. There's a kiddies' book on the back seat, *Karsten and Petra*, not the sort of thing you or your wife would read, is it? Besides that, a plastic tiara and two Pokémon cards. I'd say seven and ten years old. The younger's a girl, the older's a boy.'

'I could have three? Or just one, who likes *Karsten and Petra* books *and* Pokémon?'

'Then I'll draw your attention to the rear safety belts, two of which have been used rather a lot, the one in the middle considerably less. I'm sure there *are* children who like both *Karsten and Petra* and Pokémon, but their Pokémon interest will have been aroused by an older sibling. An only child wouldn't arrive at Pokémon on their own. Still, it doesn't matter. You *do* have two kids, don't you?'

I felt completely invaded and said nothing.

Water glittered up ahead, everything had a mossy green glow, the asphalt worn pale by years of traffic all day long.

'People often get offended when I guess right,' he said. 'Nobody wants to be easily read. Everyone wants to be special.'

'Perhaps because everyone *is* special.'

'It's a nice thought! But is it true? In a way, communism as an ideology was dead right. Everyone's the same. As distinct from identical. However, it could never work. Everyone's the same, only no one wants to accept it, not really, which of course is why capitalism is so successful. It manages to make everyone feel unique in all their sameness. That's what we used to have religion for. So it's always been there . . . Anyway, here I am yacking away! I hope you don't think I'm ungrateful. It's very kind of you to give me the lift. I'll shut up the rest of the way, if you want. I'm assuming though that you're the sort who can't sit in silence with someone you don't know without feeling uncomfortable?'

'I'm sure I can manage,' I said. 'You can talk or stay quiet, it makes no odds to me.'

'I see!'

He laughed and then went quiet.

We came past the new church that didn't look like a church, more like a municipal facility. Smoke rose up from the incinerator that cremated the dead. Then we passed the school and he looked at me.

'That where you work, is it?'

'You're the one who said I was a teacher,' I said, 'not me.'

He laughed again.

Warehouse stores and shopping centres, then the new tunnel into the big intersection above the town.

'Where do you want me to drop you off?'

'Anywhere, it doesn't matter.'

'Where are you going?'

'Høyden. You don't have to take me to the door, though! Especially as I've been so annoying.'

'You work at the university?' I said, glancing across at him. The harsh sunlight revealed his skin to be pockmarked. Not from acne, it was something else.

'Chance would be a fine thing!'

'What line of work are you in, then?'

'Communications.'

'Do you live out there, or were you just visiting someone?'

'Visiting. You *are* a teacher with two kids, aren't you? Still married to their mother and voting Red Party?'

'Could be.'

His laughter was infectious, high up the scale, and I smiled. The traffic in town wasn't too bad and soon I was able to drop him off at Høyden, between the old university buildings and the church. Still with the engine running I checked my phone for any messages. Kathrine would be giving her paper soon and I texted her to wish her good luck.

Thanks, but I've already given it, she replied.

How did it go?

OK, I suppose.

What's happening now?

Plenary discussions. Then group work.

Time for a chat?

Later. I'll give you a ring.

OK.

When I looked up I saw the hitchhiker standing over by the church talking to some people. They were sitting on the steps, and although they were some distance away I could see they were rather beggarly looking. Dossers, or not far off. He was gesticulating, apparently trying to explain something to them. I turned the car and drove back through the town and home, arriving only a few minutes before Marie and Peter got in from school. It wouldn't have mattered if they'd got there before me, Peter had a key, but still I was glad to be there when they got home, I remembered how cheerless it had felt when I was their age to let myself into an empty house in the afternoon.

I took them with me to one of the big hypermarkets on the outskirts of town and did the shopping for the weekend. They liked that, both of them, because I let them have what they wanted. Back home I made pizza – or rather I made the dough and they did the topping. We ate in front of the TV while they watched their favourite film, about a father and mother who for a whole day have to do as their children say. They'd seen it at least ten times, but that didn't matter. After the pizza I gave them the sweets they were allowed on Friday nights and by nine o'clock they were both in bed.

Kathrine didn't phone as she'd said she would. She'd probably just forgotten the time, it was a big seminar and she was friends with a few of the other participants. I could have called her again but didn't want to be clingy, so I didn't contact her until I went to bed, when I sent her a short text.

Had a good day?

She didn't reply. I lay awake for some time thinking about what she might be doing. The gleam in her eye in the days leading up to her going away, she'd been looking forward to it. Better there than here, more exciting? Old friends from her student days. Perhaps someone she'd particularly liked back then. They'd be married too now. A sudden opportunity. No one would know. One as guilty as the other, and guilt can be tempting when it's a secret.

I checked my phone even though it hadn't lit up there on my bedside table the last hour.

Surely I couldn't stoop so low that I'd demand to know what she was up to?

It was probably nothing anyway.

But she'd been distant for a while now. Disappearing every spare moment to get some work done.

I looked in on the kids. Both were fast asleep. At least they had a good life. I was sure about that. The routines we kept made them feel secure. Everything was familiar and good. They never came anywhere near the holes you could fall into, they didn't even know there were any.

I sat with a glass of wine downstairs and gazed out at the road that lay so empty in the still of night. Why couldn't I allow her a bit of fun? Let another man go to bed with her. Fuck her there on her hotel sheets.

She hadn't even asked how the kids were. Two days without them. Not a sign of interest.

When I went back up to bed I saw that she'd replied.

Yes, it's been good! Sorry not to call, I met Torunn and we went out for dinner, so it was late by the time I got back. Speak tomorrow? Sleep well!

I put the phone down on the bedside table again and sat down on the edge of the bed. There had to be a way I could check. Maybe I could call Torunn and say Kathrine wasn't answering her phone. Work something in about them having dinner together.

Dinner? What do you mean?

I couldn't sleep now in any case.

I put my T-shirt and trousers on and went out onto the veranda. The decking was still warm under my bare feet. A faint grey light shimmered above the black outlines of the fells. Everything was so still. I propped myself against the railing and stood there staring for a while, then went back inside and opened another bottle of wine, it was Friday, so it wasn't going to matter much. I poured myself a glass and took it back out with me, pulled a chair over into the corner and sat myself down.

I wasn't often up at night. I certainly never sat outside.

The summer I turned seventeen, when I was staying with my grandparents, I was out every night then. I was so infatuated with a girl that I couldn't bear to sleep or even sit still. I used to put my headphones on, *Harvest Moon* in my ears, and just wander off. Up the empty valley behind their house, to the falls and beyond, along the shore of the lake above, gleaming and silent in the light of the night, to a place I'd discovered, a flat area of rock on the fellside where I'd sit and listen to music, atomised by feelings of love.

It was Kathrine who'd been the object of my affections. She was fifteen then, I was two years older. She sang in the choir. I played bass in the band. She was the best-looking girl there by a mile. Gorgeous in a hesitant sort of way. I would smile at her, try to catch her eye as we played, so she already knew who I was when later I went and sat down beside her at summer camp by the fire one evening, and she didn't shy away when eventually I put my arm around her. Anything but.

'I've been waiting for you,' she said.

That sentence said so much about her. She knew what she wanted and was able to envisage how things would pan out. She was determined, but self-effacing at the same time, which meant that her strong will was hidden, a surprise when it came to the fore. I've still not seen that combination again in anyone that age, and as a teacher I've seen a lot of fifteen-year-old girls. She started going to Ten Sing in protest against her mother, I soon gathered. Her mother, Synnøve, was as cold as ice. Nice enough on the face of it, but she radiated cold, it was impossible not to feel it whenever you met her. Synnøve's husband, Mikael, was rather unsociable. Not actively, he wasn't unfriendly as such, it was just that he never took much interest. Not in us, anyway. Synnøve did, but she always thought she knew better. Kathrine's brother, Håvard, was a professor of art history, eight years older than his sister, divorced with two teenagers. None of them had much time for me. I don't think they disliked me exactly, it was more me being just a schoolteacher and the fact they could see that I was quite happy with that.

I felt sure Synnøve thought Kathrine deserved better. And that she would have found someone more suitable if I hadn't turned up in her life at such an early stage. But she accepted me at the time. No doubt she found me harmless enough, and we were so young then. Besides, we were in a Christian environment where you didn't have sex before marriage. We did, of course, though Synnøve would never have imagined it.

It was a big thing for us. It built up gradually. I'm not ready yet, Kathrine would say whenever we got close. Then one night when I was on my own at home, she came round with some frozen prawns, some bread and lemons. Prawns were the best thing I knew. As I tipped them onto a dish to thaw, she whispered in a low, bashful voice that she was ready now.

It was tender and gentle, and I loved her for bringing the prawns.

You didn't have to be a shrink to understand I had something she wanted. Everything she didn't get from her family. She found a haven at our place, my parents liked her and spoiled her as if she'd been their own daughter.

For three years we saw each other nearly every day, did nearly everything together. Then, the summer she completed gymnas and was about to move to Oslo to study at the university, she broke up with me. Just like that, out of the blue. She cried and said we'd grown away from each other. But you're crying, I said. You're feeling one thing and thinking another, can't you see? She shook her head, unable to talk. I phoned her every day after that, until she asked me to stop. I did. But I couldn't get over her.

The next few years we basically had no contact. I saw her every now and again when I came back for Christmas and the summer holidays, usually only from a distance, though we did speak to each other a couple of times, never on our own, though, and only superficially.

I got together with someone else, her name was Unn, she was a student at teacher training college like me. We bought a flat together out in Sagene when I started working. One of the first days after we started living there I bumped into Kathrine, she was standing right in front of me at one of the refrigerated displays at the supermarket. She was genuinely pleased to see me. It turned out she lived just round the corner. We agreed to have coffee together and reminisce about the old days. It felt innocuous enough, it had all been such a long time ago. But then sitting with her there at that table, seeing her smile, hearing her voice and her laughter, did something to me. It was as if the years just rolled away. By the time we parted, I was consumed by her. All I wanted was to see her again. Unn was good, better than I deserved, so I knew I had to dismiss the whole thing, that I couldn't see Kathrine again and had to stop thinking about her. But there I was with Unn completely oblivious on the sofa next to me, in the flat we'd only just bought and done up together, and all I could think was that a life with her would be a false life. I could go along with it, at least I could if we had children, but I only had one life and surely it wasn't meant to be only a half life?

Unn was crushed, couldn't understand it, our life together had only just begun. She grieved as if I'd died. And to her mind I suppose I had. I said nothing about Kathrine. We sold the flat, Unn moved back in with her mother and I rented a bedsit, felt lousy, like a traitor, a selfish and altogether bad person. I had Kathrine's number, but out of respect for Unn I couldn't bring myself to dial it. I'd have felt like a widower getting married the day of his wife's funeral. Not until a couple of months later, as Christmas approached, did I call her and ask if she was going home for the holidays. She was, and we agreed to see each other.

Kathrine still didn't know the whole story. She knew I'd been living with a woman called Unn and that I'd left the relationship feeling it hadn't been right for me. But she didn't know exactly when that had happened, and she certainly didn't know that it had happened because of her. That would have been too cynical, too calculating.

This time her mother was against us. She was polite towards me, but to Kathrine she expressed her doubts over several years, until we had Peter – I suppose she realised then that there was nothing more she could do.

I put the cork back in the bottle, rinsed my glass under the tap, put it in the dishwasher and went back to bed. I kept picturing Kathrine with another man, and in each case tried to put it from my mind, but it was as if some part of me wanted to go there, because the images kept coming back, and with them an accumulating, dismal sense of despair.

I woke up with Marie standing in the doorway in just her knickers, watching me. I propped myself up on my elbows and mustered a smile even though I was drained and not in the mood for smiles.

'Why are you still asleep?' she said.

'What time is it?'

She gave a shrug and I picked up my phone.

Ten to nine.

'What are we doing today?' she said.

'We're going to get you dressed for a start. And then we'll see. Is the weather nice?'

She nodded.

'We could go swimming?' I said.

She smiled.

'You run along and I'll get up in a minute.'

'Promise?'

I gave her a look of exasperation and she padded off.

The thoughts of the night before seemed excessive now. Of course she wasn't unfaithful. She was a mother of two young children, well organised, sensible, it wouldn't even occur to her.

I stepped into the shower and turned the water on. Maybe we could take one of Marie's friends with us, I thought. But then I'd have to ask Peter if that was all right. He would say no, and then possibly dwell on it the rest of the day, the fact that he had no friends of his own he could go swimming with. It wasn't unlikely he'd start crying either.

On the other hand, I couldn't go on shielding him all the time. He had to learn to manage his emotions, as Kathrine always said.

I put on a pair of shorts and a T-shirt, took one of Marie's summer dresses from her wardrobe and went downstairs to join them.

When an hour later I parked the car at Nordnes and felt the heat of the asphalt at the same time as a breeze filled my nostrils with the smell of the sea, just as Marie opened her door and Peter his, I was struck by a sense of complete freedom. I could do exactly as I wanted. It felt like a revelation. They each gripped a hand and together we walked down the hill towards the outdoor swimming pool that after a short while came into view in front of us, a glare of white wooden buildings in the sun. People everywhere. We found a spot on the grass and spread our blanket out before going down to the pool and jumping in. I tossed them about a bit, swam towards the bottom with the two of them clinging to my back, stood on the edge and watched them swim back and forth. Afterwards we bought ice creams and sat in the sun to dry.

What would I do, if I could do what I wanted?

Exactly what I was doing now.

But doing it with the feeling of being free was another thing altogether.

Why?

I couldn't fathom it. But it felt compelling, more than just a whim.

On the way home we stopped off at the food hall. I wanted to make something nice for when Kathrine came home and bought two matured ribeye steaks, a head of broccolli, tomatoes and potatoes, then a pricy bottle of red at the off-licence. The kids sat in the back, content and exhausted, with damp hair, occasionally saying something to each other.

'Anyone want a hamburger from Burger King?' I said as we stood waiting for the light to change at a crossing in the town centre.

'Yes!' Marie cried.

Later that afternoon I was mowing the lawn and was almost finished when Kathrine phoned.

'Hi!' she said. 'Just thought I'd check and see how you're getting on.'

'We're fine,' I said. 'How about you?'

'It's been very intense. Interesting, though, and all very good.'

'What did Torunn have to say, anything interesting?'

'Torunn?'

'Yes, didn't you have dinner together yesterday?'

'Oh, yes! Yes, we did. Oh, she's fine. We had a nice evening. Sorry I didn't manage to phone like I said I would.'

'You're phoning now.'

'Yes! Are Peter and Marie around?'

'They're inside. Do you want to call them on FaceTime?'

'Good idea. Speak to you soon!'

I got started making the dinner while the kids were talking to her. My head didn't know what my hands were doing. I was almost certain she hadn't been out with Torunn. The surprise in her voice when I mentioned her name: *Torunn?* Now she was laughing and chatting with the kids. She hadn't been out wth Torunn. But she told me she had. She'd been lying. And why would she lie about something like that?

There was only one explanation. She'd been with someone else. Writhing and moaning underneath him like a whore.

I tipped the pasta shells into the boiling water and began to set the table. I couldn't be sure. I didn't have proof. Probably never would have, either.

But she'd lied to me about what she'd been doing.

Over on the sofa, there was a flapping of hands as the kids said their goodbyes. Once they'd hung up, they darted across in unison to hand me back the phone, then sat down at the table to wait for their dinner. It felt good having them there. They were so sparkling, and such friends for each other too, and their being there helped me take my mind off things until they went to bed and I was on my own again.

Kathrine was the most rational person I knew. It was inconceivable that she would risk everything we had. What was an hour's thrill compared to a whole life together? She'd never do that.

Never.

But maybe that was what drove her? Always sensible, always rational, always ready to assume responsibility. Couldn't that eventually give rise to a destructive longing for the opposite?

My thoughts shuttled between the two possibilities.

I knew her so well.

Which only gave substance to the suspicion. If I didn't find it unthinkable, she wouldn't either.

She texted me late that night.

Just wanted to say goodnight, she wrote. *Sleep well!*

I didn't reply at first, but then realised I'd be playing into her hands, she'd know then that I suspected her of something and would be able to take precautions. It would be better just to act normal, make her feel safe, then confront her when she was least expecting it.

Goodnight, I typed. *Love you more than anything.*

After the kids had gone to bed the next evening I took the steaks from the fridge and put them out on the worktop to allow them to come to room temperature before cooking. I didn't know exactly what time she'd be home, only that it was going to be late. I texted her, as cheerfully as I could manage.

When do you land? Entrecôte and red wine await!

No answer.

I sat out on the veranda and phoned first my sister then my mother, more out of a sense of duty than anything else, and then had a longish talk with Martin. I said nothing about what was eating away at me, though I wanted to. Martin was married to one of Kathrine's best friends and I didn't entirely trust him, I knew how hard it could be to keep your mouth shut with the person you live with. In any case, he was going out, he was a film buff and there was a showing of 'the great Dane Dreyer's *The Word*', he said. Shortly after we hung up, a reply came from Kathrine.

I couldn't believe my eyes.

Missed the plane. Having to stay over at Gardermoen. Catching first flight in the morning then going straight to work. Really sorry. Maybe the wine and the entrecôte will keep till tomorrow?

How stupid did she think I was?

What did she take me for?

Go to hell, I typed. *And stay there.*

I sat for a moment and looked at the words. I needed to keep a cool head. If I sent the text, she'd know that I suspected her and would have all the time in the world then to come up with an explanation.

I deleted what I'd written and typed another.

Not like you at all. What happened?

The typing bubble with the three little dots appeared as soon as I'd sent it. Seconds later came her reply.

Went out with Camilla and Helle after the seminar, couldn't get a taxi and the train didn't move for an age.

She'd had the explanation ready, it was obvious. It was far too matter-of-fact and came without delay.

I put the light on in the living room, went into the kitchen and threw the steaks in the bin.

I was too gullible by half. Had to stay calm and think clearly.

A lot of misfortune all at once! All well here, kids asleep and I'm working. Miss you.

Miss you too, came the reply. *Sleep well.*

I googled hotels at Gardermoen and found nine. None of them knew anything about a Kathrine Reinhardsen.

Oddly enough I fell asleep almost immediately and slept soundly until the alarm went off the next morning. I was no longer angry, only despondent. I saw the kids as if from a distance, as if they weren't really anything to do with me. I put my best face on, they didn't notice there was anything wrong. They had their breakfast, packed their school bags and got in the car, ran gleefully, all limbs, into the school playground before I carried on to work. After parking the car I checked my phone and saw that Kathrine had sent a text. She wrote that everything was fine, reminded me that Peter needed his PE kit today and Marie a couple of library books, and asked me to make sure to pay a garage bill before it got passed on to a debt agency.

I didn't know whether to laugh or cry.

Either she was more cynical and calculating than I'd thought possible, or she hadn't done anything.

But I'd caught her out in what was patently a lie. She hadn't stayed at any hotel at Gardermoen.

Why was she lying?

Students were streaming past the car, I turned off the phone, grabbed my briefcase and got out to start the day.

We had biology first lesson. The plan was to kick off a project they'd be spending the whole autumn term on. They'd be learning about biotic and abiotic factors of an ecosystem and usually I connected this up with human impacts on nature on the one hand and conservationism on the other, both important elements of the syllabus. With the climate crisis as my hammer, I'd also be knocking a hole through the wall between science and social studies, for which reason I'd insisted on taking them in that too. The idea was to do as much as possible outdoors and then round the whole thing off by taking them to an island in the fjord where we'd spend the night. I'd been doing just that with my classes for several years now, so they knew what was in store for them, having heard the older students talk about it, or so I gathered.

I only thought about Kathrine fleetingly.

Gudrun was still absent. No one in the class had spoken to her, and her mother had neither phoned nor emailed to say she was staying off. It concerned me a bit, something clearly wasn't right.

I gave her mother a ring in the break, but again there was no answer.

After a double lesson with year nine, I had an hour's gap in my timetable before year eight were to have me for maths. It was time enough to drive out there and back again.

Or should I just leave it?

I didn't want to compromise them. Outside school itself, teachers no longer had much authority, but they still had a bit. A second visit would be putting the screws on.

Øyvind and Kamilla were sitting chatting in an otherwise empty staffroom when I came in. Øyvind had been form teacher for two members of the band that had gone missing. He seemed to be sunning himself in having known them first-hand, at least that was what it sounded like as I sat down, and was laying out the theory that they'd entered into a suicide pact and were now dead.

'I remember how pleased I was when they took up music and started playing together in a band. I suppose I thought it could be their redemption. Well, not so much theirs as Mathias's. Sander was just following suit, you know. Tagging along. But Mathias was serious about it.'

'You knew them pretty well, then?' said Kamilla.

'Oh yes. Mathias's parents were quite open about the problems they were having with him. When he was twelve he tried to stab his father with a knife. Couldn't keep his temper under control. It always seemed to come out of nowhere, too. The parents were decent, middle-class people. So there was nothing traumatic about his background, at least not as far as I could see.'

'Any problems with him here?' I asked.

'Nothing to speak of. He was a bit unsociable, kept himself to himself. That was all though. Then he started hanging around with Sander. Music ought to bring brightness and joy . . .'

'Lots of light and lots of warmth, as the song goes.'

'Exactly! But what they were doing was dark and morbid.'

My phone rang. I went out and answered it in the corridor.

'Hello?'

'Is that Gaute Reinhardsen?' a woman's voice said.

'It is, yes.'

'Hello, it's Maren Antonsen speaking. Gudrun's mother.'

'Oh, hello! I was trying to call you. How is she?'

'That's what I wanted to talk to you about.'

'Yes?'

'She's not ill, you see. She's just very tired. Too tired to go to school.'

'Why would she be tired?'

'That's just it,' she said.

I looked down the corridor as I waited for her to go on. It was striking how different it was in winter when coats hung from all the pegs. Now they were bare and standing there felt so much lighter. It was a place you could walk away from now without a thought.

'Is she not getting any sleep?' I said when nothing more seemed to be forthcoming.

'She's been having nightmares. She's tired out in the mornings.'

'I see. Nightmares, you say?'

'Yes. She'll be shouting and screaming in her sleep. Sometimes she claws at her face.'

'How long has this been going on?'

'It's been a week today.'

'Have you talked to anyone about it?'

'There's nothing to talk about. It's nightmares, that's all. But I thought you'd need to know why she's off school.'

'Perhaps you could talk to her GP about it?'

'Yes, or why not a psychologist?'

'Good idea!' I said, not getting the sarcasm at first.

'What for? It's only dreams. There's nothing wrong with the girl.'

There was, but that was something that lay far beyond the bounds of my own responsibility, not to mention my expertise.

'But she must attend school,' I said. 'There's no getting around it.'

'She's running a temperature too at the moment. So she'll be off a few days yet,' she said. 'Thanks for your time.'

She hung up before I managed to say anything more. Back in the staffroom, the party of two had broken up and I sat down on the sofa and drank a cup of coffee while scrolling through some of the newspapers' online editions. At some point I paused and typed *debilitating nightmares* into the search bar. A page about chronic fatigue syndrome came up. A long list of symptoms included *Sleep problems*: a) Irregular sleep patterns: insomnia, frequent waking, dreams/nightmares, need for sleep during daytime, b) Weariness after full nights of sleep.

Not that long ago it would have been unthinkable that a fourteen-year-old girl should be deemed to suffer from something like chronic fatigue syndrome. But things had changed unfortunately, I thought as I followed a link to something about narcolepsy that said:

Narcolepsy is a rare long-term condition causing excessive daytime sleepiness (hypersomnia). The brain is unable to regulate sleeping and waking patterns, which can result in loss of muscle control (cataplexy), sleep paralysis, hallucinations when falling asleep or waking, sleep attacks and excessive dreaming.

That seemed to fit too. She was extremely tired during the day, and the terrible nightmares she was having at night could well tick the *excessive dreaming* box.

She needed to see a doctor. My job now perhaps was to make sure she did?

I was about to phone Kathrine for her opinion on it when I remembered what had happened. Instead, I muted my phone, put it in my pocket and went into the workroom to see if there was anything coming up in the next few days that required me to be particularly prepared.

As I stepped into the hall at home I was greeted by the smell of her perfume a second before she appeared smiling in front of me, barefoot in blue jeans and a white top.

'Hi,' she said. 'Do you want some coffee? I just made some.'

There was an airy kind of beauty about her that hadn't been there before she'd gone away.

I followed her into the kitchen and dumped my briefcase on the floor.

'Are you home already?' I said. 'I thought you were at work?'

'I missed you all,' she said, and kissed me on the cheek.

It incensed me immediately.

'Coffee, then?'

'Yes, please,' I said, keeping calm. She turned towards the counter and I decided to seize the moment. If I waited, everything would just be back to normal again and it'd be too late then.

'Can I ask you something?'

She spun round.

'Of course.'

Looked at me enquiringly.

'Have you been unfaithful?'

Her face went red.

She hadn't been expecting it. Wasn't prepared. Two seconds of guilt radiating from her face before she collected herself.

'I can't believe you're asking me that. Don't you trust me any more?'

'Have you?'

'I won't even answer that,' she said, and turned away.

It felt good. In some warped kind of way it felt good that she was guilty.

'So you have, then,' I said, sat down on the sofa and leaned back. Perhaps it was having the upper hand that felt so good. Not having to bother about what she thought or felt.

She clattered about a bit in the kitchen behind me. Came in with the coffee. She'd got herself together now, her face was relaxed as well.

I wasn't going to let her off the hook.

'Why don't you trust me?' she said.

'You just told me you've been unfaithful.'

'No, I didn't. I told you I wasn't going to answer you.'

'And why wouldn't you want to do that? No, I'll tell you why. Because you won't lie.'

She stared at me. I avoided looking her in the eye.

'I want you to trust me,' she said. 'You think badly of me. That's up to you. But don't come to *me* expecting to have your paranoid suspicions confirmed or dispelled.'

I smiled.

'You blushed when I asked you.'

'I was angry.'

'So why can't you just tell me you haven't been unfaithful?'

'This is an all-time low, Gaute.'

'Is it?'

'Yes.'

'What hotel did you stay at?'

'What does it matter?'

'So you won't tell me that either?'

'No, not when you're asking like that.'

At that moment the kids came bustling into the hall and Kathrine, saved by the bell, went out to greet them. Greedily, she soaked in their warmth. She didn't look at me once as she came back through the living room before going upstairs with them to their room.

A few minutes later Peter came down on his own. He fetched his school bag from the hall, then came back in and sat down at the table.

'Homework?'

He nodded.

'I thought we might have chops for dinner. How does that sound?'

'Good,' he said.

'With potatoes.'

'Mm.'

'And cauliflower. And maybe some peas?'

I stood up, ruffled his hair as I stepped into the kitchen. Opened the fridge.

'Have you been talking about that missing band at school?' I said.

'A bit,' he said as he looked up at me.

'One of my colleagues was form teacher for two of the lads in that band. I was talking to him about it today. One of them had tried to stab his father with a knife when he was the same age as you.'

'What for?'

'I suppose he was angry,' I said, and put the white parcel containing the chops on the worktop, the bag of potatoes next to it. 'Haven't you ever felt like doing the same to me?'

He shook his head.

I laughed.

'Glad to hear it!'

It was as if I'd split myself into two. One part babbling away to Peter without a care in the world, the other a dead weight in the pit of my stomach. As soon as we stopped talking I was back in the pit again.

I took the potato peeler from the drawer, but when I opened the bag I saw the potatoes were so thin-skinned they didn't need peeling at all, so I put it back, emptied the potatoes into the sink and started scrubbing them instead.

'What's that you're reading?' I said without turning round.

'Science.'

'About what?'

'Extinct animal species. I have to write about one.'

'I read a book about the great auk when I was your age,' I said, and took out a saucepan into which I put the potatoes one at a time after each had been scrubbed. 'Some boys were on a canoeing trip with their dad and they saw a great auk. It might have been the last one ever. Even if it wasn't, it was still very exciting. Do you know about the great auk?'

'No.'

'It was a very common bird in the Viking age. A big, heavy thing it was. A seabird.'

'Was it like the dodo?'

'A bit, I suppose. The dodo of the Viking age.'

'The book says nothing about it. Can I google it?'

I unlocked my phone and handed it to him, then put the saucepan on the hob and switched it on.

'It died out in the nineteenth century,' he said behind my back. 'The last observation was in 1844.'

I heard the water start running in the pipes upstairs.

'You could write about the great auk, then,' I said.

He didn't reply and I turned round to look at him. There were tears in his eyes.

It couldn't be that bad, surely?

'What's the matter?' I said. 'Are you sad because it died out?'

He shook his head, picked up his book and locked his eyes on the page. I left him alone, turned the heat down under the potatoes, chopped some onion, switched the extractor on and started frying the chops in a frying pan, the onion in another. Kathrine was giving Marie a bath, I could hear little squeals every now and then.

How could she carry on as normal, when the night before she'd been screwing someone else?

What was it all about?

Was I just being paranoid?

What was I going to do? Force a confession out of her? Trust her and simply move on?

I couldn't think clearly when the one thing I had to do was think clearly. The feeling of hurt clouded everything. I felt like I could throw up.

I went over to Peter and ruffled his hair again.

'The world can be a bit unfair sometimes,' I said. 'A species can die out.'

'It's always our fault.'

'Not always. But often it is, yes.'

I tried to think of something positive to say, but couldn't. Nothing he'd take seriously, anyway.

'Did you enjoy yourself at the swimming pool on Saturday?'

He nodded.

'Maybe we can swim in the sea next weekend? It should be warm enough. Not like last year, do you remember that?'

'When you had to fix the jetty?'

'That's right. It was freezing cold!'

The bathroom door opened upstairs and I heard the two of them come out. I pictured Marie wrapped in a big towel, she loved that.

A true enjoyer of life, she was.

I took the chops off the heat and started on the gravy.

Kathrine said nothing as we ate. The children were silent too. Usually, I would try to lighten the mood if we'd had an argument, I couldn't stand that sort of silence, didn't want to be part of a family that wouldn't speak to each other. But now I didn't care. I wasn't going to give her even the slightest concession. She glanced at me now and then. Beseechingly, or so I imagined, though I refused to look her in the eye. After we'd eaten I went and sat down with the paper and left the dishes to her. Stared at the headlines without reading them, following what she was doing with all my senses.

She withdrew to the refuge of her study.

I persuaded Marie to come downstairs and watch television with me as the dusk fell. She snuggled into the crook of my arm. It felt good to have her there, so near to me.

It started to rain, gently at first, almost imperceptibly, but before long great globs of the stuff were dashing against the rail of the veranda out there.

Just as I was thinking about getting Marie ready for bed, Kathrine emerged.

'I'm going out,' she said and walked straight past us.

'At this hour? Where are you going?'

'No idea. Just out.'

She didn't even acknowledge Marie, who must have wondered what was going on. And it didn't seem to bother her at all that she hadn't put them to bed for several days now. All she thought about was herself.

'As long as you're back before their bedtime.'

She flashed me a look that was full of rage.

'You're here, aren't you?'

And with that she went out. I heard the car start and then drive off down the road.

'Where's Mummy going?' Marie said.

'I'm not sure. Perhaps she needed something from the shop. Anyway, it's time for bed soon.'

'No.'

'Five more minutes, then we'll go and brush your teeth. OK?'

She nodded and stuck to her promise. Once they were in bed, the light in their room switched off and the door closed, I sat down on the veranda and gave Martin a ring, then Endre, then Joakim. I didn't mention Kathrine's behaviour to any of them, even if it was the only thing I could think about. Still, it helped just to hear some other voices, share in other people's thoughts. I enjoyed talking to Martin especially. His life was in three compartments with watertight dividers between them. The first was his research, which he hardly ever talked about, presumably because he realised it didn't interest me. The second was Sigrid and his life with her, which he never touched on either, apart from when he was drunk. The third was everything else he did that interested him, and that was what we talked about. This time it was the Danish film he'd been to see – it had left an impression on him. I promised to watch it too as soon as I could, so we could discuss it properly.

Kathrine came home late, crept up the stairs and into the bedroom. She thought I was asleep, but I lay watching her, through narrowed eyes at first, which looked to her like they were closed, then, when she sat down on the edge of the bed and got undressed, with eyes that were fully open.

Apart from the first years we were together, a time when I had quite a head start on her and was the more experienced of us, she'd always been so sure of herself, there was something supreme about her, as if she was someone who couldn't ever make a mistake or do anything wrong.

Not any more.

She reached behind her back and fumbled with the catch of her bra before she managed to open it and let it drop from her shoulders. Straight after that she lifted her side of the duvet and climbed into bed. Lay there with her eyes open.

I felt her despair in every fibre of my body.

But then my thoughts returned to her deceit and I turned my back to her, my heart thudding in my chest with anger.

The next morning I avoided her. It was so unpleasant that in the car on my way to school I decided I'd either have to confront her once and for all and demand an admission, regardless of the consequences, or else put it all away and never mention it again. She obviously wanted us to stay together, if not she wouldn't have bothered denying anything, it wouldn't have made sense.

I decided to hold off on any decision until I saw her again, then let it depend on the moment. I'd go with whatever feelings were strongest in the situation.

Gudrun's desk was empty again. And everyone carried on talking when I came in, they didn't even stop when I sat down.

'Thank you, that's ENOUGH!' I said, raising my voice.

It was as if all the noise in the room flew into the wall like a bird and fell down dead to the floor.

'Right!' I said. 'Everyone here minus Gudrun.'

'What's wrong with her?' said Jesper.

I gave him a frosty look without saying anything. He glanced around him a couple of times with a hesitant smile on his face and tipped his chair back on two legs.

'OK,' I said once he'd suffered enough. 'Let's pick up where we left off yesterday, shall we? Nature. What's that exactly?'

Mrs Ferner's hand shot up. I looked at her and gave her the nod.

'Everything that isn't made by humans.'

'Exactly. But what about us? Don't we belong to nature? We're made by humans, aren't we?'

Some of the boys laughed.

'I'm not trying to be funny. It's a serious question. Are we human-made or are we nature? Are we created by us, or did something else create us? In which case, what?'

'Nature?' said Jenny, my favourite student in the class.

'Good answer,' I said, and got to my feet. 'It's not my intention to make this difficult for you. At least not yet! Because actually this is quite simple. We're going to be talking about nature, and as we already know we can divide nature in two – that which is living and that which is not. You'll remember we talked about the biotic and the abiotic. And then we have everything that isn't nature. What do we call that, if we're to use an umbrella term?'

'Culture,' said Astrid.

'So pollution is culture?'

'Isn't it?'

'Yes, it is!'

It perhaps wasn't fair to be questioning the concepts before they'd properly ingested them, the weaker students would just be confused, so I wrote them out in block letters on the board and spent the rest of the lesson establishing them.

Only when the bell went and they all suddenly broke up did I remember about Gudrun, and then, with a rush of mind-darkening anguish, Kathrine.

I poured myself a coffee and went and stood by the window. Clear blue sky, the playground filled with light.

She couldn't just stay away from school day after day without an acceptable reason. Her mother had to understand that. It couldn't be my responsibility either. I was just the one who had to report it. But I knew the system. It followed the rules blindly and unbendingly. And Vroldsen was no help.

I didn't care much for the school pyschologist either. But at least she seemed like someone who stepped carefully.

I put my coffee down and called her. She remembered me, and remembered Gudrun too. I explained the new development and asked for her advice.

'She can't stay off school indefinitely without a doctor's note. So you must tell the mother to take her along to her GP so everything's above board. If not, then she'll have to attend.'

'But she won't go to her GP,' I said. 'That's just the problem.'

'In that case the school will have to take steps. Tell her that. I'm sure she'll get the picture.'

I phoned the mother. To my surprise, she answered.

'Thanks for calling,' she said. 'I was going to myself.'

'How's Gudrun?'

'Still the same. No improvement.'

'She can't stay off school much longer without a note from her doctor,' I said. 'Do you think you can get that? If not, I'm afraid I'll have to refer the matter further up the line, which won't make things any easier for you.'

She gave a laugh.

'I'll send you a video clip,' she said. 'You can see for yourself.'

The second we ended the call, the bell went for the next lesson. It wasn't until the next break, sitting at a desk in the workroom, that I opened the message she'd sent.

What do you think the doctor would say about this? she'd written.

The clip she'd attached was grainy, recorded in a dimly lit room.

Gudrun was lying in bed, thrashing her head from side to side. Her eyes were closed. Her face was pale and bathed in sweat. Now and then she said something, hissed was probably a better word, through clenched teeth.

Then all of a sudden she sat bolt upright and screamed.

It was the most unsettling thing I'd seen. Her eyes were wide open, her head thrown back, and the scream she emitted seemed to be produced with every ounce of strength in her body.

She fell back on the bed and writhed as if receiving a series of electric shocks.

The clip stopped.

I watched it again, this time with my earphones in so that I could turn the sound up.

Amini shamini amini shamini, it sounded like she was saying.

And then the scream. So full of dread it scared the daylights out of me.

It looked like she was having some kind of attack. Epilepsy, perhaps?

Whatever it was, it was definitely outside my field of responsibility.

I phoned the counsellor.

'Hi, it's Gaute again. Sorry to be such a pain, only the girl's mother just sent me a video clip. It's Gudrun having one of her nightmares. Do you think you could have a look at it?'

'I don't see how I can help.'

'Just have a look at it. We can talk again afterwards.'

The staffroom next door was a hum of laughter and chat. I took my packed lunch from my briefcase and went in, standing for a second while I scanned for somewhere to sit.

'You can sit here, Gaute,' said Kari, making room on the sofa.

'Thanks,' I said, and sat down next to her before unwrapping a sandwich.

'Lovely weather we're having,' she said.

'Yes, it's incredible, isn't it?' I said. 'You can even swim in the fjord without getting hypothermia.'

'Speaking from experience?'

'No. Not yet, anyway. I did promise Peter we'd give it a go at the weekend, though.'

My phone thrummed in my pocket. I took it out and saw that it was the counsellor calling.

'I need to take this,' I said to Kari with an apologetic smile, and went towards the door. 'Hello?'

'I've seen the clip you sent,' she said.

'And?'

'I understand why you wanted me to watch it.'

'You do?'

I closed the door behind me and ambled along the corridor.

'Nightmares aren't unusual, particularly in children. But if they happen too often and become the dominant pattern – if they're routinely disrupting sleep, and so on – then usually there's some underlying problem. High levels of psychosocial stress, for instance. Anxiety and depression. Or they can be caused by PTSD.'

'I didn't realise,' I said. 'So nightmares are a diagnosis?'

'No, but they're part of a bigger picture. Her not talking is part of the same thing.'

'What do you mean exactly by *the same thing*?'

'She may have experienced something traumatic. Something very traumatic. Abuse, for example. Perhaps she's been threatened to stay quiet about it. In a case like that it would be quite rational to simply stop talking altogether. And then she'll relive it all in her dreams. Or it could be anxiety. But that doesn't come out of nowhere either.'

'No, quite,' I said, pushing the door open and stepping out into the playground, narrowing my eyes against the sun. 'So what do you think? What's the right thing to do?'

'I'd like to talk to Gudrun. The mother too. Is there a father anywhere, do you know?'

'I'm not sure to be perfectly honest. I've only ever spoken to the mother. She's the one who comes to the parents' evenings. I think perhaps they're divorced. I don't know for certain, though.'

'OK. I'm actually fully booked tomorrow, but I think I can find time. What time would suit you?'

A lorry backed slowly into the playground at the far end. A man in orange overalls stood waving it in. Some of the smaller kids had gathered to watch.

'I've a full day of teaching tomorrow. This is all a bit beyond my responsibilities, I have to admit. Still, I'll send you the mother's name and contact details right away.'

'I understand if you think it's a bit unpleasant. But you are her form teacher. I'm assuming both the girl and her mother have some sort of trust in you. So I want you to speak to the mother and tell her we're coming to see them.'

'Have you got the authority for that? I mean, can you just tell me to do something, anything?'

'Have you informed your headteacher about the situation?'

'Not yet, no.'

The lorry stopped and some kind of winch or crane was deployed, reaching out towards the yellow skip behind it. Then the bell went and the kids dispersed.

'You'll have to. I can have a word with him too, if you like. It is a he, isn't it?'

'Yes. Vroldsen, his name is. That won't be necessary, though. I'll take care of it.'

'Shall we say one o'clock? Meet at your school?'

'One o'clock sounds fine, yes.'

After we'd hung up I felt an urge to phone Kathrine. I felt rather humiliated, and it always helped to talk such things over with her. It was like airing things out, I could laugh about whatever it was and to a certain extent make fun of myself. And why *shouldn't* I call her? What if I *had* resolved not to make up my mind until we saw each other next? It wasn't seeing her that was the important thing, it was allowing my feelings to decide.

And my feelings at that moment were good.

I rang her number. But her phone was switched off. She was probably in church. A wedding or a funeral. Normally I'd have known.

The situation was untenable, the two of us not speaking to each other. It was almost worse than what it was about.

The skip swayed in the air at the other end of the playground, as bright yellow as the sky was bright blue.

I was going towards the door with my phone in my hand when Kathrine texted me.

I'll call you in a while.

The sofa in the staffroom was empty now and my coffee and lunch were the only things that hadn't been cleared away. I quickly ate the sandwich I'd unwrapped and dropped the other two in the bin along with the paper, put my cup in the dishwasher and went and sat down at my desk.

I'd have to phone Gudrun's mother and tell her I'd be coming round with the counsellor tomorrow. I wasn't looking forward to it.

What was I going to say if she refused?

I put my earphones in and watched the video again.

What was it she was saying?

Was it amini shamini?

Probably just nonsense words. It sounded like a rhyme a child could make up. Hocus pocus. Amini shamini.

I phoned the mother.

'Do you see what I mean now?' she said.

'Yes, I do,' I said.

'It's nothing a doctor can do anything about. Apart from give her sleeping pills, maybe. But she's only fourteen.'

'Actually, I've spoken to an expert on the subject,' I said. 'She told me it's not uncommon, especially among children. But in order to be able to help she needs to see Gudrun and have a chat with her.'

'Is she a psychologist?'

'Sort of, yes.'

'There's nothing wrong with the girl. I've said it before, and I'll say it again.'

'No one's saying there's anything wrong. But it's possible to do something about her nightmares. I don't think we should be turning that opportunity down, do you?'

She was quiet for a moment.

'All right, then,' she said.

I was relieved when I hung up. The horrible feelings that had been churning away in the pit of my stomach felt like they were almost gone. Life wasn't so bad, after all. Problems arose and problems were resolved. Sooner or later they always were.

I went through into the staffroom, got myself another coffee and was standing at the window looking out at the fells that were tinged blue in the distance, when Kathrine rang.

'Hi,' she said. 'You called. I was in a meeting.'

'Yes,' I said, putting my cup down on the windowsill then seeking a bit of privacy at the far end of the room, away from the workroom where others sat working. 'I wanted to apologise, that's all.'

'For what?'

'For my accusations yesterday. I don't know what came over me. I'm very sorry about it.'

'I understand,' she said.

'What, that I'm sorry?'

'No, that you suspected me. I haven't been quite myself for a while. It's better now though.'

'Is it?'

'Yes.'

'What was the problem?'

'I'd rather not talk about it over the phone. Tonight, perhaps? I could buy some wine and something nice to eat?'

'How about a barbecue?' I said. 'The weather's glorious.'

'Good idea,' she said. 'Perhaps we could have some people round too?'

Something sank inside me. Didn't she attach any more importance to it than that?

'I thought the two of us were going to talk?'

'We can talk afterwards. Shall I ask Sigrid and Martin?'

'Yes, all right,' I said, hoping my lack of enthusiasm was detectable.

'Great! I'll call them right away then. See you later!'

That was the night the new star appeared in the sky. I'd just come out onto the veranda when it rose up as if out of the sea in the west. It was unsettling, all of a sudden it was just there, silently brilliant.

Kathrine and Sigrid were sitting in the garden talking.

'Hey! Have you seen that?' I shouted.

'It's hard not to,' Sigrid shouted back.

Martin came out too and stood next to me, staring without a word at the star. He followed me as I went down into the garden.

'What do you think it is?' I said. 'A UFO? Ha ha ha!'

'It's a supernova,' said Martin. 'A star flaring up somewhere in the galaxy before burning out.'

'But it's so close,' said Sigrid.

'It only looks close,' said Martin. 'The reality is it's very distant. What we're seeing now is actually something that happened hundreds of years ago.'

Kathrine said nothing, she just sat there gazing at it.

'What do you think, Kathrine?' I said.

'I don't know. But what you say sounds convincing, Martin.'

Their eyes came together, and although neither of them smiled, there was nonetheless an intimacy about the way they looked at each other.

As if I couldn't have said it was a supernova.

After a while we cleared the table for dessert. Martin and Sigrid helped carry the things inside. I was rinsing the plates and loading them into the dishwasher when Kathrine disappeared into her study. It wasn't like her at all. I waited a bit, then went after her, opening the door without knocking so she wouldn't have time to hide whatever it was she was doing.

She was on the phone. I glared at her without saying anything, then closed the door again, carried on with the dishes, got some coffee on the go.

'Do you need a hand?' she said when she came back out.

'You could go and look after our guests, now that you've finished on the phone,' I said.

'I'm sure they can look after themselves for a few minutes without my help. Is something the matter?'

'No, not at all.'

'OK. I'll take as much of this as I can manage.'

She took the big serving tray and began putting cups, bowls and glasses on it.

'Who were you talking to?' I said.

'My mother.'

'At this hour?'

'Yes,' she said, looking me in the eye as if to say now she was being genuine. 'She said she was going to call when she got to the summer house, only she hadn't, so I wanted to check on her.'

I would never stoop so low as to go through her things. But my suspicions were now so strong that I had no choice, I had to know, not just believe. So when she went outside with the tray I opened her bag and rummaged through the contents.

I found a pregnancy test.

I stood there dumbfounded, holding it in my hand. It was like being told someone had died.

In a cold haze I went upstairs into the bedroom and left the test on her bedside table so that she'd know that I knew. Back in the garden she carried on as if nothing had happened. We watched the kids put on a play Peter had written. She clapped and enthused over it, and after the kids had gone to bed she sat chatting with Sigrid and Martin and me about whatever came to mind, the way you do when you've got friends round.

If she'd told me and said she regretted it, I'd have forgiven her. I wasn't inhuman, I knew how easy it was to be tempted into doing something stupid, especially now that we'd been together for so long. If she'd told me, it still would have been us together. It would have been something that had happened in *our* life. But I couldn't forgive her being false with me, lying and trying to deceive me. That wasn't us. That was her and him, her and him hidden away inside her, and me.

That was the deceit. Her not being sincere. She was a liar. An actor on a stage. Now that I *knew*, I could see it was all a performance, that she wasn't real, she was a liar. What if I hadn't found out? I wouldn't have seen it was all a play, I'd have thought she was sincere and authentic, that such was the life she was in.

Maybe it had *always* been an act.

Although I was dead inside, neither Martin nor Sigrid appeared to notice. They'd had wine, they'd had cognac, it was summer, they were having a nice time in their friends' garden. Kathrine didn't seem to notice either. She would do soon though.

I began to savour the thought of unmasking her. Shredding her lie, forcing her back into the realm of the truth.

Letting her squirm.

I wouldn't give her an inch.

Not an inch.

I gulped my cognac and poured another, looked up at the supernova, which of course was what it was. I remembered the winter when Hale Bopp, or whatever it was called, had shone and lit up the nights. The thought of the universe being so vast and open that we perhaps were unable to imagine what might come travelling from afar. A bit like driftwood turning up in a bay.

Tomorrow I'd call an estate agent and put the house up for sale. It didn't matter how much she was going to beg and plead. And then I'd find an apartment for me and the kids.

These were good thoughts.

She talked to Martin for a while about trees. How important they were in the Bible. The tree of knowledge and the tree of life, and the ancient notion that the wood used to make the cross of Christ came from the latter. But Martin didn't seem that interested and was trying to explain to her that what he was going to write about was the tree as a tree. No more, no less. And that was fantastic enough in itself.

Sigrid rolled her eyes at me and I smiled back at her.

We'd always got on well.

She'd stick up for Kathrine though outwardly, she was very loyal.

'What about the burning bush Moses saw?' she said, and laughed. 'That was God, wasn't it? God isn't even a tree, but a burning bloody bush!'

Kathrine smiled.

'Something really strange happened today,' she said. 'It began when I was on my way home. I met this very intrusive bloke at the airport. It turned out we were on the same flight. A proper pain in the neck. The sort that keeps turning up wherever you look. Anyway, this morning I buried a man, a man with no family or friends. We get them sometimes. The church was empty. When I looked in the coffin it was him, the same man! The exact likeness. Same age, same build, same face. It was an unusual face too, completely round, and with the oddest scars, you couldn't possibly mistake him. The thing is, the death had occurred eight days before! So it *couldn't* have been the same man, I only saw him two days ago!'

'Twins?' said Sigrid.

'You'd think so, but wouldn't the other twin, the one I'd seen on the plane, be at the funeral?'

'Two days ago, you say?' I said. 'That was Sunday, wasn't it? But you didn't fly home until yesterday, Monday?'

'A day and a half, then!' she said. 'The point is that it was the same man. And what's more I saw him again at the supermarket this afternoon. How likely is that?'

'Triplets!' said Sigrid with a laugh.

'It's simple,' Martin said. 'A man dies. His twin brother flies to his funeral. You see him on the plane, and then again at the supermarket.'

'But he wasn't at the funeral! No one came forward as next of kin. Not a single person. He was buried in the deepest loneliness.'

Martin shrugged.

'Why did you say it was two days ago if it was yesterday?' I said.

She ignored me. But Sigrid threw me a glance.

'Of course, there could have been a conflict between them,' said Kathrine. 'And the deceased could have lived here.'

'I can't see any other explanation,' said Martin.

We sat quietly for a minute before Sigrid looked at her watch.

'Well,' she said. 'We'd better be making tracks if we're to get up in the morning.'

'Yes, it's not the weekend yet,' said Kathrine.

We all got to our feet. When Martin and Sigrid made to start clearing the table, Kathrine and I both protested and they complied without objection. After following them out to the car, we started doing it ourselves. It was the last thing we'd do as a couple, it occurred to me. I said nothing, I wanted to give her one last chance to confess. But she didn't say anything either.

I went back out to fetch the rest of the things under the strangely bright night sky. By the time I returned to the kitchen, she'd already gone upstairs.

I poured myself another cognac and drank it standing by the sloshing dishwasher, half expecting her to call down to me. She had to know now that I knew.

I made a round of the downstairs rooms. Everything was tidied away.

No reaction.

In which case I'd have to react myself.

I put my glass in the sink and went up. She was lying in bed with her eyes closed, but opened them as I stood in the doorway.

'So who got you pregnant?'

'What are you talking about?' she said, obviously buying time. She sat up and stared at me.

'I've a right to know, I think.'

'Goodness me, Gaute,' she said, trying her best to come across all nice and innocent. 'Is that what you think?'

'What else would a pregnancy test be doing in your bag? And why have you hidden it now?'

'You mean you've been rummaging in my *bag*?'

She always took an attack-minded approach when we argued. Always gaslighting me. After a while it felt like I hadn't a leg to stand on. Well, it damn well wasn't going to happen this time.

'That's beside the point,' I said. 'Answer the question.'

She clutched the duvet to her chest with one hand and lowered her gaze.

'I've been feeling sick, and the idea came to me that I might be pregnant.'

'By whom?'

'By no one. I'm not pregnant. But if I was, it would only be you, of course.'

She looked at me.

'We don't have sex any more,' I said.

'It's not that long ago. Anyway, this is absurd. I can't talk to you if you're presuming things like that.'

'Who were you phoning earlier on, when you slipped away to your room?'

'Oh, stop it. I told you, I was phoning my mother.'

'Let me see your phone, then.'

'I certainly will not. You've gone too far now, Gaute. I won't have you not trusting me. Do you seriously believe I'm lying to you?'

'Yes,' I said, and went downstairs again. I put on *Slow Train Coming*, lay down on the sofa and stared at the ceiling. There was such force in denial. I'd never be able to prove anything, all I had was circumstantial evidence. But I knew. And I'd had enough.

I drew the curtains, turned the music off and curled up on the sofa to sleep, until it occurred to me that it was the wrong thing to do, I hadn't done anything, why should *I* be lying there? She was the whore, she could sleep downstairs, not me.

She pretended to be asleep when I went back up. I couldn't be bothered making a scene, so I flopped down onto the bed, took my shorts and T-shirt off and climbed under the duvet.

'Are we friends?' she said.

I didn't answer her, just turned my back on her.

'Don't be so childish, Gaute.'

I said nothing. If I engaged with her, she'd only turn everything upside down.

'Nothing's happened. I don't understand what you're doing. Do you?'

I turned my head towards her.

'Just shut up.'

'But, Gaute – '

'SHUT UP, I SAID!'

Silence then.

If only she wasn't going to lie there crying.

I couldn't check. Anger was the only thing I had now. I couldn't lose that as well.

The next morning we did what we were supposed to. Were chatty with the kids, who didn't notice that we weren't talking to each other, we made sure they got dressed and gave them breakfast. I told them about the new star and we went out onto the veranda to see it shining in the blue expanse.

'It's actually bigger than the sun,' I said. 'It's just that it's so incredibly far away.'

'But it's right there,' said Marie.

Peter laughed.

'It only looks that way.'

At school, at least among the students in the playground, the star was old news. No one seemed to be bothered about it, the same way they weren't bothered about the fells, the forest or the fjord, all they thought about were their groups of friends, forever forming, forever dissolving. We weren't that different from other animal species as far as that was concerned.

Was my family going to dissolve too?

Was that really what I wanted?

It wasn't a question of wanting. It was a question of necessity.

In the staffroom, where my colleagues were as busy as ever in the mornings, I clutched my coffee cup and was white with terror on the inside, smiling and chatty on the outside.

In the classroom I felt a bit better. The previous day was a dreadful backdrop that I was aware of the whole time without necessarily paying it much heed. I talked about the little expedition we were planning to the islet and what we were going to do there. It was too early really, but I wanted us to have something to look forward to, it would be motivational for them.

Shortly before one o'clock the schools' mental health counsellor emerged from a car in the car park. She walked through the playground with a confident stride wearing a pair of overized aviator sunglasses and a cross-body bag. I went to meet her in the corridor. She pushed her sunglasses up on top of her head, gave a smile and put out her hand.

'Shall we get going right away?' I said.

'Why not?' she said. 'Did you get someone to take your lessons?'

I nodded.

'The headteacher's deputising.'

'Vroldsen – was that his name?'

'That's right, yes. My car or yours?'

'It might be best if you do the driving, you know where it is.'

She was rather thickset, and her face rather flat. Jeans, despite the heat. A white top.

I unlocked the doors and we got in.

Could I see myself with her?

Not without thinking about Kathrine every day.

She sat with her knees together, her bag on her lap with her hands on top.

'What do you know about the mother?' she said.

'Not much,' I said, indicating before turning out onto the main road.

'Seems decent enough. Sceptical towards mental health professionals, though.'

'Who isn't?'

'Not me,' I said, and smiled at her.

'Have you ever been to one?'

'Can't say I have. Never had the need, thank goodness.'

Neither of us said anything for a moment. I opened the window slightly on my side. A shudder of air came in.

Was I really going to tell her tonight that I wanted a divorce? Would I be able to do that?

I could if I was angry enough.

'I remember her,' the counsellor said suddenly. 'Gudrun, that is. I thought at the time that something had happened to her. But there was nothing I could do.'

'What made you think that?'

'A teenager doesn't stop speaking for no reason.'

'There could be a social explanation,' I said. 'She's different. Most likely been teased, bullied. Certainly ostracised. And because she's different she doesn't stop eating, as many girls her age would do, she stops speaking.'

'I'm not sure calling it a social problem makes it any better. Bullying is bullying, whatever the circumstances.'

'No, but you mentioned the possibility of abuse over the phone yesterday. That was what I meant. It doesn't have to be the case.'

'It's more common than most people think.'

'Yes, I'm sure.'

'I see it every day.'

'I don't doubt it. But I think the mother here is OK.'

She took her phone out and started typing. After she sent a couple of texts I noticed her check the news from NRK. There was something breaking, the story highlighted on a black background.

'What's happened?'

'They've found those young men from the heavy metal band.'

'Oh?'

'Three of them killed. Bestial murders, it says here.'

'How awful. What about the fourth one?'

'They haven't found him yet. Looks like they think he did it.'

She put her phone to sleep and dropped it into her bag.

'Two of them went to my school a few years ago,' I said.

'Really?'

'Yes. Did you have any contact with them?'

She shook her head, sighed, and gazed out of her window in silence. A few minutes later we turned off the main road into the valley. Before long I saw the house come into view up on the ridge.

The mother came to the door as we parked and got out.

'This is Yvonne Pedersen,' I said with a nod to indicate the counsellor, who again pushed her sunglasses up on top of her head.

'Ah, the shrink,' the mother said. The counsellor gave a hesitant smile and put out her hand. Fortunately, it was accepted.

'I'm Maren,' the mother said.

A man was sitting looking at us, his legs splayed apart on a sun lounger on the veranda of the house next door. Wasn't it the guy I'd given a lift the last time I was here? No sooner had the thought occurred to me than he waved. I raised my hand in a half-hearted response. The mother and the counsellor both looked at me, then at the man on the veranda.

'I gave him a lift into town last time I was here,' I said. 'How's Gudrun?'

'You'd better come in and see for yourself,' the mother said. 'It's why you're here, isn't it?'

We followed her up the stairs into the lounge. It was unconventionally furnished, to put it mildly. The dining table at the far end was just a tabletop on two trestles. Around it were four crudely fashioned stools. Paintings done on plywood boards covered the walls, abstract images in vivid reds and greens, or naivist depictions of animals and people, like drawings done by a child. The curtains were home-made too, a grey, canvas-like material on which various figures were printed. Pushed back against the wall on the kitchen worktop were a number of empty wine bottles that I wished she'd cleared away before we came.

'Would you like something to drink? A glass of water?'

'No, thank you,' the counsellor said.

I shook my head too.

The mother sat down heavily on the sofa. It was deep, with several throws dumped on it, and bits of food and crumbs.

'So, where is Gudrun?' said the counsellor as she took the place in. I could see her working on her report already.

'She's asleep.'

The mother picked up a pouch of tobacco and began rolling herself a cigarette.

'She hasn't been to school for a week now, is that right?'

'That's right.'

'And that's because she's too tired?'

'Yes. She's been having these very severe nightmares. It's made her afraid to go to sleep, so she stays awake as long as she can. There's nothing I can do about it. You can't force people to sleep.'

'Why do you think she's having these nightmares?'

The mother shrugged, put her cigarette in her mouth and lit it.

'Does there have to be a reason?'

'Often there is,' said the counsellor. 'Disrupted sleep patterns can be a sign of stress or anxiety, they may even be a post-traumatic reaction. Has she had an unpleasant experience of any sort? Perhaps someone close to her died?'

'Died? No, everything's been normal. She wasn't looking forward to going back to school, mind. But that's normal too, isn't it? Listen, can't you sit down? You're making me nervous hovering about like that.'

We sat down.

'Why wasn't she looking forward to starting school again?'

'She's not happy there.'

'I understand she won't speak when she's at school?'

'So they say,' the mother said.

'Why would that be, do you think?'

She looked at me.

'Haven't you said?'

'Said what?' I said.

She turned her piercing gaze to the counsellor.

'Gudrun has an unusually deep voice for a girl, especially a girl of her age. She sounds almost like a man. It makes her embarrassed. The other kids haven't exactly ignored it. So I suppose she just decided to keep it to herself.'

'Is that right?' the counsellor said, looking at me. 'Why didn't you mention this?'

'I've never heard about it before,' I said. 'No one said anything to me about it when I took over as form teacher. All I was told was that she wouldn't speak.'

My phone vibrated. I pulled it out of my pocket just enough to see who it was. It was Kathrine.

'Does Gudrun have friends outside school?'

'What's that got to do with anything?'

'I'm trying to form a picture of her situation.'

'Listen. There's nothing wrong with Gudrun. She's a self-respecting girl and upset about her voice. That's all it is. We're fine.'

'Does her father play an active part in her life?'

'What father?'

'Is he dead?'

'Not as far as I know. But you're venturing onto thin ice there. That's a private matter. It's none of your business.'

I stood up.

'Could I use the loo, do you think?'

'In there,' she said, indicating a door over by the stairs.

I closed it behind me, sat down on the toilet seat and read Kathrine's text.

We can't go on like this. We need to talk. Properly. Have you got time tonight?

It could only mean one thing. She wanted a divorce. She'd been thinking about it for some time. Now she'd come to a decision.

I knew her.

All I felt was an emptiness inside.

I pressed the button to flush, washed my hands and returned to the living room. The mother stubbed her cigarette out in a bowl. Her movements indicated impatience and increasing hostility. The counsellor was sitting with her back straight and her legs crossed. She exuded what she probably thought to be composure, but which to me, and no doubt to the mother too, looked more like arrogance.

I mustn't be tempted to reply to her text. I couldn't just hand her the initiative like that.

'Perhaps I might speak to Gudrun on her own,' the counsellor said.

'The girl needs to sleep.'

'I understand that. But it's important to know what she's thinking.'

'Is this an evaluation?'

The counsellor smiled and shook her head.

'Gudrun's been off school for a week. She's experiencing severe sleep problems, possibly due to an anxiety disorder. We can't simply step back and hope for the best.'

'Gudrun does not have an anxiety disorder.'

'But she's afraid to sleep, you say. And since it's having such an adverse effect on her, we need to look into it more closely.'

She stood up.

'Where is she?'

The mother stood up too.

'Are you allowed to come interfering like this? Aren't you supposed to have some kind of authorisation?'

'All I want is to help Gudrun. I'd prefer not to have to pass it up the line that you've been keeping her away from school. That's quite a serious matter, as I'm sure you know.'

'I'll tell you what's a serious matter. Living in a society that runs on control and surveillance. That's a serious matter. The schools are only there to control the kids, and control their parents too for that matter. If you're the slightest bit different, the slightest bit alternative, the authorities are going to come after you. Anyone would think we were living in East bloody Germany. I'm a free person. I gave birth to Gudrun as a free person. We ought to be able to do exactly as we see fit. We're all individuals, every one of us different. But oh no. Oh no. School's destroying her, yet no one's talking about that, are they? The girl's having sleep problems and before you know it in come the shrink and the teacher. To *help*, they say. Can't you see?'

'You may be right,' the counsellor said. 'But you're also missing the point. I'm here to help Gudrun, not to control her, or you for that matter. She clearly isn't well. We can do something about that. But first I need to speak to her.'

'And if I won't allow it?'

'I'd prefer not to entertain that eventuality. You can help Gudrun by helping us. Doesn't that make sense? You must be worried about her too.'

'Of course I'm worried. I'm her mother.'

'Then let me help.'

'I don't believe in your sort of help.'

'That's fair enough. But I won't be making matters any worse than they are, so why not let me have a word with her? It can't do any harm.'

The mother sighed.

'Her bedroom's downstairs.'

We followed her down the stairs to the door at the end of the passage, which she opened for us. The first thing I saw were the bands of light that fell in between the slats of the blinds. Then Gudrun, asleep in a big double bed beneath them. She was lying on top of the duvet in a T-shirt and shorts. Terribly thin. Her collarbone and hip bones pronounced. In the dim light her skin looked yellow.

'It's almost a shame to wake her,' the mother said. 'You can see she's fast asleep.'

The counsellor said nothing and the two of them hesitated a moment before the mother bent over her daughter, took her hand and softly said her name.

Gudrun threw her head from side to side a couple of times. The muscles of her arms tensed until they trembled.

The mother looked up at us.

'She won't wake.'

The counsellor stepped forward.

'Gudrun,' she said. 'You must wake up now.'

Her voice was by no means loud, but the stillness of the room made it sound like she was shouting.

Gudrun gasped and opened her eyes.

She sat up and shuffled slightly so as to lean back against the headboard.

'There's someone from the school to talk to you, Gudrun,' the mother said.

Gudrun shook her head. Her eyes were empty and staring.

'He's here,' she whispered.

'Who's here?' said the counsellor, leaning closer. 'Who's here, Gudrun?'

Gudrun shook her head again.

'Is it your father?'

'Now listen here –' said the mother.

'Are you frightened?'

Gudrun nodded.

'What is it you're frightened of, Gudrun?'

'He's here,' she whispered again.

'Who? Who's here, Gudrun?'

'There's no one here, Gudrun,' the mother intervened, smoothing her daughter's hair. 'You've been dreaming.'

'Who do you think is here?' said the counsellor. 'Is it someone you know? Is it someone who did something to you?'

Gudrun stared at her as if unable to grasp what the counsellor was saying. Then she looked at her mother.

'Can I have a blanket, Mum?'

'Of course you can,' the mother said, and went over to the cupboard. Gudrun lay down again, drew her legs up and clasped her arms around her knees. The mother put a thin blanket over her and she closed her eyes.

'Do you want something to drink?'

Gudrun lay without moving, without answering.

'I think we should leave her alone now,' her mother said.

'Gudrun?' the counsellor said.

I thought about Peter when he was a couple of years old, the way he'd close his eyes and pretend to be asleep if anyone approached his pushchair and tried to get his attention.

'Perhaps we should go now,' I said.

The counsellor nodded and we went back out with the mother. Concerned not to put any more pressure on the woman, I went straight to the front door.

'Thanks for your help,' I said.

'I think there may be more to talk about,' the counsellor said.

The mother threw up her arms as if in despair.

'When would it be convenient for me to come again?'

'What do you mean?' said the mother. 'What good will it do?'

Glad that I wasn't been included in any return visit, I unlocked the car remotely as we stepped outside. Next door's veranda was deserted now. But as I went towards the car the pushy bloke appeared and came over. He must have been keeping an eye out at the window.

Gudrun's mother closed the door without saying goodbye. The counsellor stood for a moment and stared at me, obviously annoyed.

'So, we meet again!' the man said in a loud voice, still some distance away.

I gave him a nod, opened the car door and got in without closing it. It was boiling hot inside. Yvonne got in the other side.

'Do you want another lift?' I said, looking up at him as he halted by the car. He rested an arm on top of the door and smiled.

'No, I'm all right today. Just wanted to say thanks for the last time. This would be the mental health counsellor, if I'm not mistaken?'

From the corner of my eye, I saw Yvonne turn her head towards me. I didn't return her look.

'Relax,' the man said. 'An educated guess, that's all. Who else would the teacher bring when Gudrun's having mental health problems? Kristian Hadeland's the name, by the way. Neighbour of sorts. I don't live here, but I'm here quite a lot.'

'Shall we get going?' Yvonne said. 'I've an appointment back in town.'

I nodded.

'Nice to see you again,' I said. I gripped the door handle and looked up at him. He made no move to take his arm away.

'You must say hello to Kathrine,' he said.

'You know *Kathrine*?'

'I wouldn't put it like that. I met her the other day, on the plane up from Oslo. We chatted a bit. I had no idea you were married to her last time I saw you.'

He smiled.

'She's a public figure though, isn't she? Being a pastor, I mean,' he said. 'You must run into people who know her all the time. Or at least people who know who she is. Anyway, I shan't keep you. See you again soon, no doubt!'

He stepped back and waved as I drove off.

'Who was that?' said Yvonne.

There were beads of perspiration on her brow.

'Haven't a clue. I only met him last time I was here. He wanted a lift into town.'

'Rather unpleasant, if you ask me.'

'He is a bit, yes.'

'How did he know I was a mental health counsellor?'

'I've no idea. I certainly didn't tell him. He did say it was an educated guess though.'

She breathed in deeply and gave a shudder, then looked out of her window. The fellsides shimmered green in the sun. The sky was deep and blue and without a cloud. A space so vast it made everything down here feel small and inconsequential.

I opened all four windows.

We need to talk.

What could that mean other than her wanting out?

Was I supposed to just agree? Sit down and listen while she told me she wanted to leave me? Just accept it?

I see.

OK.

That's what you want, is it?

Well, if you say so, that's what we'll do.

Go upstairs and go to bed. Talk about the practicalities the next day. Who buys who out. Divide up the furniture, the books, the pictures on the walls and God knows what else.

If that was what she was thinking, she could damn well think again.

I'd give her hell.

Starting with who she was shagging.

Humiliate her.

She was the one who was leaving. So it was only right that I kept the house and the furniture. We'd do the whole thing through the solicitors. I'd refuse to speak to her. Stonewall her completely. Cold as you like.

'It makes me so angry,' Yvonne said suddenly, as if to herself, still staring out of the window.

'What does?' I said.

'The neglect. The girl was a skeleton. How can you be a parent to an anorexic fourteen-year-old and not seek help? Hide her away at home? All that crap about freedom and East Germany when you've a child starving herself to death!'

'She was very thin, yes. But the mother did seem to care about her. Quite a lot, I thought. Besides, it doesn't have to be anorexia. She might just be naturally thin. Or she could simply be missing meals because of her sleep being so irregular.'

Yvonne looked at me.

'But it didn't look good, I agree with you there,' I added.

'She was frightened too. I don't think I've seen anyone frightened quite like that before.'

'Yes, she was.'

I wasn't ready yet to ask what she was going to do about it, but she told me anyway:

'I'll set up a meeting with child welfare. It would be useful if you came too. You are her teacher, after all. And you saw what I saw.'

I nodded.

'I'll try to find time for it.'

We joined the motorway. I closed the windows and switched the air conditioning on.

'Isn't it a bit drastic though?' I said after a while. 'Involving the child welfare department? I mean, you haven't actually talked to her yet. I know she was a bit thin and that, but still . . .'

'I'll be telling them what I saw. It'll be up to them to draw their own conclusions. It's my job. I'm doing my job. We must think of what's best for Gudrun and nothing else.'

'Yes.'

'You'll be able to put forward any reservations you might have, of course.'

'Yes.'

I dropped her off in the school car park, by which time it wasn't worth me going back to work, so I drove straight home instead. I needed to think, come up with a plan. I couldn't just meet her unprepared.

I changed into shorts and a T-shirt, took a beer from the fridge and sat out on the veranda where it was boiling hot even in the shade of the parasol.

There was something about Gudrun. Something other than what the counsellor had seen. It wasn't anxiety. She was frightened, but the fear she was experiencing wasn't generalised, it wasn't an unease that we'd seen. She was scared of something specific.

Could it be the father, as the counsellor believed?

I swallowed a mouthful of beer and looked out across the houses.

What was I going to do here when Kathrine moved out?

How was I going to stop her?

Could I stop her? Was there anything I could do?

I got to my feet and went down to the greenhouse. The tomatoes were looking good, a bit hard maybe, but I took one nonetheless. No, as a matter of fact, they were just right. Couldn't be better.

The small, twisted cucumbers. The lettuce. The red peppers. The lemons, still green.

I watered everything, then took a lettuce, some tomatoes and a cucumber back up into the kitchen with me. I'd cook us some mackerel we could have cold for dinner, with cucumber salad.

But why? Was I really going to make dinner for us the day she told me she wanted a divorce? Was I supposed to pretend I hadn't cottoned on, that I didn't know? Or should I just go out and leave her on her own before she got the chance to say anything? I could give Martin a ring, see if he fancied meeting up. Yes, why not? We could sit outside somewhere and have a few beers, it'd be good.

I sat down again and opened the video Gudrun's mother had sent me. It was just as unsettling again now. Especially her chanting or whatever it was. What *was* it she was saying?

Amini shamini?

I googled it on the off chance.

Amini was a Persian name, apparently. It meant *reliable, loyal, trustworthy, wholehearted*.

Shamini existed as well, it too was a name, though this one was Hindi rather than Persian. It meant *heavenly star*.

Loyal to a heavenly star.

Was that what she was saying? In her sleep, two days before the new star appeared?

It could only be coincidence. She didn't know Persian. She didn't know Hindi. And she couldn't have had any idea a new star was going to appear in the sky.

But *could* it be coincidence?

It had to be, there was no other explanation.

I heard a car pull up round the other side of the house. I got up and went into the kitchen and looked out. It was Kathrine. I stepped back so she wouldn't see me, and watched her get out of the car, open the boot and take out a carrier bag full of shopping.

A calm came over me. She wouldn't have been to REMA 1000 and done the shopping if she was thinking of telling me she wanted a divorce the same night.

HELGE

It was just a day like any other. I'd got through all of them so far, so presumably I'd get through this one too, I thought, locking the car and then crossing the quayside to the Warehouse, as we called the building, even though it had been completely renovated and no longer had anything to do with the maritime trade of old.

Inside, the place was oddly quiet. Not a living soul to be seen.

I slipped my sunglasses into my shirt pocket and puffed a couple of times on my vape before going up the stairs.

Voices broke abruptly into song as I got to the top.

Of course.

The whole crew were assembled. Sverre in the middle with a huge cake in his outstretched hands. I stopped and forced a smile as they sang.

Hip, hip, hooray to you on this day!
Hear now, we'll sing you our praises!
All in a ring around you this day,
we march and sing you our praises!
We bow, nod and curtsy and turn with a swing,
dance you a dance with a hop and a spring,
our hearts they all wish you most ev'ry good thing!
To you on this day – hip, hip, hooray!

'Once again I'm reminded that Norway surely has the world's silliest birthday song,' I said as they completed the verse. 'But thanks all the same!'

'Do you recognise the cake?' said Sverre, and beamed from ear to ear.

I stepped closer, all eyes upon me as I considered the vague representation of our Malmö church project done in marzipan.

'Ha ha,' I said.

'Blow the candles out now, Helge, then we can all tuck in!' said Helle. 'Oh, and many happy returns!'

She reached up on her toes and gave me a peck on the cheek.

I blew out the candles they'd arranged to form a six and a zero. They all cheered and clapped, Sverre put the cake down on the nearest table and cut me a piece in the uncomfortable transition from community and togetherness to individuality and dispersal.

Three years already since we did that church.

It must have occurred to them too when they hatched their plan.

I took a bite.

'Delicious,' I said. 'Very kind of you, Sverre.'

'Your interview with *Aftenposten* was excellent,' said Helle, standing beside me now with a cup of coffee in one hand and a plate with a piece of cake on it in the other.

'Thanks,' I said. 'It was quite good, I thought.'

'What do you make of this new star?' she said.

'Yes, an avid reader of popular science must have a theory,' said Sverre.

'It's a comet,' said Børge.

'But it's not moving,' said Sverre. 'Comets move.'

'If it's far enough away, it'll only look like it's not moving,' said Børge, jabbing his fork towards the ceiling as if to emphasise his point.

'But it's Helge's view I'm interested in,' said Sverre.

'It's not necessarily anything we've seen before,' I said. 'It could be a completely new phenomenon for all we know. But don't ask me what.'

'You're talking about the new comet?' Paul said in English, stepping over to join us.

'Indeed,' said Sverre.

'Well, the comet is a comet,' said Paul.

'A comet is a comet is a comet?' I said.

'Exactly,' he said with a smile. He was bearded and wore glasses, unceasingly upbeat and socially untroubled in the way of so many

Americans, conviviality itself. What actually went on in his mind, I had no idea. He was impossible to read. Sverre was an open book by comparison, in fact I knew where I stood with everyone but Paul.

'Maybe it's something living,' I said, if only to pitch in with something nobody would have thought about. 'An extraterrestrial organism of some sort.'

'Right, like a kind of flower. A flower made of fire,' he said laughing.

'Yes, for instance. Or some sort of intelligence monitoring us.'

'Well, we take care of that ourselves well enough,' he said, glancing round exaggeratedly then laughing again.

I put my plate down and poured myself some more coffee.

'Well, must get some work done,' I said.

Sverre and Paul exchanged glances.

It was a very quick exchange, but nonetheless an exchange it was. It was obviously something they talked about. What I did when I said I was *working*.

I went into my office and closed the door behind me, pulled the blinds down in front of the glass wall that separated my own space from the open plan and then sat down with my feet up on the desk, only a moment later to sit properly and wake up my desktop Mac.

I opened the *Aftenposten* interview and started reading it again.

IT'S NOT ABOUT ME, IT'S ABOUT THE ARCHITECTURE

Visionary. Self-effacing. Loner. Socialist. Helge Bråthen embraces contradiction. Now, as he turns sixty, his view of the future is bright.

'Yes, and so what?'

Helge Bråthen, our only architect of true international renown, looks at me challengingly. We're sitting outdoors at a restaurant on the city's old wharf, surrounded by tourists, and I've just asked him a question about the criticism aimed at him and his previous firm Fuglen when a few years back they were awarded a prestigious commission to design a building for one of the most oppressive regimes in the world, the moneyed emirate of Qatar.

'Do you want me to say we did it for the money? Or do you want me to say I'm sorry, we didn't know what we were letting ourselves in for?'

He leans forward, planting his elbows on the table and spreading his hands without releasing me from his gaze. His face is tanned and leathery, cheeks and chin roughened by designer stubble, his signature mane of hair intact, though these days completely white.

'You have to understand that while architecture is politics, it is so in a different way. A democratic building is a different thing from a democratic country. Architecture can bring people together. A building doesn't care about your political convictions. A building can open up an urban space and create life there, but it can also close a space down and make it lifeless. In Qatar we were given free rein. We wanted to seize that opportunity and do something good for people. Should we have turned it down because the regime under which those people live is suspect?'

'You were paid an enormous amount of money . . .'

'Architecture is expensive. Hugely expensive, in fact. But the utility value is difficult to measure.'

He leans back with a smile.

'If I'd been a king, my motto would have been: *For all*. But don't include that, people will think I'm deluded. Shall we go?'

Tall and loose-limbed, clad in a pristine white shirt and beige-coloured chinos, he leads me through the narrow alley and out onto the quayside.

'What made you move here?' I ask, the waters of the Vågen harbour glittering in front of us in the sunshine.

'It's delightful here,' he replies, turning towards me. 'Don't you think? A small urban pearl. And I needed a change of scenery.'

Sifting through the search results for Helge Bråthen, what's striking is the sense of restlessness that emerges. The first time his name appears is in 1979 when as a member of an Arendal punk band he was interviewed for the local newspaper. The accompanying picture shows a sweaty-browed teenager with piercing eyes and – no surprise – an impressive mane. Two years later he turns up on the Oslo music scene, now on vocals and guitar for new-wave outfit Kongstanken. They put out three singles and two EPs (if anyone remembers the format?) before disbanding and disappearing. Bråthen, however, did not disappear, and the following year he resurfaces as an actor in cult movie *Sons of the Night*. Later he appears in its sequel, *Oslo Night*. Then there's a lull. Six years. The rest of the story is familiar. He founded the Fuglen firm of architects which ran away with the very first international competition it entered before going on from one prestige project to the next, acclaimed for its innovation, originality and environmental awareness – an area in which the firm were early frontrunners. High-rises, airports and railway stations made of wood rose up in London, Vancouver, New York, Tokyo. Rock-like art museums, mountainous skyscrapers. Ten years ago he jumped ship, relocating from Oslo to set up a new, considerably smaller, more locally oriented firm he called MÅR. Along the way he married, became the father of three sons, divorced, and married again, this time to the curator Vibeke Hjelmeland Jensen, thirty years younger than Bråthen, with whom he now has a daughter not yet a year old.

As we get into his car, I find myself thinking he comes across as rather content with the way his life has turned out. His hands gripping the wheel are big as slabs, though his wrists are surprisingly slender. My nose detects a faint waft of aftershave. The watch on his wrist is discreet, though fabulously exclusive.

'What took you into architecture exactly?' I ask as we head out of town in the direction of the Elvenes complex, MÅR's first major project close to the lake known as Birkelandsvannet.

'I could have been an artist,' he replies. 'I always liked to draw and paint when I was growing up. You can safely say I was a child who needed to express himself. Then in my teenage years I became very interested in politics. Architecture is the only field I can think of where those two interests, art and politics, come together. In another sense I suppose you could say I wanted to be an architect while still in the womb, nice and snug in that good, soft space. We're never as secure after that, are we? Nor should we underestimate the yearning we have to recreate that space. A home, a good home, is a secure and warm family surrounding.'

'Yet a womb doesn't immediately come to mind when I think of, say, the Sail in Chicago,' I venture.

'No, you're right, it doesn't!' he says with a suggestion of irony, and laughs loudly before continuing more seriously: 'And that's just the point with the Sail. That's where we're heading out into the unknown, into the future. Leaving all that we know and are so familiar with. What awaits us there?'

From a distance the Elvenes care home looks almost like it belongs to the hillside. Bråthen takes me out to an observation point a short distance away where he talks about the building with childlike enthusiasm, gesticulating eagerly.

'What was the first thing that came into your mind when you set about this project?'

'Light. The interface with nature. The views from here are so splendid. At the same time, we had to protect the idea of the private space. And of course it had to be functional! We couldn't for a moment lose sight of the fact that what we were designing was a care home.'

The rooms are rectangular boxes stacked on top of each other, each storey displaced in such a way that the overall impression is one of drawers pulled out of an item of furniture. The roof of one box becomes the balcony of the next. Everything is in wood and glass. Inside, Bråthen explains, a space emerges organically, almost like a grotto, and this is where the communal areas are situated, with the staff spaces on each side.

'Are you proud of it?'

'Proud?'

'Yes. Are you?'

'No, I wouldn't say proud. It's not about me, it's about the architecture. That applies more generally too. So-called signature buildings that you admire as buildings for their aesthetic qualities alone, that's just nonsense. Architecture is functionality – and perhaps there's a symbolic value in it too, for those who actually use a building. The best thing is when nobody pays the building any attention, but uses it without thinking about it. There's so much that we never notice. Smells, sounds, light. Everything works together and is a part of the building's aura. You sense it, but you don't think about it.'

'The socialism of his early years would be important to the star architect too, wouldn't it?'

'You could say so. Though I'd prefer to do without the *star* prefix.'

'So what's it like being a wealthy socialist?'

Immediately, Bråthen shows annoyance at the question.

'Listen,' he says, 'I do what I do because I like doing it. And I do it because it helps people. Yes, I make a very good living out of it. But what bearing does that have on anything?'

Back in town we meet up with the photographer, who arranges a photo shoot on the quayside in front of MÅR's offices, before continuing indoors.

Bråthen says hello to everyone he meets, joking and laughing. His assistant brings us coffee and we sit down on the sofa in his office.

'You're sixty now,' I say. 'How do you feel about it?'

'It feels good, definitely.'

'You're father now to a small child. Does that keep you young?'

'I don't know. But she does bring joy and happiness into my life, so it would be pretty much impossible for me to sit down and mope about life's autumn setting in.'

'Having married again, what has your new partner brought into your life?'

'What kind of a question's that?'

'Well, this is a feature interview, it's going to be about you and your life. I'm assuming she's an important part of that?'

He laughs.

'We're good together. Put that.'

It's an office devoid of personal markers. No family photos, no diplomas, no image of any building associated with his name. A series of framed drawings of trees are displayed along one wall, on the other three abstract paintings in vivid colours.

'If you look back at what you've achieved, what gives you the most pleasure?'

'Professionally, you mean? That's a bit like asking me to pick which of my children I like best. But we did a church in Malmö a few years ago. That turned out very well.'

'Are you a religious person?'

'Quite the opposite!' he says, and runs a hand through his hair. 'But I do believe in the equality of individuals. And I believe that what arises when people come together, what is created in that encounter, is more than the sum of what we are individually. I believe too that there may be some form of divineness therein.'

'Are you ever afraid of coming across as pretentious?'

'Never.'

I couldn't be bothered reading any more than that and went and lay down on the sofa. Apart from the horrendous condescension it was interesting to see how one appeared to others. How little of one's inner being came out, and how enduring earlier opinions could be – an interview from 1998 could still determine what an interviewer saw and believed twenty-five years later.

What would a truthful interview look like?

HELGE BRÅTHEN TURNS SIXTY WITH A BITTER TASTE IN HIS MOUTH: I'M NOT THE PERSON I USED TO BE.

HELGE BRÅTHEN AT SIXTY: I'VE STAGNATED.

Nothing much had actually changed. I could still do what I was good at. It was a mental thing, something had got in the way.

HELGE BRÅTHEN, STAR ARCHITECT AT SIXTY: I'VE LOST IT.

Maybe if I started smoking again.

Such things couldn't be underestimated. Creativity is a delicate business.

I could still do what I was good at. Nothing had changed. It was the thought that I couldn't that made the difference. A thought I'd failed to nip in the bud and now it had got out of hand. It was doubt itself that was the problem, not the object of the doubt.

If the mere thought was enough to make me grind to a halt, then the opposite thought would surely be enough to get me going again?

Nothing had changed.

I got to my feet and then sat down at the desktop, put my earphones in and opened Spotify, selected one of the suggested playlists without looking to see what was on it, and felt a tingle in my spine when 'Oh Baby' began.

Status Quo had to be the world's most underrated band! Their seventies albums were the business. And who would have thought 'Pictures of Matchstick Men' had come out thirty years before the Charlatans and the Stone Roses?

I sat vaping for a few minutes, gazing out at the deep blue and improbably still expanse of the fjord, the vegetation on the other side. I felt a stomach ache coming on, as always when I sat here. It was a Pavlovian reflex. The closer I got to the computer, the bigger the ache.

Among the projects we were working on I'd been stupid enough to insist on doing one on my own, no prying eyes. Only now I'd got to the point where I couldn't bring anyone else in, it would be so patently obvious how helpless I was.

It was a project that looked tailor-made for me. A big new centre on the island of Mors in the Danish Limfjord, dedicated to the writer Aksel Sandemose who'd been born there. Unusually, we'd been commissioned directly without having to submit a project to any competition. We were the ones they wanted, or rather I was. The building was to be situated in deciduous woodland outside Nykøbing, the site was particularly beautiful, and with Sandemose the seam of possibilities was rich indeed. I'd read up on him, of course, and had inspected the site. But none of the ideas I came up with would work. Sandemose was synonymous with the Law of Jante, the very essence of Scandinavian culture. But he was also about the shadows of the past and the human condition – not openness and light, but something psychologically impaired and marked. Sandemose himself was a rather obnoxious character, so I gathered. None of this could be swept under the carpet, I felt, so the building couldn't be wood and glass and light, neatly integrated into the landscape. But how could I make it un-integrated, how could I bring out the crimes of the past, the social oppression, without building a prison? Nick Cave had recently said that bad people making good art was a cause for hope. I liked that thought, it turned the idea of censorship on its head. I didn't have to chain the writer or his work to the building. But what was it I wanted to percolate up out of all of that, sixty years after the man had died?

I'd toyed with the idea of a longhouse – it was a form that at least was deeply rooted in Nordic culture even if it had little to do with Sandemose – and the thought was to make it a timeline of sorts, start with a ruin or something like that, then move on to some kind of enclosed space, parts that were separated from one another, allowing no overview, a heaviness at every point, and no sense of flow, then gradually open it all out until everything became light and clear and connected with the sky. Art as a redeemer of man.

But it was too abstract a narrative for people to grasp in one go, and the building itself as I'd imagined it would be hideous to look at. It would be false too. It's history that changes, not the human condition, be it individual or collective.

So I divided it up into several buildings. Which only made it worse.

My strengths had always been in conceptualisation, in giving ideas a simple, striking form. The Malmö church was a rotunda with a central roof opening. The heavens and the circle of life were above us, but also togetherness and closeness. The cross, enormous and constructed out of timber, rose up outside, next to the building. The thoughts behind it all were perhaps not that sophisticated, but the effect was immense – even I, who believed in nothing, felt the presence of something divine there.

I also liked the wholly unintended sense of the pagan that came with the wood. And it was true, was it not, that Christianity here had pagan roots?

But Sandemose?

I was a complete blank.

I could always do a tower, as they'd done for Hamsun, but then again I'd seldom seen such a horrendous and utterly confused structure in my life.

Do not think you are anything special.

No, because you're *not*.

Sandemose was bad karma to me.

The crimes of the past. But they weren't my fault. I hadn't had anything to do with them.

And anyway that wasn't the reason I was stuck.

Stuck? Was it that simple? That banal? Had I just got stuck?

I hadn't done anything of note in three years. Oh, I'd contributed, directed, advised, but I hadn't created a thing. In three years.

Getting in the car every morning and driving to work had become a charade. I was like one of those men who get sacked and never tell anyone, they just carry on leaving home in the mornings and coming back in the afternoons to talk about how their day has been in a job they no longer have.

For distraction I reached into my pocket for my phone, only it wasn't there. After a moment's panic I realised I must have left it in the car.

I didn't want to have to field the looks I was going to get as I went through the open plan, but I needed my phone, so I opened the door and stepped out, nodding and smiling to my left and right as I ran the friendly gauntlet that so accurately summed up what my life had become. Outside, the heat was like a wall. Some gulls screamed, angered perhaps by the weather. The car interior was boiling hot. I retrieved my phone and went back in, closing my door behind me again, relieved that I'd insisted on having my own office separated from the open plan, even though openness and egalitarianism, the equality of everyone involved, whether senior or junior architect, project manager, canteen worker or receptionist, had been fundamental premises in starting the company in the first place.

Everyone was equal, except me.

I sat down on the sofa and decided I might as well send replies to all those who'd sent me their congratulations. That was work too, wasn't it? But then Vibeke rang.

'Hi!' I said. 'How are my two favourite girls?'

'We're fine,' she said. 'We're at the shopping centre getting a few things in.'

'Like what?'

'Like some flowers, for instance. It is your birthday, after all. And Åse's had an ice lolly, which she liked very much, and now we might just go to a cafe or somewhere. What are you up to?'

'Nothing much,' I said, looking out at the cerulean blue of the fjord. 'It's too hot to work, so I'm just hanging around really.'

'Haven't you got air conditioning?'

'Yes, yes. It's the general mood more than anything. Too much summer, it makes a person restless. Anyway, where are you exactly? I could come and meet you. Have you had lunch?'

'Who has lunch at ten o'clock?'

She laughed. Perhaps I was coming on too needy.

'All right, how about in an hour then? Can you endure the inferno until then?'

'Well, *I* can. Not sure about Åse, though.'

Why was she so reluctant? Didn't she want to meet me there?

'We needn't have lunch just to see each other,' I said. 'Where are you? I'll come right away. I could do with some new shirts. A pair of shorts too, in fact.'

'Listen,' she said, 'it's not that convenient just at the moment.'

I froze.

'OK,' she continued after a pause. 'I might as well come clean. I'm busy with something secret.'

'Ah, I'm with you,' I said, though I was annoyed with myself for lapsing into such weakness.

'It's just a little thing. But I can reveal that it's something special that I think you'll like. That's what I'm hoping, anyway.'

'As long as it's not a cake in the shape of some church in Malmö,' I said.

'Was that their surprise?'

'Yep.'

She laughed.

'Did it taste nice?'

'Yes, as a matter of fact, it did.'

'They obviously love you,' she said. 'I do too!'

After we'd spoken I accessed my sketches for the Sandemose centre.

What was it they loved, if they loved me? A shell, that was what. Something they saw and could fill up with whatever they wanted. Because I was hollow.

I couldn't ever talk to Vibeke about it. I had no illusions, I knew why we were together. I was thirty years older than her. It was the creativity, the status, the self-confidence, perhaps also the money. All of which was OK, because that was me too. But if I told her the creativity was gone, and my self-confidence with it, she would know as well as me that it was only a question of time before the status and the money would be gone too. She'd be left with just a skinny old man.

For one thing, she didn't need to know. For another, it didn't have to be true. It was like a tennis match. You can lose every ball for two hours, but as long as you win the last one you're still in the game and everything can be turned around, then suddenly, suddenly you're no longer the loser but the winner.

If I got on top of this, which could happen in a split second, the time it took for an idea to strike a person, a three-year barren spell would suddenly mean nothing. I might even be able to talk about it.

The first thought is often the best. Even if it's hardly yet a thought at all.

I took my notebook out and leafed backwards through the pages.

There.

The Pond

Static water.

Unchanging.

Black.

Surroundings in flux. Not the pond. Though the pond may become overgrown. It remains the same. Deep. Mirror. Black. Old. Has always been there. No movement. Still. An eye. Looking up at the sky. Trapped.

That was it, yes. A whole week I'd played with the idea. Dig an actual pond there in the woods and somehow build downwards around it. And then, when the impossibility, the impracticality, the ridiculousness of it all eventually occurred to me: how about a well of some sort? In the middle of the building. A building with a centre to it. Another rotunda? But what would the well be *for*? It couldn't just be a symbol, it had to have a function. Perhaps it could be a kind of tank running from top to bottom through all the floors? A tank? Full of water? Was I losing my mind?

I'd always been open to the ideas that came to me, nothing was ever too stupid, only this time, this time I felt embarrassment, shame.

Why a pond?

It may have been relevant in respect of Sandemose, but its only *direct* relevance was to me.

The car in the murky depths with its headlights on. The man who died in it. While I just stood there staring. The parallel had been clear to me all along and I'd thought it was a good thing, it connected me to the project and lent to it a very particular authenticity. But it was only now that I understood what it was that had got me thinking along such lines at all. I wanted to make amends. I wanted to atone for myself. And in that light there was so much at stake.

Was that why I'd ground to a halt? Was that where I'd reached the impasse? Had what happened back then suddenly caused me to seize up?

No. I'd come to terms with what had happened. I'd been just a boy then, eleven years old, and the enormity of the situation had been such that a child wouldn't have known what to do.

That was the truth.

But still. There *was* a connection. I'd put it behind me and enjoyed success. A lot of success. And it wasn't right, I hadn't deserved it, though had accepted it all the same. In a way I'd known all along that eventually it would turn. That it was only a matter of time before fairness would prevail. Before what I had would fall away bit by bit, until finally I'd be standing there again, on that bridge in the darkness with the murky waters beneath me and the headlights shining in the depths, alone with my guilt.

I'd failed in other respects too, not least when it came to my children, though not only them, and it was clear to me that sooner or later the weight of it all was bound to halt my momentum. The flow, the buoyancy, that part of me that always said yes and never hesitated, never saw the limitations. That part of me that until now had been all of me.

I didn't really believe that, did I?

What you believe to be real, becomes real.

But I was only eleven. A child. And what happened then had nothing to do with what was happening now.

I googled *car accident drowning Gjerstad 1977*.

1977? I'd have been fourteen then, not eleven.

What made me think I'd been eleven? I'd always been eleven, whenever I thought about it.

Nothing came up.

Fortunately.

Why fortunately?

Could I not face it?

Someone knocked on the glass. I closed the tab and went to the door rather than telling whoever it was to come in. It was Sverre.

'Are you in hiding today?'

'I've never been the sort of boss whose door is always open, you know that. Is there something you want me to look at?'

He nodded and I went with him to his desk where Paul was standing waiting.

They'd been working for a while on a bid to build a new comprehensive school in Bodø. I'd seen lots of outlines, but so far all we'd talked about had been adjustments, the basic idea had been the same all the way through. The building was in the form of a star with an auditorium, study space, a library, staffroom and canteen all in the middle, the classrooms located in the five arms as it were. The idea had come from the starfish – the building was right by the sea – and the North Star. And then, rather more tenuously I thought, the notion that learning emanated from the centre and then made its way outwards into the world.

Glass and wood, with the structure, steel beams, ventilation ducts and all, open to the day.

It would be a splendid building. I listened as they pointed out various details and explained them to me, but said nothing, trying instead to think of some objection I might offer, though finding none, at least none of any significance, and anyway I didn't want to be seen as nitpicking and pedantic.

'Excellent,' I said when they'd finished. 'I'm impressed. It's going to be a fantastic building.'

'Yes, isn't it?' said Sverre.

'Amazing, Paul. Really great,' I added.

'Thank you,' Paul said. 'Actually, the main idea, to have a centre and a periphery, is yours, from the Elvenes building.'

Why was he saying that? Why did he think I needed commending?

'No, no. This is completely original. Well done, both of you. With this, we'll walk it. Nothing else is possible.'

They beamed at me.

'How's it going with Sandemose?' said Sverre. 'Are you ready to show us something soon?'

'Yes,' I said. 'A few details to sort out, but it won't be long. Next week, perhaps.'

'Ever the perfectionist. It doesn't have to be the finished item, you know. Rough drafts will do!'

'I love the Norwegian for that,' said Paul. '*Utkast* – throw-outs!'

I gave them both a thumbs up and went back to my office.

Everything there filled me with loathing. Bad, bad karma.

Why? Because it reminded me of myself?

When did I get to be like this?

Gutless, racked with fear.

I hardly knew myself.

I had to find my way back, to the person I'd been before. No, for God's sake, the person I *was*.

A person who just got on with things.

All I had to do was face the terror. Look it in the eye.

The accident would probably only have been reported in the local paper. That was why nothing appeared in a regular search. Back issues were all behind a paywall.

I signed up for a four-week subscription.

Two articles came up. Immediately, I felt sick. I didn't want to read them, I couldn't, I hadn't the stomach for it. But I made myself. I had to face it, eyes open, no matter how much it hurt.

MAN DIES IN TROMØY CAR ACCIDENT

A single-vehicle accident involving a Volvo estate car late Thursday night at Gjerstadkilen, Tromøy, proved fatal for the vehicle's driver. The victim was named as Mr Syvert Løyning of Vindsland. In a statement, police spokesman Kai Ommundsen told reporters that inspections indicated that the vehicle had skidded in slushy conditions before careening off the bridge into the inlet. The stretch of road in question sees little traffic, especially at night, and the accident was not discovered until the following morning when police were alerted by a member of the public who had noticed that one of the kerbstones on the old bridge had been dislodged. Rescue services were quickly on the scene to recover the vehicle.

Mr Løyning, 37, was a native of the Vindsland area, where he lived with his wife Evelyn and their two children. An engineer, he worked for a number of years in the service of the Royal Norwegian Air Force before taking up a position with U-Tech. At the time of the accident, Mr Løyning had been working in a consulting capacity on a project at Tromøy's Pusnes shipyard.

The news has sent shock waves through the local community. People gathered in numbers at the site of the accident yesterday morning to lay flowers and pay their respects, among them representatives of the Pusnes yard. Safety concerns about the bridge have previously been raised on a number of occasions and will be made no less pertinent by this tragic event.

The office, the fjord reaching into the town, the bright blue sky, everything around me blanked out. The article was like a window through which I now peered into that day in the 1970s. The accompanying picture showed a car being lifted out of the water by a crane. I'd seen that happen in real life. I'd been standing above the bridge looking down on the rescue services, the curious bystanders. The water was quite black, the rocks of the shore white with the snow that had fallen in the night. But it was the typesetting too, the adverts and the layout, I could almost smell the newspaper print. It wasn't me remembering the time and place, it was the time and place remembering me, and they pulled me in.

The person I'd seen drown wasn't some nameless anyone, it was *Mr Syvert Løyning*. He had a wife. *Evelyn*. And their two children had lost their father.

Not because of me. No one could say that.

I had no blame in what had happened. I could just as easily have been somewhere else and he'd still have driven off the road.

His children would be around my age now. Possibly younger, but people had kids when they were in their twenties back then, so my own age seemed like a reasonable guess, give or take.

They wouldn't be hard to find. I could phone and say I was there the night their father died.

But what good would it do? It wouldn't benefit them, all it would do was open the wounds again.

Had I told myself I was eleven to make myself more innocent?

There had to be hundreds of Løynings, so I typed the name of the father into the search bar and added *son daughter*. Fifty-odd hits, most with *son* and *daughter* struck out, and all to do with a funeral director by the same name. He was my age. Could he be a son? But who would have named their son after themselves in those days?

I put the Mac to sleep, dropped my phone into my pocket and went out. It was lunchtime in twenty minutes and the last thing I wanted was to sit small-talking with other people, especially on a day like this with a looming threat of speeches and celebratory activity.

Sitting in the car I had no idea where to go. The thought occurred to me I could simply drive off the road somewhere into the sea. Find a bridge, put an end to it all.

But I didn't mean it. The thought wasn't fastened to any reality.

I turned the air conditioning on full and decided to go into town, parked on the roof of the multi-storey and walked towards the shopping streets. Urban pearl, my arse. A small town with delusions of grandeur, that was what it was.

Maybe I should get my hair cut? Get rid of the *impressive signature mane*? It would be a new start.

But to what?

More self-denial.

How unusually hot it was today.

I turned and looked up at the sky and was surprised to see the star. I'd forgotten it was there. It was pale, like the sun's ill sister. I got my phone out and opened *VG*'s news app. It had its own dedicated in-depth section now, everything gathered under the heading 'The Mysterious Star', as if it was some silly Hardy Boys or Bobbsey Twins book. The expert they interviewed had a high forehead that made him look like a parody of a boffin. But he seemed sensible enough. *It could be something we've never seen before*, he said.

But then the name.

Løyning.

It was always the way, I told myself, and slipped the phone back into my pocket. As soon as you started thinking about a thing it cropped up everywhere. It had nothing to do with coincidence, it was to do with attention, and was as clear an indication as any of how our worlds were shaped by our conscious presence in them.

Joar Løyning. The age was right, but there were lots of Løynings and the chances of him being the son of the man I saw die were negligible.

I walked on, still undecided as to where I was going, crossed the Fisketorget with its milling throngs, carried on up Vetrelidsallmenningen and then along Øvregaten, and when I saw the grey towers of the Mariakirken I decided I might as well go there. I'd always been fond of the solid, grounded nature of the Romanesque churches, as opposed to the Gothic ones with their soaring steeples and spires which had something Babylonian about them, all hubris of man, striving towards God that he might form himself in His likeness. The Romanesque churches were more human, blocks of stone balanced in thrusting arches, they could feel almost subterranean at times, and in any case more appropriate: God had to come to us, not we to God.

Not that I cared about God!

I paused for a moment, looking up at the two grey towers with their green caps of lead, trying to grasp the thousand years that had passed since they'd been erected here. I couldn't. My mind hadn't the reach, my thoughts had no lift. Was that why we said the mind could be *burdened*? Yes, my thoughts were heavy, weighed down with emotions, unable to leave my body.

The doors were open and I went towards them and the alluring darkness within, but then my phone rang.

It was Vibeke. I held it in my hand for a moment, looking at it without answering. But she wasn't giving up, it kept on ringing and eventually I took the call.

'Helge, you've got to come! Come at once!'

'What's happened? What is it?'

'There's a man in our storage room! He's broken in!'

'What? Calm down. Say that again.'

'A man, he's broken into the storage room! I went into the basement and there he was.'

'Christ.'

'I locked him in. He's still there.'

'Where are you now?'

'Upstairs in the apartment.'

'Have you called the police?'

'I'm calling you first. I've got Åse to think about as well.'

'All right. Call the police now and I'll get there as quick as I can. OK?'

'OK.'

'Are you scared?'

'Not now. But I'm not going down there again. He was out of his mind.'

'Call the police, they'll deal with it. Stay in the apartment until they arrive. You're quite safe there.'

We both hung up and I walked as fast as I could without running, through the town centre back to the multi-storey. It could only be a drug addict, no one else would risk breaking in somewhere in broad daylight. They were harmless. Weak. But she'd locked him in!

I couldn't help but laugh to myself. She really was amazing. Resourceful, a doer.

At the same time, I'd only ground to a halt when she came into my life.

It was a fact.

Whether it was coincidence or not, I didn't know. How could I?

Come on, get a grip. Focus. There was a burglar in the storage room. Vibeke and Åse were upstairs in the apartment, they were afraid.

I got into the boiling hot car and sped away down the ramp into the town. When I got through the tunnel I called her number. It was busy. Probably the police she was talking to. Ordinarily it was unlikely they'd make a priority of something as petty as a break-in, but surely it made a difference him still being there?

There was no sign of any police presence when I arrived. I parked the car and called Vibeke's number again. This time she answered.

'I'm here now,' I said. 'Are you upstairs?'

'Yes.'

'Good. You're safe there. Have you called the police?'

'Yes. They said they'd be on their way.'

'Well done, Vibeke. I'll be up in a minute. Just need to check on the guy in the basement first.'

'No, don't do that! I told you, the police are on their way! He's dangerous.'

'Junkies aren't normally dangerous. And if he thinks he can just break into our storage room and frighten the wits out of you, he's got another think coming. Besides, we don't know what he might be doing there now. He could be smashing everything up.'

'Helge, don't. You don't need to. You could be putting yourself in danger.'

Thankfully, she didn't realise it could be an opportunity I'd been looking for.

'I'll be careful, I promise,' I said. 'I'll be with you in a few minutes!'

I hung up and opened the heavy steel door of the basement.

Someone was screaming in there.

A madman, screaming insanely.

An elderly man who also lived in the building was standing in the stairwell with his phone in his hand and looked at me as I came in.

'I've called the police,' he said.

'Good,' I said. 'Vibeke's called them too.'

'He's in your storage room.'

'Yes, Vibeke locked him in.'

The screams sounded like they were coming from an animal.

I went closer.

'You in there,' I said. 'Calm down now.'

He started pounding on the door, screaming like he was in hell. It was a solid door and the padlock was a heavy-duty thing, but even so I stepped away. I glanced back at the old man, who shook his head. OK, maybe I wouldn't unlock the door. There wasn't much point anyway, not with the police on their way.

At once, sirens sounded. I hurried through the garage and out the side door. Two patrol cars with flashing blue lights had pulled up. Two more were tearing down the hill.

'He's in here!' I said to the first officer who got out. He was as big as a brick shithouse.

'Do you live here, sir?'

'Yes. It was my wife who rang. But why so many of you? There's only one guy in there.'

'And he's in there, in the basement?'

'Yes.'

'Locked inside a storage room?'

'Yes.'

The place was teeming with police now. All were heavily armed.

'Show us the way, will you, sir?'

I nodded and led them through the garage, then as I opened the door into the passage where the storage rooms were, the giant officer held me back.

'Which room is it?' he said in a low voice.

I pointed. Whoever it was, he was quiet in there now. He must have heard the sirens.

'Have you got the key to that padlock?'

'There's a code,' I said, my voice as low as his. 'Do you want me to open it?'

He shook his head.

'Just tell me the code, sir.'

'1998.'

He held two fingers in the air and then indicated the door. Two officers drew their firearms and positioned themselves on either side of it. With a nod of his head the commanding officer signalled for me to get out of the way and another gave me a gentle shove to get me going, as if I were a kid they didn't want hanging around. He followed me out, and as we stepped into the garage and the door was closing behind us, I heard the one in charge give a shout.

'Police! Move away from the door!'

'Isn't this a bit overkill?' I said. 'I mean it's only a burglary. Some poor junkie, I imagine. Am I right?'

'You live here, don't you, sir?' said the officer. 'So I suggest you go upstairs to your apartment now. We'll speak to you later.'

'Yes, all right,' I said. I stood for a second, pretend-rummaging in my pocket, certain that in a moment or two they'd bring him out, and I wanted to be there to see him. To see who it was.

'*Now*, if you don't mind, sir,' the officer said. 'Or shall I go with you?'

'No, no, that won't be necessary,' I said and went grudgingly over to the lift. My finger lingered on the button. I couldn't drag it out much more, the lift was already there. All I could do was step inside and go upstairs.

Vibeke stood waiting with Åse on her hip.

'At last,' she said. 'What's happening?'

'The police got to him before I could,' I said and kissed her lightly on the lips. 'I had to show them the storage room. Are you OK?'

'Yes. Just a bit shaken, that's all.'

'You will be, it's understandable,' I said. 'What I *don't* understand is all the manpower, there are loads of police down there. What did you tell them exactly? Was there something you didn't tell me? Did he have a weapon of some sort?'

She shook her head.

'They've found those guys out of that death metal band. Three of them have been murdered. The fourth one's on the run. It must be him. Don't you think?'

There were tears in her eyes. She looked away and went inside into the living area.

Only then did I see the flowers, the bottles of wine and the bags of shopping on the kitchen worktop.

I followed her in. She put Åse down on the floor and turned round to face me.

'He's just killed three of his friends,' she said. 'And I was alone with him in our storage room.'

'Did he threaten you?'

Again, she shook her head.

'He seemed confused and very, very scared. He asked me to help him.'

'What did you do?'

'I locked the door. He started screaming. And then I came upstairs and phoned you.'

'You did brilliantly,' I said, wrapping my arms around her. 'Vibeke, you did brilliantly. The police have got him now.'

What I wanted to say was, *For Christ's sake, Vibeke, didn't I spell it out that I didn't want a party?* But I couldn't, not now. Instead, I smoothed a hand over her back and held her tight.

'I'm all right,' she said, extricating herself. 'Have you had lunch?'

I nodded.

'But I can keep you company, if you want.'

'No need. I'll just have a quick bite of something. Thanks for coming.'

'Thanks for coming? Now you're being silly!'

She smiled.

'You'll be going back to work, won't you? I've got lots to do here, as I'm sure you've noticed.'

'Vibeke,' I said.

She put an index finger to my lips.

'I told you I didn't want a party.'

'Shush,' she said. 'No one said anything about a party. You go back to work and I'll see you this evening.'

LINE

Mum was standing at the sink doing the dishes when I came down. Gran was in the living room watching TV by the sounds of it, unless she'd fallen asleep in there.

'Going for a walk,' I said.

'Good idea,' Mum said. 'Where were you thinking of going?'

What did she want that information for?

'Up to the waterfall, maybe,' I said.

She nodded and I went out in the direction of what Thomas and I used to call the Troll's Forest when we were little. Age-old spruce trees all close together. Dark even in the middle of the day. Or not dark exactly. Dim. And always still. Long veils of foliage as if draped from the branches. Thick moss carpeting the rocks. I thought about Valdemar as I went, wishing he could see it. My heart jumped like a small hare in my chest. If he'd been like anyone else, I'd have taken a photo and sent it to him. Just the photo, no explanation or anything. But he's not like anyone else.

Am I?

Before I met Valdemar I'd have said yes to that. I'm just like anyone else. He says I'm not. And I'm not so stupid that I don't realise that's exactly what men say to women when they want them. You're not like anyone else. You're special. Fast-forward an hour and all of a sudden you're more than that, you're gorgeous. But Valdemar isn't like that. He says what he means, always. That doesn't mean he's right when it comes to me. Just that he means it.

A tinge of doubt accompanied every thought I had about Valdemar.

What was I going to do?

What the hell was I going to do?

Even among the trees, where the sun was excluded, it was hot. Midges danced in swarms. In the pool below the falls, dark slender shadows moved below the surface. Small trout. I sat down on a rock and watched them. After a few moments I reached for my phone, but then remembered I'd left it behind. Immediately I felt pangs of withdrawal. But I'd consciously decided not to bring it with me.

One of the fish rose. Its spine was grey and speckled as the rocks all around.

I forced myself to remain a while and looked up at the fellside, the tumbling water. The trees at the top stood luminously in the last rays of the day.

Of all the places in the world I'd always liked it best here, at Gran and Grandad's. Especially when Thomas and I had come to stay on our own here with them. It had felt like pure joy then. A winter holiday one time when the forest pond was frozen and we skated on it and got to know some of the other kids from around about. A couple of summers when Mum and Dad were in Germany.

Now Grandad was dead and Gran was so ill she probably wouldn't survive the winter. Thomas had shut himself away in his bedsit and saw no one, Dad was drinking himself to death in Portugal, and Mum was pretending everything was all right.

My hand moved for my phone again. The same sinking disappointment when I realised it wasn't there.

I gazed in the other direction, my eyes picking out the big rocks further inside the forest, which Grandad used to say were trolls that hadn't been quick enough to return to the fell before the sun came up. We wanted to believe him and so we did. Gleefully we balanced on the backs of those dead trolls, safe as long as the sun was shining. We asked him if they could wake up again when the sun went down. With great solemnity he said he didn't know.

Dad couldn't stand Grandad. When I was a kid I couldn't comprehend why. Grandad was wonderful. Full of stories that came babbling out of him. He laughed such a lot too.

He probably hadn't cared much for Dad. And of course Dad would have picked up on that, and before long he'd have turned it about so that he was the one who didn't care for Grandad, rather than the other way round.

When Gran was diagnosed with Parkinson's, Dad told me it was hereditary and that if I got it when I grew up I should remember it wasn't from his side of the family.

What kind of a thing was that to tell an eight-year-old?

Nothing more was moving in the pool and my eyes searched a while before I located the trout again, now almost motionless near the bottom. I picked up a stone, craned over the surface and released it directly above one of them like a depth charge. But the trout I'd targeted darted away even before the stone got near.

I splashed my face. The water wasn't much cooler than the surrounding air, but it was nice anyway.

I didn't really feel like going back to Mum and Gran, but then I couldn't exactly sit here all night either. The half-hour without my phone that I was imposing on myself was already gone, but thirty minutes more would mean I could dispense with tomorrow morning's stint. It was all the same.

Valdemar had told a story about Hitler. They'd been talking about charisma. Hitler had possessed enormous charisma, Gerhard said. People wanted to be on his side. Valdemar had read a book written by Hitler's architect. He'd been completely infatuated, Valdemar said. But then after the architect introduced his father to Hitler, his father had gone completely white, he said Hitler was a dangerous man. He'd seen something no one else had seen.

'That sounds a bit like my dad,' I'd said.

Valdemar had laughed. He didn't very often.

'You're living in your own little bubble,' he said.

I felt stupid, like a kid. He picked up on it.

'Hitler was just a human being too,' he said. 'The same as your father.'

Valdemar wasn't a Nazi, even if a lot of people thought he was. When he spoke about the Third Realm, it wasn't the Nazis he was talking about but something people had believed in the Middle Ages, that the First Realm was the age of God, the Second Realm the age of Christ, the Third Realm the age of the Holy Spirit.

'We're entering the Third Realm,' he said. Not to me, but to the others.

*

Outside the house I heard a loud and insistent peeping noise. I looked around. It sounded like baby birds. But where were they? They weren't on the roof or underneath the eaves.

There it was again. Was it coming from the gateway?

Yes, it was!

There, among a wilderness of climbing plants, was a nest, and in the nest a clutch of young with their beaks wide open, peeping loudly.

'Where have your mum and dad got to, eh?' I said. 'Are they out finding food for you?'

They were so delicate, so helpless that tears came to my eyes. I wanted to hold them in my hands, but I knew that my smell would perhaps cause the parents to disown them, so I contented myself with just looking. A moment later a bird came swooping in over the slope of the roof and I stepped away so as not to disturb and went back into the house. I called out to Mum.

'We're in here!' she called back from the bathroom.

She was standing with the hairdryer poised in one hand, a hairbrush in the other. Gran was sitting on a stool in front of her. Her trembling hands held in her lap.

'Have you seen the baby birds in the gateway?'

'Aren't they sweet?' Mum said.

'Yes, but why didn't you say anything?'

'There was no occasion,' she said.

'What sort of birds are they? I only saw the babies.'

'There's a pair of wood pigeons that nest there.'

I was about to ask if it wasn't odd for them to be having young now in late August when she abruptly changed the subject.

'Are you hungry? I could make us a snack before we go to bed?'

I looked at her. She met my eye fleetingly before glancing to her right, where liars look when they're lying. But there was nothing to lie about here, was there?

I shook my head.

'We'll be finished here in a minute,' she said, and switched the hairdryer on again with an expression that appeared to be relief. She lifted an area of Gran's thin hair with the hairbrush.

*

Feeling a bit put out by Mum's strange behaviour I lay down on my bed and scrolled through my Insta feed. Josefine was in Greece, tanned and in a bikini, posing on a beach with a big smile on her face and a turquoise sea in the background, then seated, still tanned, still in a bikini, at a small cosy-looking restaurant, another big smile on her face. It looked like she was having lamb chops with chips. I felt like texting her but didn't, there was too much to explain. Julie had posted a picture of the stack of books she had to read in the coming week, then one of herself next to her mum on the veranda at theirs, two streets away from where I grew up. Kristoffer and Magne had thrown a party in the houseshare. I spread my finger and thumb to enlarge the image on the screen and studied the faces of those who'd come, mostly people I recognised, some I knew the names of, some I didn't.

The window was open and darkness fell into the room. I'd have thought it would make the air a bit cooler, only it didn't. A crow squawked somewhere. A moment later the whole sky seemed to be full of them, squawking crows. Their noise died away without me noticing – the next time I looked up it was quiet out there.

Half an hour had gone since I'd put my phone down. Pleased with myself for having such discipline, I sat in the window and stared in the direction of the fjord. Its waters were as black as oil. The sky above it lighter, ethereal.

The thing was I didn't even know if we were together or not. There were lots of others who wanted him. People who wanted to be near him. Not just girls either.

Did I?

There was no one else to ask but myself. And I didn't know.

Or rather, I knew I did. Something inside me wanted to.

But I didn't know if I could.

The first time I saw him I hadn't known who he was. I was glad about that now, thinking back. I wasn't interested in him then. He knocked into me in the queue for the bar at Palasset. I turned and he looked straight at me.

'Lucky me,' he said.

I looked away again with the most superior air I could muster. *Likewise*, I should have said, only the moment had gone by then. I carried the drinks carefully back to where I was sitting with Josefine and Klara, but said nothing to them. There was nothing to say. But I scanned the room until my eyes picked him out. He was sitting at a table over by the window. His straw-coloured hair fell about his shoulders like an angel's. His eyes, bright and strong. A sensitive mouth. Thin, wiry frame. He was so incredibly beautiful. But that wasn't what made him attractive, it was his aura. Even from a distance I could feel it.

He didn't look once in my direction. And yet he came over to our table shortly before closing time.

'I'm Valdemar,' he said. 'Who are you?'

'Line,' I said. Josefine and Klara gawped at him, at me, at each other.

'Line . . . ?'

'Kvamme.'

'A good West Norwegian name,' he said.

And then he left.

'Have you been talking to *him*?' said Josefine.

I shook my head.

'I've never seen him before. Do you know who he is?'

'He just told you,' said Klara. 'Valdemar.'

'He used to play in one of those black metal bands.'

'Really? He doesn't look the type.'

'He's proper bad news,' said Klara. 'Stay well away.'

'What do I know?' I said. 'He came over, that's all. Anyway, what black metal band?'

'I can't remember what they were called.'

'Corpse. They were called Corpse,' said Josefine. 'He turned up at a lecture in a Nazi uniform once.'

'He did what? But he looked so straight!'

'Well, he isn't.'

'Stay well away,' said Klara.

'If you say so,' I said. 'He's not got my number or anything. I never spoke to him until now.'

I dropped into Palasset the next few nights after that on the off chance I'd see him there. But I didn't. I'd never seen him there before either, so I supposed it wasn't a place he normally went. I resigned myself.

Until one day he came into the shop. All of a sudden he was just standing there. He'd had his hair cut, it gave him a harder look, but I recognised him straight away. He scanned the place and came over as soon as he saw me.

'So this is where you hide out,' he said.

He looked me straight in the eye. It was uncomfortable and I looked down while continuing to fold the items in front of me.

'In H&M of all places.'

Renate stared at us from where she was standing at the payment point. Maybe she thought he was my boyfriend.

'How about the two of us just leave together?' he said.

'Now?'

'Yes.'

'Where would we go?'

'We could buy a couple of beers and sit in the park.'

'I can't.'

'Why not?'

'I'd get the sack.'

'You can choose between H&M and me, and you choose H&M?'

'That's it, yes.'

'OK,' he said, smiled with his eyes still fixed on me, then turned and walked away.

Renate came over wanting to know who he was.

'A boy I met in town one night. I hardly know him.'

'What was he doing here, then?'

'He wanted me to leave my job and go somewhere with him.'

'I would have done.'

'I know *you* would.'

She laughed in that chirpy way of hers.

'Talk about godlike!'

'Yes, I know.'

I found a few mentions of his band on the internet. They'd split up a few years back and didn't seem to have put anything out. There was no trace of them on Spotify or YouTube, or anywhere else either. It felt a bit spooky that he'd found out where I was working. But a lot of people came into the shop, so maybe one of his mates had seen me there and mentioned it to him that night at Palasset.

I waited for him to come back every day after that. But he didn't.

Then one night a few weeks later someone threw a handful of grit against my window in the houseshare. I opened it to see him standing in the street below.

'Are you going to come with me now, then?'

'Yes,' I said, and at once hurried down the stairs, pausing for a moment behind the front door so as not to appear too eager before stepping out.

He was waiting on the pavement looking absently up at our living-room windows, wearing a pair of wide army-green trousers that were cropped above the ankle, a grey T-shirt.

The short hair suited him. It was more severe, but at the same time made him appear younger and more boyish.

He turned towards me as I came out, stepped up close, put his arms around my waist and kissed me.

'What are you *doing*?' I said, and pulled away.

'Kissing you,' he said.

'Well, you can't.'

'Never?'

I didn't answer. He smiled and put a hand on my shoulder.

'Do you want to come and see a film with me?'

I nodded. He started walking. I followed. He said nothing. It was as if I wasn't there any more, or as if he no longer cared.

But he'd come to take me out. And he'd kissed me.

'What are we going to see?' I said.

'*Orpheus*.'

'Never heard of it. Where's it showing?'

'At the Cinemateket.'

'An old one, then!'

He didn't say anything.

I gauged him to be around five years older than me, maybe more. Perhaps he'd changed his mind already.

'Have you seen it before?'

He nodded.

'Is it any good? I suppose it must be if you want to see it again.'

Silence. Sunlight in the tops of the trees, sunlight glittering in the windows of the big concert hall.

'What's it about?'

'You'll see soon enough.'

His aloofness now was almost unbearable. Thoughts flew around in my head. But not in his, so it seemed. He didn't look like he was bothered about anything.

I'd never been to the Cinemateket before. Their posters never appealed to me. How absurd to run a cinema dedicated to boring films! The people who went there looked boring too, I'd often thought so, seeing them go in from the wharf. Languid figures and gloomy expressions. They thought they were so intellectual.

'Do you often go to the Cinemateket?'

'When there's something I want to see.'

He wasn't exactly working hard to get me. Maybe he never found it necessary.

At least like a gentleman he paid for my ticket. Even if he didn't offer to buy me something to take in.

I felt like having some popcorn and a Diet Coke.

It didn't look like they had popcorn. But I could see they had M&Ms, and Bamsemums too.

'Do you want anything?' I said.

We were the only people there. It wasn't surprising considering the fine weather outside.

He shook his head.

I was about to go over and buy something when he put his hand on my arm.

'There's nothing here you want.'

'What do you mean?'

'It's just crap.'

'Are you having me on?'

'Why would I?'

I shrugged.

'Buy what you want then,' he said. 'If you really must pollute yourself.'

'Not if you feel like that. It's not important.'

'OK,' he said.

The mood between us was awkward now as we went inside the small cinema space. It was empty and the screen was still dark. We sat beside each other, in the middle.

He slid down in his seat, bracing his knees against the back of the one in front.

'You'd think the adverts would have started by now,' I said.

'They don't have adverts here.'

He turned his head and looked at me.

'So we'll just have to entertain ourselves.'

I met his gaze. It made me feel warm inside.

His eyes were so unbelievably beautiful. So deep.

'How old are you, Line?'

'Nineteen. And you?'

'How old do you think?'

'I've no idea.'

'Guess.'

'Twenty-five?'

'Did you know?'

I shook my head.

'Do you know about me?'

'No.'

'Nothing?'

'Just that you were in a band.'

He nodded a couple of times.

'Anything else?'

'No.'

'There are rumours about me. Don't listen to them.'

'Like that you're a Nazi?' I said without thinking, and immediately wished I hadn't.

But all he did was laugh.

'Yes, for example! Who told you that?'

'A couple of friends of mine.'

'The two you were with?'

'Yes.'

'What are their names?'

'Klara and Josefine.'

'Are they good friends?'

'Yes.'

'What do they do?'

'Klara's first-year law. Josefine does Spanish.'

As I spoke the screen lit up and he turned to face it.

He glanced at me and smiled.

The film *was* boring, and rather confusing too, but of course that's not what I said. When it was finished he walked me home. There was no suggestion of having a drink somewhere or that we should go back to his place. He didn't ask if there was anything I fancied doing, just started walking towards the town centre as soon as we stepped outside, as if he hadn't noticed how lively the wharf's outdoor restaurants and bars were now, packed with people.

He walked beside me as if I wasn't there. Hands buried in his pockets, eyes picking out the fjord between the houses and other buildings, scanning the sky, fixing on the square at the end of the street. Looking at anything but me.

'What did you make of it?' he said into the air in front of him.

'The film, you mean?'

He didn't answer. Of course it was the film he meant.

'It was very interesting,' I said.

'You liked it?'

'It was really good!'

'Yes, it was.'

He seemed pleased that I'd liked it. So I supposed I did mean *something* to him. He wouldn't have taken me with him to see it again if I didn't. I wasn't going to shove him away if he put his arms around me again, that was for sure.

Ten minutes later we were back outside mine.

'Thanks for coming,' he said, still with his hands in his pockets, a full two paces from where I was standing.

'Do you want to come in? It's a houseshare, but you don't have to meet the others, not if you don't want to. We can sit in my room.'

'I'll be on my way, if it's all the same.'

'OK.'

He walked off, no umming and aahing about it, and after standing there a moment I let myself in.

'Been out on a date?' said Julie, emerging from the kitchen with some big wedges of watermelon on a plate.

'No,' I said. 'Can I have one of those?'

'Who was that who walked you home, then?' she said, holding the plate out to me.

'Did you see us snogging?'

'No.'

'Did he come in with me? Did we go up to my room?'

'OK, I get the picture. A friend, then?'

I smiled at her and took the watermelon to eat in my room, where I stood at the grimy window and looked down on the street below. The sun shone orange on the roof of the house opposite. Thinking about him, it was as if my thoughts were little arrows of joy shooting through my body.

I went downstairs into the living room. Kristoffer was lying on the sofa in only his boxers, the remote clutched in his hand. Julie sat at the table eating her watermelon.

'What are you watching?'

'An old movie.'

'What's it called?'

'*Premonition*.'

'Any good?

'It's all right.'

'You wouldn't have any of that white wine of yours left, would you?'

'In the fridge.'

'Mind if I have a glass?'

'Help yourself,' he said in English.

'Do you want some?'

'Yeah, why not?'

'How about you?' I said, turning to Julie.

'Oh, go on then.'

The kitchen was a mess after the weekend. The worktop was full of dirty dishes covered in solidified food remains, used glasses, bottles drunk down to the dregs. The packaging from the meat we'd eaten the previous evening had been left on the windowsill, the paper in the bottom slimy with blood. Basically it was disgusting, but it was Kristoffer's turn to do the dishes and no way was I going to bail him out. I took three glasses from the cupboard, placed the box of wine on the table with the tap over the edge and filled the glasses one by one, took them into the living room, put one down on the table in front of Julie, handed Kristoffer one and sat down next to him on the sofa with mine.

I'd never felt anything like this before.

'Cheers!' I said.

Julie smiled at me and took a sip.

'Shall we put some music on instead?' I said.

'This'll be finished in a minute,' said Kristoffer.

'You said it was just *all right*,' I said.

'I still want to see how it ends.'

'Where are Magne and Ida anyway?'

'Magne's in his room. Ida went out for a jog,' said Julie. 'Why?'

'No reason.'

The wine was deliciously cold and as sweet as squash. I went into the kitchen for a top-up and decided I might as well bring the box back in with me.

'Like that, is it?' said Julie. 'Thinking of going out somewhere?'

'Could do. Fancy coming along?'

'No, I'd better stay in. Got to get up early.'

'How about you?' I said and looked at Kristoffer.

'Not in the mood really.'

'Come on! Going out's always more fun when you weren't intending to.'

The front door opened. I heard Ida panting for a moment before heading for the bathroom.

'It's not even ten o'clock yet,' I said.

'You're a bit eager,' said Kristoffer.

'No, I'm not. It'd be nice, that's all.'

I felt stupid sitting there. Like I'd played all my cards too soon. There was no going back now. I certainly couldn't just go upstairs to bed.

'That time you got dumped, we all went out together, remember?' I said. 'It was a Sunday.'

'I won't ever forget it,' said Kristoffer.

'What's the matter – is there someone you're trying to get over?'

said Julie. 'I didn't even know you were going out with anyone! Was that him, the one who brought you home tonight?'

I shook my head.

'It's the opposite.'

'You're in *love*?'

'I think so.'

'With *him*?'

'I think so.'

'Are you going out with him?'

'No.'

'Who is he? Anyone we know?'

'I can tell you when we go out.'

Julie laughed.

'OK, only joking,' I said. 'You don't have to come, not if you don't want to.'

'I'll come,' said Julie. 'And Kristoffer will too. He just needs to put some clothes on first. Don't you, Kristoffer?'

When we went outside into the street I could hardly believe I'd said what I'd said. It was so totally unlike me. There was nothing in it. I'd been to the cinema with a boy who'd barely said a word.

'Where do you want to go?' said Julie.

'Does it have to be up to me?'

'It's for your benefit we're going out, of course it's up to you!'

'How about Bakgården?'

'Right, Bakgården it is.'

We crossed over, walking past the concert hall then along the quayside. The fells above the town were aglow in the fading sun. There were quite a few people out, though nothing like the numbers on a Friday or Saturday night when great parties of punters would swell through the streets and everyone was in high spirits, drunk or desperate. Shouts and cries, laughter, bass rhythms thudding from the cars. Always someone puking in a doorway or sitting splayed on the ground somewhere. People sauntered tonight in pairs or groups of three or four and were sober.

'I don't think I've ever sat down here,' said Julie when we saw that Bakgården's small courtyard still offered a couple of empty tables.

'I'm always erect here too,' said Kristoffer, and we laughed.

'What are we on? I said. 'White wine?'

'No reason to switch now,' said Julie.

I went inside and stood at the bar. Everything was light-coloured wood. Bottles gleamed from the shelves on the wall. A man in his fifties, slightly pot-bellied, wearing shorts and a Metallica T-shirt, turned towards me.

'What'll it be, love?' he said. 'Oh, sorry, not allowed to say that any more!'

His eyes creased as he laughed.

'A bottle of white,' I said. 'Have you got one that's a bit sweet?'

'That would be a Liebfraumilch,' he said. 'That do you?'

I nodded and looked around the room.

I couldn't believe it.

He was sitting right there. On the raised area up against the wall, leaning forward in conversation with another guy who seemed to be listening attentively.

I turned away.

My heart thumped in my chest.

He hadn't seen me.

Oh, fuck!

The bartender dropped a scoop of tinkling ice cubes into a metal wine bucket, nestled the green bottle among them and pulled out three glasses from the rack above the counter.

'I'll bring it out to you,' he said.

I paid and went back to the others and sat down. Julie had lit one of the long thin menthol cigarettes she ordered online from abroad somewhere. Kristoffer was looking at his phone.

'Here we are,' said the bartender, appearing a moment later to arrange everything on the table for us. 'Ashtray?'

'Yes, please,' said Julie, a wry look above her little cloud of smoke.

She smiled at me.

'Well? Who is he then?'

Kristoffer slid his phone back into his pocket and filled the glasses, raising his own to call a toast.

'To our little sis, and to love,' he said.

'Cheers,' said Julie.

'It's nothing really,' I said, casting a glance to my rear. 'Nothing's actually happened yet.'

'But you've met someone?'

'Yes. And you won't believe me now, but he's sitting in there.'

'What?'

I nodded and widened my eyes.

'Why don't you ask him to come and join us?' said Julie.

I shook my head.

'I don't even know him. Oh, this is so embarrassing! How did it get to this?'

Julie gave a laugh and put her hand on mine.

'You still haven't told us who he is.'

'Listen, can we swap places, Kristoffer?' I said. 'I don't really want to find he's standing behind me all of a sudden while I'm talking about him.'

'Sure.'

'He knocked into me at the bar at Palasset,' I said. 'He came over afterwards and introduced himself. His name's Valdemar. Then he came into the shop one day and wanted me to drop everything and go out somewhere with him. I said no. He turned up again tonight throwing stones at my window to ask if I wanted to go and see a film with him.'

'How did he know where you worked?' said Julie. 'Had you told him?'

'No, no, I only told him my name!'

'And where you lived and which window was yours,' said Kristoffer.

'I hadn't even thought about that.'

'So what happened then?'

'He kissed me.'

'OK!'

'And that's it. We saw the film and he walked me home afterwards. He hardly even said anything.'

'But who *is* he?' said Julie.

'Is he good-looking?' said Kristoffer.

'Of course he's good-looking,' said Julie.

'He's not your type, Kristoffer.'

'Oh?'

'Far too skinny for your liking.'

'Nothing's far too anything for my liking.'

'Ha ha!'

'A bit more info, if you don't mind,' said Julie. 'How old is he?'

'A year older than you.'

'Aha . . . and what does he do?'

'No idea. I know nothing about him. He used to be in a band, that's it.'

'And the name of this band?'

'Corpse.'

'Urgh! What kind of music?'

'They split up five years ago. I don't think he's into it any more. But it was black metal.'

They both looked up.

'A black metal dude? Are you joking?'

'He doesn't look like one. He's not like that at all.'

'I only hope you're right,' said Kristoffer. 'Best not to get involved with that lot. Not that it's any of my business. But you know what I mean.'

'I am old enough to do as I like, you know.'

'We care about you, that's all.'

'So does my mum. And you know what she's like.'

Kristoffer sat back and threw up his hands.

'I'm sure he's a very nice guy.'

'Of course he is,' said Julie.

'At least I know now that I've never been in love before,' I said. 'I thought I had, but I haven't.'

I looked up to see Valdemar now standing behind Kristoffer. He ran a hand through his short hair and smiled at me.

'Hello, Line,' he said.

Kristoffer twisted round and looked up. Julie lit another cig and feigned indifference. I felt my face go warm and didn't know where to look, what to do with my hands.

'Aren't you going to introduce me to your friends?'

'Julie and Kristoffer, this is Valdemar. Valdemar, this is Julie and Kristoffer. We share a house together.'

'Why don't you join us?' said Julie.

'Don't mind if I do,' said Valdemar. 'Let me fetch my pint.'

As he turned and went inside, Julie's eyes met mine and she raised her eyebrows. I couldn't figure out if she was impressed or sceptical.

'Well, there you go then,' she said, which didn't make me any the wiser.

'He's a specimen, isn't he?'

'You're telling me,' she said.

'He's definitely interested in you,' said Kristoffer.

'Why does it feel like I'm having my boyfriend round to meet my parents for the first time?' I said.

'You know us, we don't judge people,' said Julie. 'We're open towards everyone.'

'As open as the grave,' said Kristoffer.

'Graves are silent, not open,' I said.

'*First* they're open. *Then* they close around you.'

'What are you going on about?'

'Haven't a clue,' he said, and laughed. 'Sounds good, though!'

Valdemar came back out with a pint glass in his hand, half full, put it down on the table and pulled out the chair next to Kristoffer.

'Funny you should be here, we were just talking about you,' said Julie.

'About me?' he said, and gave me a smile before sipping a mouthful of his beer.

A feeling vaguely like pride welled in me.

'Yes,' said Julie. 'Line was saying you were in a black metal band?'

'It's true. A while ago now, though.'

'Apart from that, she said she didn't know what you do with yourself.'

'We only just met.'

'What *do* you do?'

I almost hoped he'd tell her to mind her own business, but he didn't.

'I'm supposed to be doing my master's in philosophy. But most of the time I work as a porter at the hospital to earn money. How about you?'

'Psychology, final year.'

'And you?' he said, turning to Kristoffer.

'Information science.'

'A bit of a catch-all that, isn't it? A very broad field?'

'It is, yes.'

'What do you specialise in?'

'Cognitive computing, it's called. Information systems that behave like humans, to put it simply.'

'So the two of you are involved in much the same thing in a way,' said Valdemar. 'You work with people that behave like machines, while you work with machines that behave like people. Am I right?'

'Ha ha,' said Julie.

He looked at me and smiled again.

'Actually, it's just the opposite,' said Julie. 'Psychology's about the most human things of all.'

'If you say so.'

'You don't agree?'

'No, as a matter of fact.'

'Is that a qualified opinion or just an opinion?'

I tried to catch her eye to get her to stop, but she was glaring at him now.

'I've some experience with psychologists,' he said. 'I was in therapy all through childhood. I saw a shrink for four years without saying anything, until they let me go.'

'There are good and bad therapists,' said Julie. 'You can't generalise about people.'

'No, exactly. That's the problem.'

'How do you mean?'

My eyes met Kristoffer's and I threw a glance.

He took the hint and pushed his chair back.

'It's getting late,' he said. 'And it's Monday tomorrow.'

He turned to Julie.

'Are you coming?'

She nodded, drained her glass and got to her feet.

'Nice meeting you,' she said to Valdemar before turning to me. 'See you later, Line.'

After they'd gone I filled my glass and sat with it in my hand, studying the windows of the wonky wooden structure where the bar was situated, my eyes then fleetingly meeting his as I moved my gaze in search of some other neutral thing they might consider.

His expression was more serious now. Was something bothering him? I'd seen he could be social and engage with people. So why wasn't he talking to me as he'd talked to them?

He lifted his pint and drank.

'Nice friends you've got,' he said as he returned his glass to the table.

Was he being sarcastic?

'Yes, I like them,' I said.

He shifted on his chair, rested his forearm on the back, a hand left dangling. His other hand was placed flat on the table. Some symbols were tattooed on his fingers, I hadn't noticed them before, just beneath the knuckles.

'Kristoffer's gay, isn't he?'

'Yes – and?'

'Useful to know, that's all.'

It was impossible to decipher what they meant. They looked like characters from some other alphabet. Sanskrit or something, I didn't know.

He ran his hand through his hair again as if he hadn't yet got used to it being so short.

'Are you going to work at H&M the rest of your life?'

'Don't you like me working there?'

He smiled.

'You're on the defensive.'

'It's only for a few more weeks, until I start university.'

'Ex.phil?'

'Yes.'

'What do your parents do?'

'My parents?'

'Yes.'

'My mum's a nurse. My dad's an alcoholic.'

He laughed a bit awkwardly and glanced at the floor.

'That sounds like hard work. What did he do before that?'

'He was a teacher.'

'Primary, secondary, gymnasium?'

'Gymnas. Why do you ask?'

'Just want to know who you are.'

'Well, I'm not my parents.'

'But who your parents are says something about what class you belong to, doesn't it?'

'So I'm middle class, am I?'

'I'd say so.'

'Isn't that everyone?'

'Is it?'

'We don't have a caste system here as far as I know.'

He liked that comment, so I understood, the way he smiled before lifting his glass to his mouth and draining the contents. He wiped the froth away from his lips with the back of his hand.

'A few years ago I took a DNA test,' he said. 'I wouldn't do it now, but I didn't know any better then. Anyway, it turns out there are people in India with almost the exact same genetic profile as me.'

'So someone there looks like you?'

'Yes, that's what it amounts to.'

'Isn't that a bit weird?'

He shook his head.

'Actually, it's perfectly natural. People migrated from Northern Europe to northern India thousands of years ago. They're the ones who called themselves Aryans.'

'Isn't that a Nazi concept? The Aryan race?'

'No, Line, this is historical fact. We mustn't be afraid to talk about Nazism. It doesn't mean there's a master race! The language we speak is Indo-European, meaning that the Indian and the European come from the same source. That's all.'

He was leaning forward now and had begun to gesticulate, something I hadn't seen him do before.

'Is that why you've got Indian symbols on your fingers?'

He stared at me first, then at his hand, then back at me.

'They're runes,' he said. 'Don't you know your own history?'

My cheeks burned.

'They're so small, I couldn't see them properly,' I said. 'What do they say?'

'You can learn the alphabet and read for yourself,' he said.

'The Futhark?' I said.

He smiled but said nothing. Instead he stood up, ran a hand over his head and looked at the sky.

'I'm going home now,' he said. 'But we'll see each other again.'

He crossed through the courtyard into the street outside without turning to see if I was watching or following. I resigned myself to sitting there with the rest of the wine, only then decided I was far too restless and left a few minutes later.

When I let myself in, Julie was sitting in the living room. I didn't feel like talking to her, but as I went through the hall on my way to my room she called after me.

I put my head round the door.

'How did it go?' she asked.

'It was fine,' I said.

'*Are* you going out with him?'

'I don't think so, no,' I said and smiled. 'But listen, I'm really tired and a bit drunk. I think I'll just go to bed.'

'OK. Sleep well!'

'You too!' I said, and went up the stairs, closed my door behind me and plonked down on the edge of my bed. She came up herself not long after and I heard her door close as she turned in for the night.

A good thing she hadn't been there when he'd started on about Aryans. She'd have hated that.

I pulled my phone out of my pocket and googled *Aryan*, scanning the article that came up on Wikipedia. He was right. A migration, about four thousand years ago, and they'd called themselves Aryans.

The runic alphabet was history too, though nothing to do with Nazism.

Why hadn't I asked him for his number?

What if I didn't see him again for another fortnight?

I couldn't handle that.

I flopped back, then put my legs in the air, stretched them, drew them back to my chest and wrapped my arms around my knees. After a moment I dropped onto my side and lay there like that for a while.

I'd never known anything like this before. It felt like I was just a single tensed-up emotion. And every time the thought of him went through me that single emotion seemed to detonate into a thousand smaller ones, like a car windscreen that shattered. My toes tingled, my fingers tingled, my stomach tingled.

I imagined what could have happened if he'd come home with me. Imagined him lying there next to me now. His beautiful head on my chest. Eyes closed. My hand running through his hair. Both of us blissfully exhausted, sated, content as a pair of foxes basking in the sun.

There was tension in him too, I'd sensed that, but I could ease it, I knew that now as I lay there, and at that moment I was a little girl no longer, I'd grown up, was more grown up now than anyone I knew. More so than Julie, more so than Kristoffer, more so than Thomas, more so even than Mum and Dad.

I sat up, almost alarmed by the realisation. It was that strong, that certain.

Where did it come from?

Mum had always said I was like a bird. Watchful, timid. I could see that.

It was him. Valdemar. It was him who made me feel like this.

In the days that followed I clocked every customer who came into the shop. Every night I waited for the sound of grit tossed against the pane. He didn't come. He didn't come on the Monday, he didn't come on the Tuesday. He didn't come on the Wednesday, he didn't come on the Thursday. Maybe he was holding off until the weekend I thought when Friday came. He had a job to go to, it stood to reason. But he didn't come on the Saturday, and he didn't come on the Sunday either.

I went through everything that had been said between us in my mind, searching for a reason, something that could have made him want to stay away, but I found nothing. Maybe I was just too young for him, too young and too stupid. Maybe it was Julie and Kristoffer that had put him off, maybe he didn't like them and had cooled his interest because he knew that I did.

There was no one I could talk to about it. It was driving me up the wall. So many emotions and nowhere to put them.

It wasn't entirely inconceivable of course that something had happened to him. His mother could have been taken ill, I had no way of knowing.

But the most likely explanation was that he just wasn't interested any more.

Maybe he'd met someone better?

Ten days it went on. And then, one late afternoon when I got in from work, there was a letter for me on the table in the hall. I knew straight away it was from him. But I didn't open it, not immediately. I put it down on my bedside table before going back downstairs into the kitchen where Magne and Julie were having their dinner.

'There's enough for you too, if you want some,' said Julie.

'Looks nice,' I said. 'What is it?'

'Macaroni cheese,' said Magne. 'And Julie made a salad.'

'I wouldn't mind some salad if there's any going,' I said.

'What about the mac and cheese? I've made a ton of it. We can't just chuck it out.'

I didn't know what to answer. Julie didn't say anything either, so Magne's protest remained in the air while I fetched a plate and some cutlery. Magne was a friend of Kristoffer's from when they'd been kids together. I supposed they'd had a lot in common then, but now they were as different as could be. Magne mostly stayed in his room reading or playing computer games, and whenever we came back to ours for an afterparty he was the type who'd appear in his underpants and tell us to keep the noise down. I never thought he liked me much, I annoyed him for some reason, even if I hadn't a clue what it was.

There was some avocado left, on a little bed of lettuce with some bits of tomato and cucumber. I took two slices, dark green and grey along one edge, brighter green and near-yellow along the other, and put them on my plate together with some of the lettuce before sitting down at the table.

'There was a letter for you,' said Julie. 'I left it on the table in the hall.'

'I saw that,' I said.

'Who was it from? Not many people write letters these days.'

'No idea. I haven't opened it yet.'

'Your dad, maybe?'

I frowned at her.

'My dad?'

'Why not?'

My dad had taught her in the first year of gymnas when he'd still been working. I was only ten then and knew little about that side of him. She often said he was the best teacher she'd ever had. I think she knew it pleased me to hear it.

'I'm not sure he could string two words together these days,' I said. 'I'd be amazed if it was.'

'That boy of yours, then? Valdemar.'

'Why would he write a *letter*?'

'How should I know?'

'Have you met someone?' Magne mumbled into his macaroni cheese. I looked up at him in surprise. Hadn't he heard?

'Line's in love,' said Julie.

'Not any more she isn't,' I said. 'It was a passing fancy, that's all.'

'All right, so Line *isn't* in love,' said Julie and laughed.

Someone came in through the front door.

'Anyone in?' It was Kristoffer.

'In here,' Julie called back.

I got up, rinsed my plate at the sink, put it in the dishwasher, said hi to Kristoffer, and went upstairs to my room. I sat down on the bed with my back against the wall, put my AirPods in, selected the playlist that started with Central Cee's 'Day in the Life', and turned up the volume. Ignoring the letter on the table at my side, I texted Josefine and Klara to see what they were doing. Josefine was packing, she was off to Greece in the morning. Klara wasn't doing anything really, she asked if I fancied going over to hers. I wrote back and told her I was tired but we could see each other tomorrow, maybe grab a latte together in the morning or after work. Kendrick's 'DNA' came on, but then Thomas rang. I didn't answer, just let it ring. I couldn't be bothered. I took a photo and sent it to Josefine who sent one back of her open suitcase with a pile of clothes next to it that wouldn't fit in. *Could do with a hand packing all this*, she wrote. I didn't reply but started searching for a song that could play while I read the letter. Cypress Hill, maybe, 'Tres Equis'. It was so short I put it on repeat. I put my phone down and picked up the letter. Reading it wasn't going to change anything. What it said was there whether I read it or not. Still, I hesitated, let the track play. Then I tore through the top edge of the envelope and took the letter out. A sheet of A4 copy paper. The handwriting was big and awkward like a child's.

Dear Line,

I haven't forgotten you, in case you thought I had. The thing is, I've been away. I'm organising a gig in Sweden. There's been a lot of work involved. You could come, if you want. If you can be at the train station in Karlstad, Saturday at 3 p.m., I'll come and meet you there.

Valdemar

I didn't know what to think. But it could only be positive, surely? He wouldn't be asking me to go all the way to Sweden if he wasn't interested.

I googled Karlstad and concerts in August. Several bands came up, but none Valdemar would have been involved with. One, who called themselves the Real Thing, looked like a dance band, the same applied to the Queen of Sheba, whereas Joachim Forström, who was going to be playing in a park, was pure dad rock.

Where *was* Karlstad, anyway?

Not far from the Norwegian border. I worked out I could take the night train to Oslo on the Friday. Then another train on to Kongsvinger, after that a bus and another train. Arriving Karlstad 3 p.m. Saturday.

He'd checked it out. There were direct trains to Karlstad from Oslo, but none that connected conveniently with the overnight run from Bergen.

Should I?

Of course.

If I didn't, I'd regret it for the rest of my life.

JARLE

The fells that only a few minutes earlier had seemed liked papier-mâché models painted in greys and whites and greens now loomed massively on the other side of the windows as the small plane dipped towards the airport that as yet remained out of sight but hopefully lay waiting for us somewhere in the valley below. The odd thing was that the landscape suddenly became so vital. Up there in the blue sky it was as if nothing had concerned me, certainly not the five other passengers on the flight. I could have been anywhere or anything. But now! I saw trees, white and crooked stems with green foliage, I saw moist green mosses, I saw yellow bog, I saw becks frothing white, plunging into gulleys, I saw walls of spruce, I saw narrow paths and gravel tracks, I saw weathered grey farm buildings. I related profoundly to all these things. How was it to be explained? None of it belonged to me in any way, I had no connections at all with this part of the country. Yet the contrast was enormous and moving. Either it *did* belong to me. Or else I belonged to *it*. Whatever it was, it released in me a wave of something that felt almost like triumph.

Barely twenty metres above the ground, the plane still wobbling in the air, I saw a road beneath us, and there, there, as I craned closer to the window, the tarmac. A patch of grey-black surrounded by trees on all sides. Rather like the crown of a scalp shaved to permit surgery.

I was only staying the one night so rather than packing a cabin case I'd simply dropped a couple of things into a leather briefcase. It was elegant and made me feel good as I lifted it down from the overhead locker, the handle gripped snugly in my hand as I went down the aisle, down the steps and out onto the tarmac where here and there the air hung shimmering, thin, transparent barriers of warmth. How unnatural then to look up and see the white glacier peeping from between the peaks!

An airport worker wearing shorts and a hi-vis orange safety vest over his T-shirt sheathed the propeller blades in what looked like long fat socks, another opened a hatch in the fuselage. I followed the five men who had disembarked before me, to what was no doubt referred to as the terminal building, though it was so small the designation would be appropriate only in a land of miniatures.

Inside, I glanced around in search of the wall-mounted box where the woman from Avis had said I would find the key to my car rental. I couldn't see it anywhere and reasoned it to be hidden behind the frame of the corpulent gent standing with his back to me who was engrossed in something hidden from my view.

An abrupt feeling of sympathy came over me. His white shirt clung in places to his skin, stuck with perspiration, and something told me he was unaware that the sight through the flimsy fabric of his bare body could be considered by others to be improperly intimate. There was always something painful about a person not knowing that something about them perhaps might be perceived as aberrant and therefore showing no embarrassment about it. It was a thought I'd had ever since I was a boy and had been at the swimming baths with my mother, she'd been wearing a white bathing suit that turned transparent in the pool, revealing her nipples to the world. I was seven or eight years old at the time and the experience made me feel physically ill. And then there was the occasion my father came straight from work to the end-of-term festivities at school one Christmas in his overalls and wellies and his donkey jacket on top, when all the other parents had put nice clothes on. I felt so sorry for him. And the girl from my class at gymnas who spent her money on a shoulder bag the same as the one some of the other girls had and who brimmed with pride and joy without realising that hers was an imitation and the others all had the real thing.

In front of me, the man now moved towards the exit with a car key and a crumpled envelope in his hand. And there was the key drop I was looking for, he *had* been standing in front of it.

They'd given me a VW I discovered when I looked at the key, but I didn't know what model until I pressed the remote outside and the lights flashed on a white T-Roc.

Not bad, I thought, dumping my briefcase on the back seat. I'd never driven one before, but I'd seen them and had wondered what they were like.

A high-up car that offered a good view of the road, I noted as I left the parking area. It was responsive too, surging away onto the main road as I put my foot down.

I connected my phone up and called Henriksen as soon as the road straightened out.

'I've arrived,' I said, my eyes drawn by the wide, glittering fjord whose shore the route was following.

'Already? This one's got you excited!'

'I thought I'd come by as soon as I've checked into the hotel. How's that with you? I'd like to see the patient and compare notes.'

'All fine by me. As long as it doesn't drag on!'

A white articulated lorry came sailing majestically over the plain towards me on the other side of the road. Again, it struck me how big and important everything was down here on the ground.

A god, descending to man on earth, would surely have felt the same.

'It's a nice image that, isn't it? Dragging on,' I said, hugging the side of the road as a tiny fear went through me of meeting the lorry head-on. He'd used an expression one didn't hear so much any more. 'Is it something you say often?'

'I wouldn't know. Perhaps it's your old-fangled nature that prompted it.'

The noise of the wind changed as the lorry swept past, like an intake of breath.

'Old-fangled, there's another good one.'

'Collect them, do you?'

'I write them down, yes, as a matter of fact. Without really knowing what for.'

He laughed.

'No doubt they'll come in handy,' he said. 'When are you going back?'

'Tomorrow afternoon.'

'Ah, that excludes dinner tomorrow, then. How about lunch instead?'

'Sounds good. See you in a bit.'

I hung up and glanced through my playlists on Spotify as I drove. The road was all bends now, so it took a while before selecting something that I felt suited both inner and outer landscapes: Brahms, *Ein Deutsches Requiem*. Vainglorious and pretentious? Certainly! But intensely beautiful too.

After checking into the hotel, a hideous concrete block that fell far short of Brutalism's ugly appeal, I strolled up to the hospital, a half-hour walk, the building looming like a castle on the plain of the river. It was disproportionately big for such a small town, but it served the entire region and there was an element of regional politics involved too: a few years back the college here had been given university status and several specialist centres that would normally have been located in the larger cities had been placed here, among them a neurosurgical unit, the only one outside of the university hospitals.

I went into the reception area and asked for Henriksen.

'I'm afraid he's busy at the moment,' the woman behind the desk said, casting a brief and sorrowful glance at me before looking down at her computer screen again.

'I do have an appointment. Tell him it's Jarle Skinlo. Dr Jarle Skinlo.'

'I'm sorry, only there's been a major accident. He's in theatre as we speak.'

'What sort of an accident?'

'A road accident. A bus. Quite a number of serious casualties. It's chaos up there now.'

'I understand,' I said. 'I'll come back in the morning.'

'You're welcome,' she said and returned to her work. I walked back down to the hotel and settled into my room to study the material Henriksen had sent me that same morning regarding our patient. The first attachment was an MRI scan showing irreversible damage that was incompatible with anything but death, the second an EEG with no recorded activity. The third, however, also an EEG, did show activity, and the accompanying MRI scan that had been done at the same time showed the damage to the brain stem to have *lessened*. It was unbelievable. And so I didn't believe it. There had to be some kind of error. No one comes back from the dead. There had to have been activity all along. But consciousness?

I was longing to find out.

The afternoon had me wandering aimlessly for a while before sitting down to a cappuccino at a coffee shop by the river. I'd asked for a cortado, which to the fair-haired girl behind the counter apparently was unknown territory. I'd bought myself two shirts and a pair of socks in the shopping centre and found a couple of interesting books in the bargain bin outside the bookshop. It was one of the good things about small towns, I found, that readers in such places aren't always that sophisticated, for which reason the quality books the bookshops were required to stock often could be had for next to nothing. Thus, I'd picked up a collection of poems by Pessoa, or more exactly his heteronyms de Campos, Reis and Caeiro, as well as himself under his own name, the title was *It Is Not I Whom I Depict* and I sat and read it from cover to cover there by the river, turning down the corners of the pages to which I would later return. And then a book about Schubert's *Winterreise*, the song cycle he completed in the final months of his life, which I intended to read that evening while listening to the songs. I was already looking forward to it. I'd also bought, though for the full retail price, a popular science book about dreams entitled *The Oracle of the Night*, it looked quite promising.

I'd been up since 5 a.m. so I had a nap and eventually woke up with my head feeling heavy, realising thereby, and by the light, that the weather had changed. Drawing the curtains apart, I saw banks of black cloud like a wall above the peaks.

After showering I switched the TV on and got dressed with one eye on the evening news. Clearly news desks around the country had been busy. The triple killing in Bergen, the mysterious phenomenon in the sky, and then this road accident, a school bus apparently, that Henriksen was up to his ears in. The presenters were dramatically grave in their delivery, their voices imbued with the singular intensity that is peculiar only to newsreaders, spelling it out to us: these are important matters!

I shuffled into the bathroom to attend to my dental hygiene. My dentist had alerted me to a new kind of toothpick, which I now took from my sponge bag. They were orange with a flexible tip covered in tiny rubber bristles that could clean between even the smallest interdental spaces. They'd actually improved my standards, which wasn't to be sniffed at. Such matters too were important!

A few months from now, today's news would all be forgotten. It was a fact viewers ought to be reminded about, I thought to myself as I stood with my mouth wide open, wiggling the soft pick in the space between two teeth that were particularly close together. *The following news stories are considered important at this moment in time, and are indeed important to those directly affected, but for the rest of us, and in the greater perspective of time, they are in fact nothing but single occurrences among many. In a few years they will reside only on memory's furthest outskirts, waiting to be activated, which for the vast majority of us will never happen. Our selecting them and presenting them to you today as crucial events is down only to the fact that it is nevertheless in the present that we live. Some would say it is in the present that we* are. *This is our time, this is our day, this is our hour. With that, I now hand you over to the news team.*

So speaks a man time has abandoned, I told myself, examining for a moment my reflection in the mirror before dropping the toothpick into the waste bin. Thin, angular face, thin skin, thin lips, thin glasses, bald head.

If I'd glimpsed such a face in passing, what would I have thought?

Probably nothing. A man, sixtyish. Civil servant? Social services manager? Doctor? A regular life, comfortable but bored. Married, kids moved out. An empty-nester as they called it nowadays.

It wouldn't be far off the mark. Apart from being married with kids. And being bored. Only idiots get bored, that was my motto.

But *boring*, that was a different matter, and probably true.

A boring person who was never bored. That was me. Jarle Skinlo.

I could hear the TV saying the police had taken a twenty-year-old man into custody in connection with the triple murder. They weren't saying his name, but it didn't take a genius to understand it was the fourth member of the band.

I brushed my teeth, turned the TV off in the middle of someone explaining something about comets, slipped my key card into my wallet, put my jacket on, picked up the book I'd bought about dreams and left the room.

On the wall by the lift someone had pinned a sheet of A4 with a picture of a dark-haired woman and some obscure text about a demonstration of crystals in room 324. It was carelessly done and hard to believe the hotel had anything to do with it.

Strange. What sort of a person would be flogging crystals at a hotel typically used by business people?

Only as I was crossing over the car park did it occur to me that the woman would be a prostitute. And that I, or any other man staying on his own at the hotel, could just go to room 324 and knock on the door, if that was what I fancied.

The thought quickened my heart. Why the *heart* should find such a thing exciting wasn't by any means clear; the heart would never have sex with anyone no matter what happened, all it could do was sit there and beat in its little cage.

If the heart had been able to think, it would have stopped beating altogether, Pessoa had stated so wisely. Pessoa, that champion of the meaningless. Wasn't that what he was? Uncovering and cultivating meaninglessness at one and the same time. For there was pleasure in the nihilistic certainty: as soon as it was affirmed, nothing mattered any more, not even evil, and man was free.

I was free to enter room 324. But even if I wanted to, I wouldn't.

Why not?

Never the nihilist, Skinlo?

A quiet night in with Schubert's *Winterreise*? Is that more like it?

The foolish nonsense of a brain sensitive to vagaries of the weather.

I followed a footpath along the river and came to a restaurant, a pavilion-like building a few hundred metres from the centre of town. It looked pleasant enough and so I sat down at a table by the window, ordered an entrecôte and a glass of red and started reading the book about dreams while waiting for the food to arrive.

The meat was tough and burnt at the edges, the béarnaise cold, the fries limp. But the wine was all right and the view faultless: the inky waters of the river running its course, the clouds congregating like a motorcycle gang in the sky above, dark and foreboding, the feeling that the sunshine earlier in the day had been only a theatrical backdrop now drawn aside to make way for the drama proper: the plunging darkness and rain.

I'd reached coffee when the sky crashed apart. Raindrops as big as pebbles dashed against the patio tiles outside, ran a myriad holes in the surface of the river, turning it into what looked like a bubbling soup, while the branches of the trees along the bank lifted as if in unison. Above it all, lightning flashed, and thunder rolled from the fells.

It occurred to me that I didn't need Henriksen there to see the patient. All I had to do in order to gain access was present myself and refer to our appointment.

It still wasn't that late. And a glass of claret under the belt had never stopped any doctor from working, even if the medical community did want to give another impression.

'Not the best of weather to be out and about in,' the waiter said, placing the bill in front of me on a little metal dish. 'I trust you're driving?'

'I'm afraid not,' I said. 'Perhaps you could call a taxi for me.'

'Certainly,' he said. 'Where would you like to go?'

'Up to the hospital.'

'That should be no problem,' he said. 'Give me a sec and I'll check for you.'

While I waited I called Henriksen's number just to be on the safe side. Against expectations he answered.

'I heard you came by,' he said. 'Sorry I couldn't spare the time. Run off our feet here. You'll have heard, I supppose?'

'The bus crash?'

'That's it. Never seen anything like it. So many serious injuries all at once. Anyway, I'm done for the time being. On my way home to get some shut-eye. Where are you?'

'On my way to the hospital, as it happens. I thought I'd look in on the patient and prep him before we get started in the morning.'

'Prep him? You can't prep him. He's a vegetable. There's no one in.'

'I'd like to see him all the same.'

'Listen, I'm not far away. I'll meet you there, if you like?'

'Not necessary, really. You get yourself home and get some sleep.'

'No, I'm fine. You did have an appointment. And besides, he is *my* patient.'

The taxi slid with a hum through the rain that was already gushing through the gutters, occasionally flooding at the roadsides. The area in front of the hospital was deserted, but the car park was almost full. The cars looked like big, unmoving beetles and it didn't require much of an imagination to cast them as victims of some form of natural disaster such as that which had occurred in Pompeii when the lethal fumes had come on the wind and left everything dead yet intact.

Henriksen was standing over by the lifts, long and gangly, his face too was drawn out and narrow, his head lowered as he studied his phone.

'Jarle!' he said, looking up when I approached. He gripped my hand in both of his, like a president. 'You're looking well!'

'You too,' I said.

He laughed. It made his eyes, which often seemed cold and fishlike in a way, gleam.

'That I doubt. It's been a long, hard day.'

'How many fatalities? They didn't say on the news.'

'None! That's what's so bloody odd! I've never seen so many serious injuries all at once. But no one's died. Not yet, anyway.'

He puffed on his nicotine inhaler.

'Shall we?'

I nodded and he pressed the floor button.

'His wife will be there,' he said and leaned back against the wall of the lift. 'She barely leaves his side, as they say.'

'And she's given her permission for me to take a look at him?'

'She has. We had a meeting this morning. She doesn't know the details, though. We might want to hold back a bit in that respect. I don't want her building her hopes up. Have you seen the material I sent?'

'Yes. All rather hard to believe, I'd say.'

'Something obviously went wrong. Nevertheless, the damage is so critical there's hardly any point in keeping him alive.'

'What does his wife have to say about that?'

'She hasn't objected.'

'Has anyone? Parents? Siblings?'

He shook his head.

'No other family. Just the wife and two kids.'

The door slid open and we entered the ward. Henriksen knocked on a door and opened it without waiting. A woman was sitting on a chair next to the bed. Neat and small, delicate features, a faint blush to slightly rounded cheeks. She looked up at us as we came in. Eyes with no spark of life.

'Good evening,' said Henriksen. 'I've brought that colleague of mine I was telling you about. Jarle Skinlo.'

'Hello,' she said.

'Nice to meet you,' I said and smiled at her before stepping forward to the bed where her husband lay. His eyes were wide open, though vacant. They saw nothing, and there was nothing to see in them. A man in his mid-fifties, dark beard, greying hair. His face was fresh and ruddy.

The windowpane reflected a flash of lightning. The thunder that followed was loud and close by. He didn't bat an eyelid.

'And you must be Jan,' I said. 'As you may have heard, my name is Jarle. I'm a neurologist. I conduct research into the workings of the brain. Tomorrow I'll be doing a scan of your own brain together with a colleague of mine. After that we must see if there's any way we can communicate. I hope you're comfortable.'

'What do you mean?' the man's wife said. 'Communicate? How?'

'Just covering all bases,' Henriksen interrupted. 'An ethical precaution, if you like. Not to be taken literally.'

'He's not there,' the woman said.

'Much would indicate so,' I said. 'But as long as we're not certain, the best way to proceed is to assume that Jan can hear us.'

'Not certain? But he's been taken off his IV. He's lying here dying. How can you say you're not certain?'

'We are indeed certain, of course,' said Henriksen. 'Your husband's brain is so damaged that he won't ever return to any kind of life one would deem to be worth living. Hardly life at all, in fact. He can't think, he can't perceive, he can't feel pain. The man you knew as Jan is no more, I'm afraid. He won't be coming back.'

'But why is he saying you're not certain?' the woman said, gesturing in my direction while her eyes remained fixed on Henriksen.

Henriksen gave me a glare.

'In a very few cases, people in clinically vegetative states have been found to be conscious, in the sense of continued awareness or perception,' I said. 'The chances are minimal. But as long as they exist, we must address the possibility. An ethical precaution, as was said.'

Tears ran down her cheeks.

'It's a routine examination,' Henriksen said. 'No more, no less. Realistically, I'm sorry to say that there is no hope of either consciousness or recovery. Isn't that right, Jarle?'

'I'm afraid that is the case, yes,' I said. 'I'll be in touch with you as soon as we have some results available.'

'Thank you,' she said.

'You bloody idiot,' Henriksen said as soon as we'd shut the door behind us. 'Why did you have to go and say that? You know as well as I do, that brain is damaged beyond repair. For crying out loud, you saw what it did to her?'

'I couldn't exactly lie to her, could I?'

'Lie? What do you think I spend my time doing every day when I'm talking to patients' families? It's all about telling them what they need to hear. Not babbling on about what you happen to know or think or believe. Just hang on here a minute.'

He went into the duty room and then appeared again with a well-built red-haired nurse in her thirties who immediately made a beeline for the room we'd just left.

'You've always had that touch of naivety about you, you know that, don't you?' he said as we went towards the lifts.

'No,' I said, 'I think you're wrong about that. You may be a good doctor, but you're a poor judge of people.'

'Ha!' he snorted.

'When I told her there have been very few cases where vegetative patients have been found to be conscious, I was lying. The figure may be as high as ten per cent. Perhaps even fifteen.'

He pressed the button for the lift and the door opened.

'I don't believe it for a moment.'

'I know you don't. Nonetheless, it happens to be the case.'

'When the brain is as damaged as Ramsvik's, the man's as good as dead. You know that. You've seen the data. Any kind of awareness there is inconceivable.'

'There can be small pockets.'

'*Pockets*?'

'That's right.'

He smirked as we stepped out onto the ground floor and went towards the exit. The warmth outside was almost tropical, and surprising too. My mind must have prepared me for something more autumnal from what I'd seen through the windows, the towering black clouds, the driving rain.

'How are you getting back to your hotel?' Henriksen said. 'Have you got a car?'

'I'll walk.'

'In this? Let me give you a lift.'

We went over to a black Range Rover that was parked right next to the building. It was in perfect nick, the seats looked almost unused and not a sweet wrapper in sight.

'Listen, Jarle,' he said, twisting his body to reverse out of the parking bay with his arm around the back of the passenger seat, 'you don't operate on people. You don't have to take the risks I do every day. Who's worth the surgery, who's to be left to lie there and die. You're not the one who has to turn off the life support on someone's child.'

He threw the gear lever into first and pulled away.

'You do research. You've no responsibility. It's no wonder an old hand like me feels provoked when you start coming on like a social worker, telling a vegetable you're looking forward to having a nice chat with him while his wife's sitting there listening. You do understand, don't you?'

'Yes, I understand,' I said. 'But do you understand what it might – and I stress *might* – be like to be inside a person like that, unable to talk or communicate in any way, when everyone around you thinks you're a vegetable and treats you like an object? To lie there and listen to doctors making decisions about ending all life-sustaining treatments? Hearing, in other words, your own death sentence be pronounced and knowing that you're going to be lying there for days on end while you starve to death. You can't talk, you can't move, you can't purposefully control any function of your body. The only thing you can do is think and feel.'

'I get you, of course. It would be horrific!' Henriksen conceded with a smile, his eyes on the road, the windscreen soft and malleable-looking as if shuddering almost imperceptibly in the rain that the wipers swept aside, the car following the river, the road a gentle bend. 'Fortunately, it never happens!'

We passed a bus stop. The view of the river was blocked by some tall deciduous trees, dark, black almost, apart from the crowns of light thrown on them by the lamp posts. The green seemed to come from out of the darkness. As if it were growing from it organically, an evolutionary step ahead.

'Hey!' Henriksen suddenly blurted out, instantaneously slamming on the brakes. My body wanted to continue its forward momentum but was restrained by the safety belt that tightened forcefully around my chest.

A deer was standing in the middle of the road. It stared at us, unmoving in the beam of the headlights.

'Are you OK?' said Henriksen.

'Yes, I'm fine,' I said. I couldn't take my eyes off it. The great antlers that looked like they were part of a tree. The slanting, sardonic eyes. The strong, sleek body.

Henriksen tooted the horn and the beast bounded off into the trees at the side of the road.

'Well, you don't see that very often,' I said as we drove on.

'Fine animal,' he said.

'Yes, but what's it doing here?'

'Don't ask me. The heat, maybe? Anyway, where were we? Ah, I know, you were talking about the inner life of vegetables! I suppose it is *possible* that some of them may retain, should we say, a *remnant* of consciousness. But nowhere near enough to afford them any kind of life. And fifteen per cent? Never in a million years. Nought point one five, more like. And besides, isn't the fact of the matter that we can measure brain activity, not consciousness?'

'Indeed. That's the whole point. In other words these people may be conscious without our realising. And it does in fact happen, you must know that. People have emerged from vegetative states after several years and reported having been able to perceive everything that went on around them the whole time.'

'You don't say,' he said dismissively.

'Not many, I grant you that. I read about a case in Canada. But one case is enough, as you know. It means it can happen.'

'Quite the opposite. One case means nothing. It's not enough.'

He threw me a glance. His annoyance had passed, now he looked more like he felt sorry for me.

'But let's stick to Ramsvik,' he went on. 'You brought his wife to tears and you instilled in her a hope where there is none. On top of that, you put me in a bad light to say the least. Made me out to be the insensitive doctor intent on killing off his patients, while you were the knight in shining armour talking to the vegetable like all he had was a head cold.'

'Is that what this is about? Your vanity?'

'The vanity's all yours, not mine. I save lives. You poke about in people's tragedies in order to make a name for yourself.'

Nothing more was said until Henriksen, belligerent for as long as I'd known him, swung into the car park in front of the hotel and pulled up.

'How about a drink?' he said, killing the engine. 'For old times' sake?'

I looked at him, mildly astonished.

'I'd have had one anyway when I got home. Might as well have one here, with you.'

'Yes, all right. Why not?'

'That's the spirit!'

We went into the hotel bar and sat down at a table where we studied the drinks menu.

'You know me, I've always found it hard to come back down again,' he said. 'What'll you have?'

'A glass of red. How about you?'

'Never go wrong with a Scotch.'

He glanced around the room.

'Do they come to the tables?'

'I doubt it,' I said, getting to my feet. 'I'll get these.'

I'd known Henriksen ever since we'd been medical students together, when the two of us ran the film club. He was never called anything but Henriksen even then, it was basically only his parents who called him Lars Atle. He was the same now as then, drank just as much, though was never quite as cynical in those days. For a while we'd been interested in the same girl, Inger, who I ended up marrying. I wasn't quite sure if he'd ever forgiven me for it. He was the sort you could spend a lot of time with without really getting to know him. I knew his opinions and could predict to a certain extent what he was likely to say in a given discussion, but I had no idea what he was like on the inside. What it was like to be him. Some people were like that. Personable, but impersonal.

'Seriously though,' he said when I returned with the drinks. 'Pockets of consciousness? What's that all about? It doesn't sound particularly scientific, if you ask me. You've not got caught up in some New Age rubbish, I hope?'

'New Age rubbish?'

'Yes. Postmodernist relativism or whatever you want to call it.'

'Not at all. You've nothing to worry about there.'

I saw no reason to involve him in what I happened to think and believe, not Mr Zebra, Mr Black-and-White, so I simply smiled and lifted my glass.

'Cheers, good to see you!'

'Cheers, and likewise. But I am still wondering about what it is you actually do. I'm genuinely interested, believe it or not.'

'Well, it's like you said before. We can't really measure consciousness. There's no real way of going about it. Scientifically, I mean.'

'I knew it! You *have* gone hippie on me.'

'No, I'm just a bit more hesitant, that's all.'

'Than me, you mean?'

'If we don't know what consciousness is, how can we know if people in vegetative states, people who are comatose, are conscious or not? An injury that prevents a person from building new memories, for instance, sets up a different kind of consciousness, at least in part.

What happens to our consciousness if the brain is no longer able to build new memories and at the same time cannot receive new visual, aural or other sensory input? While all the old memories remain intact.'

'What a lot of hypothetical questions all at once.'

'Yes, but it's not beyond the bounds of possibility that there are people in clinically vegetative states who are living in their memories. And are cognisant of the fact.'

'What's the relevance here?'

'The relevance is that many patients who are comatose or in vegetative states aren't vegetables or zombies, but are actually living their lives on the inside.'

He snorted.

'If they're not receiving any sensory impressions, if they're not seeing or hearing anything, how can you know? How are you going to get through to them?'

'I can't. But some people in vegetative states who *can* see and hear, but nothing else, have been responsive. You must have heard about it? Inside the scanner they were asked to think about tennis to answer yes and about passing through their apartment to answer no. Their replies could be read off the scans, because different parts of the brain were activated.'

'Yes, I've heard about it. But those patients hadn't suffered anything like the same haemorrhaging as Ramsvik.'

'Well, we'll see in the morning.'

He'd slid down on the uncomfortable sofa, it was without proper support for the back, and was now almost reclining, drink held against his chest.

'But where's it all leading? That's what I want to know.'

I said nothing.

'Anyway,' he said after a minute, 'enough of all that. How's things? All right?'

'Yes, all good.'

'Do you hear from Inger?'

I shook my head.

'Anyone new in the picture?'

'No.'

'No, I suppose not,' he said, straightening up slightly.

'How about you?'

'I'm fine. Sanna's started cutting herself, her forearms. And Hugo won't talk to us about anything. I mean, he's polite and civil and all that, not difficult as such, we just don't get anything out of him.'

'How old are they now?'

'Sanna's sixteen, Hugo's fifteen.'

'Sounds tough.'

'Tough? I'll say it's tough. And so bloody meaningless too. Why can't they just enjoy a nice life while they've got it? We've never done anything to harm them. At least not as far as I know. But there they are, suffering. You may have made the right choice, not having kids.'

'Not my choice, as you know.'

'No, they're lovely kids,' he said, more to himself than me.

'Yes, they are,' I said.

An hour later, after five drinks, he got up to go.

'You don't think it'd be better calling a taxi?' I said. 'Pick up the car in the morning? I can drive it up to the hospital for you, if you want.'

He shook his head.

'There's hardly ever a police control here. At least never in midweek at this time of night.'

'It wasn't actually being caught I was thinking about. It was more the danger, that you could crash the car or run some poor sod down.'

'There'll be no one out now,' he said and patted my shoulder. 'Jarle, always the little old lady! But thanks for your concern!'

Upstairs in my room, standing at the window in the dark, it occurred to me that the reason he'd suggested having a drink was so he could talk about his kids. In which case I'd failed him. I'd shown not the slightest interest, not a single question had I asked to pursue the subject.

Perhaps it was the first time he'd ever mentioned it to anyone.

That was what it was like to be a narcissist, I thought, and switched on the bedside lamp before propping myself up on the bed with a pair of pillows behind my back, the *Winterreise* book in my hand, headphones in place.

It was perhaps the greatest advantage of living on one's own, not having to find the right stance in relation to another person. I represented no one. Had no one else's needs to fulfil. And I could always pick up the thread about his children the next day over lunch. Knowing Henriksen he would bat it away. To his mind, a confidence was the same as a weakness. No doubt he had despaired at himself on the way home.

I leaned back, listening to the songs without reading. How sorrowful they were, so crammed with snow, darkness, loneliness, the lights of the village forever there in the distance, and spring but a dream. Although their origins were remote to me, penned as they were by a dying young German two hundred years ago, they touched me. No, more than that, they possessed me. For a while the songs and I were one and the same, their moods seeping through me and leading my thoughts in directions that even moments earlier I could not have predicted.

Had I played any other musical work something else would have moved in me, not only other feelings, but other thoughts too. *The Rite of Spring*, for example – was that not the very opposite of *Winterreise*? Full of life, intense, vibrant, complex, wildly imperfect, in some respects rather primitive, whereas *Winterreise* was sophisticated and decadent, full of longing for something that could never and should never be attained, for the longing was precious in itself. *The Rite of Spring* was the attainment and therefore was oblivious to the longing. *The Rite of Spring* was life at its outset, *Winterreise* was the journey that set out from there. 'I must travel a road from which no man has ever returned.'

But was *I* lonely. Was *I* longing to die?

Not at all! The feelings that welled in me were not my own. Or rather, were not of my own making. In that respect they were immaterial. Unless the fact that it was good to feel longing, good to feel sadness, good to feel wretched, was meaningful in itself.

Perhaps it was the case that a person had no need at all of others in order to live a full life. Perhaps life could be lived through art alone, that reservoir of human emotions, encounters, thoughts and experience.

Why not?

A study was conducted once involving a handful of patients with locked-in syndrome, which required them to assess their quality of life, and a majority stated that they were no less happy than they had been before. People with this disorder are able to communicate only by moving their eyes or blinking and have no control over the rest of their bodies. They are, as it were, locked inside the body as if it were a prison. And yet they are happy. Or at least not particularly unhappy. But what do they have when all they have is themselves? When they live only in thoughts? *Are* they then thoughts? What *are* thoughts anyway? They come to us as neither images nor sounds, but as something else, a kind of presence that is partly linguistic, partly – well, what?

I got up and went over to the desk, plugged in my laptop and opened the document that was my book.

Maps of the Brain

by Jarle Skinlo

I still liked the title, it was representative of the book's contents, which together constituted some sort of map of the brain, a chapter for each of its regions, general observations about the kinds of activity that took place there as well as anecdotal content based on patient records, and a personal perspective that took as its point of departure the fact that the brain I was describing was my own as seen from the outside, in the form of scans I presented and described, and from the inside, relating lived experiences from my own life. The maps of the title were of course a collected overview of the cerebral terrain, but I wondered now if it might be better in the singular, with the indefinite article, *A Map of the Brain*. Or perhaps something else altogether?

I opened a separate document and stared at some earlier suggestions:

A Journey into the Brain
Into the Brain
Journey to the Centre of the Brain
Brain of Darkness
Our Great Brain

Brain of Darkness was better than *A Map of the Brain*, but was more obscure and perhaps promising of something else. Besides, there wasn't much darkness in my life! So I left the title as it was and cast an eye over the introduction.

> More often than is healthy, I try to catch hold of my thoughts in flight, to consider them as they flutter by, but the problem of course is that the only thing I have to catch them with are other thoughts, which themselves cannot be captured unless by – yes, exactly! – other thoughts.

Here I wanted to have something about Alan Turing and his excellent observation to the effect that 'the explanans must be of a higher order than the explanandum', but I found it a bit heavy to introduce Turing at such an early juncture, and the same would apply to a footnote – both entailed the risk of frightening the casual reader away. The thing was, I hadn't found anywhere else where it could naturally be inserted either. Of course, I could always include a chapter on artificial intelligence, a field in which Turing was a central figure, and tuck the quote in there. Indeed, there were only two things more expansive than human consciousness, both hypothetical: God and AI. The problem again though was that I couldn't work out where it would go in the book's overall scheme of things. On the other hand, a space might conceivably present itself towards the end and resolve the whole issue.

It's a bit like that children's game in which two or more participants place hand upon hand, the one that is underneath at any given point being withdrawn and placed once more on top, a continuous piling up of hands into a pile that never gets any taller.

What is a thought? This is the most fundamental question in what I do, much as the question 'What is a brick?' would be to a bricklayer. But unlike the bricklayer I have no answer to my question. It isn't the chemical and electrical signals that are relayed between the cells of the brain – most of that activity takes place beyond our awareness, within automated systems whereby information is processed and forwarded at dizzying speed, impossible to compare with anything else in our world until the advent of computer technology gave us machines that could process information with similarly mind-boggling rapidity. These systems are made up of modules and they pay each other no heed. Although we know that thoughts, and thereby human consciousness, derive from those same simple modules, such a system is clearly of a different character – and it is approximately here, at this 'different character' that our insights reach an impasse and become speculation.

No one knows what a thought is. No one knows what consciousness is.

No, you might object. That's not true. Everyone knows what a thought is. Everyone knows what consciousness is.

And in a way you would be right. We think and are conscious, therefore we know from experience what these things are. We feel it, we sense it, we know it – but we cannot capture it.

Here, of course! Why hadn't it occurred to me before?

I began to type.

> The British mathematician Alan Turing, best known perhaps for having cracked the German military's Enigma code during World War II, put this paradox elegantly into words when he wrote: 'the explanans must be of a higher order than the explanandum' – which is to say that a brain cannot explain the brain, consciousness cannot explain consciousness. For that we need a more general principle to explain the particular phenomenon. Something of a higher order.

Even as I typed I sensed it wasn't going to work, it wouldn't lead into what came next. Turing's reasoning made the text race, but only into a cul-de-sac – everything ended there. I deleted what I'd just written and read on.

> The leap from mechanical to self-experiencing system is a bit like the leap from non-life to life, only at a level above. What does it take for a system to become aware of itself? Automated systems such as the one that controls our motor functions, allowing us for instance to reach out and pick an apple from a bowl of fruit, involve huge numbers of incalculably minute computations, and considering these alone our first impression is one of near-endless complexity. Yet the work performed by the individual module is relatively uncomplicated: the module receives two inputs, one conveying the relevant instruction as to what to do, another with information about current status, whereupon the former is adjusted according to the latter before being sent on with a view to effectuation.
>
> Consciousness is quite a different type of system, in which information is integrated and all components interrelated, and it is in this coordinated interaction, this networked device, that the experience of the self arises. But how it happens no one knows. No one! Working with this problem, studying the literature, it's

easy to fall into the trap of believing that consciousness is a kind of thinking system, something technical and in some way constrained and manageable. The arrival of the computer has without doubt strengthened this misconception, since both the brain and the computer break down information into signals they then relay and store. That computers are now able to learn and develop on their own terms makes the analogy only that much more appealing. A few short decades from now they will doubtless be capable of independent thought. Which raises some interesting questions about what it is to be human, as well as making my first question all the more pertinent: what is a thought? Where exactly do they come from? What is their relation to us, the individuals who produce them? It is not the case that all thoughts are rational, that all thoughts are objectively directed, as algorithms are. We humans think dark thoughts too, shabby thoughts, evil thoughts, wild, sick thoughts. Why? The ancients distinguished between mind, soul and body, and one need only listen to one of Chopin's piano pieces to understand how profound a distinction it is. A system being consciously aware of itself is one thing – a system that may fill with longing is quite another.

For that reason, I will often conclude a series of lectures by reading out a poem or playing a piece of music. I know that many of my students, perhaps most, find it pretentious, but as long as some of their number understand what I'm getting at, and take it seriously, it's worth it. I take pains never to use the word 'soul', which I consider to be rather too laden with God and immortality, instead I want my students to at least try to even out the difference between themselves, the lives they live and the brain they study. The brain is so quickly cast as something external to us, an object with certain functions, isolated and compartmentalised into various zones, a thing – a miraculous thing, certainly, but a thing nonetheless. Even the most ardent idealist may end up thinking so. But just as consciousness arises in connection and coordination, where no cell acts on its own but comprises a part of the whole, the brain as a complete entity is connected too, the brain too is one node among many in a network it shapes and by which it itself is shaped. Through this network, which is language, which is culture, which is society, Chopin's piano music streams. Only when these two poles have been established, the mechanically precise functions within and the fluid social domain without, can our discussion about consciousness begin. For consciousness is neither one thing nor the other, but emerges somewhere in between. But where? Is it a purely physical phenomenon or does it possess a non-physical dimension too? And what of the self? Is the self a purely physical phenomenon? Where is the boundary between the self and human consciousness? Or perhaps the self is human consciousness?

The answers to these questions will depend on the direction from which we approach them. Consciousness as a phenomenon will appear differently to a psychologist than to a neurobiologist or a philosopher. The only thing on which everyone can agree is that what is central to consciousness, what it does and which is unique to it, has to do with experience. Our experience of reality. Processing information from our surroundings and acting accordingly in relation to that reality is one thing, quite another is to experience. What is it like to be a bat? This was a question posed by the American philosopher Thomas Nagel in a famous paper he published in 1974, and consciousness may be defined in much the same way, i.e. what it is to be something. Vast quantities of information circulate in the brain, information of which we are unaware insofar as it is processed automatically, but since this information is not manifest to consciousness, it remains as it were unexperienced, and for this reason it is as if the information, and the neurons involved in its processing, do not exist to us. Indeed, it is as if what happens does not happen at all. For the world to become real, it must be made real to us – and this is what consciousness does. Well-known experiments have shown it is possible to physically map the movements of unconscious information by scanning the brains of subjects exposed to the briefest flash of an image – the readouts look like the path of someone scaling a very steep mountain and then falling back down again. Information that becomes conscious, however, progresses further and reaches a plateau – and here, suddenly, it becomes manifest to the subject, which is to say that it becomes part of the subject's experience. This not only corroborates to us Freud's theory of the subconscious, it also demonstrates in striking manner the very mystery of the unconscious mind – for what is it that causes the same signals that blindly pass through the neurons of the brain to actually become manifest to a person? Could it be one and the same thing – that we become someone as the signal becomes something? Is it the case that we humans emerge as conscious beings only in the instant the world around us becomes manifest within us?

If consciousness somehow consists in the very experience of something, then the self is that which claims ownership of the experience. This exists, says the conscious mind. This is mine, says the self, and it too exists. Whether or not this sense of ownership is already in place in the newborn infant is of course impossible to say. Presumably we are talking about some kind of process here, slow no doubt, and quite imperceptible, beginning in those very early stages of infancy when the world and the people in it float in and out of the fields of perception and where no distinctions yet exist between inside and out, between states of sleep and waking, between dreams and reality. The infant sees, but what it sees does not stick and is instead fluid. It captures the baby's attention, but is as yet unowned by it, it is fluid, as the infant mind itself is fluid. Gradually, a pattern emerges, of repetitions, a hazily dawning conception of boundary, the blurred awareness of within and without, of here and there, and in this within, this here, the self emerges, cautious and hesitant at first, soon increasingly confident, increasingly greedy, until at some point it has taken possession of everything and has become the sole proprietor of experiences, boldy proclaiming: me! me! mine! mine! This self, this I, brand new and unfamiliar in every new individual, is vulnerable too; all psychology stems fundamentally from this notion of ownership and how it is encountered and managed. The self conquers the inner mind, retaining its grip by laying down memories, much as an animal retains a grip on its territory by laying down markers in the form of its sprayed urine. In time the self will stand secure and may be shifted only by disorders such as schizophrenia and psychosis, or by severe brain damage, which may redraw the self completely, and yet, to the individual, the self will remain the self, regardless that everything about it may now be different.

But: it is I who sees, I who does, I who thinks – and how does this come to be, and in what does it consist? Studies have shown that the brains of people watching the same film are quite synchronised, the activity that occurs then in the various regions of the brain occurring in exactly the same way in each individual. When the subjects see a face, a small area known as the fusiform gyrus lights up at the back of the brain. When they see a car driving along a road, another, similarly located, lights up in the same way, this one called the occipital lobe. When someone fires a gun, the auditive area of the cerebral cortex lights up, and, in a form of chain reaction, other areas too, and networks, among them the amygdala, which has to do with emotional responses, including fear. And yet in each individual the experience feels unique, and this is the case in any circumstance. Religious ecstasy is basically about one thing only, which is the dissolving of the self's sense of ownership. What fills the conscious mind in that instance is a powerful sense of belonging not to the individual self but to the universal everything. Music too, and literature, are all about the dissolving of this same ownership. But there, in the realm of the unpossessed, we are no one, merely a locus through which impressions pass, as a river runs through a plain, or cars will proceed along a motorway.

This is a book about the human brain. Since there is no such a thing as a general brain, it is a book about a particular brain. Moreover, because the most significant part of that which goes on in a brain may only be understood and experienced from the inside, it is a book about my brain. And because I am a neurologist by trade, the inside of my brain is more concerned than is usual with how the brain appears from the outside. My hope is

> that in this way I shall be able to draw a picture of the brain that is simultaneously objective and subjective – the darkness of the soul illuminated by the light of science.

Would *The Darkness of the Brain in the Light of Science* be a good title?

No, far too clunky, and pretentious too!

Better to stick with the one I'd got.

I closed the laptop, went over to the window and looked out over the town. It was only just gone eleven. I wouldn't be able to sleep for some time now after stupidly having slept in the afternoon.

Perhaps go for a drive somewhere?

Or have a nightcap in the bar?

Go for a wander through the empty streets?

Take a couple of sleeping pills and conk out for the night?

Watch some East European porn and masturbate into the early hours?

Maybe a combination? A nightcap, a bit of pleasuring, then a few pages of my book about *Winterreise* to compensate before calling it a day?

Not a bad plan actually.

On my way to the lift I noticed that the mysterious crystal woman's poster had been taken down. Fair enough, no decent hotel would want to be advertising that kind of private initiative. The fact that it had been removed only reinforced my theory that the woman was a prostitute drawing attention to her services without mentioning their nature. Maybe there was some kind of code involved, common knowledge to everyone but me.

Room 324.

I bought myself a glass of red wine at the bar and sat down at a table with a view of the car park. The wine, a cheap Côtes du Rhône, was too light and tangy to my taste, but maybe the impression would improve after a few sips when the taste buds got used to it. It was often the way.

There weren't many in. A couple of uncultured young men in their thirties in white shirts and ties, a woman around forty sitting by the bar with untidy hair and poor posture, a man my own age with his laptop open on the table in front of him. The two men in their thirties radiated the kind of self-assurance such men have when they're accustomed to everything going their way. They weren't bound by anything here and paid no attention at all to their surroundings. I guessed they were consultants of some sort, a legal team perhaps, flown in to fix a company issue. The woman was clearly in transit, in the wider respect too. Everything about her suggested she had fled from something whose alternatives, even sitting on her own drinking in a near-empty and soulless hotel bar, were in every instance an improvement. The man my own age, who more than likely had been sent out from some main office or other, or perhaps worked in public administration, kept glancing occasionally at the woman at the bar, though without her appearing to notice. He was not averse to a bit of adventure, it seemed, whereas she, who looked to be completely on her own in the world, clearly had no time for anyone just now but herself.

A car swung slowly, hesitantly almost, into the car park. The rain was made visible by the beam of its headlights, and the asphalt glistened. Above the fells the light of the comet shone dully through the blanket of cloud. The trees at the riverside stood like stooping giants in the dimness, the river itself discernible here and there between their trunks. I knew it was flowing there, but the movement of its waters was hidden to me; it was as if the darkness absorbed it.

The car stopped, the front doors opened and a young couple, teenagers, or perhaps in their early twenties, got out. She was stringy-looking and dressed all in black, in a short skirt and top; he was wearing jeans and a white T-shirt. The contrast in dress made me think they didn't know each other that well. They came through the entrance into the hotel together, though without holding hands as they perhaps would have done if they were going out with each other.

I sipped my wine, noting that it was just as disappointing as before, took my phone out of my pocket and saw that both Henriksen and Roman had texted me.

Jarle, Henriksen wrote, *thanks for this evening. Afraid I can't make it tomorrow. Get in touch with the head nurse, Solveig Kvamme, she knows you're coming. (Lovely woman, single, but not your type.)*

He must have been even drunker when he'd written that than when he'd left the hotel. Where was his judgement? As if I'd make a play for anyone in a professional situation. It was counterproductive too – he'd obviously got his eye on her himself, in which case he was hardly doing himself a favour drawing my attention to her.

Hi Jarle, Roman wrote. *Landing at 8, driving straight to the hospital. Meet you there, OK?*

OK, I wrote back, and without thinking took another sip of my wine before shoving the glass away across the table and going up for another, this time an Amarone.

The young couple had sat down a few tables away. Their conversation looked to be sporadic. He would say something, perhaps ask a question, and she would reply in one or two words. After that there'd be a silence, before he asked her something else. They clearly didn't know each other beforehand and were obviously out on a first date.

What did Henriksen know about my type, anyway?

All he had to go on basically was Inger. And she was as far from my type as could be. Bubbly, outgoing, inviting, a person you couldn't help but notice. I thought of her freckles, her cute little upturned nose, small mouth, sparkling green eyes. She was doing media studies at the uni and we'd met in the film club, all three of us – Henriksen, Inger and myself. I didn't care for her much until Henriksen started going on about her and I began to look at her the way he did. Why she went with me I never knew, not even when we got married, I just supposed it was a case of opposites attract and that we complemented each other in bringing different things to the table. She was easy to get on with most of the time, but when she did get angry she invariably reached the heights, even if it was all over and done with very quickly. I, on the other hand, had never had much of a temper and rather enjoyed the energy of her force field, while being content to remain the person I was. After three years I eventually realised what a lot of other people had known and probably talked about for quite some time, that she was sleeping with others besides me. I was appalled more than I was angry, but the bombshell was so great that I could hardly do anything else but confront her with what I'd found out. She denied nothing, and showed no remorse. The only thing she was sorry about was that I had to know. I was far too good for her, she said, and she didn't deserve me – and then she was gone.

I had no contact with Henriksen during that period. When we did meet again, it wasn't a topic. He had got married himself by then – and would soon be divorced, though he didn't know at the time. I never talked to anyone or even thought much about Inger and me. It was an episode, nothing more, and it was over. It hurt, of course, when she married again and then had a child – she'd always been very clear when we were together that she didn't want children – but it was never something I was going to have a breakdown about.

I must have bored her out of her skull, I thought to myself as I gazed through the pane and a shimmer of light moved on the peaks. It was the cloud dispersing, allowing the light from the comet to filter through.

In order for it to have come as a surprise in our day, the path it followed had to extend over centuries. No observations of it since the Middle Ages, and the celestial phenomena they observed and described in words and pictures in those days were so numerous and often so unbelievable that this one had passed under the radar. It was as simple as that. But people wanted excitement, they wanted mysteries, they wanted the unknown.

The young couple got up and went over to the reception desk. Apparently, they were familiar enough now to go to bed with each other. But there was still a metre's distance between them, and as far as I'd been able to see no physical contact had yet taken place.

Over by the bar, the man from main office was now standing next to the woman who had run away. He was in the process of ordering another beer, but it was a long counter and the woman was seated at one extreme, making his intentions rather plain.

Indeed, he smiled at her now and said something. She shook her head, leaned forward and scratched her unstockinged calf, her hair falling curtain-like in front of her eyes.

The solicitors had gone, so the man and the woman were the only ones left.

Besides me.

I drained my glass and stood up. I didn't really feel like going back to the room. It was only just midnight and I wouldn't get any sleep for at least a couple of hours, but there was nowhere else to go and so I took the lift up, walked down the carpeted corridor and let myself in. I took my shoes off while sitting on the edge of the bed, then washed my face and hands in the bathroom and brushed my teeth.

At night was the best time to work. All I had to do was sit down, open the laptop, read through the last couple of pages I'd written, and then carry on where I left off. Work was a den into which I could relax and retreat from the world. When I was there I saw nothing else, wanted nothing else.

Only it was different now. It was as if a big, empty space had opened up inside me. There was nowhere to go, I knew it. Work wouldn't do, music wouldn't do, the books I'd bought wouldn't do. Everything felt so inconceivably trivial all of a sudden.

At the same time, a thought had latched onto me. It was like a fever now. One of those thoughts that made your throat feel swollen, your palms sweaty, your face warm. A thought that was as tempting as it was terrible. The riches it promised would be brief and tainted by the wildest, most painful regret, but that didn't matter: it grew in me as I stood gazing out through the window at the lights of the town.

It was the thought of room 324.

Downstairs in the bar it had kept itself to the perimeters of my mind, had lain motionless there, as an adder in spring sun, but now it had slithered to the fore and I could think of nothing else.

No one knew me here.

On the other hand, if it got out, it would damage my reputation enormously. Irreparably even.

I put my shoes on.

I could barely believe what I was doing when the next moment I found myself on my way towards the lift. Was it really happening?

The bald man with the thin-framed spectacles looked back at me from the mirror.

I ought to be sensible, turn back, find another way altogether of melting the ice in my chest. Or perhaps it didn't need to melt. Why should it?

I could go back to my room at any moment, I told myself as I went through the lobby to the cashpoint. I withdrew an amount and tucked the notes into my wallet. All I had to do to save myself was press the button for the sixth floor instead of the third.

But I pressed for the third. Followed the corridor in the direction of room 324. Nothing would get out, my secret would be safe with me. If I met anyone now, I would simply carry on walking past the room. But I met no one, the corridor was empty.

With my heart pounding, I clenched my hand and knocked.

No answer. I waited a moment, then turned to go back to the lift.

But behind me the door of the room opened. The woman from the poster appeared. Pale, dark-haired, dark-eyed. In a black dress, with a plunging neckline. Young, but not that young. Thirty, perhaps.

'Did you just knock?'

I nodded, my head felt heavy and warm.

'I . . . saw your ad,' I said softly.

'Sorry?'

I stepped closer.

'I saw your ad,' I said again, and directed a nod along the corridor. 'On the wall by the lift.'

'It's gone midnight,' she said. 'I've packed everything away.'

Packed away? What did escort girls use that would have to be packed away?

My cheeks burned.

'I'm sorry to have disturbed you,' I said.

'No, no,' she said. 'Come in, if you like. I can unpack them, it's no bother.'

'As you said, it's late.'

'You're the one who knocked!' she said with a laugh.

'Yes,' I said, and forced a smile. 'Yes, I suppose I did.'

She stepped back into the room and held the door open for me. I ought to have just walked away, but somehow it felt like I'd committed myself. And if I did walk away, there was a fair chance I would run into her again at breakfast the next morning, she might make a scene.

I glanced up and down the corridor before going inside.

She drew the curtains. The room was considerably smaller than mine, the air inside dense and sweet-smelling. Joss sticks, perhaps, or scented candles. The bed was unmade. Some black items of clothing and a black bra were draped over the back of a chair.

'You don't look like the sort who'd be interested in crystals, if you don't mind me saying,' she said, smiling fleetingly before bending over a suitcase that lay on the floor beside the bed.

'I suppose not.'

She produced a black cloth from the case and spread it out on the floor as if it were a picnic blanket. Then a small rectangular box she put down on the cloth and opened. Inside was a red stone with a label carefully placed beside it.

'What line of work are you in?' she said, taking from the suitcase another small box.

'I'm a neurologist.'

'Oh!' she said. 'Brains and stuff?'

'That's right.'

'I'm very interested in all that, as it happens,' she said, beaming at me now. 'Do you believe in telepathy?'

'Not really, no.'

'The night my grandmother died – we were very close, I should add – she came to me in my sleep. "I'm going now, Evelyn," she said. "But don't be afraid. I'm fine. And I'm so glad to have known you." '

'Really?' I said, unable to look at her.

'My brother fell off his bike once too. It was all very serious, he cracked his skull open and broke a load of ribs and was in hospital for weeks, and do you know what happened?'

As she spoke she continued to put out her little boxes, occasionally looking up at me while smiling. The impression it gave was unnerving.

'I heard him say my name. "Evelyn," he said inside my head. I was in my best friend's bedroom and he was still in hospital. I was only about ten. What do you make of that? As an expert, I mean. Weird, don't you think?'

'Weird indeed, yes.'

I hadn't the heart to tell her that the brain could sometimes produce a realistic auditive experience without any physical sound waves being involved.

'There's such a lot we know nothing about. We're surrounded by so many forces. It's quite possible to connect with them, as long as you're open to the idea and know what you're doing.'

She got to her feet, flicked her hair back over her shoulder with a practised movement and planted her hands on her hips.

'Ready now,' she said. 'How much do you know about crystals?'

'Not much, I'm afraid.'

'Is it for yourself or someone you know? There's a big difference, you know!'

'It's for myself.'

'OK,' she said. 'Let me think.'

She put her forefinger to her mouth as her gaze passed over the boxes and their contents.

Her nose was rather broad for someone with her narrow face and high cheekbones. Her brown eyes were warm and lively. Her lips were in constant motion, interrupting nascent little smiles, and when she spoke they seemed somehow to be moving even before a sound came out. She wasn't beautiful, but she wasn't unattractive either. Not by any stretch. Her bosom was ample, her hips curvy and inviting.

'Do you know anything at all about crystals?'

'I can't say I do,' I said. A growing erection prompted me to step away from her as I studied the stones in front of us, trying hard to focus. 'I'd like you to tell me about them, if you would.'

'Well, crystals have been used for healing purposes through many thousands of years. The Druids used crystals, that's a fact. They're used for two reasons, you could say. The first is for *seeing*. If you stare long enough into a crystal, you can see things. Things in the future or the past, whatever. The second is because crystals can trap and enhance energy forces, meaning that whoever owns the crystal can embark on a process of development they wouldn't otherwise have been able to. Do you understand?'

I nodded.

'Some of them can have very strong effects on the human body and mind. But not all of them work on everyone. You have to find your *own*, you see.'

Her fingers drew quotes in the air.

'What you need to do when choosing your stone is to be aware of its signals. Your body will tell you. The stones you're attracted to are going to be the ones with the properties you need. But you mustn't think about what they look like! Appearance has got nothing to do with it.'

She crouched down in front of them. I thanked my lucky stars there were no witnesses and crouched beside her.

'So, this is a mountain crystal,' she said, picking out a specimen and holding it up. 'Also known as clear quartz. It's good for both mind and body, but you must carry it around on your person the whole time. It'll protect you from negative energies and unblock your energy flows when they get clogged up. It's known to enhance personal development too. But the neat thing about mountain crystal is that it also works on people who don't believe in the powers of crystals. It works on the unconscious. Something tells me that's you. Am I right? You're a doubter, aren't you?'

'I don't know, really,' I said. 'You're very persuasive, though.'

She bubbled with laughter.

'Do you think so? Well, there you are, then. Maybe it's started working already!'

She picked up another.

'This one's called smoky quartz. It's good for stomach problems, digestion and the like. Would that be you?'

'No.'

'It's very effective in the case of depression and thoughts of suicide. Are you gay?'

'Gay?'

What kind of a question was that? Had she been expecting me to come on to her? And was now disappointed?

'Why do you ask?'

'Because this stone is the business for young girls, artists, gay people. It makes you more open towards colours and art, music and all that.'

'I see.'

'This one's a green garnet. What's called a universal stone. It works for pretty much everything. In particular it helps you let go of the past and find your true self.'

'What about that one?' I said, indicating a red stone next to the green one. 'That looks rather nice. What's it good for?'

'That's a red garnet. A very exciting stone. It's interesting you're attracted to it. It represents death and rebirth, boundaries and mysticism. It's good for strength and pride and success. It's also a great help when it comes to sexuality. But the most awesome thing about red garnet is that if you place it against the third eye it facilitates contact with your previous incarnations. Do you believe in that sort of thing? Reincarnation, I mean.'

'There are more things in heaven and earth, I suppose,' I said. 'But what's this third eye?'

She put the tips of two fingers between her eyebrows.

'The third eye is here. And here too,' she said, moving her fingers to a point at the nape of her neck. 'At the top of the spine, right where the brain begins. But you must open it first.'

'Have you done that?'

'Yes, I have. I took a drum journey with a shaman at an alternative fair I visited, and took part in a ritual to open the third eye.'

'What does it do, this third eye? Do you see with it?'

She laughed.

'That's what a lot of people think. But no. It's all about opening oneself to the other worlds. Taking them in. This world is so forceful and demanding it can drown out all other signals. The only thing we've got that can allow us to transcend that is intuition. When you open the third eye, what you're doing is strengthening your intuition. You become more clear-sighted.'

'Is that what happened in your case?'

She nodded.

'What do you see now, then?'

'I see my guides. Now and then I see the dead, too.'

'The dead?'

'Mm.'

'Sounds a bit dramatic. Are they here now?'

She nodded again.

'Where? In this room?'

'No, silly! You're quite safe! What I meant is they remain in the place they died for some time. In this world, that is.'

'In that case,' I said, getting to my feet again, 'the hospitals must be overflowing!'

'It sounds to me like you need a mountain crystal.'

'The one that works on doubters?'

'Mm.'

'I think I'd rather have the red one. Is that OK?'

'Of course!' she said, and stood up too. 'Another thing about that one is that it can help you discover hidden things.'

'You've convinced me. How much does it cost?'

'Two hundred. Or two for three hundred. How about a mountain crystal and a red garnet?'

I was filled with a vague sense of disappointment. Not because the spiritual side was now suddenly displaced by business, I wasn't bothered about that.

'Why not?' I said, dipping into my pocket to get my wallet out.

The transaction concluded our encounter and I didn't want it to conclude. It was that. I wanted to stay.

I handed her the three notes.

'Thank you,' she said. 'Long may you benefit!'

I slipped my wallet back into my pocket.

'So you travel around selling crystals? Is that what you do for a living?'

She shook her head.

'Not only. I give courses mainly, and sell the stones on the side.'

'Have you been giving a course here?'

'Yes.'

'On what?'

'Crystals.'

'Oh, so your courses are about crystals too?'

'Yes.'

'What do you talk about on these courses?'

'Oh, it varies,' she said, sitting down now on the edge of the bed. 'Anyway, thanks for stopping by. It was nice meeting you.'

'Same here,' I said. 'You'll be moving on tomorrow, then?'

She nodded.

'Where to?'

'Off home.'

'Where's that?'

She looked at me, wearily now, without answering.

I smiled.

'Well,' I said. 'It's getting late. Thanks for the crash course in crystallography!'

Back in my room I placed the two stones on the bedside table, undressed, put the light out and got into bed, still rather bewildered at what had happened. She wasn't stupid, but then not exactly intelligent either. A naive, confused soul. So why on earth had I wanted to stay? It certainly hadn't been in the hope of erotic adventure – getting into bed with a stranger, a small bald man in his sixties at that, had felt like the last thing on her mind. The thought probably hadn't even occurred to her.

She wasn't beautiful, no, wasn't smart, and she was thirty years younger than me.

Perhaps I'd just got myself worked up earlier in the belief that she was on the game, perhaps the excitement of the fantasy had simply carried over, detaching itself from its original motivation in the process. Or perhaps it was the feeling that at any time life could open out into something new entirely. If room 324 was full of dead souls, guides and three-eyed soothsayers, what might there be in room 323 or 325?

Waking the next morning with a thumping head, my mouth parched, I realised I must have been a bit drunk the night before. That explained all, the inappropriate desires and the sentimentality. I downed a glass of water, then another, showered, dressed, then made myself a coffee, reasoning that I could avoid meeting her in the breakfast room if I skipped breakfast altogether, and by the time I went out to the car I was feeling fresh and ready for the day to begin.

I sat down on a sofa in the hospital reception area to wait for Roman. The sun had returned, the sky was clear and blue, and the thin veil of mist that had covered the fells when I got up had evaporated. The beating noise of a helicopter taking off intruded for a moment from outside. A steady flow of people passed through the doors, most with a confident stride, others more hesitant, pausing a moment to get their bearings and find out where they were meant to go. The mood was rather buoyant, as is often the way on sun-drenched days of summer, contrasting with the dark, wind-battered, rain-drenched days of autumn and winter when so many withdrew from the outside world in favour of the inside one. The intrinsic connections between emotional states and meteorological conditions were seldom talked about. But sun and rain were fundamental to our existence, and so ancient was our dependence upon them – not just millions, but billions of years – that we were utterly blind to it. This was related to the fact that we were always in a certain frame of mind, a certain mood, that it connected us with the moment, our only point of contact with existence, while the significance of mood in that respect was something we never thought about or paid any heed. Existence was huge and universal, rain and our annoyance at it small and local. That was probably why I found such pleasure in the thought that humanity had once comprised but a very few individuals, a couple of hundred perhaps, or even fewer.

It spoke volumes!

My mobile chimed in my briefcase and taking it out I saw that it was Roman texting me to say he'd be slightly delayed. I went over to the coffee machine and bought myself a cappuccino, drinking it standing while leaning back against the wall, briefcase at my feet.

The brain then was the same as now. A smooth, dense lump enclosed within the more or less pleasingly formed encasing we referred to as the head. They too must have had a name for it. A word for the brain, the head, the nose, the eyes. *Bool*, *kla*, *moofu*, *olanka*, whatever. Why not? The blood that ran from their bodies now and then – *agoma*? *knittu*? If not something more onomatopoeic. Blood: *tssh-tssh*. Heart: *do-domp*. Then eventually just *tsh* and *domp*.

Roman, easily recognisable through the glass entrance doors, came scurrying across the concourse, his wheelie case trundling in his wake. He hadn't yet reached thirty but looked like he was in his late forties. Corpulent and waddling, thin-haired, cerebral, with kind eyes and a sense of humour that was sufficiently self-deprecating as to have seen him through his more youthful years relatively unscathed.

I went towards him.

'Apologies!' he said breathlessly and came to a halt in front of me. 'Have you been waiting long?'

'No, not long. What happened? Did you get stuck in traffic?'

'What, here? No!' he said, without grasping the joke. 'Hardly a car on the road. No, it was the flight that was delayed.'

'You got here, that's the main thing. Are you prepped?'

He nodded and gave his cabin case an exaggerated shake.

'Are you ready, or do you want a coffee first?'

'Some water, maybe,' he said, and glanced around.

'There's a machine over there,' I said, indicating towards the wall over by the lifts.

He glugged half the bottle in the lift on the way up. Wiped his mouth with the back of his hand and twisted the lid back on.

'We'll be speaking to the head nurse to begin with,' I said.

'OK,' he said. 'Have you seen the patient?'

'Yes. He's completely gone.'

The lift door slid aside and we stepped out onto the ward, where busy activity prevailed. The head nurse's office was tucked off the main corridor. I knocked and a voice inside told us to come in. It belonged to a woman around forty years old, she was seated at a tidy desk and looked up at us from her computer screen. Thick, dark blonde hair, a round face, faint circles under her blue eyes.

'I'm Jarle Skinlo, and this is Roman Johansen. We're here to examine one of your patients, Jan Ramsvik. I believe Henriksen mentioned it to you?'

'He did, yes,' she said. 'Nice to meet you.'

She stood up and shook our hands. There was something dulled about her, as if she were enclosed within a membrane that served to deaden whatever she said or did.

'We're a bit busy today,' she said. 'There was a rather serious road accident yesterday. So I won't have much time for you, I'm afraid.'

'As I understood it, we've been given a room in the basement. Is that right?'

'Yes. I've made sure there's a technician on hand for you.'

'Well, the only thing we need is to have the patient brought down to us. We can manage the rest ourselves.'

'Good,' she said. 'I'll see that it's done. Do you want that right away?'

'We'd like some time to set up first, if that's all right? Half an hour, say?'

She nodded.

'What sort of examination is it, exactly? If you don't mind me asking?'

'We'll be measuring brain activity. Looking for signs of consciousness.'

She looked at me blankly. An open, unconcealing look.

'You know what happened, don't you?' she said.

'In theatre, you mean?'

She nodded.

'I was present as part of the surgical team. He was clinically dead. It was beyond doubt. And then he woke up and was alive. On the operating table. I was there. I saw it.'

'There must have been something wrong with the apparatus. He obviously can't have been clinically dead. He must have been alive all along. You weren't able to detect it, that's all.'

'Yes, that *must* have been it, mustn't it?' she said, looking almost beseechingly at me.

'Unless he's the first person in two thousand years to rise up from the dead,' said Roman, and laughed.

She didn't, but seemingly took no offence either.

'It's a terrible thing,' she said. 'He has two small children. And he survived the first stroke. He was about to be transferred to Sunnaas for rehab when he had the second one and was declared dead. I can't imagine what it must have been like for his wife. Stroke, hope, stroke, dead.'

'Terrible indeed,' I said. 'But perhaps not uncommon?'

She smiled faintly.

'No one's ever come back from the dead on my ward before.'

The fMRI scanner loomed like an altar in the otherwise empty room, gleaming white in the glare of the ceiling lights. The radiographer was seated in a booth, visible through a glass pane, behind a bank of monitors and apparatus. His name was Jarle too, it turned out as we introduced ourselves. I noted with satisfaction that he'd laid his hands on everything I'd asked Henriksen to make available to us. Besides running the patient through the scanner we'd be using some pretty low-tech equipment: a transcranial magnetic stimulation coil that delivered magnetic pulses into the brain to stimulate the nerve cells in the targeted region, as well as a good old-fashioned EEG machine Roman had brought with him – because we travelled about a bit, occasionally even visiting patients at home, we'd put together a veritable little mobile lab, inconceivable in my early days, but functional and practical in an age in which software had been developed to handle just about any task. The EEG machine, basically an antique from a modern medical perspective, with more than a hundred years to its name, was still one of the best pieces of equipment we had once it was hooked up to a laptop. For although the brain was almost infinitely complex, the way it worked was surprisingly simple and mechanical. The scanner could provide us with a more precise visual representation of the brain's activity, but the EEG delivered in superior time resolution. They complemented each other well.

I opened the laptop and ran through the images of Ramsvik's brain for Roman's benefit. He was one of the brightest postdocs I'd worked with and I was excited to know if he was going to see anything I hadn't.

'It all looks pretty hopeless,' he said, studying the first of the images. 'And that's putting it mildly.'

'He was declared brain-dead. Then when they took him off the life support, his heart stopped beating after only a few seconds, so there would seem to be no error of judgement there. But now look at this!'

I moved on to the next image.

'It can't be the same person,' was Roman's immediate reaction. 'It's not possible. The damage we've seen is irreversible.'

'But here it's been reversed!'

He looked at me.

'So what happened?'

I shook my head.

'I've never, and I mean never, seen anything like it. The same sort of damage, yes, many times. But never repaired like this.'

'So there must be an error somewhere.'

'Yes, there must. Unless we're to start believing in miracles.'

I put the laptop back in my briefcase.

'I heard about something else that was strange yesterday,' said Roman. 'Not this strange, obviously. But strange, nevertheless. A young man, comatose after attempting suicide. A few hours later, his father lapses into a coma too, and is admitted to the same ward.'

'Oh?'

'That's strange enough as it is. But the really weird thing is that the father has no signs at all of any physical injury. His heart's pumping fine, brain function normal. Have you ever heard of anything like that before? Comatose with no physical cause? I mean, he's not responding to anything. The blood tests come up with nothing unusual.'

'Where on the scale is he?'

'Three, they said.'

'Yes, it does sound strange. But it's got to have something to do with his son's suicide attempt, surely? Some kind of shock or trauma?'

'You don't want to have a look at him, then?' he said with a smile on his face.

'I wouldn't say that. Only I thought you wanted to get back to your Parkinson's patients as soon as possible?'

Just then, the door of the room opened and the porters wheeled Ramsvik in on a hospital bed. His eyes and mouth were open. I stepped towards him. Saliva had dribbled from the corner of his mouth. A faint guttural sound escaped him, a groan almost. It was unnerving, unwilled as it was.

'Do you need any more help?' a porter said.

'No, we're fine,' I said. 'Thanks a lot!'

As they closed the door behind them, I bent forward and peered into Ramsvik's vacant eyes.

'Hello again, Jan,' I said. 'Good to see you. We met briefly yesterday. I've brought a colleague of mine with me today. His name is Roman.'

'Hello, Jan,' Roman said.

It was impossible to imagine that he was there, behind those vacant eyes, looking out. But that didn't mean he wasn't.

'What we're going to do now, Jan, is we're going to run some tests on your brain. You've had a couple of strokes and we're going to have a closer look now at what sort of damage you've suffered. But we're more interested in what you *can* do rather than what you can't. For that reason we'll be asking you to think of something specific once you're inside the scanner, so we can ascertain if you're able to hear us. It's very important you give it all you've got.'

His head moved slightly. I grabbed his hand.

'Squeeze if you can hear me, Jan.'

Of course, there was nothing.

'Worth a try,' I said quietly to Roman.

'Sure,' he said. 'Shall we get started?'

Together we transferred Ramsvik to the scanner's patient table.

'We're going to put a pair of headphones on you now, Jan, so that you can hear us in there. The scanner makes a terrible racket, but there's nothing to be afraid of, and we're right here. But it's important you do everything you can to follow the instructions we're going to give you. OK?'

I joined Jarle in the booth while Roman remained standing beside Ramsvik. Through the pane I watched as Ramsvik's body slid into the body of the white machine. A moment later an image of his brain appeared on the screen in front of us.

I never got used to it. We could actually watch the brain working in real time. The scanner measured the amount of blood that was transported to the various neural regions, allowing us to see where in the brain activity increased in response to our instructions. In healthy individuals that meant that in principle we could *see* their thoughts, the ones they were aware of and the ones they weren't – the problem of course was that we couldn't distinguish conscious thoughts from all the other activity and were unable to gain any sort of reliable picture of what was going on until all the data had been processed at a later stage.

Still, the thought that those tiny impulses in there represented entire worlds was magical. How could such an abrupt and microscopic electrical impulse occurring in such total darkness represent a face? A voice? A landscape of fells and fjords?

It was like looking into the unknown. It was a language, but one so foreign and incomprehensible it might just as well have been delivered to us from outer space. The truly unfathomable thing was that it was ourselves we were looking at. That what was made manifest to us was our very coding of the world around us and all that we were. The mystery was that from the inside it didn't feel like code at all, but the world itself.

I leaned towards the microphone.

'Hi, Jan. Jarle here. I hope you're not too uncomfortable in there. I'm going to ask you now to think about something very specific. Can you imagine for me that you're at home in your house and that you're walking from room to room? Start in the kitchen, then go into the living room, then into the bedroom.'

The screen showed no sign of activity. There was nothing happening.

'You sure he can hear me?'

'Quite sure. I tested the connection before we got started.'

'OK,' I said, pressing the microphone button again. 'Hi, Jan. If you can hear me, would you think of strawberries, please? Delicious, fresh, juicy strawberries.'

Nothing.

'Can you think about the birth of your first child for me, Jan?'

Nothing.

'Looks like there's no one home,' said Jarle.

'Looks like it, yes. But then it's possible he just popped out for a minute. Jan, can you think about playing tennis? Think about standing on a tennis court with a racquet in your hands, playing a game of tennis with someone.'

Completely dead.

The door opened. It was Henriksen. His hair was untidy, his doctor's coat worn nonchalantly on top of the same shirt and trousers he'd had on the day before.

'How's it going here?' he said. 'Any sign of life?'

'None so far,' I said.

'There's no one home,' Jarle said again.

'Of course there isn't!' said Henriksen. 'We knew that already.'

He slapped my shoulder a couple of times condescendingly.

'I admire your optimism! But if by any slim chance his brain does produce a thought, it'll no doubt be something to do with food by now.'

I gave him a despairing look. He held his hands up defensively, palms towards me.

'Easy now. I actually came down to ask if you could have a look at something for me.'

'What would that be?'

'Some images I can't quite figure out.'

'We're a bit busy just at the moment.'

'No rush. But come up when you're finished. See you later!' he said, and breezed back out again.

Annoyed, I tried to refocus and gave Ramsvik some more instructions, but when the results came up as before, no reaction, I called a halt to the proceedings and with Roman's help returned Ramsvik to the hospital bed on which he'd arrived. As I wheeled away the TMS equipment, Roman moistened in a bowl of water the EEG sensors that dangled from their wires. The apparatus, which looked rather like a handful of seaweed, was more sensitive when the sensors were moist, and we'd found out that water conducted electricity a lot better than the gel the hospitals used. Jarle watched with an expression of mild perplexity, but said nothing. His reaction seemed to underline the primitive nature of the method. Directing electric current into the brain was something the medical community had been doing for more than a hundred years, for various reasons. Measuring the brain's electrical discharges had been going on for almost as long. The point of this procedure was to ascertain whether the increased activity caused by the TMS remained local or spread to other areas, and if so whether this occurred in an integrated manner or was simply haphazard. Unlike the fMRI scan, the EEG would give us no real-time indications, so any conclusions could only be drawn later on.

But when I saw him lying there as Roman fastened the electrodes to his skull, there was nothing to indicate anything other than that Jan Ramsvik had departed his body, and done so for good.

Once Roman was ready, I connected the EEG to the laptop.

'OK?' I said.

'Mm,' said Roman.

Having no pain receptors itself, the brain could not feel pain, so the electricity that streamed into the smooth, compact lump, did so without being perceived, though efficiently – the neurons responding by transmitting their signals much as they would during an epileptic seizure.

If you looked at an exposed living brain, as during surgery, such activity was undetectable, which was at least as strange as watching the patterns emerge on the computer screen, the brain was quite silent and, apart from its faintly pulsating blood vessels, motionless too. Moreover, if you looked at the brain through an electron microscope, during surgery to remove a cancerous tumour, for example, this mystery was enhanced, because in such instances one would observe something else entirely. Not the neurotransmitters flourishing now here, now there on a screen, nor the bare, fatty lump itself inside its skull, but a kind of landscape: the blood would resemble rivers running through strange, oddly coloured terrains, through deep gorges and caves, out onto great valley plains, where suddenly a glacier, gleaming white against the river's red, could rise up like a wall from the floor of the valley, and this would be the tumour. Only a few centimetres away, quite different landscapes, quite as strange, would manifest themselves. And how impossible to grasp that this was where our human thoughts and emotions came into being. In these other-worldly landscapes that seemed to belong to other planets entirely, at the very edges of the universe.

'Aaahhhhh,' said Ramsvik.

I jumped and glanced towards him. He was lying as before, his head slightly to one side, mouth open.

'Just a reflex,' I said as my gaze met Roman's.

'I know.'

'I had one that started talking once. *Did you lock the door?* he said. Frightened the life out of me. But that was a reflex too. He didn't know what he'd said or what it meant. He wasn't even aware he'd said anything. That part of him was destroyed. But parts of the motor centre for language were still intact. So there was still the occasional sentence coming out, a bit like a tape loop.'

Roman shook his head.

'Whenever I'm with you, I have to remind myself to start wearing a bike helmet. All the time. Even when I'm asleep.'

'Sounds like a good idea to me.'

After a short while, Roman removed the TMS equipment while I accessed the sound file on my laptop. I placed a wireless earbud in each of Ramsvik's ears and then played the sound file while monitoring him as he lay there motionless on the bed. The file was steady noise, as if from a radio tuned between two stations, and then pairs of words coming out of the hiss at various intervals. I'd selected the words myself and had a female doctoral student speak them as I recorded.

Cycle – Car
Tree – Flower
Coffee – Tea
Monkey – Submarine
Day – Night
Cat – Skyscraper
Clouds – Sky
Food – Drink
Mushroom – Corridor
Woman – Man
River – Pistol

And so on. The point was to establish expectations as to the nature of the word that followed, and then foil them at intervals. If there was a conscious mind present, the brain would create waves of activity the computer would be able to pick up and register. Strictly speaking, what would be measured in such cases was memory, and although I'd been working a while on the notion that memory could exist without consciousness, it was hard to imagine it could happen in practice.

After the word pairs came a few sentences telling little stories.

He was out cycling when the sky clouded over and small sofas began to fall through the air.
In July the lilacs in the garden began to vomit.
The dog miaowed, the cat barked.
Ole looks at the sun at night.

The file was half an hour in length, with prolonged periods of white noise in between the words and sentences. Roman called it torture and when I told him it was poetry he said it was the same thing.

Torture or poetry: Ramsvik didn't care. He lay without moving, his mouth gaping open, his eyes empty, through half an hour of noise and words. Although I knew that in theory there was a tiny possibility some part of him would hear and react, I didn't believe it would happen, and when the porters returned to collect him and we packed our things together, I apologised to Roman for having dragged him all the way there in vain.

'The break will have done me good,' he said. 'And besides, what you're doing *is* actually exciting.'

'What *we're* doing.'

'All right, *we*, then.'

I went upstairs to the ward to thank Solveig Kvamme for her help and give her a rundown, mainly because I assumed Ramsvik's wife would be there and would want to know how things had gone.

But the head nurse wasn't in her office or in the duty room. I looked into the staff kitchen area and a nurse who was sitting there immersed in her phone, presumably on a break, directed me to one of the rooms where I found her in conversation with a patient, seated at his bedside. She stood up when she saw it was me, and we went out into the corridor.

'We were in the same class at primary school,' she said.

'Who? You and Ramsvik?'

She smiled, and looked away bashfully.

'No, the patient I was talking to just then.'

'Ah,' I said.

'You're finished now, I take it?'

'Yes. I just wanted to thank you for your help.'

'Did you find anything out?'

'Too early to say for sure. But everything would seem to indicate a complete vegetative state, I'm afraid.'

'What about what happened? He was declared brain-dead.'

'I don't know. It's a mystery. Which means either that there was an error somewhere along the line or that something else occurred and we don't know what.'

I met her gaze and was again struck by how open it was. It wasn't hard to see why Henriksen might be interested. She was his complete opposite: well rounded, mild and hesitant, where he was lean, temperamental, over the top. Pleasant, where he was a pain.

'I'll never forget it,' she said. 'It was like a horror movie.'

'It must have been very disconcerting, yes,' I said. 'But he can't have been dead. It's the very definition of dead, isn't it? That it's irreversible.'

'Henriksen said exactly the same thing.'

'We were students together,' I said. 'That's probably why! Do you know where he is, by the way? He wanted a word before I left.'

'Try his office. If he's not there, he's most likely in theatre.'

I discovered him sitting behind his Mac in his office. I'd never visited him there before and found myself glancing around the room somewhat in surprise. I couldn't quite grasp that the place was so tidy. The desk was as good as bare, in fact there was hardly anything at all in the room besides the few items of furniture.

His car had been like that too. Clearly, the slob he'd been in his student days was no more.

'Ah, there you are,' he said, glancing up at me without lifting his head. 'Just let me get this done first.'

I sat down on his sofa to wait. My fingers found the red crystal in my pocket. It felt good to hold it in my hand, so the money hadn't been entirely wasted.

It represented death and rebirth, boundaries and mysticism, was what she'd said. And it gave a person strength and success. But if that was true, why wasn't everyone walking around with a red garnet in their pocket? I should have asked her.

'Have you ever heard of the third eye?'

Henriksen shook his head, his attention still directed at the screen in front of him.

'It's situated in the forehead, between the other two. It has to do with with intuition, so I'm told. Allows you to look inwards as it were. Makes you more clear-sighted.'

'Clairvoyant, you mean.'

'Yes.'

'Grab that chair over there and come and sit here, would you?'

I did as he said, sat down next to him as he went back to the first of the images he wanted to show me.

'Tell me, what do you see?'

'Is it a trick question?'

'No. What do you see?'

'Death.'

'A bit more precise, if you don't mind.'

'The brain stem is completely dead. A full-scale epidural bleed. Massive injuries to the cerebral cortex.'

'Would you be surprised if I told you the patient is alive?'

'I would say that was impossible.'

'How about this?' he said, a new MR image now appearing on his screen.

'The same. Almost identical.'

He leaned back in his chair, legs apart, and threw his hands in the air.

'Those two patients are here now in intensive care. Both with extensive chest injuries to boot. From that road accident yesterday.'

'The images must be misleading in some way.'

'I'm afraid not. And I think the same is true of Ramsvik. He was brain-dead. His heart had stopped. And there was nothing wrong with the balloon we used. I'm certain of it. All of which means he was dead. Only now he's alive. These two *ought* to be dead. But they're alive too.'

'What does it all mean?'

'I was hoping you'd tell me. After all, you study extreme cases like this. All I do is perform surgery.'

'I can't help you there.'

'Then who can? What am I supposed to do?'

'I don't know. All I can suggest is send the images to the neurological department at the Rikshospitalet and have a word with them down there.'

He snorted.

'They know no more than we do.'

'But they'd be alerted, was more what I meant.'

He stood up and went over to the window, put his nicotine inhaler between his lips and took two rapid puffs.

'Do you mind if I send *you* those images?' he said without turning round. 'There must be someone in your circles who's seen something similar.'

'Living Death syndrome?'

'Ha ha.'

'I'll ask around, if it'll give you peace of mind. But it's only twenty-four hours or so since the accident. The fact that they're still alive is extraordinary, but in all probability it's no more than a freak of fate. An extreme physical reaction that can't be sustained.'

'I almost hope you're right. The last thing I need is a bloody mystery on our hands.'

I stood up.

'Good to see you, anyway,' I said. 'Send me the images, I'll keep in touch.'

The flight home took just forty minutes and the drive back to the apartment around the same, so by seven that evening I was already sitting on the veranda with the door open listening to Gluck's *Orpheus and Eurydice*, which I'd seen performed what seemed like an age ago, though it was no more than three days since. As I listened I gazed out at the fjord and the fells beyond, which were illuminated by the faint red blush of the sun, and sipped a glass of ice-cold Chablis.

I thought about my uncle Harald and his smallholding up in the hills, a place I'd often stayed as a child, my parents being in the habit of dumping me there whenever they needed time on their own or were going somewhere together. Harald was unmarried and had little interest in looking after me, whether it was because he didn't know how or simply didn't care, so most of the time I was left to my own devices and passed the days exploring the farm and its surroundings. He kept hens – not the usual white ones that my grandparents had, but big brown ones – they ran freely around the yard and when I was very small I was rather afraid of them, especially when they flapped their wings, but later they became as natural a part of the world there as the tall tree in front of the house, the old rusty tractor, the shed and the woodpiles – and then one frosty morning, in autumn or winter, I found two dead chicks in the henhouse. I picked them up carefully. They were stiff and cold. The hens didn't seem to mind about me or the chicks, but sat motionless in the cold air, clucking occasionally, now and then giving an ebullient little shake of their feathers. They were as stupid as could be, I knew that, but my uncle would defend them, he said they were as intelligent as they needed to be and that they would have been ill-served by a bigger brain, it would have been counterproductive.

Tears came to my eyes at the fluffy little chicks being dead, and at their parents' indifference. When I went inside to tell my uncle about it, I first wiped my eyes on the sleeve of my sweater, he didn't care for sentimentality, the world had to go on regardless. He sat there in his worn-out armchair, smoking while gazing out of the window. I stood in the doorway.

'Two chicks have died,' I said.

'Well, there's a thing,' he said with a smile. 'Dead, you say? Then we shall have to bury them.'

We went to the henhouse, where he picked up one of the chicks in his big hands and began to rub it gently on the chest with his thumb. After a moment, he picked up the other one too and then took them both inside into the house, put one of them down on a blanket and angled the reading lamp towards it while rubbing the other in the same way with his thumb. Then he swapped them round and after a few minutes first one then the other gave a little shudder and soon they were peeping cheerfully.

'There we are, Jarle!' he said. 'Arisen from the dead!'

He laughed when he saw the look on my face.

'There's nothing mysterious about it. Their bodies were cold, that's all. Like a car engine in winter. It needs a few goes before it'll start. Well, the same applies to chickens!'

No, there was nothing mysterious about it. Some very simple organisms could lie dead for thousands of years and then come to life if conditions around them suddenly changed, and seeds could flower after long periods of passive time. Scientists had frozen bats and seen them wake up again when warmed, and even humans could be revived after significant lengths of time submerged in sufficiently cold water. Cold slowed the body down, and in some instances its functions came almost to a standstill, as if held on standby, ready to be resumed once the temperature again began to rise.

What I'd seen in the cases we'd examined earlier in the day was different. Ramsvik, so it seemed, actually *had* come back from the dead. Whereas the two road-accident victims were still alive – despite everything indicating they *should* have been dead, they were clinging on, against all odds.

In a way, the body *was* like a machine, a biological machine, gurgling and bubbling, its innumerable, infinitesimal parts all running together in sync. A burst artery was essentially no different from a burst fuel pipe, the result was certainly the same, complete breakdown. So when Ramsvik died and then woke up, there must have been some part of him that *hadn't* broken down, some activity in the brain that had remained intact all along, or else some process, unfamiliar to us, had been taking place, a process which then, somehow, had kick-started the heart and got it working again – and with it the brain that had simply been on hold. The brain could be paused, countless cases had shown this to be true, often following an accident. The only problem was that cardiac arrest deprived the organism of oxygen, which in turn triggered massive cell death and increasingly irreparable damage the longer it lasted.

Raised voices came from the veranda below, and I realised now that the music had come to an end.

'It's not you I'm turning down, for God's sake! It's Rome!' the architect shouted. A memorable sentence, for what it was worth, but I felt a strong sense of distaste come over me, this wasn't something I wanted to hear or know about, so when his young wife shouted back, 'You're spurning us, can't you see? All you think about is yourself,' I went back inside and browsed my CDs, eventually putting on Brahms's first symphony, and turned the volume up a notch. I poured myself another glass and by the time I returned to my chair on the veranda, downstairs had all gone quiet again. This time I wanted to actually listen to the music, to immerse myself in it, instead of allowing it to become just a backdrop to my thoughts.

I loved it when the strings took over the theme from the flutes and oboes at the beginning of the allegro, adding fullness and depth as the music descended into wistful calm, as beautiful as it was sad, though not mournful, it was more like when something secret reveals itself to us in a glimpse and is then gone. Yet before it goes, whatever it may be, sighing so softly, so darkly, it returns and rises, ever so briefly, ever so delicately, rising as it also dissolves, as if turning one last time to meet our gaze.

Yes, I loved the strings of Brahms, perhaps more than the strings of any other composer. It was as if somehow they unlatched me, transported me into havens I'd never known to exist, new with every listening. The marvellous thing about music was that it meant nothing, contained no specific meaning to be derived, made no claim upon me in that sense, and the emotions to which it gave rise were not specific either, yet rich and boundless. Music was not integral to us as living organisms, we created it outside of ourselves. Yet the fact that humans had been making music from the very dawn of mankind suggested that music was essential to us. What separated man from the beasts was language and our highly developed awareness of the self, and from there it required little in the way of imagination to make the connection to music, which no animal possessed. Language and self-awareness opened up vast spaces of possibility, but entailed a loss too, of the nearness to the here-and-now that was so distinctive of the animal realm, and it was to compensate for this loss, as a counterweight or counterforce to those human faculties, that music was created and had accompanied human beings from the very beginning. A culture without music was as unthinkable as a culture without language – it simply did not exist, and never had.

In music, thought did not obtain, there was no reason, no rationality, no obligations or expectations, no past or future.

Music was the third eye.

This notion, which came to me abruptly, brought with it a tingle of joy. I took the stone from my pocket and clasped my hand around it. If she sold crystals, and most probably told fortunes too, wouldn't she have her own website? Evelyn was an uncommon name too, I thought, as I picked up my phone and typed *Evelyn crystals fortunes* into the browser's search field.

There she was!

She could tell your fortune over the phone. A woman of many talents, obviously.

With Brahms swirling, I went to the end of the veranda, folded my arms on the rail and stared out across the fjord, deep blue and still now in the dimness of evening. Not a sound came from the neighbours below, I supposed they were sulking in their separate rooms. Loud music thudded from an apartment across the way, mingling into a babble of voices: someone was having a party.

My stomach complained. When had I last eaten? Not since lunch? But I'd given lunch a miss. Not since last night, then.

I went back inside into the kitchen. I hadn't been home much of late, so there was nothing in the fridge from which anything could have been concocted. There were some noodles in the cupboard, though. That would have to do.

As I filled the saucepan from the tap, my phone rang. It was Roman.

'Have you seen the results?' he said.

'No, I've been a bit preoccupied. Why, have you?'

'Yes. And they're positive, too. That's what it looks like to me, anyway.'

'Positive?'

'Yes, there's consciousness. He's conscious. He's thinking and feeling in there.'

'Ramsvik? Are you sure?'

'As sure as I can be.'

'The test's not a hundred per cent reliable, you know that.'

'True. But have a look yourself. I'm certainly in no doubt. He's thinking and feeling.'

'Christ almighty. Is that really possible?'

'Looks like it,' Roman said. 'But we need to run some more tests, don't you think?'

'Yes, I do think. And we need to tell Henriksen to get him back on IV, as quick as he bloody can.'

GEIR

A tooth towards the front of my lower jaw had broken and started to come loose, it rocked when I pushed my tongue against it. Hell. How could that be? I'd only just had root canal surgery on the bloody thing!

Up ahead, at the bottom of the gently sloping hill, the traffic was clogging up. Alexander put the sirens on. It was complete overkill, but I said nothing, just leaned back in my seat with a sigh. I couldn't keep my tongue away from the tooth, it kept sidling up to give it another shove.

'Do you know any of these KRIPOS people?' he said without looking at me. And thank goodness for that, we were on the wrong side of the road.

Alexander was one of those beaming people. Some people, not many, have the brightest faces, they beam. Most are young, a few are able to keep it up into middle or even old age. Alexander was young and his face beamed with a bashful kind of life energy. I liked him, but I wasn't sure if I'd want him with me if the shit really hit the fan.

'I know the guy in charge, Follo his name is. No idea who he'll have brought with him, though.'

'Is he good?'

'Absolutely. You don't get to be chief investigator for the national crime investigation service if you don't know what you're doing.'

We swept through some traffic lights into the narrow streets of the town while I checked the news on my phone. Nothing yet. Maybe it hadn't been such a good idea tipping Jostein Lindland off like that. But he needed a break, anyone could see that. Besides, it would have got out anyway. The story could just as well be his as anyone else's.

The three dead lads flashed into my mind's eye. As the night had gone on I'd almost got used to them lying there, but now, away from the scene, I shuddered. The worst thing wasn't the bodies being skinned. It wasn't even their throats being cut and their scalps removed. That was horrific enough, of course, but a body was a body, no matter how mutilated. No, the worst thing was there was something comical about them. Their faces hadn't been skinned, they were intact, and it made them look like masks. Their mouths hung as if they were smirking. Their heads had been wrenched so far round that their backs were where their chests should have been.

Comical perhaps wasn't the right word. It was humour blacker than night. Past the tipping point where it turns into pure malice.

Grotesque was what it was. So unbelievably grotesque. Nothing else came close, not even in the sickest movies I'd seen.

Who could have done something like that? And how? And *why*, for Christ's sake?

I needed to find out how long it took to skin a human body. What sort of implements were required. Where those lads had been before they ended up there. But first I needed to get hold of Jesper Holm Jensen.

Still no reporters, no TV cameras outside as Alexander swung up in front of the building then swept down the ramp into the basement where he parked as close as he could next to the lifts.

'Is that just to wind me up?' I said.

He gave me a puzzled look as he locked the car with the remote.

'No lifts, no potatoes, no pasta, rice or bread for me the next couple of months. I thought I told you?'

'Oh, that,' he said. 'You did mention it a few times, yes,' he said as he went towards the lift, then punched in his code and grinned all over his face. 'See you upstairs in about half an hour, then!'

There was no coverage in the stairwell, so when I got to the ground floor I went out into reception so I could give Helene a ring.

'Oh, you're *alive*, are you?' she said.

'Yes, sorry. Only we've got a huge case on our hands. I'm afraid it's going to be round the clock for a while yet by the looks of things. Is that OK?'

'Have I got a choice?'

'Not really, no. Sorry.'

'It'll have to be, then, won't it?'

'Are the kids around?'

'Ella's gone. William's sitting here with his breakfast. Do you want a word?'

'Course I do.'

Your dad's on the phone, I heard her say.

'Hello?' said William.

'Hello, son. Listen –'

'You can't come anyway?'

'I'm really sorry, I can't. You see. I'm working on a very serious case. Very serious indeed.'

'That's OK. You can come next time instead.'

'I wanted to be there tonight. Still, all the best, eh? Play a blinder for me.'

'I'll be on the bench. But thanks anyway.'

I hung up and carried on up the stairs. I didn't know how he kept so cheerful. Didn't matter that I couldn't come. Didn't matter if he didn't get a game. I was only glad he had no idea how much it pained me whenever he came on as a sub or more rarely was picked to start. He was so eager, but he couldn't play for toffee. I paid just as much attention to his teammates, the way they reacted to him. Always hoping they weren't going to throw up their arms in despair and roll their eyes, give him a hard time. The important thing, I kept telling myself, was whether he enjoyed himself, that was all that mattered. And he did. I knew that, but my feelings didn't.

A couple of floors up and my heart was thumping hard in my chest. It always got me a bit scared, but I pressed on and didn't stop until I reached the fourth, where I stood for a moment with my hands on my knees to get my breath back. There was no real danger, but after my father died I was always more than a little wary when it came to physical exertion. Hale and hearty one minute, with a snow shovel in his hand, the next minute dead on the ground. Same age as I was now. A bit overweight, but not that much. About the same as me.

At the furthest extremity of every heartbeat was a tiny pain, funnel-shaped it felt like, first dull, then sharp and stabbing. That bloody tooth wasn't making it any better either. It was an old man's thing, your teeth falling out.

I opened my mouth wide and stuck my thumb and forefinger inside, pinched the tooth between them and gave it a wiggle.

The better part of it came away, though I'd barely even touched it. I spat it out into my hand and was staring at it, my tongue investigating straight away the crater it had left, when the door opened. I closed my hand around the tooth and held my phone up in front of me to give me a reason for standing there.

'Oh, hello,' one of the young officers said, stepping past. I couldn't remember her name. 'I think they're waiting for you in the conference room.'

'Thanks,' I said, and smiled at her. 'Thanks, Frida.'

She smiled back dutifully. I slipped the tooth into my pocket and followed her along the corridor. Four people were sat in the conference room, all with laptops in front of them. A young woman, a young man, a middle-aged woman and then Follo, of course, who got to his feet as soon as he saw me through the glass wall and stepped out into the corridor.

'Geir Jacobsen,' he said. 'Good to see you!'

'Likewise,' I said. 'How's things?'

'Oh, not so bad,' he said. 'But listen, there's no time to waste. Come inside, will you?'

'I'll be with you in a sec,' I said, and darted into the office, where I cast a quick glance at my emails and plugged my phone in to charge, before nipping off to the loo. My piss was yellowy brown, which wasn't unusual in this heat. Nothing to worry about there, anyway.

I washed my hands and dried them, smiled into the mirror to see what I looked like with half a tooth missing. Any hope I'd had that it wouldn't be noticeable evaporated immediately. It was the first thing you saw. I looked like a drug addict.

I'd have to start smiling the way my mother had done all those years, with my hand in front of my mouth. Or stop smiling altogether.

In the conference room, Follo was talking into his phone while the other three were bent over their laptops.

I'd always thought there was something rather annoying about Arne

Ivar Follo. It was the way he looked. He had this extremely high forehead that was emphasised by his curly hair being short at the sides and piled up on top, at the same time as his face was oddly squashed together, that too highlighted, by a trimmed beard without a moustache. His eyes were brown and mild, though. It was easy to think he was a harmless sort, perhaps not that bright, but in that case you'd be making a mistake: he was as sharp as a knife.

'Say hello to the team, Geir,' he said, putting his phone down on the table in front of him. 'Aksel Risnæs, Camilla Solberg, Mia Kristoffersen.'

'Nice to meet you all,' I said.

The two younger ones – soft, puppy-like faces both, though in different ways – looked like they'd just got out of university. The older woman had a square, rather flat face with a flat nose, cropped hair, glasses and a steely gaze. If she'd been in my class at school, she'd have been asked what happened – was she dropped on her face while it was still warm?

'Sit down, Geir,' Follo said. 'You're the senior investigating officer on this one, is that right?'

'For the minute, at least.'

'And you've come straight from the crime scene?'

'Yes. Been there all night. Horrific.'

'We know a little, but I don't think we're fully in the picture yet. Perhaps you'd give us the rundown.'

'The short version is that all four members of the black metal band were reported missing five days ago and that last night three of them were found murdered in what looks like a ritual killing. The fourth member, Jesper Holm Jensen, appears to be on the run, last seen at his parents' house just before midnight yesterday. I take it you'll want me to elaborate on that?'

Follo nodded.

'OK. The four missing persons were Mathias Vågsnes, Sander Ellingsen, Jesper Holm Jensen and Johan Larsson. All nineteen to twenty years old. The band they were in was called Kvitekrist. They were known to us, the scene they were involved in, and previous incidents involving individuals linked to that scene meant we kept an eye on them, but none of the four had any kind of criminal record.'

'Who reported them missing?' the young female officer, Mia, said.

'The parents did. But to be quite honest, we didn't take it that seriously. They could have just decided to take off somewhere, couldn't they? Berlin, Warsaw, Gothenburg – the vocalist's from there. They weren't exactly responsible young men. But two of the parents in particular were quite insistent, they were convinced something must have happened to them. So on day three we launched a more systematic search. Culminating so far in three of them being found murdered last night.'

'If I can just stop you there for a second,' said Follo. 'What about their phones?'

'They didn't have any.'

'When you found them?'

'No, I mean none of them owned one. We thought it was a bit unusual too, but there you are.'

'Where does that information come from? It's easy enough to find out if a person owns something, but it's a different matter altogether to ascertain that they don't.'

'The parents told us. And the people we talked to from the black metal scene confirmed it. It may have had something to do with their image. It probably looks a bit daft to be checking your Instagram when you're made up to look like a corpse.'

The one called Mia smiled.

'Still, we'll look for phones,' said Follo. 'OK, so you got a search under way on day three. And they were found on, what, day five?'

I nodded.

'Who found them?'

'Male in his forties. Surname Espeseth. He'd been out hiking on the Ulriken, said he'd got a bit lost in the forest while looking for a shortcut. More likely he was out looking for funny mushrooms, if you ask me. Anyway, the call came in just before eleven last night.'

'What do we know about him?'

'Seems to be clean. Social worker with the local authority, lives on his own, rented flat. We're checking him out. I believe he's in an interview room as we speak. The data we've pulled from his phone confirms his story, so there's nothing yet to suggest he had anything to do with it.'

'OK.'

'The crime scene is up at Svartediket, a small clearing in the trees. We got there half an hour after the call, which is to say about half eleven. Three of the lads had been killed – Sander, Mathias and Johan. They were lying next to each other at the bottom of the clearing. There'd been no attempt to hide them and there was no one else around when we arrived.'

'What about the man who found them? Espeseth?'

'He was waiting for us down by the road. He was too scared to hang around on his own at the scene itself. Can't blame him either. I've never seen anything like it.'

'Had he touched anything? Disturbed anything while he was there?'

'He said he panicked when he found them and just ran away. He phoned us a few minutes later. And he didn't see anyone else, either before or after.'

'You called it a ritual killing. What makes you think that?'

'All three had been killed and mutilated in exactly the same way. They'd been skinned, scalped, their throats were cut and their heads nearly torn off. Like I said, I've never seen anything like it. But if there's such a thing as a ritual killing, I'd say this was it.'

'So the clearing in the woods was deserted, there was no one there but the three bodies?'

'That's right. Though there was a fire. It had gone out, but the embers were still warm. Some stones had been arranged next to it. And two backpacks had been left over by the trees, and two cameras. I'm going to have a look at what's on them as soon as we're finished here.'

'Stones? What kind of stones?'

'Just your normal grey rocks, about so big.'

I held up my hands as if gripping a small melon.

'Were they part of this fire?'

'No, they didn't seem to be. They were spread out. I can show you.'

I took my phone out of my pocket but Follo held up his hand.

'We've got the photos. It's your first impressions we're interested in.'

'Right,' I said, suppressing my irritation at the rebuke. 'They were laid out in a certain pattern. One in the middle, five at different points around it.'

Mia and the flat-faced woman whose name I'd already forgotten exchanged glances.

'What do you think was their purpose?' said Follo.

I shrugged.

'No idea. But given the context I don't think it would be unreasonable to assume they were part of the ritual.'

'What about the backpacks?' said Mia. 'What was in them?'

'Items of clothing and food. But they're not finished analysing them yet.

'You say the fourth member of the band was observed at his parents' house,' the flat-faced woman said. 'When was that exactly, and where would the house be located with respect to the scene?'

'He was seen around about the same time as we received the phone call from Espeseth. The parents' house is just down the hill from the hospital, so it's not far. Twenty minutes' walk, I'd guess. Ten if you run.'

'Can you get someone to check that?' said Follo.

I nodded.

'What took place at the house?'

'The witness is a lodger there. Iselin Rasmussen, twenty years old. Works at the Bunnpris supermarket in the centre of town. Rents a room on the top floor. Besides Iselin, the house is empty – Jesper's parents are living in Africa at the moment. She'd never seen Jesper before. He was yelling and screaming and hammering on the door. She went down and let him in. She raised the alarm, but by the time the patrol car arrived he was nowhere to be seen. Hasn't been seen since. According to the witness, he was highly confused and aggressive, probably psychotic.'

'The crime scene,' said Follo. 'Was the ground particularly trodden, would you say?'

'No.'

'Any signs of a struggle?'

'None. The whole area was as pristine as can be, apart from the fire – oh, and a book that had been burned.'

'A book?'

'Yes, sorry, I forgot to mention that.'

The young male officer opened his mouth for the first time.

'But the fire was still hot?' he said.

I nodded.

'Well, warm.'

'How does that add up?' he said. 'You've got all these signs of activity. A fire not long gone out. Rocks arranged in a pattern. As well as the three mutilated bodies, of course. And yet you say there were no signs of any tramping about, no struggle?'

'That's what I said, yes. I thought it was strange too.'

'Hm,' said Follo, fixing his eyes on me. 'What's your theory, Geir?'

'That it was choreographed.'

'Meaning?'

'Theatre. A performance. Three bodies meticulously presented. Book burning, a pentagram, fire. All stage props.'

No one said anything. Then Follo spoke:

'OK,' he said. 'Let's take this from the beginning. You had to go through the woods to get there, right?'

'Correct.'

'So you've come through the woods and you emerge into this clearing. What do you see? What do you feel? What are your thoughts?'

They were patronising questions, the sort you'd ask a witness who had no idea what might be important. But this was my job, the questions were relevant, and I tried to reset.

'It's almost midnight, so it ought to be quite dark. Only it's not. Light is shining down from that new star or comet, whatever it is. It feels spooky in a way, unnatural. I see the three bodies almost at once, they're lying there at the opposite end from where we come in, close to the trees. And so I go over.'

'You've seen them, so in a way you're prepared for what's to come. But is there anything that surprises you, before you go over?'

'No, nothing. Not until I see the bodies close up. What I see then is definitely something I hadn't been expecting.'

'What about the fire?' said Mia. 'Did you see that? The backpacks?'

'Not at first, no. I was focused on the bodies, naturally. Now you mention it, though, there was a burnt smell in the air. A whiff of sulphur, in fact.'

'Gunpowder?'

'Yes, that's it.'

'But you didn't think that at the time? That the smell was of gunpowder?'

'No, just that it reminded me of something. I couldn't think what it was, and then I forgot all about it.'

'What was the first thing that struck you when you saw the three bodies lying there?'

'It was the horrific nature of it. And as I said, they looked almost like they'd been put on display. There's no doubt in my mind they'd been left there to be seen. It was a statement.'

'About what?'

'I've no idea. You'll have to see for yourselves.'

'Was there anything else that struck you?'

'No, only what was mentioned just before, that the place was so, well, *tidy*. The bodies were laid out so neatly, the rucksacks were packed and closed, like they'd been arranged too. There was no rubbish or debris of any kind, no sign really that anybody had been there at all. Apart from the fire, of course. Nothing besides that, though.'

'You think they were killed somewhere else and then taken there afterwards?'

'It certainly looks that way, yes.'

'I need a list. The facts, times, everything we know. An inventory of what was found at the scene. Names and addresses of the parents and everyone connected with the black metal scene, as well as the two witnesses, of course. And then a list of everyone who's going to be working on this. Tick the ones you can rely on the most, just so we know. Then meet back here in half an hour. OK?'

'Right,' I said.

'And I'll need to see those images as soon as you've got them.'

'The photos of the bodies?'

'I've got them already. No, the video material on the two cameras that were found.'

'Oh, of course.'

I got up and went to my office. The video files hadn't been sent yet and I typed an irritated email to have them get a move on before I called Alexander and asked him to send me the parents' names and addresses, as well as any others he could get his hands on with connections to black metal circles.

As far as I could work out, it looked like my role was going to be a kind of liaison between the KRIPOS lot and the in-house team. Not having the overall responsibility for the tactical and technical sides of things suited me down to the ground, it would give me more time to think. Maybe I'd even make it to William's match later.

I wondered, was my strong desire for him to do well communicated to him even though I tried to hide it as best I could?

They were kids, not flowers. It was their genes that steered them, not Helene and me.

Again, the image of those bodies.

The skin of their hands, like gloves, glistening in that ghostly starlight.

Membranes here and there enclosing the flesh, like slaughtered animals.

The tuft of hair on top of the head.

Those gaping eyes. Joyless, drooping grins. A little incision at each corner of the mouth, I supposed.

Who could have done something like that? They were just kids, for Christ's sake.

I sat down and put my feet up on the desk, tipped my head back and stared up at the ceiling for a moment, then closed my eyes.

What did I actually know about Kvitekrist and the scene they were a part of?

The third wave, they called it. The most important bands were from this town. And they were bigger abroad than at home. That was about it.

Jostein would know more about it than me.

I leaned forward, picked up the phone and called him. No answer. So I googled *Norwegian black metal third wave* and scanned what it came up with, newspaper articles mostly, and then a book about the subject. I must have put it to the back of my mind at some point, because I recognised the title straight away: *Darkness: The Second Coming. Heksa and Norway's Extreme Black Metal*, by Ivar Abelseth.

He'd know more than Jostein.

I looked him up and wrote down his number.

What else had I been thinking about?

The skinning, that was it.

A hunter would know how long it took.

Magnus wasn't in my contacts, so I discovered, but then I remembered I'd bought a new phone. Not having spoken to him for years, I assumed his details somehow hadn't migrated over.

I googled Magnus Aasen, Askvoll. His number came up and I phoned him straight away. He had a smallholding out there, no other work, just a bit of fishing in the winter to make ends meet, it was like he was living in the seventeenth century. He'd be awake, no doubt about that.

'Yes?' he said at the other end.

'Hello, Magnus. It's Geir here. Geir Jacobsen. It's been a while!'

'Geir?' he said. 'Well, I'll be . . . What do you want from me now, then?'

'Who says I want anything?'

'Oh, give over.'

I laughed.

'I'm wondering how long it would take to skin an elk. I don't know anyone else likely to know besides you.'

'Well, that would depend. If you've got a winch, you can pull the skin off like a sock in only a few minutes. With a knife it takes longer. If you're not bothered about the quality, you can do it in half an hour. Maybe less, if you've done it before. As quick as fifteen minutes, I'd say.'

'As quick as that?'

'I take it you're investigating the murder of an elk?'

'Not exactly, no.'

'If we're talking about skinning a man, that would take much longer. An elk's got a lot more membrane, so the hide will just slide off. A man is more like a pig, I imagine. All fat and subcutaneous fibre. It would be a very delicate and complicated task. A winch wouldn't help much either. With a knife it would take you ten times longer than an elk would.'

'So somewhere between two and a half and five hours?'

'Something like that. It's just approximate, mind. Why don't you ask those pathologists of yours? I'm sure they'd be more exact.'

'Good idea. Thanks a lot. How's life out there, anyway?'

'Can't complain.'

'You're managing all right, then?'

'Just about.'

'Well, let me know if you come into town. We'll have a beer together.'

'Why don't you come here instead? I brew my own beer, as you know. And I make a very nice redcurrant liqueur.'

'I'll bear it in mind,' I said. 'Be nice to see you, at any rate. But listen, I must be off. Thanks once again for your help.'

I hung up, woke my computer up, opened a new document and started to type:

What: Murder of three adult males, 19, 20, 20 yrs old. Members of band Kvitekrist.
Why: Not known.
When: Victims discovered around 11 p.m. Monday, presumably killed some time earlier in the day, time unknown.
Where: Victims discovered in forest surrounding Svartediket. Scene of crime possibly elsewhere, though in vicinity.
How: Killed with sharp object (knife), subsequently skinned and scalped. Planned.
Who: Not known (immediate suspect: Jesper Holm Jensen).

Jesper was the key. If he wasn't the perpetrator, he was a witness. And if by some remote chance he hadn't witnessed the actual killings, he was almost bound to know who carried them out and why. Assuming of course they weren't indiscriminate, but for one thing indiscriminate killings were rare, and for another everything we knew so far pointed in the opposite direction. Kvitekrist flirted openly with evil and the forces of darkness, and the way they'd ended up could only be seen in relation to that fact.

Hypothesis 1: Jesper Holm Jensen alone killed the other three band members. In which case he must have cut their throats while they were asleep. What motive could be strong enough? Possibly psychotic (a witness suggests so) or under influence of hallucinogenics. The acts of mutilation possibly explained by psychosis or intoxication. Against this, a great deal of planning must have been involved, implements to skin the bodies, bodies presumably moved, etc.

Hypothesis 2: Killed by a rival band from the same circles. Unlikely, but can't be ruled out. Black metal scene known for transgressive behaviour, including killing. One or three, makes no odds. May have been egged on by previous cases. Drugs possibly involved. Mutilation clearly in keeping with visuals (pigs' heads on stakes, buckets of blood, swastikas, satanic rituals).

Hypothesis 3: Killed because of money. Money owed to criminals, or stolen from same. Mutilation then explained as warning to others. On the other hand, could have made do just cutting their throats and scalping them – why bother skinning them?

I couldn't think of any other scenarios.

I yawned and stretched my muscles, swivelled round on the chair a bit to look out at the jagged ridges and the green fells in the distance. My tooth didn't hurt, which was one good thing. The root canal surgery meant it was dead, as far as I knew.

I sometimes dreamt about losing my teeth.

It meant something specific, only I couldn't remember what, so I googled it.

Fear of ageing, fear of falling short or simply of dental decay. Perhaps you feel in danger of losing face, or have suffered some defeat. Perhaps someone dented your pride.

There was a knock on the open door. I closed the tab and looked up. It was Follo. He was holding his phone up.

'It's out. It's everywhere. How do you explain it?'

'A reporter turned up last night. Jostein Lindland.'

He gave me a puzzled look.

'You allowed a reporter onto the *crime scene*?'

I nodded and gave a faint smile.

'Tell me, Jacobsen. Have you lost your mind?'

I shrugged.

'Who tipped him off?'

'Haven't a clue. Besides, it's not important. It was going to get out anyway. Unless you were thinking of keeping it all a secret?'

'Did you call him?'

'Me? No. No, I didn't.'

'But you do know him?'

'Vaguely, from the old days. We're not friends or anything, but I know who he is.'

'Why didn't you send him away? This is a discplinary matter, you do know that?'

'I thought it would be useful to us for him to know what's what. We're going to be dependent on information from the public, after all.'

I looked out of the window, knowing it was going to annoy him.

'What kind of policeman lets a reporter onto the scene of a triple killing and shows him the victims? And why didn't you mention it in the meeting just now?'

'I forgot,' I said. I was still looking out of the window, but swivelled back now to face him. 'Sorry about that. I should have told you.'

'Allowing a reporter access to the scene of a crime isn't something you just forget.'

'Well, I did,' I said. 'Anyway, it's nothing to get worked up about. The reporter we're talking about, Lindland, was the one who gave us Heksa, in case you remember? He got kicked down the ladder at work because of it. He took a bullet for us.'

'I want him interviewed. I'll do it myself, only it'll have to wait. We're meeting again in three minutes.'

He spun round and walked out. I pulled my phone out of the charger and followed him.

The conference room was packed, people were standing, lining the walls. Alexander got to his feet as soon as he saw me, to give up his chair.

'No need to suck up,' I said. 'Sit down.'

He did as I said, but looked a bit crestfallen.

'Right,' said Follo, facing the horseshoe of investigators. 'Let's get cracking, shall we?'

He gave a quick briefing of what had happened and how much we knew up until that point, before then outlining the two main prongs the investigation would be pursuing in the hours that followed. Finding

Jesper Holm Jensen was priority number one. Number two was pinpointing the location where the killings had taken place. The possibility of the skinning having been carried out somewhere else entirely apparently hadn't occurred to him. No one else brought it up either. Their clothes had to be somewhere too, maybe at the original crime scene, maybe where they'd been skinned, maybe in a different place altogether. No doubt it would occur to them before long. Perhaps it already had and they didn't want to mention it here in front of everyone else.

A swarm of officers was sent out to talk to friends, acquaintances and family. Anyone who lived along the road below the path that led to where the bodies were found would be interviewed. CCTV at the waterworks had to be checked. Flights, trains, buses, car rentals. My thinking was that I'd be working closely with Follo, in the office sifting through and evaluating whatever information that came in, but to my surprise he sent me out into the field as well.

'Jacobsen, you and Sæverøy go and talk to the witness who saw Jesper at his parents' house. As far as I understand, they're on their way home now. If we're in luck, they might already be here. In which case, talk to them too.'

'Right you are,' I said.

It didn't go unnoticed, but I couldn't have cared less. Follo seeing himself as a hard and uncompromising leader of men, while still being unable to grasp the difference between leadership and small-mindedness, wasn't my problem. It wasn't something he'd appreciate being told either. At least not by me.

Lene Sæverøy came over as soon as the meeting was adjourned. She was rather short and compact, some might have called her squat. Her face though verged on the triangular, with high cheekbones and a narrow chin. Her hair was red, and her lips glistened. As a person she was doggedly serious and like so many others on the force she did and said what she thought was expected of her, and nothing else. On a couple of occasions, though, I'd seen another side to her – in the company of colleagues the same age she appeared quite differently inclined to laughter, it didn't take much at all to set her off.

'We'll take my car,' I said.

It would give me a bit of leeway later on in the day. I might even be able to pop round to Elisabeth's before catching William's football match.

'OK,' she said, too careful to protest.

'Impressed?' I said as we got in. It was a white Citroën C3 with a black roof and black airbumps on the sides. I'd bought it second-hand for next to nothing.

'Very,' she said, and smiled politely.

'What do you drive yourself?'

'A Kawasaki.'

'No car?'

'No.'

'What about the winter?'

'Bus or tram.'

I picked my sunglasses from the little shelf under the dashboard and put them on as we emerged into the sunlight. I sensed she wasn't going to do small talk without being prompted. She was too guarded and didn't know me well enough.

'I'd like you to handle the questioning,' I said. 'She'll be more comfortable talking to you than me. Is that OK?'

It was as if she visibly swelled after taking in what I'd said. She looked out of the window, perhaps to find the right facial expression. When a moment later she turned towards me, she signalled composure and professional assurance.

'Is there anything in particular we want to know?'

'No.'

'OK.'

Not a ripple on the water as we crossed the bridge. It looked like the buildings that were scattered up the slope of the fell reached down into the fjord as well. The temperature gauge on the dashboard said 39 degrees. It couldn't be right. It was the sun, surely?

I pulled up at the Danmarksplass junction. It was almost impossible to see what colour the traffic lights were.

My phone rang. It was Follo.

'You're on speakerphone,' I said.

'It seems that reporter friend of yours has had a stroke or something.

Whatever it is, he's in a coma at the hospital. So he's not going to tell us anything now.'

'Bloody hell.'

'Exactly,' he said. 'Catch you later.'

I turned left past the old stadium and on up the hill. The address we were going to was directly below the hospital. Maybe I could look in and get the lowdown on Lindland once we were done?

'This'll be it here,' I said, pulling up opposite a yellow-brick house at the bottom of a cul-de-sac. 'Are you ready?'

'Ready as I'll ever be.'

The heat hit me as I opened the door. Crossing the street, I squinted up at the sun burning in an empty blue sky. Lene rang the bell. At the bottom of the road there was a flight of steps running up the steep bank to the main road above. It must have been the way he'd come. But someone who'd planned and carried out a triple killing would never have panicked and run off home to their mum and dad, would they? Certainly not when they'd taken the time to skin the bodies first.

My shirt was already clinging to me. Sweat trickled from my armpits. I scratched myself, wiped my brow with the back of my hand. Thought about those buildings reaching down into the depths of the fjord. The cool, blue-green waters.

Someone came down the stairs inside. The door opened and a girl about twenty years old put her head round. A rotund, chubby little face with a small mouth and heavily made-up eyes.

'Iselin?' Lene said. 'We're from the police. I was the one you talked to on the phone earlier. Do you mind if we come in?'

She nodded, opened the door wider and stepped aside to let us in.

'I've already told you everything I know.'

'I realise that,' said Lene. 'But quite often people remember things, little details they hadn't thought about before that can turn out to be important. Are you OK?'

'Just a bit shaken up, that's all.'

She stared emptily into space for a moment with cheerless, mournful eyes. Her stomach bulged out between her cropped black T-shirt and tight black skirt.

'I quite understand,' said Lene, and placed a comforting hand on the girl's shoulder. 'It must have been awful for you. If you feel the need to talk to someone about it, someone other than us, I mean, we can arrange that.'

'No, I'll be all right,' she said. 'Nothing happened really, did it?'

'You're a brave girl, I can tell. You live here on the top floor, is that right?'

Iselin nodded.

'Do you mind if we go upstairs and talk there?'

'No, that's fine.'

The room was small and boiling hot. An electric fan whirred on a desk. The bed, which took up half the space, was unmade and strewn with cuddly toys and cushions. On the wall above it, ten or so photos had been pinned, mostly herself as a kid, together with what presumably were her parents and brother: on a beach, in a town in what looked like Southern Europe, skiing in a forest. Similarly, above the desk, some postcards, Monet and Van Gogh as far as I could tell at a glance, and a poster of a teenage singer with elf-like ears. I recognised her from when Ella was younger: Ariana Grande.

Iselin sat down on the bed.

'I've only got the one chair, I'm afraid.'

Sæverøy glanced at me.

'You have it,' I said. 'I don't mind standing.'

She pulled the chair up and sat down.

'We're going to be recording the interview,' she said, producing her phone. 'It's just for internal use, though.'

Iselin nodded. The new crater in my jaw provoked a tingle of horror and fascination as my tongue again investigated.

'Right, Iselin,' Lene began. 'Your surname's Rasmussen, is that right?'

'Yes.'

'And you're, what, twenty years old?'

'Yes.'

'Tell me what happened here last night.'

'Well, I'd been out and after I came home I basically went straight to bed, but then I woke up because someone was banging on the door, shouting and screaming.'

'What did you do then?'

'I got up and went to the window to see who it was.'

'And what did you see?'

'A guy my own age. He was off his head by the looks of it. Shouting and carrying on.'

'Had you ever seen him before?'

She shook her head.

'But I knew who he was. He was the son of the couple who live here.'

'How did you know that?'

'Well, I didn't know as such. But he kept shouting *mother* the whole time. *Mother, let me in*. So I just assumed.'

'What happened then?'

'I went downstairs to let him in, didn't I?'

'You were OK with that?'

'No, I was really scared. But I thought I had no choice. That he had a right to come in, do you know what I mean? And besides, it could have been an emergency, something could have happened to him.'

'What made you so scared, exactly? Did he threaten you?'

'No, he was just out of it. I thought he must have been on acid or something.'

'And there was no one else in the house at the time besides you?'

'No, his parents are in Africa. I'm supposed to be looking after the house in a way as well.'

'OK, so you go downstairs to the door and you let him in?'

'Yes. He runs straight past me then, up the stairs to the first floor. I think to myself that's where his room is.'

'When you opened the door, did you get a good look at him? Can you describe him to us? Anything that you remember would be a great help.'

Iselin shook her head.

'It happened so quickly. He just barged past and ran up the stairs. But . . . well, he was quite small. And he seemed scared out of his wits. It was like he didn't even see me.'

'Anything else you noticed?'

'No.'

'What sort of clothes was he wearing?'

'I can't remember. Or rather, I didn't really notice, not properly.'

'Try to recall. You open the door and he's standing there. Dark-coloured clothes or lighter?'

She shook her head.

'I've no idea.'

'OK, so he barges past you and runs up the stairs to his room.'

My phone rang. It was Ella.

'I'm sorry, I need to answer this,' I said. 'Just carry on.'

Lene gave me a look of surprise, perhaps even anxiety, before composing herself again with a nod. I went out onto the landing and closed the door behind me. For some reason, it didn't feel quite as hot there, though the sun was beating in through the window. Specks of dust whirled about in the rays. My phone rang and vibrated, as insistent as Ella herself. It reminded me of the Donald Duck comics, when you knew it was Scrooge McDuck phoning because the cord shaped itself into the outline of his face.

'Ella,' I said. 'What's up?'

'It's just that . . . remember I was telling you about that boy in my year who I got in an argument with that time?'

'About feminism?' I said, to let her know I did remember. And that I cared.

'Yes. He was a total idiot. But he was with his mates then, wasn't he? He might not have meant what he said. And now he's just texted me and asked if I want to go to a party on Friday.'

'So now you're wondering if you're allowed?'

'No, don't be so stupid. Of course I'm allowed. But do you think I should? Go to the party with *him*, I mean. It was terrible, what he said. But do you think he meant it?'

'How should I know?'

'But what do you think?'

'I think you should follow your gut feeling. And it sounds to me like you want to.'

'Does it?'

'Yes.'

'So you think I should?'

'That's not what I said. Try and gauge how you feel.'

'OK, thanks. Got to go now,' she said, and hung up.

I stood there for a moment. The voices from inside the room were faint, almost undetectable, as if they were no more than a shimmer in the air. The distant rumble of traffic on the main road likewise. I put two fingers to the pulse in my neck. It felt like a little animal in there. A wriggling snake.

I needed to get a check-up, make sure my heart wasn't going to stop on me.

I called Elisabeth now I had the chance.

'Geir,' she said.

'Hello, you,' I said. 'I thought I'd come round for dinner tonight. If you're not doing anything, that is?'

'I haven't heard from you in three days.'

'You've seen the news, though?'

'Yes, I have. And I realise you're busy *now*. But those bodies weren't discovered until last night. So what were you up to before then?'

'I've been working on the case.'

'Before?'

'Yes, of course. The media don't know everything that's going on. But if we're going to start arguing about my work, let's give it a miss.'

'I don't want to argue. But you could have sent me a text at least. Two seconds of your time, just to let me know?'

'You're right. I've been a bit pressed, that's all. Anyway, it'd be lovely to see you.'

'Then come over.'

'Yes, I will. I can't stay, though. I'm run off my feet here.'

'Are you making any progress?'

'I'll tell you about it later. Can't wait to see you.'

I hung up, slipped the phone into my pocket and went back in. Trying to be invisible, I stood quietly by the door, but Iselin stopped talking and looked up at me.

'Don't mind me,' I said. 'Go on.'

'You wanted to help him and so you went downstairs to the first floor,' said Lene.

'Yes,' said Iselin. 'He was so far gone. He could have topped himself, for all I knew.'

'It was very courageous of you, Iselin.'

Iselin smiled fleetingly. It was a chink, the first real suggestion of a living person that she'd shown. She may have been answering the questions all right, but apart from that she was decidedly dull to the world. I reckoned she was medicated. Antidepressants flattened out the peaks and troughs, only sometimes they left you with not much more. Ella was a torrent of energy in comparison. She could light up a room, which wasn't always a good thing, I supposed.

'When I opened the door, he was kneeling on the floor praying.'

'Praying?'

'Yes, with his hands folded.'

'Was he saying anything?' I asked.

She shook her head.

'He was just kneeling there without moving, with his eyes closed. But as soon as he realised I was there, he freaked out again. Jumped back against the wall like he'd seen a monster. I tried to calm him down. Told him I was just the lodger. Only it was as if he saw something other than me. He shouted at me to show him my hands. I was holding the knife behind my back, right? And then when he came at me I ran upstairs again and phoned his parents. They were the ones who called the police.'

'And he was gone by the time the police got here, is that correct?'

'Yes.'

'But you didn't hear him go?'

'No, I didn't hear anything. And I was *really* listening, you know?'

'I'm sure you were.'

'Do you know for certain that he was here?' said Iselin, now turning her attention to me.

'What do you mean?' I said.

'Did anyone else see him?'

'What, here?'

'Yes.'

'No. So far you're the only person we know that saw him. Why do you ask?'

She shook her head.

'No reason. It's just weird he could get away like that without me hearing him.'

'I suppose he was just very quiet about it,' said Lene. 'Is there anything you want to add? Anything we haven't talked about?'

'No, I don't think so.'

Lene got to her feet.

'Thanks ever so much, Iselin. This has been very useful.'

'You're welcome,' said Iselin, she too now standing.

'Do you think he's the one who did it?'

'I'm afraid I can't say,' said Lene.

'I can,' I said. 'It wasn't him.'

Lene looked at me with astonishment.

'Have you got any friends or family here in town, Iselin? Someone you can stay with a few days?' I said. 'Sometimes it's a good thing to have other people around you after a nasty scare like that.'

'I've got a brother who lives here. I'm going to see him now, as it happens.'

'Good.'

'Do you think you could come down to the station and talk to us again tomorrow?' said Lene. 'For a more formal interview?'

'Another one?'

'If you could?'

'I suppose so.'

Lene thanked her once again and we left her joyless, sweltering hot den behind us and went back down to the car.

'What about the parents?' Lene said, clicking into her seat belt as I turned the key in the ignition.

'I was thinking you could deal with them.'

'On my own?' she said in a tone of voice that made me think she was becoming sceptical about my judgement.

'You can take Alexander with you, if he's available,' I said. 'Or someone else.'

'OK.'

I drove a different way back, through the sweep of 1950s residential outskirts, the houses with their little gardens of sandy soil, the grass now parched yellow-brown as the summer reached a close.

'What do you draw from all this?' I said.

'Not much,' said Lene. 'Other than that he definitely sounds psychotic to me.'

'What do you base that on?'

There was something forbearing about the way she looked at me. I smiled and wondered if I should focus more on how I came across.

'What she said about how it was almost as if he saw something other than her, and that she was a kind of monster in his eyes. It does indicate a distorted perception of reality, wouldn't you say? And then his screaming on top of that?'

'Can't he just have been scared? If you'd just seen your friends have their throats cut and then be skinned, maybe you wouldn't act rationally either.'

We emerged onto Danmarksplass again. The windows of the new buildings where the old shipyard had been glittered in the sunlight. The High Technology Centre on the other side of the bridge, once state of the art, looked like a Playmobil house.

'Why did you tell her he didn't do it?' Lene said eventually. 'When we don't actually know. Or do you know something I don't?'

'No, not at all. But all our information would suggest that it's highly unlikely. I'd say inconceivable. If he'd done something like that, he'd have to have planned it. Not only that, he'd have to carry it out very methodically. It would have taken hours. And I can't marry that with the state he was in. I just can't see him running home screaming for his mum and dad afterwards, can you?'

'He could have just panicked. That's not hard to imagine.'

'A person would have to be exceptionally cold-blooded in my book to cut the throats of their three best mates. They must have been asleep or knocked out on something, don't you think? Certainly defenceless. Then, after cutting their throats, you've got to stay focused and skin them. That doesn't suggest panic to me.'

'Perhaps not,' she said. 'But he could have had an accomplice, maybe more than one. You made it sound like we know for certain it wasn't Jesper. Instead, it's just your own hypothesis.'

'It makes things easier for Iselin. It wouldn't be much fun to know you were on your own with a triple killer.'

I dropped her off on the corner by the police station and drove back the same way we'd come. Parked in front of the hospital. The heat that shimmered above the asphalt reminded me of the time I'd stuck my head out of a train window at a station in Italy. I'd been on my way to Brindisi and I remembered the shock of the heat, so much hotter than inside. It had made me feel so claustrophic, because what if it didn't let up? What if it was never going to be possible to go outside again?

It had been 40 degrees, but that was the south of Italy.

I'd have to have a shower at Elisabeth's, put some other clothes on.

I yawned, stepped inside into the reception area and phoned my namesake Geir Jakobsen, the pathologist.

'Hello there,' he said.

'Busy day?'

'I'll say.'

'Anything new?'

'Yes. We found some biological traces on the victims.'

'Semen?'

'No, no. Some matter under the nails, some in the corners of their mouths. We're not quite sure what it is yet. We're waiting for the test results.'

'Excellent. Anything else? In the blood, for instance?'

'Again, we don't know yet.'

'OK. One more thing: how long would it actually take to skin a man? Approximately.'

'As I told KRIPOS, it's hard to say. It depends what sort of implements you're using, whether you're skilled in that sort of work. But at least three hours would be my guess.'

'All right, thanks a lot. Catch you later.'

'No problem. Bye.'

It was barely believable. How could they have been so meticulous about killing them and putting them on display like that, and yet so careless as to leave DNA traces behind?

I yawned again as I went over to the reception desk. I showed my ID to the woman behind the computer and asked after Lindland. They had him up on the neurological ward on the second floor, she told me, and gave me the name of the consultant I could speak to. Before going up I bought myself an ice-cold Diet Coke in the Narvesen shop and drank it on the spot while standing in front of the magazines.

What a strange case this was. Nearly all the other murder cases I'd worked on had been decidedly by the book in comparison. Nearly all followed a familiar pattern. Killings were pretty much a feature of human life, people had always bumped each other off, for the same reasons and in the same ways, whether the year was 1944, 1998 or 2017. As a rule, the killer was related in some way to the victim. If not, it usually had something to do with attempts at wrongful gain, drug- or alcohol-induced behaviour, gang conflicts – or else was sexually motivated. Those left over were the so-called unusual cases such as serial killings, mass murder, terrorism, killings committed by children, and killings without motive. That just about exhausted the possibilities. A large part of investigating a murder was therefore about looking for familiar patterns. In normal cases, the solution was in the norm, this was true ninety-nine out of a hundred times. In unusual cases, which by definition hardly ever occurred, it was the unusual aspect that was significant.

In this case everything was unusual. From the number of victims to the way they'd been killed and mutilated.

I dropped the bottle into the bin and ambled over to the lift. As far as I knew, Descartes was the first scientist who wanted one method for everything, a system in which all knowledge was gained in the same way, independently of the object of investigation. It was such a clever thought that it soon gained traction. It was Descartes too who saw the value of breaking the whole down into its constituent parts. He was a true genius – even such a trivial thing as a roadmap for a murder investigation would be unthinkable without him. But his method *began* with intuition. It was worth bearing in mind. I'd always enjoyed thinking along such lines, considering states of affairs or events on their own terms, as much as in the context of a given method of inquiry.

An elderly woman was standing in the lift when the doors opened, her arm connected by a tube to a bag of clear fluid that hung from an IV drip stand at her side. When she stepped out, wheeling the stand as she went, a little cloud of red puffed out into the fluid. I shuddered and looked away, pressed the button for the second floor and leaned back against the wall.

Jesper had knelt and prayed to God in his room at home.

Iselin had asked if we were certain he'd been there.

There'd been a smell of gunpowder at the scene of the crime.

The lift stopped and I went out into the corridor and asked the first person I saw, a young male nurse, where I could find the consultant. He directed me to a room at the far end, where I found him sitting on a sofa with his feet planted wide apart, a baguette sandwich gripped between his hands.

I introduced myself and asked about Lindland. The doctor wiped the crumbs from his mouth and put the baguette down on a paper napkin before answering. His eyes were slightly bulging, his lips thick and moist-looking, and his hair had thinned into a good old-fashioned bald spot on the crown.

'Are you a friend, or are you here in an official capacity?'

'Both, as a matter of fact,' I said. 'Could I see him?'

'Certainly,' he said and got to his feet, took a swig from a carton of apple juice and picked up his baguette again. 'Just follow me.'

He strode along the corridor, it was all I could do to keep up.

'He was comatose when admitted,' he said. 'We thought it was a stroke at first, but that wasn't the case. His heart's perfectly all right as well.'

'So what happened?'

'We've simply no idea. I don't know if you heard about his son? He tried to kill himself last night.'

'Oh? No, I hadn't heard. Kill himself?'

'Yes, he shot himself in the chest with a shotgun. So it may well be a case of shock. An emotional trauma of such dimension that his body just had to switch off.'

'Is that possible?'

He gave a shrug.

'We're going to have another look at him.'

He opened the door into a small room. Jostein was lying in a bed amid a tangle of tubes and wires, surrounded by monitors and apparatus. Looking a bit peakier than the last time I'd seen him, but otherwise much the same. His big, fleshy face with its multiple chins, his belly like a hill under the cover.

'He looks like he's asleep,' I said.

The consultant shook his head.

'Unfortunately he's in a deep coma. Unresponsive to any stimuli.'

'And Ole?'

'Sorry?'

'His son. I'm assuming he's alive? You said he *tried* to kill himself.'

'Yes, he's alive. He ought not to be, given his injuries, but it appears he'll survive.'

'How about his mother?'

'She's with him now. He's on another ward.'

Looking at his face, it was just about possible to see the man Jostein had been ten, fifteen years ago. The high cheekbones and hollow cheeks, the keen eyes, a gaze that was always measured, even when sparkling with humour or darkened by scorn. More than once I'd wondered if he was actually malicious at heart. Now his face was bloated, the keenness of before all gone. It seemed like he'd given in. But to what?

'Thanks,' I said to the doctor. 'Let me know if there's any change.'

'I will.'

Outside in the car park I phoned the dentist. His secretary gave me an appointment in two days. With so much of the tooth having come away, the rest would probably require surgery. And then they'd have to make me a new one. It was going to cost the earth.

Follo called as I turned onto the main road. As soon as he was finished, as I got to the bottom of hill where Alexander had put the sirens on earlier in the day, what seemed like an eternity since, I phoned Helene, just to take the top off any annoyance she might be harbouring at me having been away so long. She didn't answer, but sent a text: *In a meeting. Will phone later.*

So, another cold front. No *hi*, no exclamation mark, no *miss you*.

What was I going to do about that?

Send flowers?

Don't make me laugh. The only remedy was to stay at home more. Spend more time with her. Make more of an effort. Little things that said I cared. Something nice for dinner, bottle of wine, fresh flowers in a vase. How about going to see a film tonight, love? Not all at once, obviously. Never go straight from zero to a hundred. Nice and gently was the way, let it become apparent. Then everything would be all right again.

Only I couldn't at the moment.

As I went towards the underground car park, I saw the TV crews had arrived and taken up their positions on the pavement. Thank goodness I wasn't leading the investigation, I thought to myself and remained seated in the car for a few minutes to reflect on what I knew so far. The lads had been missing for five days. To start with, they must have gone off of their own accord since they'd taken backpacks and sleeping bags with them. Where had they been and what were they doing there? They weren't exactly outdoor types. But they did have ideas about nature, the Norwegian landscapes in particular meant something to them. So they were out there somewhere for four days. Maybe they were filming. OK, let's say they were filming. Then, on the fifth day, three of them were murdered. They were discovered at around eleven at night. The actual time of death depended on how long it took to skin three bodies. Which in turn depended on how many were involved in carrying it out. At least two, I reckoned. It would have been too early for them to have turned in for the night, so they wouldn't have been killed while they were asleep – something one person on their own could have done. They could have been drugged, but that required some form of trust. Meaning it was someone they knew. Maybe Jesper. Only it wasn't Jesper. If on the other hand they hadn't been drugged and weren't asleep, there would have to have been three at least. In which case the skinning would have taken around three hours. Meaning they'd have been killed around seven or eight. If I'd had three bodies to skin out there, I'd have done it somewhere near water, a pond or a stream. Possibly the reservoir itself, though that was unlikely given that they could have been seen. A stream somewhere in the forest, then. So, killed at seven or eight o'clock at the latest, skinned by a stream, taken to the clearing where they were discovered at eleven. Jesper turns up at his parents' house not long after. Scared out of his wits. Most likely because he'd witnessed what happened. But then wouldn't he have gone to the house shortly after eight rather than eleven?

No, it was too messy. I was complicating things. It had to be simpler, not nearly as hopeless. We'd find the place where they were killed, the place where they were skinned. We'd already got the place where they'd been left, and before long Jesper would turn up again. He didn't do it, but he probably saw who did. The idea that it was down to them owing money to criminals didn't have much traction. They were hardly more than kids, I just couldn't see them getting involved in anything big enough for them to get killed for it, and definitely not like that. Which basically left only one possibility. Someone in the black metal crowd had gone mad. Lost all sense of reality. It had happened before. Heksa had killed his best friend and bandmate, and two others from the same circles had killed a dosser in a park just for the thrill of it. In addition, they'd burnt churches down and vandalised gravestones, even dug up the corpses in a couple of cases.

It wasn't unlikely, not by any stretch.

Then there was all this weirdness going on.

The new star appearing in the sky at the same time. The smell of gunpowder. No significant traces of any activity in the clearing, at least none at first blush. Jesper the satanist, on his knees praying to God – but that was just regression, surely? It had to be. The girl, Iselin, who'd seen Jesper and then wanted us to confirm that he'd been there. What was that about? Why was she doubting that she'd seen him all of a sudden? Did she think he was a ghost, that he was already dead?

Was he already dead?

Oh, don't be so stupid.

A short distance away, the lift door slid open. It was Lene and Alexander. I waited until they'd got in their car and driven off before getting out. I could take the lift this time. I didn't need to use the stairs *every* time. I was the one who made the rules, no one else.

A couple of minutes later when I went past the conference room, Follo looked up and waved me in.

'Where have you been? I tried to call you.'

'At the hospital, looking in on Lindland.'

'So he is a friend, then.'

'He's an acquaintance, like I said.'

'I thought you were going to question Jesper's parents.'

'They hadn't got back.'

'They're back now.'

'Are they?'

'Yes.'

'Sæverøy's good. She can manage fine on her own.'

'That's not exactly the point.'

I said nothing. I was disappointed he could be so petty, but that was his lookout, not mine.

'What did the girl have to say?'

'She described Jesper as highly disturbed. She thought he might have taken LSD. Sæverøy thought he could have been psychotic.'

'And you?'

'I don't know. He might just have been scared out of his wits.'

'What else?'

'Nothing, really. She couldn't describe what he was wearing or what he looked like.'

'No blood?'

'She didn't mention it, if there was. I didn't want to put it into her head either, so we didn't ask. If he'd been covered in blood, she'd almost definitely have noticed. Which apparently she didn't.'

'OK. I want you to go through the footage that was shot.'

'Of course. How much is there?'

'Quite a lot. Six hours, I think. I've had a quick look. Let me know if there's anything you think might be important. If not, we'll talk about it in the morning.'

Back in my office I opened the video file, put the headset on and started watching, mostly to appease Follo – I hadn't eaten since yesterday evening and needed to pop out and get something soon.

The first images were from a bunker-like rehearsal room. Two of the band were sitting on a shabby sofa playing around with their guitars, which weren't plugged in, while a third sat drumming on an upturned plastic tub. The fourth was standing over by a table, watching a coffee machine. The camera must have been on a tripod, I supposed, and the idea was to film whatever they were doing. The only thing that stuck out was how regular-looking they were. Standard black T-shirts, black trousers, black boots. Fleshy, unfledged faces that knew nothing about life. They all had long hair except for the drummer, Jesper, his was short and spiky, and when I paused the film for a closer look I realised he had a little Hitler moustache.

Five minutes or so in, the guitarists plugged into their amps, Jesper got behind his kit and the fourth lad hung the bass over his shoulder and started to tune his instrument. Jesper twirled a drumstick restlessly between his fingers, one of the guitarists scratched himself quickly behind his ear like a cat, the other chewing on some gum while staring vacantly into space. The next minute, with no other warning than the one who'd scratched himself looking up at the other three in turn, they started playing. The transformation was total. An enormous barrage of sound filled the room, impossible to connect to the four puny youths who'd been standing there a moment before. Suddenly, they were sledgehammers. The music was tight, as precise as a machine, hard and heavy as the fells themselves, wicked and full of darkness. The two guitarists, who seemed completely unfazed by the inferno of noise they were producing, stepped forward to the mics and started singing in unison. Singing wasn't the word, it was a grotesque, gutteral growl, a screaming, spitting, aggressive murk.

I felt shaken. Not by the music itself, but by how good they were. I'd had no idea.

I tried to work out what they were singing. It was impossible to decipher.

Something kept being repeated. It sounded like *the doors*.

I googled *Kvitekrist doors*, and some lyrics came up.

'The Doors of Hell' was the title.

The Doors of Hell
The Doors of Hell
The Doors of Hell
You must open them yourself
You must want to
You must want to
Die Die
The Doors of Hell
You must want to you must need to
Die Die
The Doors of Hell
Die Die

Die Die
The Doors of Hell
Die Die the Doors
Die Die the Doors

It wasn't exactly great poetry. But the insane wall of noise transformed not only the lads themselves but also the lyrics, making them seem like they were coming from *within* something. It was, to put it bluntly, terrifying.

I paused the video, swivelled round on my chair and stared out over the rooftops on which, here and there, seagulls were perched, lethargic in the heat. Somehow, what I'd just seen made the murders more real. How could that be? The bodies were in no way unreal. Maybe it was the hideous way in which they'd been presented, so far from anything that was normal. Now I'd seen them as they'd been when they were alive. And I'd felt the force of their music.

No, I needed something to eat.

I got to my feet and went out. On my way to the lift it struck me I could ask Helene if she'd like to come and have lunch with me. It would be a smart move. It would free me up to have dinner with Elisabeth and get them both off my back for a couple of days, or maybe just hours.

On my way for some lunch at Pascal. Fancy coming?

She replied straight away, brief and to the point.

Yes.

The restaurant was only five minutes away, so I didn't bother taking the car and went out through the main entrance. From the cluster of reporters I heard my name called out. It was the veteran, Ellingsen, he'd been a crime reporter for as long as I'd been on the force. Mostly he wrote commentary pieces these days, but clearly this was a story he wanted so he'd crept out from under his stone to get in on the act.

'Well, there's a face from the past,' I said. 'What are you doing out? On holiday, are we?'

'What's going on?' he said, fixing me with his watery eyes. 'What leads are you following?'

'No comment,' I said. 'I'm sure there'll be a press conference soon. You should attend!'

'Is Jesper Holm Jensen a suspect? Do you know where he is?'

'We don't know where he is, no. But listen, I've got to get going. Nice seeing you!'

I put my sunglasses on and crossed to the other side of the street to get out of the sun as I went down towards Vågen. Not that the shade helped much, the air was as thick with heat there as everywhere else.

Helene was on the legal team of one of the big trade unions. The building she worked in was about the same distance from Pascal as the police station was, only in the other direction, so I wasn't surprised when a few minutes later I clocked her standing outside waiting for me.

I smiled and waved. All she did was take her sunglasses off.

'Have you booked a table?' she said.

'No. Do you think it's necessary? At this time?'

'What have you done to yourself? Have you lost a tooth?'

'I'm afraid so. The one I just had done. It just came out.'

'You look dreadful.'

'Beauty and the beast,' I said to provoke a smile, but she just turned round and went inside. Coming in from the glaring sunlight was like entering a cave. She halted behind another couple who were talking to the head waiter, then faced me.

'Nothing free for the next twenty minutes. I can't wait that long. I've got lots to do.'

'Shall we go somewhere else?'

'Where?'

'I don't know. A cafe would do.'

She nodded.

Back outside, with the bright blue fjord glittering between the buildings, the odd screeching gull sailing over our heads, I thought about prawns. I hadn't had prawns in ages.

'Unless you want to just get some prawns and sit down somewhere on the quayside?'

'Outside?'

'Yes, why not?'

It was a bit common for her tastes, I knew that, but she let it pass without offering any suggestion of her own and we walked over to the fish market where we bought a bagful before ambling along the quay in search of somewhere to sit down. I steered us towards a little wall over by the high-speed ferry terminal. Twenty years ago we'd have relished this. She'd have been full of joy and without a care would have plonked herself down in her baggy T-shirt and cut-off jeans, her leather sandals. Shelled the prawns, tossed the empty shells into the fjord, savoured every mouthful. She'd have laughed and kissed me. I'd been so in love with her. Now circumspection and hesitation were the order of the day. No longer the exuberance, the light-heartedness, the laughter of before. And me, with a few too many kilos around the waist, my shabby character and missing tooth.

'Ella phoned,' I said after we'd sat down with the white paper bag between us.

'And?'

'I think she's got a crush on a lad. Has she mentioned anything to you?'

'No.'

'Well, she didn't actually say as much. I'm only guessing. Something in the way she spoke.'

'You disappointed William today.'

'Is that what he said?'

'No, but he couldn't hide it either.'

'I'll try and see if there's a way I can get to his game.'

'Don't tell him unless you can.'

She pinched the head off a prawn, squeezed the ragged-looking shell at the belly where the roe was and twisted it off, dropped it in the bag, then pulled away the tail and popped the flesh, with some small golden spheres of roe stuck to it, into her mouth.

'Good, aren't they?' I said. 'I can't remember the last time I had prawns.'

'Mm,' she said.

'What are you working on, anyway? Since you're so busy, I mean.'

'A dismissal. Man got sacked and killed himself. So we're acting for his family.'

'Sounds difficult.'

I threw a shell towards the fjord. It was too light, the air held it back and it dropped to the pavement.

'Yes,' she said.

A seagull swooped, landed and snatched it up. It stood for a moment, its wings at its sides like a ski jumper at the top of a hill. It looked at us every few seconds. I shelled another prawn and tossed it the waste.

'Do you feel sorry for it or are you afraid of them?' Helene said with a laugh.

I smiled.

'You look awful without that tooth. Are you doing something about it?'

'Of course,' I said. 'I've an appointment the day after tomorrow.'

There were crowds of people on the quay, milling around the fishing pier at the end. With all their different colours, all the various surfaces by which they were surrounded, all reflecting the light in so many ways, it was a bit like looking through a kaleidoscope.

I put my hand on her knee, only wished then that I hadn't. The gesture was unreciprocated, left dangling.

If I removed my hand, it would be even more noticeable. So I leaned across to give her a kiss. She didn't turn away, but she wasn't exactly receptive either.

'Nice to see you,' I said, able now to retract my hand in a way that felt reasonably natural.

'Why are we still together?' she said.

'What do you mean? What have I done now?'

She shook her head slowly.

'No more than usual. I was just wondering. Why are we still together?'

'I love you,' I said.

'I'm not so sure about that.'

'I do, of course I do.'

'If you say so,' she said, and smiled faintly.

'What have I done? Why this sudden mistrust?'

'Who said it was sudden?'

'Do I need to *prove* I love you?'

'No. It would be enough to show that you do. So I can feel it. That's the problem, you see. I see the signs of your love, but I can't feel it.'

She avoided looking at me as she spoke and stared into the distance. I was filled with an enormous sense of annoyance. What was it with all these bloody feelings? It was the only thing women talked about, there was no let-up. Feelings this, feelings that. We were married for Christ's sake, we had a house and a car and two kids. Wasn't that enough?

'I'm sorry you feel that way,' I said. 'But it's true what I said.'

'What is?'

'That I love you.'

I leaned across to kiss her again. This time she turned away.

'Not like that,' she said.

I stared at her in disbelief. She met my gaze.

'I don't want *illustrative* kisses, I want the real thing,' she said. 'Shall we go? You'll be just as busy as I am, I imagine.'

The mood up on the sixth floor told me immediately that something had happened. I made straight for Alexander who was sitting at his desk typing away on the computer.

'What's going on?' I said.

'Haven't you heard?'

'Heard what?'

'Jesper Holm Jensen's been brought in.'

'What? Where was he found?'

'He was hiding in a basement, in someone's storage room. The owner locked him in and raised the alarm.'

'Has he said anything?'

'No. He's totally unhinged apparently.'

'Excellent news, though, all the same,' I said, and carried on into my office. The job I'd been given was degrading, but simple and well defined, and I closed the door behind me, put the headset on and started the video again. More of the same, I discovered, the band running through their repertoire, presumably wanting to document where they were at. I wasn't getting much out of it; the faces of the guitarists and the bass player were mostly obscured by their curtains of hair and Jesper was half hidden behind them anyway. After maybe half an hour the screen suddenly blacked out. Then came a long sequence from a forest at night, the camera moving between the trees, a light beam pooling on branches and leaves, undergrowth and bushes, milky grey in the murky darkness, until it reached a figure standing still, dressed in black, a knife in each hand, the face made up to look like a corpse and without expression.

The door opened. It was Follo. I paused the film, removed the headphones.

'I did knock,' he said. 'Have you got a minute?'

'Yes, sure.'

'Just thought I'd brief you. Perhaps pick your brains a bit.'

He sat down on the chair on the other side of the desk.

'We've found Jesper Holm Jensen, but you'll know about that by now, I imagine.'

'Someone did mention it, yes.'

'We couldn't get through to him. Psychotic, I believe. He's been transferred to the psychiatric ward, heavily sedated.'

'He hasn't been questioned then?'

He shook his head.

'All we can do is hope he's more amenable once he comes round.'

'Anything else?'

'No, that's basically it. No signs of blood or other matter. He could have cleaned himself up and changed his clothes, of course, but judging by the state he was in I'd say it wasn't him.'

'No.'

'The other thing is we've found their clothes.'

'Where?'

'In a stream. Blood and gore aplenty there.'

'You mean it's the scene of the crime?'

'Probably not. My theory is they were killed somewhere else, but skinned there. Then dragged to the clearing where they were found. It's about four or five hundred metres away.'

'Gave themselves a bit of a job.'

'I'll say. What do you make of it?'

'Meticulously planned, that's the first thing. The second is they must have been killed during the afternoon, meaning we can more than likely rule out that someone came and slit their throats while they were asleep. I'd say there are two possibilities. Either they were drugged and then killed. The fact that Jesper got off is of course significant. Did he slip them something to knock them out? Possibly. It would certainly explain the fact that he wasn't killed. And it would explain his terror too. He was a part of whatever was going on, only he hadn't realised where it was heading, and certainly wasn't prepared for the way it happened. If they were drugged, that could have been done by someone working on their own, but the fact they were skinned rules that out completely. Which means there were two or three. Or, the second possibility is that they were ambushed. In which case there would have to have been at least four assailants.'

'What sort of motive would they have had?'

'I think we're beyond any rational motive here. I think we're looking for someone in black metal circles who did it for the hell of it. It wouldn't be the first time, as you know.'

'If Jesper isn't an accomplice, what grounds would they have had to let him go?'

'Maybe he wasn't there when it took place. Maybe he was off in the woods somewhere, call of nature. Then when he got back they were already dead. But that can't explain why he doesn't show up until hours later.'

'Perhaps he was hiding out until it was safe.'

'Maybe. Or maybe whoever killed them actually wanted a witness.'

'Why would they?'

'So they could show off.'

'No one would be that stupid, surely?'

'Jesper's scared out of his wits. I doubt he's going to tell us anything even if he knows.'

'Well, I think you're right about that. And I agree with your reasoning. I think we're looking for someone in the same circles.'

'In which case it's only a matter of time before we find them.'

'Exactly,' Follo said and got to his feet. 'Anyway, weren't you up all night? You should go home and get some sleep.'

'I was, yes. But listen . . .'

He turned in the doorway.

'Yes?'

'What about the DNA? Any word?'

He shook his head.

'It was useless. Completely contaminated.'

*

Elisabeth wasn't in when I got to hers, so I let myself in and gave her a call to let her know. She sounded like she was in a good mood and would come as soon as she could. Not right away, she needed to get some shopping in first. I pulled off my sweaty clothes, dropped them in the laundry bin and went into the shower, conscientiously avoiding the big mirror above the sink – I didn't want to see my flabby stomach or the hole where my tooth should have been. I turned on the water and stepped underneath once it was warm enough. After I was finished I picked a white shirt and a pair of light-coloured chinos from the wardrobe in the bedroom and went and sat out on the veranda. I texted Helene and told her how nice it had been seeing her for lunch and that I'd be home in the evening sometime. I texted William too and wished him all the best with his football match, then stared out over the housing, the low-slung apartment blocks, symmetrically arranged on the sloping terrain between patches of parched yellow grass and pale grey asphalt. There was so much light outside – not just from the blazing sun, but also cast back from every surface – that it made me feel uncomfortable and after a while I went back inside. It was a rather small apartment, but nice and cosy, in fact there was nowhere else I felt so relaxed. It struck me that I always went about in my bare feet here. No doubt that was why.

I looked at the books on the shelf. Novels mostly, which I never read, but I liked her reading them, and talking about them afterwards. Through the filter of her own reading experience what happened in the novel became almost like something that *really* happened, something she'd experienced herself and was telling me about.

I checked my phone. The pathologist's report had come. I sat down on the sofa and read it through. It confirmed they'd probably all been killed at approximately the same time. There were traces of cannabis and alcohol in their blood, but no hard drugs. The biomatter under their nails and at the corners of their mouths couldn't be identified, as Follo had suggested.

I decided to call Jakobsen, the pathologist, myself, but just as I'd tapped the number I heard the key in the front door and so I hung up after a single ring and went to greet her. She dumped two carrier bags of shopping on the floor and glanced up, perspiring and exhausted too by the looks of it.

'Hi,' I said.

'So this is what you look like, is it?'

We gave each other a quick peck before I picked up the bags and took them into the kitchen.

'What are we having?'

'Mackerel, I was thinking. How does that sound?'

'Lovely. Good summer food, mackerel.'

I smiled. Her eyes widened straight away.

'I know, it looks awful, doesn't it? I'm getting it fixed, though.'

'How did it happen?'

'Bloody thing just broke off. Obviously wasn't strong enough to withstand that root canal treament.'

My phone rang as I spoke. It was Jakobsen.

'I need to get this,' I said and stepped out into the hall.

'You called?' he said.

'Yes,' I said. 'Just read your report. Good stuff. But what's the story about that DNA exactly?'

'Like it says, it was unusable.'

'Contaminated? By what? Or by whom?'

'Not contaminated, exactly. It was simply unreadable.'

'How do you mean?'

'I'm not even sure it *was* DNA.'

'What else could it be?'

'I don't know. Something chemical.'

'Not biological, then? Is that what you're saying?'

'I thought it was at first. I mean, it looks biological. But once we examined it closer, it appeared it wasn't.'

'Could it be DNA from an animal of some sort?'

'Definitely not. We'd have seen that.'

'OK. Can you have another look?'

'Another look? There's nothing more we can get out of it, that's what I'm saying.'

'All right. It's just that it's one of the few things we've got to go on, that's all. But if I'm understanding you right, it's something that looks like DNA but isn't?'

'Exactly.'

'OK, thanks, Geir.'

When I went back into the kitchen Elisabeth was scrubbing potatoes under the tap.

'Anything I can do?' I said.

'You could slice the cucumber for the cucumber salad?'

She nodded towards a cucumber that lay gleaming on the worktop in its sheath of tight plastic.

'You can use the cheese slicer.'

'Can I?'

She smiled.

'You *must* use the cheese slicer, then!'

She leaned forward to the windowsill and turned the radio on. It was a current affairs programme and they were talking about the triple murder. Normally I wouldn't have minded what she listened to, it didn't bother me, but in this case I made an exception.

'Can we listen to something else? I really need a break from that.'

'Of course,' she said, and found some music instead, classical. Not brilliant either, but it would do.

'Is it taking it out of you?' she said as she scooped the scrubbed potatoes up out of the sink and dropped them into a saucepan. The thin, flaky skin that here and there remained stuck to the tubers' pale yellow flesh made them look diseased in a way.

'I suppose it is,' I said as I sliced the cucumber into the bowl in front of me. 'I was the first to see them. It was absolutely horrific. I'd rather not think about it, actually.'

'I understand.'

'How's your day been, anyway?'

She laughed.

'No murders. No dead bodies. No devils.'

'Devils?'

'Weren't they devil worshippers?'

'Oh, I see. Yes. Yes, they were. So just an ordinary day, then?'

'Well, there was a *bit* of drama, I suppose. You know my boss, Hanne?'

'The arrogant one?'

'Yes, that's her. Well, her husband went missing yesterday. Or rather, he wasn't answering his phone. He was at their cabin, you see. She was quite worried about him. Anyway, it turned out he'd had a stroke and was lying there all on his own in the middle of nowhere. She phoned in from the hospital this morning. Apparently, he's going to be all right. Or at least he's not going to die. He'll need a fair amount of rehab though, I imagine.'

'Have you met him?'

'A couple of times, yes. Nice chap, but a bit aloof, if you get what I mean.'

The ring of the cooker spat as the rising heat took hold of the drops of water on the underside of the saucepan. Elisabeth poured some water into another, just enough to cover the bottom, and placed four fillets of mackerel in it.

'What do I do now?' I said, holding out the bowl of cucumber.

'You make a marinade. A small amount of water, a splash of vinegar, salt and pepper, and a pinch of sugar.'

'I think you'd better do that, don't you?'

She smiled and took the bowl out of my hands, allowing me to disappear into the living room and stretch out on the sofa. Fatigue seemed to have been lying in wait for me, lurking until I closed my eyes, for a minute later I was fast asleep. I woke up utterly disorientated, with someone ruffling my hair. I didn't know where I was and was immediately gripped with fear.

'It's only me,' said Elisabeth.

I breathed in deeply a couple of times, then smiled at her.

'Sorry, didn't mean to be so jumpy,' I said.

'You've seen some not very nice things,' she said.

'Be with you in a second,' I said. 'Need to go to the loo.'

My piss was just as brown as before, but then I hadn't drunk anything since the Coke I'd bought at the hospital.

I was happy to let her think my panic was because of the bodies I'd seen. It was difficult to hide when it came suddenly like that.

But now I was back in control. I was at Elisabeth's place, had a good reason not to stay too long, and could spend the night with Helene.

The constant fear of getting it all mixed up. Not a massive fear, but a fear nonetheless. It was there all the time, in one way or another. But I was good at keeping things separate, keeping myself focused on wherever I was at any given time. The only threat came from outside, being seen by someone who knew me as Helene's husband while I was with Elisabeth. It had happened a couple of times, but I'd dealt with it well, simply by introducing her on both occasions, and as long as she didn't take my hand or did anything else that suggested intimacy, no one could ever have known she was anything other than a colleague or an acquaintance. If they did mention it to Helene, she'd find nothing odd about it, I met a lot of people in my job, I had a wide network.

'It's a bit hot to eat outside, don't you think?' Elisabeth said when I came back. She'd set the table nicely, there was even a candle – white, burning with a near-invisible flame. White plates too, and gleaming glasses, the pale green cucumber salad, the grey-white fish with its blue-black banded skin. Wooden table, wooden floor, white walls. She was a bit of an aesthete was Elisabeth, even if she didn't look the type. I had no idea where she got it from.

We began to eat in silence, only the sounds of the city drifted in through the open veranda door. The bright sunlight made the living room seem dim.

'Are you staying the night?' she said.

'I can't, I'm afraid. Need to work tonight. And get an early start tomorrow. I'll just grab a couple of hours in the flat, if that's all right. It's more practical that way.'

She said nothing and the silence between us grew.

'A journalist I know is in a coma at the hospital,' I said. 'I went to see him there today. He just collapsed and went comatose. The doctor said they didn't know what it was. It wasn't his heart and it wasn't a stroke either, apparently there was nothing wrong with his brain. He said it could have been shock, because his son had tried to kill himself. I've never heard of anything like that before, have you? A shock-induced coma?'

'No.'

'I just thought of it when you told me about your boss's husband. Collapsing like that, you know? Just like my dad.'

Not even that did the trick. All she did was nod without speaking.

I needed to steer things over towards her. Something she was interested in.

Too late.

'I understand you want your freedom and that you don't want to move in with me. But I don't understand you not wanting to get married. We wouldn't have to live together. You could keep your flat and I could keep mine.'

'Do we have to talk about that now? I've had a really rough day and it's not finished yet.'

'That's what you always say. So when *are* we going to talk about it? It's inconvenient every time!'

'I'd thought I could wind down a bit here with you.'

'Can't you see how hard it is for me to believe you're actually committed here?'

'Marriage is only symbolic. You said yourself we'd just carry on as we are now. So what's the problem?'

'Symbols are important.'

'Content is more important. I love you, Elisabeth. We don't have to get married for you to know that, surely?'

She went quiet again, stared at her plate as she manoeuvred a piece of soft white fish onto her fork, then looked up at me.

'Even if it makes no difference to you, it does to me. So you could marry me for *my* sake. If you really do love me.'

'Don't pressure me. That's not the way to go about it.'

'I'm not pressuring!'

'What else do you call it? I've said quite clearly, as I've said lots of times before, that I'd like us to carry on as we are.'

Silence again.

Then, without looking at me, she said:

'I'm not sure I want to.'

'Is that an ultimatum?'

'Call it what you want. I've said what I want to say.'

She stood up and took her plate over to the sink before going off into the bedroom. I stayed put and finished eating with a gathering sense of unease. The urge to leave and let her stew was powerful, but would lead to nothing good. Going to her was out of the question too, I'd only be acknowledging the problem if I did that. I scraped my leftovers into the bin and put the plate in the dishwasher, cleared the table, then stood on the empty veranda and gazed down at the little cluster of shops that were arranged in a kind of crescent off the main road. A butcher, a baker, a florist, a bank, a Co-op supermarket and a small coffee shop, all surrounded by 1950s housing, and then the low-slung blocks that lay crosswise on the hill, the same as the one in which I stood. The light was strangely intense, as if someone had turned up a dial. I leaned out until I could see the fell to the other side. The sky there was heavy, blue-black.

I went back inside and paused in the doorway of the bedroom. She was lying on her back with her hands folded on her stomach.

'Hi,' I said.

'Hi,' she said.

'Listen, I'm not as difficult as I seem,' I said. 'I'm sorry, but we'll work it out, all right?'

I went over and sat down on the edge of the bed. She took my hand.

'I'm sorry too. It was wrong to pressure you like that.'

'Friends?'

She smiled.

'Friends.'

I stood up.

'I wish I could stay. Especially now. Only I've got to get going.'

She nodded.

'What we were talking about. You can trust me, you know. I'll have a big surprise for you soon.'

I leaned forward and kissed her on the lips. She put her hand behind my neck and drew me down towards her. I realised that pulling free and saying I didn't have time would be a tactical error, so I had no option but to go along with her sudden passion, but after a couple of minutes of lustless petting, the urge happily came over me too. Afterwards we lay in each other's arms, she with her head on my chest, while thunder clouds darkened the landscape outside the window, and the room that surrounded us too.

'Do you want a coffee before you go?' she said.

'No, thanks,' I said, and gave her a warm smile. 'I should have been back by now.'

She came with me into the hall and kissed me goodbye, and I went out into the pouring rain.

Our house was in Ålvik by the Hardangerfjord, a two-hour drive out of town. It was Helene's childhood home, a former smallholding we'd taken over from her parents fifteen years ago. The property, sloping down towards the fjord, was a haven of fruit trees and berry bushes, magnificently beautiful when everything blossomed in spring. I'd always been fond of visiting her parents when they still lived there, but was less fond of living there myself. It was fine, but no more than that. Of course, it was impractical living so far away from my job, but one of the main reasons I agreed to it at all was that it allowed me to have my own little flat for overnight stays in town. So we'd compromised, even if Helene now seemed to wish we hadn't, for my spending so little time at home had been a constant theme now for several years.

The rain that came thrashing down onto the dried-out landscape, which the windscreen wipers were barely able to manage, made me wonder if plants felt thirsty as slowly they wilted through periods of drought, week upon week without water. Or were they perfectly oblivious?

I put Dire Straits, *Love Over Gold*, on the stereo as I left town, but then when the road began to rise towards the fells it suddenly felt like I'd wasted the day doing nothing, and so I turned the music off, picked up my phone and looked up the number of the author who'd written *Darkness: The Second Coming*. It rang for a while. He was probably one of those who was suspicious of unknown callers. Eventually, though, he answered.

'Yes?'

'Ivar Abelseth?'

'Speaking.'

'Hello, my name's Geir Jacobsen, I'm a police investigator. Perhaps you've already guessed why I'm calling.'

'I'm innocent!' he said with a laugh.

'I'm afraid I haven't had time to read your book. I hear it's very good.'

'Thanks.'

'I know it's about Heksa. But I'm assuming you know rather a lot about the wider scene he was involved with, am I right?'

'I don't think there'd be anyone better to ask.'

'Right, so what I'm wondering is if you could help me out a bit regarding Kvitekrist. Where they were coming from, what kind of circles they moved in, what kind of mindset they have.'

'Had.'

'Yes, had. But actually more the scene itself.'

'I can, yes. How much do you know?'

'Not much. Only what's been in the papers, really.'

The road meandered upwards, some of the bends were so steep they had to be negotiated in first gear. The headlights of occasional oncoming cars glowed through the blue tinge of rain-soaked light.

'OK. How far back do you want me to go? Right to the beginning?'

'To the first black metal bands, you mean?'

'Yes, it's all connected. Sure you've got the time?'

'Quite sure, yes. As long as you can cut out the pointless anecdotes and other digressions, that is.'

He laughed. I got the feeling he liked me.

'OK, so basically rock has always been about going against the grain, against the establishment, the prevailing parameters. The kids are against everything their parents' generation stands for, and the way they express that is through music.'

'This might be a bit *too* basic, actually. Given that I'm slightly pushed for time.'

'All right, so to begin with we're talking about little demonstrations. Elvis with his hip wiggle. The Beatles with their long hair. A bit later the Stooges with their sheer noise. After that, two things happen: heavy metal, which flirts with the Devil and darkness – Black Sabbath around 1970, for example – and then there's punk in 1977, the aggression in that.'

'Still all a bit elementary, I'm afraid. Is the point coming soon?'

I was approaching the top now. The fell wasn't that high, the trees stood close on both sides of the road, dark and looming beneath the heavy sky.

'Sorry,' he said. 'Only it's not often I get the chance to talk music history with the police!'

'This is serious business, don't forget. Three young men have been killed.'

'I know, and I knew all three of them. Which I don't suppose you did?'

'You knew them? Personally?'

'I interviewed them loads of times. They respected me.'

Respected? What sort of a boast was that? They were just kids.

'I'm sure,' I said. 'And I will read your book. It's just that right now I need you to give me the condensed version.'

'All right, so in the early eighties extreme metal bands started emerging in Norway. They played death metal or speed metal or trash metal, like the bands they admired. But for some of them this wasn't enough. They wanted to be *more* extreme. The music had to be as dark and as ugly as possible, the vocalists didn't sing, they screamed, and they wanted to be evil. It's actually an amazing story. They came from pleasant little places in affluent Norway, they grew up in the seventies in a society that took the best possible care of them. I mean, we're not exactly talking working-class England here. And yet they were more extreme even than punk. I've seen footage of one of the bands from back then. There they are, onstage in a community centre somewhere. Made up like corpses, smeared with blood, they've got a pig's head on a stake, and the music is just so heavy and so raw, they're screaming like lunatics, and then one of them starts cutting himself with a broken bottle and ends up having to be taken to hospital. Can you imagine being an ordinary Norwegian kid and then seeing something like that? You're used to the local news on telly, pizza nights in front of the video, a bit of snogging in your bedroom, if you're lucky enough now and then. And then suddenly, this! It was like something from another world, know what I mean? Something unlike anything they'd ever known before. But anyway, even this wasn't enough for those bands. To them it was theatrics, evil as theatre, and they wanted it to be real. Don't ask me why. The vocalist blows his head off with a shotgun, they start burning down churches, the bass player kills the vocalist. Someone else from the same scene kills a randomly chosen man.'

'I know all this already.'

'Of course you do. Everyone does. But what happened then was that Norwegian black metal suddenly made it out into the wide world, straight out of these kids' bedrooms basically. The next generation profited from that. They developed it, refined it you could say, so it was no longer as primitive. They were still provoking, but that was all it was, provocation – these were self-proclaimed racists and Nazis, they said the worst things they could think of. But increasingly it was just hollow gesturing, generic convention.'

'And then?' I said, hoping he would now get to the point. It was still raining heavily, the road ahead was empty, without a vehicle in sight. The farms that kept appearing every now and again seemed likewise unpeopled, not a living soul was out.

'And that's when the third wave comes. Kvitekrist are a part of it.'

'Were.'

'Were, that's right.'

'What was the third wave all about, then?'

'Well, you could say that –'

Out of nowhere, a dog appeared on the road in front of me. I slammed on the brakes but hit it full on with a dull thud.

'Listen,' I said, 'I ran something over. I'll call you back.'

I put the warning lights on and went out into the rain. There was nothing to be seen on the road in front of the car. I crouched down and looked underneath. Nothing there either. I found it in the ditch. It was a collie. It was lying on its side looking at me. Blood was coming out of its mouth. I stepped closer and bent down. Stroked its head.

'I didn't mean to,' I said. 'You came so suddenly. I didn't see you.'

It lay, quite as still, looking up at me.

'Your owner lives up there, I suppose. I'll have to go and tell him. You stay here, all right? I'll be right back.'

I gave the dog a gentle pat. There was something wrong with its back, I could tell. The angle wasn't right.

Hell.

On the fellside a short distance away were two houses, one relatively new, the other older, from the twenties, I guessed. There were lights on in both. I went towards the new one and rang the bell.

A man in sweats who appeared to be around my age came to the door and looked at me with eyes that suggested he'd been asleep. His posture indicated he spent most of his time indoors. But there was a shotgun leaned against the wall in the corner by the door.

Inside, the hallway was bare. I guessed he lived on his own.

I explained what had happened.

He shook his head.

'That'd be Oskar's dog,' he said. 'Oskar next door. I've told him a thousand times it shouldn't be allowed to run loose.'

He stepped into a pair of boots, then looked at me.

'Thanks for stopping. I'll take care of it now. Just show me where the dog is.'

'It's next to my car on the road down there, in the ditch.'

I couldn't bring myself to walk away but stood hesitantly as the man went over and rang the doorbell of the house next door and the neighbour, an old man in a checked flannel shirt, emerged. The man said something, the neighbour looked across at me. Then he too put on a pair of boots.

'I'm very sorry,' I said once they were within earshot. 'I didn't see the dog and hadn't a chance to stop in time.'

The old man nodded, but said nothing. I went with them down to the car.

He sat down beside the dog, in the sodden grass, and put his arm around it.

'What have you done now, you silly thing?' he said. 'What have you done now?'

He looked up at me and shook his head.

'I'm very sorry,' I said again. He turned his attention back to the dog and I got in the car, turned the key in the ignition and drove off. In the rear-view mirror I saw the younger man standing motionless, his focus on the older man and his dog.

The last thing I wanted now was to talk to that pain of an author, but I didn't have far to go, and this was about the only chance I'd get.

He answered straight away.

'What happened?' he said. 'What did you hit?'

'A dog, unfortunately,' I said. 'It ran right out in front of me. It might be all right, though.'

'Glad to hear it.'

'Anyway, what I'm after is a bit of inside information on the circles Kvitekrist were moving in.'

'Well, Kvitekrist's a straightforward black metal band. They're not key to the scene in any way. They're not where it's at, as it were. They've shifted a few records, yes, they've had a few good reviews, yes, they've even played at some of the big festivals in Europe. Them and Blodhevn and Kvest would have been playing prog rock if they'd grown up in the seventies, new wave if they'd grown up in the eighties, do you know what I'm saying? They're just kids who want to be in a band.'

'So where *is* it at, then? Who *is* key?'

'Heksa. He's key.'

'Heksa's in prison.'

'That's as may be, but he's key. Musically, at least. You could say Heksa connects all three waves. He came into the second wave quite late, as a kind of first-wave nostalgist, if you like. He recorded two demos with this really shit sound and an insane vocal, everything about it was retro. He was a loner, played all the instruments himself, didn't hang out. He was only sixteen then. His development was so rapid, though, the music as well as the lyrics. His lyrics are pure poetry. The music's brilliant as well. Have you listened to it?'

'A bit.'

'Then you'll know that he started incorporating more and more folk music. Then he started going back even further and was able to find new modes of primitive expression in a remote past. Much more than just the droning guitar distortion, that is.'

'But he hasn't got much to do with Kvitekrist, if I've understood right?'

'They admired him tremendously.'

'They're disciples of a sort, you'd say?'

'You could say, yes.'

'So Kvitekrist are a regular black metal band who dabble in a bit of satanism here and there and who look up to Heksa who's in prison, and Blodhevn and Kvest are part of the same scene. Does that sum it up?'

'It does in a way. But you'd still be nowhere near what's going on.'

He was annoying the hell out of me now. Why did I have to *drag* everything out of him?

'So, what *is* going on?' I asked, mustering patience.

'Have you heard of Domen?'

'No.'

'It doesn't surprise me. Hardly anyone has. But for those in the know, they're massive.'

'OK, so who are they?'

'To answer that we need to go back to Heksa. You know what he said when they asked him why he had to go and kill someone?'

'Yes.'

'*Because it was real.*'

'Yes.'

'Well, that's the key to what's going on now. While the first-wave bands fraternised with the Devil and called themselves satanists, and the second-wave bands were all into Norse mythology and paganism – Odin and the Vikings and all that – the new bands have taken it all a step further. They refer to everything that's gone before as posturing, and they're right as well. They want to make it real.'

'It meaning evil? But they did that already, when they started burning down churches and killing people, didn't they?'

'No, it's not evil they want to make real.'

'So they're not satanists?'

'Oh yes, Satan is important to them. But to their mind Satan doesn't stand for evil. He's beyond good and evil, I think we can put it that way. He stands for all that's bestial, for blood and soil and pain and death, and that's what they've turned towards. They reject the modern world entirely. So they're not hooked up, they don't use mobile phones or computers. The sheep's or pig's heads in their live shows, they're not bought cheap from the local butcher, the way the first black metal bands did, they sacrifice the animals themselves. It's ritual, like in the Old Testament. Perhaps not exactly, but you get what I mean. They're more like a sect.'

'Sounds like a gimmick, if you ask me.'

'But it's not. They mean it. You won't find their music on Spotify. You actually won't find Domen's music anywhere. The one album they've recorded, which I know they regret having done, was something they just handed out to a very small number of people, on cassette. It's already legendary. Now even cassettes are too modern for them. They play live only rarely, and only to their own close circles.'

'So what's the point? Making music, if it's only for their mates?'

'Don't you see what kind of power there is in that? Think of all the bands and artists that have taken an anti-commercial, anti-entertainment industry stance, only to sell out as soon as they got the chance. *Everyone* is for sale. *Everyone* wants to be famous.'

'Everyone except Domen?'

'Exactly. They make their music for their own sake. And they're satanists too in the sense that they do what they want, with absolutely no constraints. Do what thou wilt, as they say.'

'Have you met them?'

'Me? No. But I've heard their album. It's incredible. Just completely incredible.'

'Did Kvitekrist meet them?'

'They saw them play, I know that for a fact. If they actually met them, they never told me about it.'

'Do you think Domen and their circle could have had anything to do with the killings?'

He laughed.

'That's your job, not mine!'

'Have you any names for me?'

'You mean who plays in Domen? I basically just told you, no one knows!'

'Someone must.'

'Someone must, yes. But I don't, I'm afraid.'

The rain had stopped by the time I drove up the hill to the house. Only when I saw the figure of Helene through the windows of the illuminated living room upstairs did it occur to me that I hadn't showered after I'd been with Elisabeth. It wasn't critical, Helene was hardly going to throw her arms around me, and there were umpteen reasons for me to have a shower as soon as I came in. Nonetheless, I felt a faint tremble of unease.

I pulled up and killed the engine, picked up my bag from the passenger seat and went in.

'Hello?' I called out from the hall. 'Anyone home?'

'Up here,' Helene called back.

I could hear the television and went up the first few stairs until I could see into the living room. She and William were sitting on the sofa, Helene with her legs drawn up underneath her, William still in his football kit.

'Hi,' I said. 'How did it go, William?'

'We won,' he said.

'Did you play?'

'A bit.'

'Good! Excellent. I'll just have a quick shower.'

Relieved, I went into the bedroom and through into the en suite, undressed, dropped my clothes into the laundry bin and got under the shower for the second time that day. Of course, she could always sniff my clothes, but burying them at the bottom of the pile would only compound any suspicion she had, because why would I do that if not to hide something? I could start a wash, but the problem would still be there: why would I wash my clothes as soon as I came through the door? That would be her first thought, and once she got thinking she might then be able to see a lot of things in a completely new light, the light of suspicion. So I did what I always did, dropped the towel I'd just used on top of the dirty clothes and hoped for the best.

'Nice to see you,' said Helene when I went back upstairs – she even smiled. She was on her own on the sofa now, William must have gone to his room.

I smiled back and sat down beside her.

'But don't forget to get that tooth sorted.'

'I won't. There wouldn't be any dinner left over for me, I suppose? I haven't eaten a thing since those prawns we had. They were very good, but they're not exactly filling.'

'I'm sorry, no. I didn't know if you'd be back. I can rustle something up, if you want?'

'No, no, no. I'll just have some cornflakes or something.'

'You must eat properly, Geir. Cornflakes won't do.'

'No, I'm fine, really.'

I got up and went into the kitchen area where I discovered two cooked sausages in the fridge, which I devoured quickly before tipping some cornflakes into a bowl and pouring some milk on top. I sat down on the high stool at the breakfast bar and crunched while Helene sat staring at the TV. I could see my reflection in the dark window behind her, a distant little gnome gazing in.

I rinsed the bowl properly under the tap before putting it in the dishwasher. Nothing stuck so hard to earthenware as soggy cornflakes gone dry.

'Any idea what the weather's going to be like tomorrow?' I said, returning to the sofa and plonking myself down beside her.

'The same as today, they said.'

'Sunny and hot, or rain like tonight?'

'Sunny.'

She switched the TV off and tipped her head back onto the edge of the backrest.

'Hard day at work?'

She didn't answer, but closed her eyes.

'Do you ever think of giving up?' she said after a second, opening them again to fix me with the clearest stare. 'Do you ever toy with the idea?'

'What do you mean? Not suicide, surely?'

'Yes, that's exactly what I mean.'

'Is it this dismissal case you're working on that's got you thinking like that? The man who killed himself after he got the sack?'

'Perhaps. But do you?'

'No.'

'Never?'

'No.'

She wanted me to ask if *she* ever toyed with the idea, I realised that. But then my phone rang. It was Elisabeth and I declined the call.

'Who was it?'

'Follo. KRIPOS bloke. He's heading up the investigation. Probably just wanting to wrap things up for the day.'

'Aren't you going to speak to him, then?'

'I'd rather speak to you. I'll call him back later.'

It was unlike her to ring me at this time. But if it was important, she would text me, I told myself, and slipped the phone back into my pocket with Helene watching me.

'Do *you* toy with the idea?' I said, if only to distract her from the phone call. 'I mean, since you're asking me?'

'Yes, I do. Doesn't everyone? Apart from you, that is.'

'Seriously? Even though we've got Ella and William?'

'It's only the idea, it's not something I'd ever do.'

'Why think about it, then?

'It's just, you know, when there's never any let-up. Get the breakfast ready, do the washing, tidy up, remember their packed lunches and their school bags, then one of them will be in a mood, there's stress at work, dinner to think about, and the dishes to clear away, and on top of it all a parents' evening and God knows what else. When it's like that I can find myself thinking how nice it would be to just let go and disappear.'

'Die, you mean?'

'I suppose that's what they call it, yes.'

'What about the kids?'

'Listen, super sleuth, it's fantasy, that's all.'

'But you're trying to tell me something, nevertheless.'

'No, I'm not. All I'm saying is that I fantasise sometimes. It doesn't mean anything. I'm fine, I want to live until I'm old and full of days.'

I felt my phone give a shudder in my pocket. There was her text.

Helene got up.

'Are you off to bed?' I said.

'Yes. Are you coming?'

'I'll come and say goodnight. There's some work I should look at, I'm afraid. Need to make up for the time I'll lose in the car going in tomorrow.'

'Will you say goodnight to Ella and William?'

'Of course.'

She went down the stairs. I waited until she was all the way down before checking Elisabeth's text.

On my way over.

What?

She knew I didn't like improvisations. I couldn't stand people just turning up.

Then I realised how stupid it had been to open the message at all. Now she would know I'd read it. It meant I wouldn't be able to say I'd been asleep and hadn't heard her at the door when she came round.

But I could be working.

Out on the job. Really sorry!

Work at this hour? she wrote back.

Can't go into detail. Come round tomorrow night! Got to go. Love you.

I turned the phone off, went and got my bag, got the laptop out and put it on the table, plugged it in and started it up before going downstairs into the bedroom where Helene was standing in front of the mirror in the en suite removing her make-up.

I came up behind her and kissed her on the nape of her neck. She froze until I was no longer touching her, then carried on as if nothing had happened.

'Goodnight,' I said. 'We probably won't see each other in the morning.'

'What time are you leaving?'

'Early, around six.'

She tossed the wet wipe she was using into the waste bin, then turned and ushered me out.

Said goodnight and closed the door in my face.

Upstairs, I unlocked the desk drawer and took out my cigarettes and lighter before going outside onto the veranda to clear my head a bit before I got started. The darkness was warm and moist, the sky still overcast. The new star shone through, faintly illuminating a patch of the fells across the fjord. I lit up and took a drag, but snatched at it too strongly and the bitter taste burned my lips and tongue. I ran an index finger over the wet rail, put the tip to my mouth and sucked in the moisture, licking my lips and then spitting before taking another drag, this time more carefully.

Did she want me to feel sorry for her with all that talk about suicide?

Who knew what women thought. Everything meant something else. Nothing was what it appeared to be.

'You've surpassed yourself, Geir,' my mum said the first time she met Helene. I didn't care for her words, it sounded like she thought Helene was better than me, a person I basically wasn't good enough for. My dad seemed to think the same thing. He kept flirting with her. Smiling and winking, his ice-blue eyes all over her, I'd never known him like that before.

I kept her away from the two of them as long as I could, they were idiots both. Her own parents were the salt of the earth, and they liked me too, I never heard a word from them to suggest I wasn't good enough for her.

I hadn't entertained the possibility either. I liked her and she liked me, so it was only natural for us to tie the knot and have kids.

I would have to put some life back into our relationship. It would have to be my number one priority.

I went back inside, hid the cigarette end in the bin underneath a soggy coffee filter that was heavy with used coffee grounds, then went and sat down at the table in the living room, put the headset on, opened the video file I'd been watching and carried on from where I'd left off.

After several sequences in the forest, all of which were much the same as the first one I'd seen, they were suddenly going berserk in a churchyard at night, roaring, overturning headstones, howling like wolves, making the sign of Satan. It looked like they were out of their heads. Still, it was no more than boyish pranks, the headstones could be righted again.

And then, the next sequence, a small clearing in the woods. Immediately, I craned closer. It was night, there was a fire going, but the place was deserted until a shrouded figure in a black hooded cape emerged from between the trees and came forwards to halt at the fire.

'Bastet,' the figure pronounced. The voice, male, was loud and compelling. 'Typhon. Fenrir. Midgard. Pan.'

With every name he uttered, a figure appeared from the forest. Each clad in the same way, caped in black, but unlike the first figure these wore no hoods, but animal masks. It was unnerving, for in the murky light they were lifelike. I saw a goat, a dog, a wolf, but the last two to step forward remained hidden behind the others.

'I am he who speaketh the law,' the first figure said, and then something I didn't catch. I turned up the volume and played it again. *None shall escape*, it sounded like. Then something about *the will is evil*. Then *run, kill and bite . . . suck the blood . . . sniff the soil . . . scrape the graves of the dead . . .*

The figure now lifted his voice and began to chant:

'Learn the law. Speak the words. Learn the law. Speak the words. Speak the words! Man is God!'

The five animal heads repeated the litany.

'Man is God!'

'We are men,' said the leader.

'We are men,' the animal heads repeated.

'We are gods.'

'We are gods.'

Then came a moment in which the leader was silent. I scanned the images of the five figures that stood in a semicircle around him, their beastly heads bowed, quite motionless.

'God is man,' he said. 'God is man.'

A movement in the trees caught my eye. So swift and fleeting I didn't see what it was. A glitch of some sort?

I went back a few seconds and watched again.

Something moved between the trees.

Was there an audience to all this?

Again, I went back, then stopped at the exact moment it occurred.

There was nothing there. Only darkness.

But then, when I ran the sequence again, there was no doubt, something moved among the trees, something sinister. Like a shadow cast by something bodiless.

I smiled at the ridiculousness of the idea. Normally, I would never have conceived such thoughts – that Jesper might be dead and that it was his ghost poor Iselin had seen; that something without substance could cast a shadow. It was as if the devilry that accompanied these young men turned my mind and directed my thoughts into the unknown.

But the killings were real, the victims were real, and somewhere out there was at least one very real killer. Whoever it was, they were now on the run, or hiding out.

That was what this was about. Nothing else.

LINE

Although it didn't leave for nearly another hour, the train was already at the platform when I arrived. I found my carriage, lifted my suitcase up onto the overhead luggage rack and sat down. I hadn't told anyone I was going to Sweden to see Valdemar – I basically couldn't be bothered listening to the inevitable arguments against, from everyone I knew who would never do anything as daring. All I said was I was going to Oslo. Which was true! I'd be spending a whole half-hour there before my onward journey to Kongsvinger and after that Sweden.

The platform was busy with travellers. Most seemed to be tourists. I was tired and closed my eyes. I must have dozed off almost immediately – there'd been so much time until departure, but when I peered blearily through the slits of my eyes what felt like a moment later we were already pulling out of the station. The next thing I saw, hours after that, was the valley opening out on the other side of the fells, the sleeping farms scattered about its slopes, the river running through the middle. And then: buildings and industry, the on-board announcement saying we'd shortly be arriving at Oslo Central.

Drained and disorientated after sleeping most of the way, I bought myself a baguette and a bottle of water before finding my next train. My head cleared even as I went down the escalator to the platform. Then it was as if I remembered I'd be seeing him soon, and the thought gave me butterflies.

At Kongsvinger I sat down in a cafe and watched *The Lion King* from beginning to end while waiting for the bus that would take me on to Charlottenberg. It had been my favourite film as long as I could remember, but I hadn't seen it for a year at least. All sense of time evaporated and I almost missed the bus – the bus station was further away than

I'd thought. The bus itself stood with its engine running and was already packed, but the single seat at the front just behind and to the right of the driver was free, so I grabbed it and sat down there.

I'd never even heard of Charlottenberg. But around here it was obviously an important hub.

Most of the passengers were elderly people. White-haired and wrinkled, saggy skin and hunched postures. I didn't find it off-putting, not exactly, but I didn't like being near them either. And eating with old people was something I really couldn't stand, not even with Gran, that really *did* put me off.

As we got going, the enormous windscreen made it seem like the town was coming towards us, rather than the other way round. The driver wore a white shirt, aviator sunglasses and a baseball cap and appeared to float up and down in his seat as we went over the bumps, arcing the big steering wheel elegantly as we negotiated the turns. He'd eyed me up a bit when I got on, so to stop him trying to start a conversation I put my AirPods in and listened to music.

It was only after we crossed into Sweden that I realised they were all coming for the tax-free shopping.

I searched for black metal on Spotify and selected the first playlist that came up. The first band were called Bathory, the song 'A Fine Day to Die'. It definitely wasn't the sort of thing I went for. I couldn't see myself getting to like it either. The next band were better. Ulver, they were called, and the song was called 'I Troldskog Faren Vild'. Listening to the first minutes of the songs as they appeared on the playlist, I tried to memorise the names of the bands so I'd be able to impress Valdemar or at least give him the impression I was interested. Emperor, Enslaved, Kvest, Third Reich, Immortal, Mayhem, Tåke, Kvitekrist, Bathory, Blodhevn, Satyricon, Bone, Darkthrone.

I could remember them all right, but telling the difference between them was another thing altogether. It was like they all played the same song.

I couldn't even pretend I liked the music.

I went back to my own playlist. It was like coming home, I thought as I gazed through the window.

Forest, forest, forest.

Sun, sun, sun.

It had to be some kind of private event he'd organised. There would have been something about it online if it wasn't private. Maybe a party with a couple of bands on. Black metal in all probability. Unless he'd moved on from there?

I basically knew nothing about him.

Part-time student dropout, former black metal band member, hospital porter. Interested in old films. Self-assured and gorgeous as hell.

What was he up to out here?

A summer get-together of some sort. With bands and everyone he knew.

Well, I'd find out soon enough.

When I got off the train at Karlstad it was ten to three. Valdemar wasn't anywhere to be seen on the platform, so I went inside into the station building itself. He wasn't there either. But I was still a few minutes early, so there was no reason to panic.

I put my sunglasses on and went to the area out front.

What if he didn't come? What if it was all some kind of practical joke?

Maybe that was why he hadn't given me his number. I realised now how inconvenient it was not having it. What if he'd been delayed and I gave up on him and was gone by the time he turned up?

I was hungry too.

I went back inside and bought a green apple and a bottle of water.

Could I have missed him on the platform?

I'd pretty much gone straight inside. Maybe he'd been sitting on one of the benches and I hadn't seen him.

I bit into the apple and went back to the platform. The juice bubbled and ran from the corner of my mouth as my teeth cut through the crisp flesh.

A guy a bit further along stared at me. He had long, thick hair and a beard, a nose like a pig's snout.

He came towards me.

'Line?' he said.

'Yes,' I said, 'that's me.'

'Hi. I'm a friend of Valdemar's. He asked me to come and pick you up. I'm Kåre.'

The smile he flashed was gone again in an instant, as if I'd only imagined it.

His eyes were a bit bulgy, too.

'So Valdemar's not coming?'

'He's tied up all day. But he'll be really made up that you've come.'

'I see.'

'Shall we go?'

'I don't know. Where *is* Valdemar? Is he here in town?'

'I've got the car over here. It's a bit of a drive.'

'OK.'

He was parked right outside the station. The car was small and seedy-looking. He opened the boot for me, but made no move to help me with my case, so I put it in myself, on top of a couple of winter coats and some carrier bags, next to a crate of empties.

He slammed the boot shut and we got in. The passenger seat was covered by a woolly blanket.

'How far is it?'

'A good hour, hour and a half,' he said, and glanced into the wing mirror before flicking the indicator and pulling out.

'What's happening tonight, anyway? Is it a party?'

'Didn't Valdemar tell you?'

I shook my head.

'In that case, I won't either.'

He drove slowly through the set-down and parking area to the way out at the far end, then turned left onto the road itself, doubling back. Everywhere was green. Between the buildings I glimpsed a river.

'Looks like a nice town,' I said.

'What, Karlstad? Nah.'

Without taking his eyes off the road he plucked a pair of sunglasses from behind the visor and put them on. I soon found out he wasn't the type who was bothered by uncomfortable silence, and I got my phone out.

'You'll have to hand that in when we get there,' he said. 'In fact, you might as well put it away now.'

'My phone, you mean?'

He nodded.

'What for?'

The thought struck me they could be terrorists who wanted to avoid being traced.

Why would I think that?

It was ridiculous.

'You'll understand soon enough,' he said.

'OK,' I said. 'I just need to check something first, if it's all right with you?'

'Sure.'

I'd received a text from Thomas without having noticed. *Can you call me, preferably as soon as possible?* he'd written. *Can't just now, will do soon*, I typed back. I DM'd Josefine, Klara and Julie to say I'd got to Oslo all right, before putting the phone to sleep and slipping it into the pocket of my shorts.

We hadn't got far out of town before we were surrounded by forest. Then farmland, forest again, farmland, forest, farmland; a lake, more forest. Kåre had rolled his window down and was driving with his elbow resting on the sill, his right hand draped loosely over the steering wheel. His hair shuddered in the wind, though he sat like a statue. Behind his dark glasses, his gaze seemed to be fixed firmly on the road ahead, without so much as a glance in my direction.

Was he being rude on purpose or was he just an airhead?

Airhead, I decided. Whatever, I got nothing from him.

'So how long have you known Valdemar?'

He gave a shrug.

'Since primary school.'

'That long? You'll know him well, then!'

'Oh yes.'

'What was he like as a kid?'

'Same as now, really. Only smaller.'

He was pleased with the joke, but at the same time tried to stifle his laughter somehow with his tongue, thereby emitting a series of little sniggers instead. Tss, tss, tss!

I wondered what Valdemar saw in him.

Still, if they'd been friends since they were kids, I didn't suppose it was that odd.

We followed the shore of a lake for some time then cut into forest again before coming to a small hub of shops and services where Kåre turned in to fill up at a petrol station. As he stood at the pump I went inside and bought a chicken wrap with a tangy dressing. It didn't occur to me until I came back out that I should have asked him if there was anything he wanted. After all, he was Valdemar's friend.

He shook his head at the suggestion, hung the nozzle or whatever it was called back in place, stepped past me and went inside. When he returned it was with a couple of bread rolls in a bag in one hand and a bottle of Coke in the other.

'Ready?' he said.

He devoured the rolls within the space of a few minutes, guzzled some mouthfuls of cola and left white gluten submarines floating in it when he was finished. He was just gross.

After that the roads we took grew more and more narrow, the houses and farms even more scattered, until sometime later we turned off onto a gravel track that led us through the forest, low-hanging branches dabbing at the roof while rays of sunlight stabbed through the trees.

'I'm guessing we'll be there soon?' I said.

'Uh-huh,' he said.

We emerged from the trees a few moments later. A cornfield stretched away a few hundred metres to the right, towards some tree-covered ridges. The road dipped between the field and the forest, and as we followed its bend a farm came into view up ahead.

'Is this it?'

'I hope so,' he said. 'Seeing as there's no more road. Tss, tss, tss!'

The farm buildings were arranged in a horseshoe and the track came to an end right in the middle. Some cars were parked there, and some more were lined up along the side of the track, which was so narrow we couldn't get past them. Kåre pulled in.

The air outside was warm and filled with forest smells. I glanced towards the main house, half expecting Valdemar to come out and greet me, but there didn't seem to be anyone around.

Kåre opened the boot for me and I took out my case, released the handle and made my way along the dusty track where the grass stood yellow between the ruts.

'Valdemar's going to be busy for a couple of hours yet,' said Kåre. 'He'll see you afterwards, though.'

'After what?'

'Everything comes to she who waits,' he said cryptically and smiled.

The farmhouse in front of us was big and neglected. The rendering had come away in big chunks and there was hardly any paint left on the woodwork. As we entered the horseshoe he indicated with his hand one of the adjacent buildings. The double doors, of gappy wooden planks, were held together by a hook.

'You'll be sleeping in the loft,' Kåre said.

'Where's everyone else?'

'How do you mean?'

'The people who own those cars, for example. And Valdemar.'

Again, he shrugged.

'Out, I suppose,' he said as he pulled the doors apart. Some light filtered through a dirty window onto the cement floor, more had found its way through the cracks in the timber walls. A wooden cart, the sort that was meant to be pulled by a horse, stood silently alongside a rusting VW Beetle. Tools and junk lay everywhere.

Something bleated.

'What was that?' I said. 'Are there sheep here?'

'Yes, but they're out in their summer pasture. That was a goat you heard. They're in there.'

He gestured with a nod towards a wall. The goat bleated again.

'We've got hens as well. And two cats. Anyway, come with me. The stairs are over in the corner. I'll go first, there's a hatch you need to open.'

It was more a ladder than a staircase. Not wanting his arse in my face, I waited until he'd gone all the way up. It was a bit of a struggle, but after a few moments I was able to manhandle my case up onto the floor of the loft above, before following on through the hatch myself.

'Yours is the back room,' Kåre said as I straightened up beside him and turned my eyes to where he was indicating. The whole loft was divided up into partitioned rooms on either side of a narrow passage.

'OK,' I said. 'And where's Valdemar sleeping?'

'He's in the main house.'

My eyes prickled. I closed them, then opened them wide and blinked a few times as if exercising the muscles. I wasn't about to start crying like a little girl.

'OK,' I said again. 'So what do I do now?'

'Get settled in? Unpack, have a rest?'

'I'm a bit hungry again, actually.'

'There's some food in the kitchen in the main house. Only don't make a mess in there.'

'I won't. Oh, and thanks for picking me up.'

He smiled and held out his hand, palm upwards. I looked at him, puzzled.

'Your phone,' he said.

'You are joking, I hope.'

'All phones to be handed in on arrival. You'll get it back when you leave.'

'Why?'

'It's the law.'

'The law?'

'I'm afraid so.'

I handed him the phone, he winked at me and climbed back down the ladder. I stepped through the passage, my case trundling behind me, and opened the door of the room he'd said was mine. There was a narrow bed, a small table with a lamp on it, a stupid little rug the size of a postage stamp on the floor. That was it. Not even a little window.

Was I supposed to sit here in this bloody henhouse and wait for him? After travelling all night and all day?

Not this girl.

I put my case down flat on the bed, opened it and took out a white T-shirt and a clean pair of knickers, my make-up bag, toothbrush and toothpaste, closed it again and went back out. Crossing the yard in front of the house I noticed that three of the cars parked there were German, two were Swedish.

The main house had two front doors, one with a glass pane that looked like the proper entrance, and so I went up the steps to that one and knocked.

No one came, and I opened it myself. The hallway was untidy. Some old clothes lay heaped in a corner, shoes were piled up in another. As if someone had simply lumped together every item they could find.

'Hello?' I called out.

No answer.

A door on the right led off into the kitchen. It was even messier than ours when it was at its worst. But the mess here was recent, not like that in the hall, which looked like it had been there for years.

To the left was a bathroom with a yellowed old bath and a sink with stains around the plughole and hardened toothpaste stuck to the sides. It was horrible. What the toilet would be like I had no idea, and no desire to find out either. I locked the door, undressed and climbed into the bath, crouching with the shower head in my hand to wash myself as best I could. Only when I'd turned the water off and stood up dripping wet did I realise I hadn't brought a towel.

There was a small hand towel beside the sink. Only God knows where it had been and how long it had hung there.

The better option was just to get dressed and dry off in the sun outside.

I was still hungry, but had gone off the whole idea of using the kitchen, so I went back out to have a look round instead.

The buildings were only slightly apart. Behind them was a big, overgrown garden where five tents had been pitched. Beyond the garden, at the fringe of the woods, stood an enormous, rather dilapidated barn.

It had to be some kind of summer bash he'd organised here. With people he knew from Germany, Sweden and Norway.

If they'd all gone somewhere, then he was probably with them. It stood to reason he couldn't come and meet me if he was the organiser.

Maybe they'd gone swimming in some forest pool.

He wouldn't have asked me to come if he didn't want me to be here. And he wouldn't want me to be here unless he was interested in me.

I went over and looked inside one of the tents. A pair of rucksacks, sleeping bags, a few items of clothing, a couple of books. There was a crate of beer too, and what looked a cooler bag beside it. Two or three bottles of vodka. Camping chairs and a camping table out front.

Just then a figure emerged from the trees behind the barn. Several more followed. Within moments perhaps twenty people were coming across in the direction of the tents. As they approached, I saw that many seemed to be wearing rather elaborate clothing. Some were sporting black hats, many wore long, loosely fitting smocks, some had waistcoats, some had braces to hold up their trousers. One or two were in leather coats, despite the heat. Some had ordinary jeans, but the trousers many seemed to be wearing looked like they'd been handed down from their great-grandparents at least, thickly woven, dark and shapeless. The men were long-haired and bearded. Most looked to be in their twenties, a few were older. There weren't many girls. I couldn't see Valdemar among them.

I felt uncomfortable. It was strange to be found standing here. But it would be stranger to walk away.

One or two looked at me quizzically as they came through the garden, but no one said anything, they just dispersed. Some went inside the tents, others sat down in the grass outside, others still carried on towards the main house.

A girl in a white dress met my gaze, peeled away from the others and came over.

'Are you looking for someone?' she said in English, smiling warmly. Her fair hair was long and fine, her earrings star-shaped.

'Yes, do you know where Valdemar is?'

'He's in the house getting ready. I haven't seen him all day. Have you just arrived?'

'Yes.'

'Why don't you hang out with us? Have a beer or some wine?'

'That's really kind of you. But I think I need to rest.'

'You do that, then. It'll be such a great night. See you later!'

'Yes, see you later,' I said, and went towards my loft. The windows of the main house were unlit and behind them I detected no movement. In the bright sunshine, the gravel gleamed white through the weeds. A goat bleated. I went through to look at them. They were standing rather close together in the dimness. They seemed to have plenty of hay, and a trough full of water. But they shouldn't have been inside at this time of year.

I went closer and patted one who stretched his head towards me thinking no doubt I was bringing him something good. The others showed annoyance, tossed their heads, stamped and shuffled as if building up to charge me down. Their smell was rank, but I liked it.

When I emerged into the sunshine again, the door of the main house opened and a bald, bare-chested guy wearing army shorts came out. He was lean and sinewy and had a bottle of water in one hand. With his deep-set eyes and protruding jaw, it occurred to me that it wasn't hard to imagine what his skull would look like after he was dead. I looked down so as to avoid his gaze and he walked past without saying anything. It looked like he was heading for the garden.

I lifted the hook off the side building's ramshackle double door and climbed up to my henhouse, lay down on the bed and stared up at the ceiling feeling an urge to share all this with someone. Klara or Josefine or Julie, or even Thomas. Being on my own here without being able to talk to anyone about it was almost unbearable.

If only I had my phone, I'd have no problem at all killing a couple of hours in my room.

It was a joke. Was it because they wanted to dedicate their focus to nature? Was that what it was all about? I could understand that, but it didn't mean they had to keep people's phones from them.

I heard footsteps on the ladder, then in the passage, voices speaking another language. It wasn't German. Dutch, maybe? Then, for a few minutes, their conversation on the other side of the partition wall before everything went quiet again.

I sat up and opened my case, rummaged through my clothes for something that looked a bit more like what the others were wearing. I could forget all about the black Adidas tracksuit bottoms which I loved and had planned on wearing. My denim skirt likewise.

Maybe I could borrow a dress off the fine-haired girl?

Ha ha.

I lay back down again and felt like crying.

But there was no reason. Was I supposed to break down just because I didn't fit in? Maybe they were the misfits, not me.

What was the worst that could happen?

That I'd end up sitting on my own all night. And that Valdemar wasn't interested any more.

If he was going to be that stupid, he wouldn't be worth having anyway.

I stood up, put my Adidas on along with a tight black top, took the little mirror from my sponge bag, sat down on the edge of the bed and made myself up. As soon as I was done I went out, round the back of the house to the garden. The shadows were long now, the air was warm and still. The field stretched away like a golden pond. People were dotted around the grass in little groups and I looked for the girl with the fine hair.

She caught sight of me and waved, and I went over.

'Do you still have some of that wine?' I said as I sat down.

'Of course!' she said, leaned over, poured some into a paper cup and handed it to me.

'So, what's your name?' she said.

'Line. And yours?'

'Hermine.'

'That's a rhyme,' I said. 'Line and Hermine.'

She laughed.

'I like your . . .' I said, but couldn't remember the English word and instead put my finger to my ear and wiggled the lobe.

'Oh, thanks,' she said. 'Yes, they're nice, aren't they?'

The guy next to her, in baggy dark blue jeans that were rolled up to halfway below the knee, a white smock-like shirt and black braces, turned his bearded face towards us.

'Gerhard, this is Line. Line, Gerhard.'

'Nice to meet you,' he said. 'You're Valdemar's girl, right?'

Immediately, I blushed. Was that what he'd told people?

I was about to say I wasn't sure, but realised how stupid it would sound, so instead I smiled and bashfully gave a little shake of my head.

A group came down from the house carrying firewood logs and kindling. A guy followed, trundling a heavy-looking wheelbarrow. It was full of rocks that he tipped into the middle of the grass where they were then arranged in a circle inside which the others prepared a fire.

'Where are you from anyway?' I said, putting down my cup and hoping they would notice it was already empty.

'Düsseldorf,' the girl said. 'And Gerhard is from Köln.'

She filled up my cup once more and handed it to me.

'That's a long way to come for a party,' I said. 'You must be very good friends of Valdemar.'

'Oh, but I've never met him.'

'Really?'

Transluscent flames flickered now from the fire. I turned my head and saw the sun hanging low over the treetops in the distance. I became aware of the hum of voices all around, rising, falling, now here, now there. Someone laughed and some others were clearly encouraged by it, for immediately their voices grew louder and more enthusiastic, as if lifted by a wave.

'I've been exchanging letters with him on and off for a couple of years,' said Gerhard. 'But I've never met him either.'

'What's he like?' said Hermine.

'What can I say? He's great,' I said.

'But you're in love with him, so you're not exactly reliable!'

I blushed again.

'Does he play his new songs for you?' said Gerhard.

I shook my head and looked away at the fire.

'Not really.'

They exchanged glances and after that they stopped asking about him. I knew some couples were like that, totally in tune with each other. A glance was enough.

'Do you know many of the other people here?' I said after a lull in which I realised that the two generous cups of wine I'd already drunk had made me tipsy.

'No one when we arrived,' Hermine said. 'But we've got to know quite a few today.'

'Are they all Germans?'

'No, they're from all over the place. Some from Belgium, some from the Netherlands. One from Spain.'

'And these guys are from England,' said Gerhard, indicating with a nod the tent next to theirs where two not very tall men in shorts sat smoking and gazing about from the vantage point of a pair of camping chairs.

'So what's going to happen tonight?' I said.

Hermine and Gerhard looked at me abruptly and in unison.

'Tonight?' Gerhard repeated.

'Well, Domen are playing. But you knew that?' said Hermine.

'Yes. Yes, of course,' I said. 'I meant before that.'

'Nothing, I guess. We're all just waiting.'

'Drinking and waiting,' Gerhard added.

I felt so stupid, so completely in the dark.

He probably wanted to surprise me. Well, he'd done that already.

I felt a sudden groundswell of pride. People had come from all over Europe to see him and his band. But it was me he wanted.

They realised how little I knew, surely? What did that make me in their eyes? An unsophisticated girl who didn't have a clue.

It wouldn't do.

'I've only met Valdemar once or twice myself, actually,' I said. 'But then he invited me here. I haven't even heard of his band, to be honest. What did you say they were called? Domen?'

'I thought as much,' Hermine said with a grin.

'Domen, that's right,' said Gerhard. 'You have something to look forward to, I can tell you. They don't record their songs, so you won't know them unless you do. They've never released an album and they only play live on occasions like this.'

'But why?'

'You should really ask Valdemar about that. But he hates commercialism in any form, and he has this idea about nearness and being present that is very important to him.'

The air in the valley was quite still and the flames of the campfire hardly wavered. The sun was now half hidden behind the trees.

'Do you want some more?' said Hermine, and her eyes were kind.

'Yes, please,' I said. 'If you've enough, that is?'

'I'm afraid we've emptied it,' said Gerhard. 'But we do have a bottle of gin somewhere.'

He got up and went inside the tent. Just then, the air became filled with a deep drone of sound. People around us immediately whooped and applauded.

'That's them!' said Hermine. 'Gerhard, they're on!'

Within seconds everyone was on their feet and on their way towards the barn. Gerhard emerged clutching a bottle. The drone, dark and hypnotic, made me tremble.

'Wow!' he said, dashing gin into our three cups, then handing me mine.

'Let's go,' Hermine said.

'No need to rush,' said Gerhard. 'We've plenty of time. Here, have some tonic in that.'

We raised our cups to each other. Gerhard immediately drained his and impulsively tossed it over his shoulder. The garden around us had emptied.

'Yeah!' Gerhard shouted. 'Yeah! Yeah! Yeah!'

I half expected him to beat his chest like a gorilla.

Hermine smiled and curled her arm around him. She winked at me as we made our way to the barn. People were still waiting to get in. As we came closer I saw why: Kåre was standing at the door searching everyone who came in. Patting them down, running his hand inside their waistbands.

'What are you looking for?' I asked him when it was my turn. 'Did you think I brought my gun with me?'

'Phones and recording equipment,' he said.

The space inside the barn seemed vast. At the far end was the stage. A torch burned on either side of it, glowing through the dim light. People had gathered at the front; the rear, where as yet I stood inside the entrance waiting for Gerhard and Hermine to come through, was empty.

The noise was almost unbearably loud.

Someone put a hand on my shoulder. I spun round and looked into the smiling face of Gerhard.

'Take this,' he said, holding out a hand. A small tablet lay in his palm.

'What is it?'

'Something that will expand your mind.'

I shook my head.

'Are you sure? It's not dangerous or anything.'

'I'm sure.'

He smiled and offered me the gin bottle instead. I took a big, eye-watering swig before handing it back and then went with the two of them towards the stage.

The audience was small, perhaps forty in all. There was an excitement, people were trying to make themselves heard above the noise; someone whistled loudly and it cut through the air; someone else shouted, DOMEN!

The drone stopped suddenly. A white-clad, barefoot man wearing a goat's mask entered the stage. The whole place broke into wild cheers. It was Valdemar. He was followed by four others, they too wearing animal masks. Valdemar gripped the mic stand, facing us off as the musicians took their positions and prepared themselves. Although he stood quite still, all attention was as if drawn towards him. It wasn't the mask, it was his presence. There was something aggressive about him, and something utterly supreme.

He glanced around at the others before turning back to face the audience.

'"And Long Was I Dead",' he announced.

With that, the band detonated into a cacophony of the most incredible noise. Valdemar craned forward, screaming and screaming. It was spine-chilling, for it was as if his voice had suddenly taken on a life of its own, as if something now had stirred within the noise. The mask made it all the more compelling. Suddenly, it was impossible to connect anything at all of what was happening with Valdemar, the boy I knew no longer existed, his place had been taken by this screaming goat-man, and the goat-man's screams too transmuted and became something other and more, something savage, mighty and brutal.

Gradually the music began to alter shape and the boundless noise occasionally and briefly stopped, and this would repeat itself, becoming a rhythm that occurred through swathes of sound, drawn out through lengthy sections, or else descending in sharp, repetitive pinpoint strikes, each musician as if immersed in his own pandemonium, and then, fleetingly, they would come together, elements of some grander system, now meeting, only a moment later to depart from each other once more. Valdemar stopped screaming, he stood with his hand on the mic stand, rocking his head from side to side, and I followed suit, it was impossible not to. The music powered on like some great and inevitable wave, and all I wanted was for it to go on and on.

'Oh my fucking God!' Gerhard yelled into my ear.

I couldn't take my eyes off Valdemar. His body followed the music with movements that were both sparing and without pretension, he belonged to the rhythm, he belonged to everything, and when he gripped the mic with both hands and began to sing, angling forward, swaying, my own body quivered in sudden transports of rapture.

I was the cockerel that crowed in the ground
I was the soul in the machine
I gave away an eye, I gave away a life
And long was I dead
Yes, long was I dead

I was the man on the fell
I saw the world and all that were in it
I saw the living
And the dead piling up

He removed the mic and spun round with it in his hand, standing with his back to us as the band played on. In the background, the drone returned. It was like a wall of darkness. He bowed his head. Behind them an image was projected. A forest in twilight. From one of the trees a human figure hung. A wind was blowing, the trees bent against it, the hanging body dangled and swayed. Still with his back to us, Valdemar again began to sing.

I was the man in the tree
I journeyed far and wide
I gave away an eye, I gave away a life
And long was I dead
Yes, long was I dead

The image faded away. The band thudded out its noise as Valdemar gripped a guitar and strapped it on. When again he turned and began to play, his chords were long, sweeping, emphatic crashes that reverberated above the wild, rhythmic machine that pounded and pounded. Not a single person in the audience stood still, all were in throbbing insistent motion, and when the band brought the song to an end perhaps five minutes later, as abruptly as if they had halted at a precipice, a murmur of disappointment at first went up, displaced then by a wave of ecstasy, wild applause, whooping and whistling.

Valdemar divested himself of the guitar as the sound of wind rushing through a forest filled the barn. He crouched and sat on his haunches. Though he again had his back to us, it was impossible to take your eyes off him. He was magical.

A folk-like theme was slowly building. Valdemar raised the mic to his mouth and began to sing.

Come cow, come cow
Come goat, come sheep
Come hawk, come eagle
Come twain worms

Come water and wind
Come forest and sea
Come suns, come stars
Come blood in whispers
Come twain worms

He drew himself up to his full height. A fuzzy guitar laden with distortion came heavily, slowly in, then drums, then bass, quite as heavy, and full of sway. In the background, a whimpering was heard, issuing rhythmically, fitfully, and some seconds passed before I realised it was coming from Valdemar and not a computer. Other sounds then swelled forth, and these *were* computer-generated. Some were as if torments of wind, others airier, more ethereal. These sounds descended then, each as if finding its designated place in the rhythm, and soon the whole piece came together as one, as compelling in every respect as the first song, though the tempo was slower.

Valdemar slipped the mic back into the stand and threw his arms spastically in the air.

Come glowing earth
Come red blood
Come twain worms

He lowered his arms and stood motionless as the music crashed down around him. When it subsided, only the drone remained, hanging in the air, and he dropped to his knees there on the stage, the goat's mask on his head, the mic again clasped between his palms.

Come mother
Come father
Come sister
Come brother

Silence settled. Valdemar stood up, turning his back to us once again. With tears running down my cheeks I cried out with the others. Hermine leaned in close to me, her hand against my back.

'This is fucking amazing! Do you understand what he's singing?'

I nodded.

'Please, you must translate for us later. I need to know every word!'

'I will,' I said, and looked around. For the first time since they started playing my eyes found something other than Valdemar. Everyone was so alike. Not necessarily in appearance, but the way they were dressed. It struck me that their clothes had something nineteenth century about them – the hats and waistcoats, interspersed with denim and leather. The young men like Gerhard with their beards, the girls with their long hair and dresses like Hermine. How exactly did they know Valdemar? When they lived so far away, in Germany?

'"Heart of Soil",' said Valdemar then. A simple, monotonous theme kicked in, the band pursuing it in unison, it was like a tethered beast trying to wrench free. On top came a choir of voices, rising, falling, rising, falling. Valdemar threw his head in time to the music. When an immense, expansive swell of strings then surged like a river, he angled forward to the mic, though did not pick it up; instead he stood with his hands behind his back and began to intone the words.

There lies a person asleep at the river
It is you
There goes a person in the town
It is you
A star falls upon the sky
It is you

You are none, you are all
Who once will fall
Your heart beats against the soil
You are filled with life's red might
You are none, you are all
Who once will fall

He stepped back. The band continued to play, wilder and wilder, and Valdemar began to dance, spastically, as if in the throes of some sickly seizure. In the background, an immeasurably deep sound began to build. As it grew in force, the band became more and more subdued until eventually they stopped playing altogether. The drone now filled the entire space, dark and mighty as the night. Valdemar craned again towards the mic.

The soil will have you
And the soil shall have you
The soil will have you
And the soil shall have you
You are none, you are all
Who once will fall

He straightened up and stood completely still. And then the dam broke, there was a crash of noise and suddenly he was holding a megaphone in his hand. He doubled up and roared at the floor like a beast, arching backwards then to direct his voice upwards into the rafters. The metallic distortion of the vocal was mesmerising. *Heart of soil, I've a heart of soil*, he roared, over and over, and the audience was again a heaving mass, the song went on and on, until abruptly it stopped and the band quite as abruptly left the stage. Valdemar remained. In utter silence. All eyes upon him. His hand drew the sign of the cross.

'Man is God,' he said.

And then he turned and walked off too.

In the aftermath, Gerhard started a chant: DOMEN! DOMEN!

'Please don't say it's over,' Hermine begged. 'Three songs? Come on! DOMEN!'

Kåre came scuttling to the front of the stage and lowered his head to the mic.

'That's all, folks. See you next time!'

The chants continued, though more and more sporadically now as people began to file out, and soon we were back sitting by the tent in the grass, the remains of the fire glowing in front of us in the darkness. I was electrified, I'd never seen anything like it before, nothing even came close. Everyone around me clearly felt the same way.

Gerhard poured some gin into three cups and handed me one.

'Have you heard the songs before?' I said.

He shook his head.

'I don't think anyone had until tonight.'

Someone replenished the fire with kindling and logs. A distant plane with blinking lights passed silently through the dim sky far above our heads.

'That was crazy,' Hermine said.

'What did I tell you? The best band in the world,' said Gerhard.

The flames rose. From the house, a figure emerged and came towards the garden. At first I thought it was Valdemar and my heart leapt, but then I recognised the loping gait of Kåre. He glanced around as if looking for someone. It didn't occur to me that it might be me, and so I made no effort to attract his attention. But it *was* me: wandering searchingly among the guests a minute later, he suddenly saw me and stopped in his tracks.

'Valdemar will see you now.'

'Me?' I said, and couldn't help but smile. Everything inside me lit up.

'You, yes,' he said wearily.

'Catch you later,' Hermine said with another wink, obviously having understood our exchange despite the language barrier.

I got to my feet and went after him towards the house. Of all the people who were gathered here, it was me he wanted to see. Of all the people in the whole world, it was me.

Outside the house, four torches were burning. The windows were dark. Above us shone the stars. It was a magical night, and as I followed Kåre up the steps and into the house I trembled with nervous excitement. We passed through the empty living room into a hall and went up the stairs.

A chatter of voices and laughter drifted towards us.

'It's the third door along,' Kåre said. 'Remember to knock.'

I gave him a smile by way of thanks. Without returning the gesture, he spun round and went back the way we'd come. He clearly didn't care for me. But he wasn't the one I wanted!

The first door was slightly ajar. There were some people inside. The voices we'd heard had been theirs. Probably the other band members.

I knocked on the third door.

'Yes?' came a voice.

'It's Line.'

After a few seconds, a key was turned in the lock and the door opened.

'Hi, Line,' he said, already on his way towards a sofa that stood pushed back against a wall, where he immediately flopped down and unfolded himself. He was still in his stage clothes, a white T-shirt soaked with sweat and a pair of baggy white cotton trousers that were cropped at the calf. His face was flushed and moist with perspiration.

Against another wall was a bed on which there was a rolled-up sleeping bag, on the floor in front of it an unzipped suitcase with the lid closed. Some books and papers were neatly piled on a table at the bedside. In the corner was a modest kitchen area with a small fridge.

'So, what did you make of it?' he said.

'It was amazing!' I said. 'Absolutely incredible!'

He smiled, then picked up the towel that lay beside him and pressed his face into it.

'Why didn't you tell me you were in a band? And such a brilliant one at that!'

He didn't answer. It was as if I hadn't said anything.

'Are you feeling all right in yourself, Line?'

I nodded.

'Then take a seat!' he said and indicated the armchair at the other side of the coffee table in front of the sofa.

I sat down in it and he stared at me in that very intense way of his.

'Do you know what dopamine is?'

I nodded and tried to keep my gaze fixed on his, but found I couldn't and looked down at my feet.

'What is it, then?'

'It's the brain's reward system. It's what makes you feel good.'

'Indeed. Do you know when it was discovered?'

'No idea,' I said, and laughed hesitantly.

'A Swede called Arvid Carlsson discovered it in the 1950s. *All* feelings of pleasure stem from dopamine being released in the brain.'

Without taking his eyes off me he sat up straight.

'Following Carlsson's discovery, two scientists by the names of Olds and Milner implanted electrodes into the brains of a number of rats. Those electrodes were implanted into the area of the brain known as the nucleus accumbens. You and I might call it the brain's pleasure centre. When the rats then pressed a lever, a stimulus was transmitted to the electrode and dopamine was released into the creature's brain. What happened then was that the rats, after discovering the connection, started pressing the lever almost endlessly, it was basically all they were interested in. They stopped eating. They stopped drinking. They stopped copulating. In fact, they stopped caring about everything else in the world other than the lever. Eventually they died of thirst. With a bowl of water next to them in their cage.'

'Is that true?'

'Yes. What do you make of it?'

I gave a shrug.

'I don't know.'

'They were feeling all right in themselves, wouldn't you say? They'd probably never had it so good. Theirs was an endlessly pleasurable existence.'

'But it wasn't genuine.'

'What is genuine?'

'What I mean is, they didn't *really* feel good in themselves, did they?'

'Oh? I think they did. They hadn't *really* ever had it so good. They were in rat heaven. Anyway, come with me! We can't sit here moping all night, can we?'

I followed him out. In the corridor he stopped at the room where the voices were coming from and pushed the door open. Four people were sat around a table. The bald guy I'd noticed before was there. He looked older than the others. Two had long hair, the third wore his short like Valdemar. The table was littered with bottles and ashtrays. A fat spliff exchanged hands as we stepped inside.

'Guys, say hello to Line,' said Valdemar. 'Line, say hello to Domen!'

Two of them lifted their hands and waved exaggeratedly, as if the gesture was purely ironic. The other two just threw me a glance and a smile.

'Come and join us when you're ready,' Valdemar said and stepped back out. He was already on his way down the stairs by the time I pulled the door to behind me and set off after him.

'They're a dozy lot,' he said once we were outside. 'But they know how to play.'

'How long have you been together?'

'Since year eight at school. Apart from Thorvald. He's the bald one. He joined three years ago.'

He seemed so much lighter and happier now, I thought. It made me feel happy too.

Pausing at the narrow passage that separated the main house from the adjacent building where my own room was, he looked at me and smiled, inviting me to go first. We went through to the garden and he took my hand.

'Are you OK with this?' he said. 'Holding my hand?'

'Yes, I'm OK!' I said, and laughed.

As we stepped into the garden, attention at once gusted towards us. Those who didn't look up at us straight away did so seconds later, prompted by those around them. Face upon face turned to us. Valdemar didn't appear to notice, or else he simply didn't care. Some looked away again, feigning disinterest, others said his name, pointed or raised a hand in greeting. Valdemar greeted them back, stopping now and then to exchange a few words: hey, it's been ages, how are you doing, *wie geht's*. He clasped the men by the hand, embraced the women. He didn't introduce me to anyone, I just stood there smiling. Everyone congratulated him on the amazing show. Valdemar was as confident as a king. There's more coming tomorrow, he told them, and at last he looked at me and with a nod indicated the fire: 'Shall we sit down over there?'

'Do you know everyone who's here?' I said after we sat down, Valdemar with his arms wrapped around his knees.

He shook his head.

'But the ones I don't know have some connection with those I do. So I trust them all.'

He glanced around, caught sight of Kåre and called him over.

'Would you fetch us some beers?'

'Sure,' said Kåre, and went off towards the house.

'So you liked it, then?' he said, turning his attention back to me.

'Oh yes! It was fantastic! You must really have rehearsed a lot.'

He laughed.

'Yes, we have. We play together nearly every day. Have done since we were at school together.'

'But . . .'

'But what?'

'Why is it all so secret?'

'It's not secret.'

'No one I know has heard of you.'

'Perhaps you just know the wrong people.'

'But you're so good! You could be really big if you wanted. I'm not joking.'

'What do you mean by big?'

'Well, it's hard to say exactly. But when you make music, don't you want as many people as possible to listen to it?'

'No. When you make music, you want the music to be as good as possible. What *you're* talking about is becoming famous. Selling as many records or being streamed as much as possible. It's incredible how powerful a notion that is. Nothing could be more subversive than black metal, but what happened? They sold themselves. Now they're playing for audiences of sixty thousand at festivals all over Europe and getting high on that.'

He fixed his gaze on me.

'Do you understand what I'm saying?'

'Yes.'

'Then we needn't talk about it any more. Have you got siblings?'

Just then I saw Gerhard and Hermine coming towards us. Valdemar's gaze followed my own.

'I just wanted to say hi,' said Gerhard, halting in front of us. 'I'm Gerhard.'

'Gerhard Rieber?'

'Yes.'

Valdemar got to his feet and shook his hand gleefully in both his. Gerhard introduced Hermine as his partner, and Valdemar gave her a hug.

'Sit here with us,' he said. 'This is Line, by the way.'

'We've already met,' said Hermine, smiling at me.

Valdemar and Gerhard started talking together in German.

'You don't understand German, do you?' Hermine said after a few moments.

'Not a word. I did French at school. Not that I know French either.'

'They're talking about a theory that Valdemar has. About the Three Realms. The first is the Realm of God, the second is the Realm of the Son, and the third is the Realm of the Spirit. That's the one we're living in now.'

She laughed hesitantly.

'According to our boyfriends, that is.'

I blushed and gave a little shake of my head to make her understand it wasn't the thing to say. I didn't want Valdemar to think I'd put it around that we were going out with each other.

But I could tell he hadn't heard.

Kåre came lumbering over with three bottles sticking up out of each hand.

'Thanks,' said Valdemar as he put them down in the grass beside us. 'Have you got a bottle opener as well?'

Kåre produced one straight away from his key chain. He prised the top off a bottle which he immediately handed to Valdemar, only for Valdemar to hand it to me while Kåre opened another.

'Have one yourself,' Valdemar said.

Kåre obliged and sat down beside us.

'I said you could have a beer, not that you could sit with us.'

'You're joking, right?'

'We're talking, as you can see. Catch you later, OK?'

'OK,' said Kåre and reluctantly got to his feet before trudging away towards the house with the bottle dangling from his hand.

Gerhard and Hermine exchanged glances before they too stood up.

'So nice to finally meet you,' said Gerhard, in English now.

'Let's speak again later,' said Valdemar, then swigged his beer and looked at me.

'Well, have you?'

'Have I what?' I said, unsure of what he meant. Gerhard and Hermine hadn't gone yet.

'Siblings.'

I gave Hermine a smile, and she took Gerhard by the hand as they made for their tent.

'I've got a brother whose name is Thomas,' I said.

'Older or younger?'

'Older.'

'What does he do?'

'Not much. He was a soldier with the UN for a while. Now he's thinking of joining the police.'

'Thinking of, you say?'

'Yes. I hope he does. At the moment he spends most of his time indoors playing computer games.'

Valdemar nodded, but did not pursue the matter, drawing his knees up to his chest and clasping his arms around them then sitting like that for a while, a bit girlishly in fact, and without speaking.

'What about you?' I said.

'Hm?'

'Have you got siblings?'

'No.'

I felt a strong urge to run my fingers through his short hair. To put my arm around him and let him rest his head against my chest.

I hadn't the courage to touch him. It was impossible to gauge how he would react.

Yet the feeling was enough. The feeling that he could rest his head against my chest and that I could hold him and be kind to him. I'd never felt anything like it before.

'Why does he do that, your brother? Spend his time indoors playing computer games.'

'I don't know. It's all he wants to do.'

'Is he depressed?'

'A bit, maybe. He probably suffers a bit from social anxiety too.'

'This goes back to what we were talking about before. Playing computer games pumps you full of dopamine. That should be a good thing. And yet he's not feeling good in himself, your brother?'

'I don't think so, no.'

'What's the opposite of dopamine?'

'I don't know.'

'Think! Dopamine is a pleasure substance. What's the opposite of pleasure?'

'Discomfort?'

'Yes. Or pain. What's best? Pleasure or pain?'

'I'd rather feel good in myself than bad, obviously.'

'But what does it mean to feel good in oneself? Isn't it having a meaningful life?'

'Yes.'

'Then isn't your brother's problem that his life isn't particularly meaningful? Don't you think it's the case that the less meaning he feels in his life, the greater his craving for dopamine? And that the more dopamine he gets, the less meaningful his life then becomes?'

'I hadn't thought of it like that before.'

'I think life is meaningful when we're present in it. We shouldn't flee from pain. We should step towards it. Accept it like the prodigal son.'

His eyes fixed me in their gaze, dark in the faint light.

'But maybe you don't know about the prodigal son?'

'No. Who was he?'

He turned his gaze to the flames without answering. For some time he simply sat there. I didn't know what to say to him and so I was silent too. The party had gathered momentum. The voices that surrounded us were more boisterous now and everyone's movements more exaggerated than before. Valdemar was no longer a part of it, I thought. Even though it was his party.

Hardly had the thought occurred to me than he got to his feet without a word and went over to a group outside one of the tents, crouched down and struck up a conversation. He was a magnet to them, all attention was immediately directed towards him, not just from the group he had joined, but from others too. One by one, people came sidling towards him. He drew himself upright, put his hand on the shoulder of one and laughed at something that had been said. There was a chinking together of bottles as people came up and congratulated him.

I could have gone over too, but I didn't want to be clingy and tag along. Something told me he wouldn't like it. Besides, he'd just stood up and left me without saying anything, with no suggestion that I should go with him.

I wasn't comfortable sitting on my own. If I called it a night, it might give him something to think about. While it wouldn't be much fun to go back to my room, I nonetheless got to my feet and made towards the side building, stopping though at one point and turning round to see if he was watching me. He would understand then, that it was because of him.

'Line!' a voice called out. It was Hermine, coming towards me. 'Are you off to bed?'

'Yes, I'm a bit tired. It was a long journey getting here.'

'Come and join us. We'll wake you up!'

Her face opened in a big smile and she pulled her long hair away from her eyes with a delicate movement of her hand.

'Thanks, but if you don't mind. I really need to get some sleep.'

She nodded, took my hand and smoothed my arm a couple of times, a bit like Mum would do, before turning and going back to the others. I'd hoped, of course, that it would be Valdemar calling out for me, wanting me to stay there with him, and so strong was that hope that I couldn't help but turn my head to look once more when I reached the barn where my room was. He was standing with the same people, his attention focused on a guy who was busy talking to him. It didn't look like he'd even noticed I was gone.

The loft lay in darkness. I didn't switch the light on, just stood there without moving until I could make out where the wall was and then follow the passage to my room with small, cautious steps. There was no lock on the door, so I didn't undress but bunched up the duvet and wrapped my arms and legs around it. For a while I listened to the sounds of the party outside. I didn't know what to believe or think any more. If only I'd been able to talk to some of my friends. Or at least chat with them online! I knew they'd be highly sceptical of Valdemar. The way he just left me to my own devices like that after his invitation had dragged me all the way to Sweden. But they hadn't seen him like I had. They hadn't seen him on that stage with his band. They wouldn't believe how absolutely brilliant he was, I'd have said. Absolutely incredible. But I wouldn't have told them how he treated his oldest friend. Nor that the first thing he did when he saw me was give me a lecture about dopamine. OK, I might have told them that. But then I'd have said it wasn't at all like it sounded, because with Valdemar everything was different. I knew they'd never understand me though, and for that same reason – because it sounded different from how it actually was.

He'd invited me and no one else to his room. He'd been pleased to see me. He'd taken my hand. Even asked if it was OK! And outside in the garden he'd sat down with me.

If I began with all that, there was nothing at all to be sceptical about. There was nothing wrong with him attending to his other guests. He had to, it was his party.

I shouldn't have left. I could have just stayed with Hermine and Gerhard and got to know some others too and just savoured watching him as he went about, and the thought that he was mine, instead of going off in a huff like that. What would he make of it? What did it look like to him? Maybe he'd think I was someone who couldn't hack it on my own and had to rely on others. The clingy girlfriend. Or someone needy who demanded attention the whole time and would sulk if none was forthcoming.

Could I go back out?

No, I couldn't muster what it would take.

I heard laughter and raucous voices from the yard outside, a door slamming somewhere over in the main house. The noise must have woken the goats, for they began to bleat. A moment later footsteps crunched on the gravel. This time it was the door downstairs that I heard, then the hatch being opened at the end of the passage. Someone switched the light on and it spilled through the cracks in the door.

'Line? Are you there?'

It was Valdemar.

I closed my eyes and lay as quiet as I could.

He knocked on my door. I said nothing. He opened it. I sensed him standing there in the doorway looking at me.

'Are you asleep?' he said softly. I didn't move. He sat down on the edge of the bed. He ran his fingers through my hair.

'Are you that exhausted?'

'Hi,' I said, opening my eyes to meet his gaze. 'I must have fallen asleep. What time is it?'

'It's not even midnight yet,' he said. 'But sleep, if you must.'

He made to get up. I propped myself on my elbows.

'No, it's all right,' I said. 'I'll come and join you. I'm really sorry. I was just so tired all of a sudden.'

He looked at me with a smile. It made me so happy I started to laugh.

'What's so funny?'

I shook my head.

'Nothing.'

'You're not laughing at me, are you?'

'No, of course not!'

'Are you sure? People don't just laugh for no reason.'

'I'm really glad you're here, I hope you know that.'

'OK,' he said.

He rose and ran his hand over his hair. I sat up and saw there was a small backpack at his feet.

'OK,' he said again. 'I thought I'd show you something.'

'Oh?'

'It's a bit of a walk. Are you up for it?'

'Yes.'

He put the backpack on and I followed him down the ladder and outside into the yard. The air was as warm and as still as before. Lights were on upstairs in the house and in the kitchen below where some people sat drinking around a table.

'We'll go this way,' said Valdemar, indicating the track where the cars were parked. After we'd walked a bit, I looked back and saw the moon suspended and almost full above the ridge of the hill on the other side of the field. It was big, bigger than usual. It shed a milky light on the landscape around us.

'Where are we going?' I said.

'Into the forest. There's a path over there.'

It was narrow and rather steep at first. I followed on behind him and had to exert myself to keep up. Soon the farm lay below us, the fire a small glow between the trees. He said nothing, but walking in single file made conversation unnatural.

'Is it far?' I said after some time.

'How old are you?' he said without turning.

I felt my spirits sink. Why was he annoyed?

'Just wondering.'

'We'll be there soon.'

The path dipped and after a while we emerged into the flat-bottomed valley of a stream and veered left onto a wider track. I kept feeling the urge to hold hands as we'd done earlier, but couldn't bring myself to act on it. And so we kept walking, now side by side, his eyes fixed firmly ahead as if he was oblivious to me being there, while I kept glancing at him. It was stupid, there was no reason why he should decide what we did or when. At the same time, I swooned whenever I looked at him, he was so close I could touch him!

We passed across an area of meadow, luminously open among the dark, dense trees. The track narrowed, and after we crossed a small wooden footbridge that led us over the stream, it again became little more than a path.

What was he thinking?

I had absoutely no idea. I knew nothing about him.

'Are your parents alive?' I heard myself say.

The trees stood thickly on either side of the path, which was only just wide enough for us to walk alongside each other, and when he turned to look at me his arm touched mine and my heart leapt.

'What? Why are you asking me that?'

'I hardly know anything about you. I don't even know your surname!'

He stopped and put his arms around me.

'I don't like my surname,' he said and without hesitation leaned forward and kissed me. His gorgeous dark eyes held mine for a moment as he withdrew and a smile appeared on his face.

'But I like you.'

'I like you too,' I said, and my heart was racing in my chest.

'We're lucky, then,' he said. 'It wouldn't be much fun out here if we didn't like each other.'

He started walking again. Before long my eyes picked out a gleam between the trees. A few minutes later we were standing by a pool, almost perfectly circular in shape. Apart from where the path emerged, crags, perhaps ten metres or so in height, rose up all around to enclose it, in some places tree-clad, in others bare.

'This is Odin's Pool,' said Valdemar.

'Is it what you wanted to show me?'

He nodded.

'Isn't it splendid?'

'Yes, very. Why do you call it Odin's Pool?'

'The Swedish name is Odenstjärn. Because it looks like an eye staring up into the sky. Odin's eye. He only had one, as you know. It used to be a holy place.'

'Not any more?'

'To me it is. Come on, there's a better vantage point than this.'

We followed a path along the edge and soon we were able to look down on the pool from above.

'How come it's so round?' I said. 'It's striking. It looks like it was drawn with a pair of compasses.'

'Because it's a crater lake, formed in the crater of a volcano.'

'Seriously?' I said, as if I was stupid.

He divested himself of his pack and sat down on an outcrop. I sat down beside him. He gazed out. I gazed out. I wanted to feel what he felt.

The water shimmered faintly in the shadows of its walls and the densely growing trees.

If what we were sitting on had once been a volcano, the lake was truly ancient. I wondered if that was what made it holy to him.

Or did he believe in Odin?

It really did look like an eye.

'Do you feel like swimming?' he said.

'What, now?'

'Yes. Now's the best time. Not a soul around.'

I hesitated and he looked at me scrutinisingly.

'Come on, give it a go.'

He laughed.

'We don't need to be naked, if that's what you're worried about. And I've brought towels.'

He patted his backpack.

'All right,' I said.

'Good!' he said, and jumped to his feet before climbing down to a ledge perhaps three metres above the surface. He turned his back slightly and pulled off his T-shirt. When he started unbuttoning his trousers I averted my gaze at first but then couldn't help looking. I didn't mind being seen in a bikini, so why was I so embarrassed at the thought of standing there in my underwear?

Now only in his underpants, Valdemar bent over and opened his backpack with one hand, his other clutching his clothes. He took out the towels and dropped the clothes into the pack. I saw how lean and wiry he was, his skin stretched over his spine, before I turned away and took my top off. The bra I was wearing was a bit see-through and so I held the top to my chest when turning back to face him. I didn't want him to see how small my boobs were either. I felt myself blush, but it was stupid, I couldn't exactly hide myself from him if we were going to be an item.

The second before his eyes met mine, it was as if he took all of me in. He smiled and looked down at the pool, then went to the edge.

'Are you coming?' he said, looking back at me.

I nodded.

'Promise?'

'Yes, of course. Are you going to dive in from there? Is it deep enough?'

'It's twenty-five metres deep here. See you down there!'

He took a step back, then lunged forward and launched himself into a dive, arms outstretched. He pierced the surface like a spear and vanished into the darkness. I put my top with my trousers and stepped up to the edge. A second later his head emerged, breaking the surface perhaps ten metres away.

'It's fantastic!' he shouted. 'Are you coming in?'

'I've changed my mind.'

'You can't!'

'Only joking!' I shouted back and at the same moment jumped, waving my legs a couple of times before hitting the water and plunging into the depths. Though I kept my eyes open, I couldn't see a thing. I let air out from my lungs as I sank. The water grew colder and colder. I became aware of every square centimetre of my skin. It was as if I didn't need eyes any more. I twisted my body and swam towards the surface, a faint taste of metal and soil in my mouth. I surfaced a few metres from the rocks and looked around for Valdemar.

'It's fantastic, isn't it?' he shouted from some distance away.

'Yes, it's brilliant!' I said, and began to swim towards him, only then to pull up and tread water, not knowing what I'd say or do when I got there.

I started to laugh.

'What are you laughing at?' he said.

'I don't know. I don't know, I'm just so exhilarated.'

He smiled, swam a few strokes and turned onto his back.

'Do you believe in God, Line?'

Oh no. What was I supposed to say to that?

I looked across at him as he lay there floating. I couldn't see if his eyes were open or closed. I didn't think for a minute that he himself believed in God. Wouldn't the best answer then be a no?

I tipped my head back and looked up at the tiny twinkling lights way up there in the darkness.

'*Do* you believe in God?' he said again.

'I don't know.'

'In that case you don't.'

'Maybe not, no. Do you?'

He spun onto his stomach and swam the few metres back to the rocks.

I followed him.

'I can't understand how you can be swimming in a forest under the stars and yet not believe in God. It's quite a mystery to me!'

He gripped the rock and hauled himself up.

'Give me your hand,' he said. I did so, and he pulled me up like I was a little girl. I noticed then that he had some kind of a star tattooed on his chest, just below the collarbone. It was quite a large tattoo, but not showy in any way.

Back on level ground he tossed me a towel. I pressed it to my face before starting to dry myself. He didn't dry himself at all, but pulled his T-shirt on and then ruffled a hand through his wet hair.

'So what do you believe in?' he said, plucking at his T-shirt here and there where it stuck to his skin. 'If you don't believe in God?'

'I don't know. Does a person have to believe in something?'

'Do you believe in this pool?'

'Yes, I do.'

'Do you believe in the trees?'

'Yes,' I said, leaning down to dry my lower legs.

'Do you believe you have a body?'

I gave a laugh and rubbed my hair with the towel.

'Of course.'

'Do you believe in the stars?'

'Yes, but you can't *not* believe in something that exists, can you?'

'So you believe in what exists, but not in what doesn't exist?'

'I suppose so.'

'Do you want to have children?'

Surprised by the question, I immediately straightened up, holding the towel against my body, aware suddenly that I was standing in my underwear.

'Why do you ask?'

'Do you?'

'Maybe. I don't know. I'm only nineteen.'

'The child you perhaps want doesn't yet exist. But you believe in it anyway?'

'That's different. It will exist, at some future time.'

'So you believe in what exists *and* in what will exist. But how do you know what will exist?'

'I don't know, how could I?'

'But you do believe in it.'

'Do I? I don't really see what you're getting at to be honest.'

He fixed his eyes on me.

'I'm just interested in knowing what you think. The way you see things.'

'I haven't really thought much about what I believe in.'

'I realise that.'

With a small flourish of annoyance, I turned away from him and put my trousers and top back on before wriggling my feet into my shoes.

'If you do decide to have children one day – would you have them with me?'

What?

I spun to face him.

'With *you*?' I said, as if to win time.

Then it occurred to me he was probably joking.

'This is a joke, right?'

'I wouldn't joke about something like that with you.'

'We've met each other twice!'

'I didn't say now. I said one day.'

My whole body warmed as he looked at me. It wasn't shame, but a close, encompassing warmth nonetheless.

'If you believe in us, that is,' he said. 'Do you?'

'Yes,' I said, 'I do,' then shook my head slowly. 'Even if you are mad, talking about kids!'

'Come on,' he said. He picked up his pack and in almost the same movement set off back the way we had come. I followed on behind. Once we got to the path I was able to walk beside him, casting little glances his way in order to gauge whether his silence was hostile or just silence. It was impossible to tell. I'd already become used to him retreating into himself. But not to the longing I felt, the waiting for him to open himself up again, I couldn't ever get used to that. It swelled in me as we went through the forest. I had so many questions. The most important one – whether we were going out with each other now, whether I belonged to Valdemar and Valdemar to me, whether we were together now as a couple – burned inside me. I couldn't ask him either, it would sound like I was still in junior school.

Children?

It was insane. But he'd said one day. That could be in ten years.

Would we be together ten years from now?

We began the gentle climb up the hill behind the farm. The moon was more distant now. I looked up at him after he moved ahead of me again to lead the way. I had no idea what would happen when we got back. What he wanted.

A fear ran through me. The next moment, it splintered exhilaratingly into a thousand tiny shards.

He turned and paused.

'What are you thinking?'

'Nothing.'

'You mean you're empty? I don't believe that. Tell me.'

'I was thinking about you,' I said. 'About us.'

He nodded and said no more. Below us I picked out the tents and the still-glowing fire. There didn't seem to be many people still around.

When we returned he went straight towards the door of the house. I didn't know whether I was meant to go with him – I'd been allocated my own room – and so I stopped.

'Aren't you coming in?' he said.

I followed him inside. Up the stairs, to the third door.

He dropped his pack on the floor and threw himself down on the sofa. As before, I sat in the armchair opposite.

'There are some bottles of wine in the kitchen bit over there,' he said. 'Do you want some?'

'Yes, please.'

He made no move to get up, and so I did.

'Are you having some?'

'Mm. The glasses are in the cupboard there.'

I didn't care that much for red wine, but now anything would do. There was a corkscrew beside the bottles and I opened one, poured two glasses and took them over.

'I'm impressed,' he said. 'I was wondering if you could.'

'I worked in a restaurant for a while.'

'When was that?'

'Year three of gymnas.'

He nodded and gulped a mouthful of wine.

'I need something stronger,' he said. 'Do you like vodka?'

'Yes.'

'I've got a couple of bottles in the freezer. Wait there a minute.'

He got up and left the room. I imagined the freezer would be in the cellar. It meant I had a minute or two to look around.

The pile of papers on the bedside table looked interesting and so I went over. They were piled so neatly that each sheet was perfectly aligned with the next, so I had to be careful. The top one was blank. The one underneath said:

DISTORTING THE FUTURE
Life in the commercial-industrial complex
by VALDEMAR STIANSEN

Stiansen! So that was his name!

I lifted the first few sheets from the top of the pile, revealing a page that was dense with text. The one underneath was the same. Had he written a book?

Maybe it was his master's thesis. Yes, that would be it.

I scanned a few lines. Although he didn't talk that way, the academic style didn't surprise me. He studied philosophy and was passionate about philosophical matters, and he was more than just bright.

I put the papers back exactly as before, sat down quietly on the edge of the bed and listened. No one was coming and so I leaned forward and lifted the lid of the suitcase on the floor. Neatly folded clothes. A laundry bag for his washing. He was conscientious, that much was obvious.

Carefully, I lifted a few items of clothing to see what brands he liked, but it was stuff I'd never heard of – Balenciaga, Auralee. It looked expensive. Who would have thought?

But what was that?

Tucked underneath his clothes was a small book. One of those bound notebooks, with Chinese lettering on the front.

I opened it.

It was a diary!

Or was it?

Hearing footsteps on the stairs, I hurriedly put it back, closed the lid of the suitcase again and darted to my chair. No sooner had I sat down than he came in with a bottle in his hand. Without a word he poured two glasses and handed me mine. He lit the fat candle on the coffee table, went back over to the door and switched the ceiling light off.

'Come and sit here,' he said.

I did so, meeting his dark, brooding eyes for a second before looking away.

'Have you been with a lot of men, Line?'

'No. Just one serious relationship, I suppose. Well . . . we were together nearly a year.'

'You're very beautiful.'

'So are you.'

He smiled.

'Not that I agree with you that I'm beautiful, though,' I added. 'But *you* are. That was what I meant.'

He swallowed a mouthful of vodka. I did the same, and shuddered involuntarily.

'Have you ever cut yourself?'

'Cut myself? What do you mean? On purpose?'

'Yes.'

'No, you must be mad. Why are you asking me that?'

'A lot of girls do. It gives them a sense of control, they say. Perhaps it's also to do with giving expression to inner pain. What do you think?'

'I've no idea. I don't know anyone who does that.'

'I'd quite like to do it to you.'

'What, cut me?' I said with an incredulous laugh. 'Isn't this getting a bit creepy?'

Valdemar didn't laugh. He sat holding his glass and stared at me.

'Why would you say that?' I said.

'Because it's something I want.'

'If you say it again, I'm leaving.'

'In that case I won't.'

Neither of us spoke for a moment. He drank some more.

'Pain can be good too, you know. It intensifies everything.'

'I'm not liking this,' I said, put my glass down on the table and stood up. 'I think I'll go back to my room for the night.'

Valdemar stood up too, and cautiously took my hands in his.

'I didn't mean to scare you,' he said. 'I'm sorry. I'm not sure quite how to behave with someone of your beauty. Can you forgive me?'

Uncertain as to what he was trying to do, I allowed myself to be steered back.

'I don't know what to make of this,' I said. 'Am I supposed to believe you?'

He put his arms around me.

'Believe the best will happen,' he said.

'I don't know you.'

'I think you do. We're soulmates. Can't you feel it?'

'Maybe.'

'And of course you agree with me about your being beautiful,' he whispered, then took hold of my top and began to pull it upwards. I reached my arms above my head like a child. He loosened the straps of my bra and undid the hooks, and after he'd removed it completely I wanted only to press myself against him, but then he took hold of my hands. He lowered his head and kissed a nipple. I realised he didn't want me to do anything, and so I stood with my arms at my sides as he knelt in front of me. When he started to take off my tracksuit bottoms, I stroked his hair. A toss of his head told me to stop, and I closed my eyes as he pressed his mouth against the fabric of my knickers. Then he stood up and took my hands again and led me to the bed. I felt a rush of warmth in my loins. I lay back and looked for his gaze without finding it. He pulled off my knickers and then I felt him against me, the tip of his tongue in the wetness between my wide-open labia. Tiny shivers of excitement ran through my whole body. His pleasuring was indescribable. I wanted more. I wanted him. I pressed his head down between my thighs. 'You're so good,' I gasped. 'You're so good. I want you. I want you inside me.'

Again he took my hands.

'The first time is special, it won't ever come round again,' he said softly.

'I want you inside me,' I whispered.

He stood up and took his clothes off. I closed my eyes. Only then did I think about contraception. I'd have to ask if he had a condom. But when I looked again he was already coming to me and I couldn't ask, wouldn't ask, all I wanted was to have him.

He placed his hands either side of me, propping himself on his arms while looking into my eyes, and then, slowly, he slid into me. At first, it was as if I felt him only as something external that was not a part of me, but then I looked into his eyes and at once the darkness there became the darkness here, filling me in long, heavy waves. It was ecstasy, and I closed my eyes completely.

Then he stopped and withdrew.

'Wait a second,' he said.

So he did have condoms. It was probably for the best.

'Hurry,' I said.

He picked his trousers up off the floor and took something out of the pocket. I closed my eyes again and arched with pleasure, I didn't want to watch him fumbling with the packet, it would be such an awkward moment.

'Don't be frightened now,' he said as he returned to the bed.

'What do you mean?' I said.

'I want to be able to really feel us.'

He held up a knife.

'No!' I said, and sat bolt upright. 'No way! Are you mad?'

He pressed the blade to his chest and slit the surface of his skin in a long incision.

'What are you doing!'

Blood began to ooze from the cut and he smoothed his hand through it while staring at me. Tears came to my eyes.

'Lie down,' he said.

I shook my head, but he forced me, gripped my wrists in one hand and pushed my arms back over my head, holding them there as he got on top of me.

'Valdemar, what are you doing! Don't, please!'

He entered me again. Again, tears welled in my eyes.

'Nothing has changed,' he whispered. 'You want me, and I want you. I'll never hurt you.'

I screwed my eyes together as I felt the blade on the skin above my chest. And then a stinging pain cut through my darkness. His lips pressed against the incision. I lay stiffly as he emptied himself into me. He curled his arms around me and held me tightly. His hands ran through my hair, his lips kissed my mouth, the hollow of my throat. He remained on top of me, still and quiet. I extricated myself and found the floor, looked around for my knickers, located them, put them on.

'Are you leaving?' he said.

I didn't answer him, but pulled on my top.

He lay watching me.

'You don't have to take it like that,' he said. 'There's no danger.'

I got into my tracksuit bottoms, snatched up my bra, flung the door open and left the room. Going down the stairs I realised I'd forgotten my shoes, but I couldn't go back and instead just carried on out through the front door. Everything was quiet outside, there wasn't a soul to be seen. Barefoot, I scurried to the adjacent building, climbed the ladder to my stupid little cubbyhole.

The cut was still bleeding when again I took off my top. I picked up one of my clean T-shirts and dabbed at the blood. I should have washed the wound, but I wasn't going to set foot in that house again, so I'd just have to leave it as it was.

I sobbed and lay down on the bed with the T-shirt held to my chest.

I had to get away. But how? I needed someone to help me. Someone would have to give me a lift. Did Hermine and Gerhard have a car? If they did, I could wake them up in the morning and ask if they could drive me to the station.

I was certain they would.

Oh, why had he done such a thing?

Everything had been so good.

And then he had to go and be a madman.

Julie had spotted it straight away. She'd seen right through him.

But I hadn't. I hadn't detected a thing.

A gullible little idiot, that was me.

I heard the door open downstairs. A moment later someone came up the ladder. Footsteps approached.

'Line?' he said softly.

'Go away!' I said, not caring if anyone heard. 'I never want to see you again!'

He opened the door.

'Didn't you hear what I said?'

'Shh,' he said. 'I want to talk to you, that's all.'

'Well, I don't want to talk to you.'

He sat down on the floor with his back against the wall. There was nothing I could do, I couldn't force him out. I was a prisoner.

I turned away from him and closed my eyes.

'Line,' he said. 'I shouldn't have done what I did. I hardly know you. But it feels like we were meant for each other. You and me. I don't know how you feel about it, but that's how I feel. Right from the first moment I saw you at Palasset, in fact. Only now I've ruined everything and I feel really bad about it. I'm sure you think there's something wrong with me. Perhaps you're afraid of me. But really, you've no need to be, I promise. I wouldn't hurt a fly. And I'm not perverse either. It's not like I get a kick out of hurting others. I'm not a psychopath. But pain is a part of life, and what it does is intensify the moment, it blots everything else out. Girls who cut themselves do so because they want to be in control of something. What I thought was that we could do the opposite – let something go, let it be free. And it was so lovely with you. *You* are so lovely. Pain makes that stronger. Do you understand what I mean? Everything else in the world is about removing pain. Eventually we become anaesthetised, everything becomes so pleasant. That's when we fade away from life. As if we're no longer present in ourselves or in the world. What's the point of living then? Line? What's the point of living then?'

My face was buried in the pillow and my eyes were closed. His words wormed their way into the hardness I felt and made everything soft. But I wanted it to remain hard and closed, not ache with pleasure that came only of hurt.

I heard him get to his feet, felt his hand smooth my spine, caress my shoulders.

'I understand if you don't want to stay here any longer,' he said. 'I can get Kåre to drive you to the station first thing. Is that what you want?'

I started to cry, but didn't want him to see me like that, so I said nothing, just lay there quietly.

'Is that what you want, Line?'

'Yes,' I sobbed.

'OK. That's what we'll do, then.'

He left the room and closed the door behind him.

I woke up a few hours later when someone knocked. It was Kåre.

'Are you ready?' he said.

'Just give me a few minutes,' I said.

I sat up, and only then did it come back to me, the night before, a barrage of hideous emotion. But Kåre was here. It meant I'd soon be away. That I never needed to have anything to do with Valdemar ever again.

I put my denim shorts on and a white top, then looked around for my shoes only to remember I'd left them in Valdemar's room. No way was I going to get them. I'd just have to leave them were they were, and strapped into my sandals instead.

Outside in the passage, Kåre was standing waiting in a pair of bright blue bathing shorts and a checked shirt, turning the car key in his hand, sunglasses hiding his eyes.

'I'll drive you to Kongsvinger, if you like,' he said.'

'Would you?' I said, and followed him to the ladder.

'Yes. It suits your train times better too. There's one leaving just before half twelve. You should be home by ten. How does that sound?'

'Good,' I said.

He went down the ladder without offering to give me a hand with my case. I put it down on the floor, descended halfway, then reached up and took it by the handle.

Outside, the weather was just as hot and still as the day before. The gravel glaring in the bright sunshine.

'Where's Valdemar?' I said as casually as I could.

'Asleep.'

I nodded, extended the handle of my case and pulled it along behind me to the car. The thought of sitting in the passenger seat next to him made me remember my phone.

'My phone,' I said.

'Got it here,' he said.

'Can I have it then, please?'

'Not yet. Not until we're off the property.'

'You're joking, aren't you?'

He didn't answer, just opened the car door. I put my case on the back seat this time and got in. He reversed onto the field so he could turn round and soon we were rattling back down the track with dust clouding in our wake. When we got to the trees he handed me my phone. I'd received forty-something messages. I started reading and replying. First to Thomas, who appeared to have something important he wanted to talk to me about. *Phone's been dead. In a car right now. Call you in a couple of hours*, I typed. Fortunately, Kåre was neither talkative nor curious, but sat silently as he drove, no doubt glad to be getting rid of me. I wasn't curious about anything either as I'd been on the way here. All I wanted was to get away and go home.

A couple of hours later he pulled up in front of the station, said goodbye as I got out, and drove off again as I went inside to buy my tickets. I ate a salad at a little cafe before sitting down on a bench on the platform and phoning Thomas.

'Why haven't you called me back?' he said.

'I'm calling now,' I said. 'What's wrong?'

'Dad's disappeared. One of his neighbours down there phoned. They've reported him missing.'

'He'll be lying drunk somewhere.'

'Apparently no one's seen him for a week.'

'I don't think it's anything to get worked up about, do you? Are you worried?'

'I don't know. A bit.'

'But not enough to go down there?'

'You must be joking, no.'

'How did they get hold of your number?'

'That's just it. He must have given it to the neighbours in case anything happened to him.'

'Maybe he's killed himself.'

'Dad? He'd never do that.'

'No, I suppose you're right. I don't know why I said that.'

'Anyway, I just thought you ought to know. I wasn't sure how you'd take it, to be honest.'

'Weren't you?'

'Not really, no. You're his treasure.'

'His treasure?'

'You are, you know you are. Aren't you?'

'Stop being silly. He wouldn't know what colour eyes I've got.'

My train came in and I got to my feet and wheeled my case along the platform.

'I'll be home tonight. I can meet you tomorrow, if you want?'

'I don't think there's any need, not really. I'll text you if I hear anything.'

'OK,' I said, then hung up and got on the train.

It was a strange week. For the first time since I moved in, I had the house to myself. The others were all away and although I went to work every day and met loads of people there, I felt lonely. It didn't help much that we were in the middle of a heatwave and the town was swarming with tourists. Or that it was my last week on the job. Or that there was no one I could talk to about the only thing I could think about. It didn't matter who I imagined telling, the scenario that played out in my mind always had them coming down on me and urging me to stay well away from him. How can you even think about going out with him after something like that? was the question I kept hearing.

And they were right.

The best thing was to put it all from my mind. Not to think about him, or think about us. Walk away from it.

But I couldn't. He had something no else had.

Thomas texted me again the day after I got home. They'd found Dad. He was in hospital. Apparently he'd lost the use of his legs. I called back, but he didn't answer.

Will he be going home again? I texted.

No idea. Are you going to go down there and see him?

Not likely. Are you?

No. Maybe you could phone him, seeing as you're his treasure.

I'll think about it.

And I actually did think about it, quite a lot in fact. I felt I ought to, that I should. But I didn't. Instead I stayed at home, went from room to room in the evenings as if in a kind of sleep, watched TV, slept a lot, ate very little. The daytimes were easier because of work, it gave me something else to think about. My last day was just like all the others. I'd thought someone might have baked a cake or something, it was the sort of thing Renate would do, but no, it was just see you and then out the door. I'd still be working Saturdays, so it wasn't that odd, I supposed, but still it was enough to make me feel expendable as I walked home, as if whatever I did made no difference to anyone.

When I got home there was a letter for me in the letter box. I could see straight away it was from Valdemar. I took it inside with me without opening it. I didn't have to open it, I didn't have to have anything at all to do with him.

My heart trembled.

I opened it standing in front of the window in the living room.

Dear Line,

I hope you're doing OK. If I could go back in time, I'd go back to Odin's Pool and our nocturnal swim. Being together with you there really was the most brilliant experience. I'd do everything we did again, right until what happened, which I'm sure you're still thinking about. I wouldn't do that again. You're a very special person and I hope that what happened isn't beyond recall and that you'll give me another chance. Please give me another chance, Line. It's a big ask, I know, but then I've a lot to lose as well. I can't stand the thought of you not wanting to see me again. Your shoes are here. Come and get them, if you want. If not, I'll send them on, of course.

Valdemar

I read it through twice, ambivalent between hurt and joy. It hadn't occurred to me that our swim in the forest had been that special to him. It made me see myself there with him, whereas before, when I thought back on it, he was always on his own. It was a lovely, shining thing to think about. But then I thought of what he'd done afterwards. No normal person would do a thing like that. I couldn't trust him. Couldn't, and wouldn't.

Tucking the letter back inside the envelope before putting it away in the drawer of my desk, I noticed he'd written his address on the back. But it was no good. It was impossible.

I showered, put some make-up on and went out into the summer night. First to Bakgården, then, when I couldn't see anyone there I knew, on to Palasset, where I ran into Renate of all people. In the year since I'd known her I'd never once seen her out. We moved in different orbits.

'Come and sit here with us, if you're on your own!' she said.

It was about the last thing I wanted.

'Actually, I'm looking for someone,' I said, and smiled as best I could. 'They don't seem to be here, though. I think they'll have gone on to Loftet.'

I walked up the hill to Høyden, past the church and the many university buildings, then down the other side, between taller structures of weathered concrete. I'd only been to see Thomas a couple of times since I moved here, he didn't much care for visitors. But he appeared glad to see me when he came to the door – he even gave me a hug.

'Do you want a beer or something?' he said when I followed him inside.

'Yes, please.'

He'd had his hair cut too, and was actually quite suntanned. I didn't pass comment, just sat down on his bright orange sofa and watched as he took a can from the fridge. Some pizza boxes were stacked up next to the bank of computers on his desk along with some empty Coke cans. But I was glad to see the place was tidier than the last time I'd been round.

'So, what's happening?' he said, handing me my beer.

'I had my last day at work today. I thought I'd come and pick up those books for the ex.phil.'

'You're not going to start prepping already, surely?'

'I was thinking about it.'

He went over to the open window and lit a smoke.

'Did you speak to Dad?'

'Not yet, no. It's not like we're responsible for him.'

'No.'

'When was the last time he did anything for us?'

'Never.'

When he smoked it was with the cigarette in the middle of his mouth with his lips as if curled around it. It looked like he'd never smoked before. If I hadn't been his sister, I'd have thought he was a bit cute.

'I didn't get in, did I tell you?' he said.

'No, no you didn't. Oh, what a –'

'It's all right. They just didn't want me, that's all.'

He smiled and turned his head back to the open window. The smoke he blew out clouded the air in front of him for a moment before dispersing.

He had the grades. He had the physical attributes. So it could only be the mental side of things that had made them reject him.

'What are you going to do when autumn starts then?'

He gave a shrug. Blew out some more smoke.

'Get a job, maybe.'

'Have you told Mum?'

'Not yet. I suppose I'll have to soon.'

He stubbed his cigarette out in an ashtray, then went over to the shelf where his books were, returning with a small pile. The audience was over.

'I think this is the lot,' he said.

I put my beer down on the coffee table and took them from his outstretched hands.

'Have you ever heard of a band called Domen?' I said.

'Of course I have,' he said. 'Why do you ask?'

'No reason.'

'Have you actually heard them or just heard *of* them?' he said.

'Heard *of* them, that's all. Have you got a bag for these?'

He nodded and went over to the kitchen area where he dug a carrier bag out of the bottom drawer.

'You know they basically never play in public? And that they've never released anything?'

'So I believe,' I said.

'There's all sorts of rumours about them. I've no idea what's true and what isn't.'

I put the books into the bag and got to my feet.

'What sort of rumours?'

'Like they're kind of a sect. They sacrifice living animals, so I've heard, and drink their blood.'

'Seriously?'

'It's only what I've heard. Why the interest?'

'Nothing really, just wondering.'

There was no hug when I left, only a nod of goodbye as he closed the door.

Julie came home early the next morning. She'd come in with the overnight train and bought fresh rolls from a bakery on her way from the station. She knocked on my door, bright and chirpy.

'There's nothing in the fridge!' she said when we came downstairs. 'What have you been living on? Fresh air and romance?'

I wanted to tell her the romance part was all wrong, but I didn't want what happened with Valdemar to be out there yet. If I gave her even a hint, she wouldn't let go until she knew all there was to know.

'It's this heat,' I said instead. 'It's put me right off my food.'

'A good thing I came home,' she said. 'So I can look after you a bit.'

She put the rolls out for us, boiled a couple of eggs and made some tea while telling me about her mother who been given an invalidity pension and lived on her own. Julie thought she was showing signs of radicalisation – she'd become more and more critical of the established media and was finding alternative outlets she for some reason trusted more.

'It's good that she takes an interest in the world around her, but it's all she goes on about. She hardly even asks how I'm doing.'

'Not much of a trip home, then?'

'Oh no, it was good in other ways. I saw all my old mates again. How about you, anyway? What was Oslo like?'

'It was fine.'

'Did you see the news about that black metal band who've gone missing? It made me think about your friend, Valdemar. Not that he's likely to be one of them, but you know what I mean.'

It was as if all the air was sucked out of me at once.

'Gone missing? Where? Who? What are they called?'

'Let me check,' she said, and picked up her phone. After a moment's scrolling she looked up.

'Kvitekrist.'

'That's not Valdemar's band,' I said. 'They're called Domen.'

'Have you seen him again, then?'

'No, I haven't.'

'Are you thinking about it?'

I shook my head.

'I don't think so. I mean, I like him and all that, he just comes across a bit too extreme for me. You didn't like him much, did you?'

'I'm sure he's all right. But I'd give him a swerve, if I were you. I don't think he's any good for you.'

'Would you have said that if I'd been going out with him?'

She laughed.

'Of course not!'

Then abruptly she looked at me as if startled.

'That's not a trick question, is it? Tell me you're not going out with him.'

'No, it's not a trick question, and I'm not going out with him!' I said, and the moment the words left my lips I knew I didn't ever want to see him again. It was all so clear to me, as I sat there with Julie.

'I had my last day at work yesterday,' I said.

'That's right, I forgot. Does that mean you've got some holiday now?'

'Not really. I want to start reading up on Monday.'

'I don't think you need to. Ex.phil's a piece of cake.'

'For you, maybe.'

'And you, our clever little sis.'

She got up and began to clear the table. I got up and helped her.

When she went for a shower I read about the missing band and realised they were one of the bands I'd checked out on my way to Sweden. Valdemar was bound to know them. Maybe they were even friends of his.

I read his letter again. Was there any doubt he was being sincere? If he wasn't sorry, and if I didn't mean something special to him, he wouldn't have got in touch. He could have whoever he wanted. Even Julie. Especially Julie. She fancied him, but knew he didn't fancy her, and so she'd gone all defensive and cast him in a negative light. It was basic psychology.

But it didn't mean I had to go back to him.

It didn't.

Oh Christ, why did everything have to be so complicated?

And why hadn't I bought a fucking morning-after pill in fucking Kongsvinger?!

Not that I believed I'd be so unlucky as to get pregnant our first time, but it wasn't exactly impossible either.

I put the letter back in the drawer. The bathroom was free now and so I went and had a shower myself. The sun was shining, the sky was blue, I'd got two weeks off if I wanted, so what did I have to complain about? OK, I might be pregnant, but if I was I could get an abortion. And if I pulled myself together I could stop thinking about Valdemar altogether. All my problems would be gone.

Only it wasn't that simple.

The first thing was that I ran into Valdemar again at Palasset that night. He was sitting at the same table as last and lit up when he saw me. No one could have faked a smile like that. He came over and said we needed to go somewhere we could talk, and asked if I would walk with him. I wanted to hear what he had to say for himself, so I did.

'Did you get my letter?' he said once we were outside.

'Yes,' I said.

'I meant every word.'

I said nothing.

'I've never felt like this about anyone before.'

Again, I said nothing. But my heart pounded.

'I know you like me too. If you didn't, you wouldn't be here.'

He stopped and put his arms around me.

'Don't,' I said.

'OK,' he said, and we carried on walking.

'What can I do to convince you?'

'Convince me of what?'

'That I'm not a violent psychopath.'

'What do you want, exactly?'

'To be with you.'

'Why?'

'I can't explain. I just know it's what I want. I don't think attraction can be explained. It's just something that happens.'

'Why did you do that to me?'

'You won't believe me, I know, but it was to pleasure you.'

'To pleasure me? By cutting me with a knife?'

'Yes.'

I turned and began walking back. He followed along silently at my side.

'Can I see you again?' he said when again we stood outside Palasset.

'I don't know,' I said.

'Next week?'

'I won't be here then. I'm going to visit my mum.'

I'd been thinking I would, but hadn't decided until then.

'How long will you be away?'

'A while.'

'I'll wait for you,' he said, and then went back inside. I texted the others and told them I wasn't feeling that good and had gone home.

The second thing was that I *was* pregnant. I couldn't believe it when I saw the test. But there was no doubt. How could I have been so unlucky? More to the point, how could I have been so stupid? Why hadn't I just gone to the chemist's and bought a pill?

At the same time, a part of me hesitated to phone the surgery, hesitated to make an appointment, even if it was what I had to do. The whole idea was unpleasant and disgusted me. Fortunately, there was plenty of time yet.

And so I went home to Mum. I didn't tell her I was coming at first, just packed my big rucksack with books and clothes and got on the bus. It wasn't until about halfway there that I paused my music and phoned her.

'Hi, Line!' she said, and her voice was bright with excitement.

'Hello, Mum,' I said.

'Is everything all right?'

'Yes, of course.'

'Yes?'

I suppressed my irritation.

'Yes,' I said. 'But I was thinking I could come out for a few days, if that's OK?'

'Of course it's OK! When do you want to come?'

'Tonight?'

'Tonight? You mean *tonight* tonight?'

'Yes, is that all right?'

'Yes, of course!'

'I'm actually on the bus now. It gets in around sixish.'

'Wonderful!' she said. 'What a lovely surprise!'

'OK,' I said. 'I'll let you get on, you're bound to be busy at work. See you later.'

'Yes, see you later. Take care!'

I hung up and returned to my music. No one could bring me down as much as she could. She was unhealthy for me. Good and kind, and unhealthy. It was like being suffocated with a soft pillow. It didn't matter to her if I was feeling well in myself or not, what mattered was that I had to look like I was. As long as I was smiling and being nice to her and Gran or whoever, she was happy. She was so superficial it hurt.

Now she could tell her friends and colleagues her daughter was coming to stay. And as soon as I got there she'd be able to pick away at my life to her heart's content. It wasn't like phoning, I couldn't exactly hang up.

I had to try and tell myself she wanted the best for me. That she was the person she was and there was nothing I could do about it.

I could read, go for walks, allow myself to be fed and looked after, sleep until late.

But she was so fucking annoying!

I always remembered too late.

The last part of the way was a journey back into childhood. I knew every hill, every bend in the road, every field, every house. They were inside me and outside me at the same time. Maybe staying here a while wasn't such a bad idea after all. Maybe I could even tell Mum I was pregnant. Nothing about Valdemar, just that I was pregnant. And that I kept thinking – because I did, didn't I? – that maybe there'd soon be a little baby, a baby who before long would be able to come here too, to run around and play.

No. I wouldn't tell her anything. She'd be worried sick, no matter what I decided. And anyway, I knew perfectly well what I was going to do. I was nineteen, for God's sake.

The bus rounded the last inlet and outside the Samvirkelaget Co-op I saw Mum standing by the car.

I waited until all the other passengers had got off before I took my rucksack down from the luggage rack and went out. She smiled and waved as soon as she saw me.

Here we go, I told myself, lifting a hand to wave weakly back before crossing the road.

'Hi,' I said.

Her face was pudgier than I remembered. And although she was all smiles and fluttery with her hands, there was something sad about her eyes.

'Hello, my darling,' she said and gave me a hug, her palms running busily up and down my back.

'Such a fuss to make,' I said, and drew free. I took off my rucksack and handed it to her.

'Can you put this in the boot?'

'Of course,' she said. 'Oof, that's heavy! What have you brought with you?'

'Books.'

I got in. Mum closed the boot and got in beside me. She looked at me, as if taking me in, but it was like it was for effect. I let it pass and she put the key in the ignition.

'Anything you want from the Co-op before we go?' she said.

I shook my head.

She started the car, glanced in the mirror, turned out onto the road. The sun shone at us from the mouth of the fjord and I put my sunglasses on.

'There's a lasagne in the oven. It should be ready by the time we get home.'

'Sounds good.'

'You're looking so tanned. Have you been out a lot during the summer?'

Now it started.

'I was at a cabin up at the lake last weekend.'

'Who with?'

Oh, for God's sake.

'Some friends.'

She held her hand up against the glare of the sun and leaned forward. She'd always been such a feeble driver. I gazed out at the fell across the fjord. It looked almost like it was resting. I remembered the time Mum and Dad went hiking there. They'd promised to light a fire so we could see them. We'd kept looking right until bedtime. When would that have been? I couldn't have been more than four years old.

'What sort of books have you brought with you, then?' she said, continuing her interview.

'Philosophy and theory of science, for the ex.phil. intro course,' I said. 'I was thinking I could do some reading here for a few days where it's quiet.'

She looked at me with a smile.

'When's the exam again?'

'In three months.'

Gran had really deteriorated since the last time I'd seen her. It was a shock to see how thin she'd become and the way she trembled while sitting in her chair, her jaw going up and down, her hands impossible to keep still. Her skin so taut around her face that her head looked like a skull.

'Hi, Gran,' I said. 'So lovely to see you!'

Her eyes lit up as soon as she saw me. I leaned over to give her a hug, though everything in me was repulsed.

She whispered something I couldn't understand.

'Yes,' I said, nodding as if I did.

Her eyes smiled.

'I'd better take my stuff upstairs,' I said. 'I'll be down again in a bit, though!'

From the window I watched Mum going backwards and forwards between the garden and the kitchen. If Gran had been better I could have talked to her as I'd done when I was little. I always told her everything then. She always knew what to say.

But no, she wouldn't have understood, of course she wouldn't.

Mum called up to say dinner was ready. I went down and the two of them were shuffling slowly across the lawn arm in arm. It had been good of Mum to move back here to look after Gran, I had to give her that. But there was always some ulterior motive where she was concerned.

She divided Gran's lasagne into little pieces for her. It was all so disgusting. Gran's shaking, the bulging veins on her arms, the slop on her plate. But I was here now and would have to make an effort, force myself to eat and smile.

Gran looked at me and tried to say something. Mum leaned towards her so she could hear what it was.

'Thomas,' she said. 'Are you asking Line how Thomas is getting on?'

'He's doing fine, Gran,' I said. 'He's thinking of going to college.'

'What sort of college?' Mum said.

'Police college,' I said. 'But he's got to meet the admission criteria first.'

Mum straightened up.

'Have you told Gran what subject you're going to be studying?'

'No,' I said. 'I'm sure you have though.'

I regretted it straight away. Mum looked hurt. She lifted a glass of water to Gran's lips as if to demonstrate what an important job she was doing caring for her mother and that my scorn was out of place.

'Psychology,' Gran whispered, suddenly quite clear.

'Gran says psychology,' Mum said. 'So yes, we must have talked about it! Are you looking forward to it?'

Gran looked at me with that joyous gleam in her eyes. I nodded, filled with guilt: I really was looking forward to it.

After dinner I spent half an hour online, then sat for some time gazing out into the dimness without thinking of anything in particular. Downstairs, the TV went off and I listened to their activity for a while, until eventually Mum came up the stairs and knocked on the door.

'Yes?'

She came in and sat down on the edge of the bed.

'Is it not too chilly for you?' she said, and put her hands in her lap.

I shook my head.

She watched me as I looked out of the window.

'How are things with you?' she said.

'Fine.'

'Are you sure?'

'Yes, I'm sure. Why?'

'You seem a little distant.'

Christ.

I took a deep breath.

'It's not a crime, is it?'

She sighed.

'We should be able to talk,' she said. 'I mean, properly.'

'What do you want to talk about?'

'You, perhaps?'

'But I don't want to talk about me.'

She sat for a moment without speaking, wanting to show me how my reply made her feel.

But her feelings weren't my responsibility.

'Fine, that's quite all right,' she said then and got to her feet.

'Good,' I said.

She paused in the doorway.

'Anita, the home help, will be coming in the morning. And again at lunchtime. If you'd rather be on your own with Gran and look after her a bit, just let me know and I'll tell Anita she needn't come.'

'I came here to study,' I said. 'Not to look after Gran.'

She smiled, hesitantly at first, then said goodnight. I felt bad after she went downstairs again and left me on my own. I shouldn't have said what I said about Gran. I didn't exactly mean it. I just wanted to make sure the opening I knew she was looking for was closed. And it was better than slamming doors and yelling at her to leave me the fuck alone, the way I usually did.

I heard her open the back door downstairs and then close it behind her. A moment later she went past under my window where I was sitting on the sill, and disappeared round the corner.

Everything was dark and still. Even the crows in the trees across the field were quiet.

It was a beautiful evening. The grey light of the sky, the dark crowns of the trees, the black fell across the fjord. But even so, I had the sense that being here wasn't going to be good for me. Mum picking away at me. Gran thinking I was such a good girl. My childhood, which was all around.

How easy life had been then!

If only I could have been eight years old again. Wake up and hey presto: a child's thoughts, a child's joys.

To go out into the sun in the morning and run around exploring all day. Grandad working the land, Gran in full vigour and looking after us.

I slid from the windowsill and went quietly downstairs. Gran was lying as if mummified in her bed. I slipped by without looking at her, to the narrow bookshelf where the photo albums were. I took two of them back upstairs with me, turned on the lamp, lay down on my side on the bed and began to leaf through the pages. There was an astonishing number of Thomas as a baby, it was almost as if they'd decided to document every hour of his life. They'd calmed down considerably by the time I came along. I paused at one of Dad with me in the carrycot, he was standing by the car we'd come back from the hospital in; another was taken in the flat, Thomas pointing at me, his eyes wide with wonder. Then Mum crying in bed with me at her breast, her feelings getting the better of her as always. Dad barely present at all. But then he wouldn't have been, in our house the business of taking photographs had always been the man's job.

I stared at one of the few where he was in the picture. He was holding me to his chest and looking at me tenderly. With pride too, perhaps. Yes, it seemed that way.

Halfway through the album, as I was looking at some photos from when I was six or seven years old, something happened outside.

The whole fjord lit up all of a sudden.

I went to the window and leaned out. An enormous light was rising into the sky behind the trees.

It looked like a UFO!

I felt scared, but I couldn't take my eyes off it.

Still it rose, and within moments it had climbed high into the sky.

It wasn't a UFO. It was a star!

The light it threw over the landscape was magical, and so beautiful that tears came to my eyes.

I stared and stared at the shining star, and all at once I knew what I was going to do.

I wasn't going to cling to all this. I wasn't going to care what people thought.

I would do what I wanted.

I would say yes to Valdemar, and I would have the child.

RAMSVIK

Pappa picks up first one then another sack of cement in the sweltering midday heat and staggers towards what will become our new house. There he dumps the sacks onto the ground, sending a cloud of dust puffing into the air. A dragonfly, hovering above the grey, freshly cast concrete floor, darts away. Pappa meets my gaze and smiles, crouches down in front of me. His face is wet with perspiration.

'Aren't you going to give me a hand, you little rascal?' he says.

There's nothing I'd rather do. But I'm confused. I thought he was dead. I thought I'd buried him.

Was it something I dreamt?

He draws himself upright again and goes back for the two sacks that remain. I go after him. I try to think of some way in which I can help him.

A great voice fills the sky.

AND YOU MUST BE JAN?

Pappa does not look up. Oblivious, he picks up one sack and clamps it under his arm to grip the other.

Dust flies up as he deposits them over by the new house which is not yet a house at all, but a grey concrete floor. Sweat runs down his face as he crouches down in front of me.

'Aren't you going to give me a hand, you little rascal?'

I wonder if Mamma is here too as I follow him towards the two remaining sacks.

The dragonfly hovers seemingly without moving, just above the concrete floor. It darts away as the sacks hit the ground. I survey the steeply sloping terrain; the river that runs slowly through the valley, hidden by the row of trees that have grown up as near to the water as they can.

WHAT DO YOU MEAN? The words echo across the sky as Pappa

crouches in front of me. I glance up and beyond him, half expecting to see a pair of enormous eyes appear above the ridge of the fell. Instead, I'm walking down a street in the rain, cautiously, for the cobbles are slippery, so much has fallen. It's dark, and the light from the lamp posts, the shop windows, the passing cars, reflects in the paving. The rows of buildings stand like faces of rock through which the streets have eroded their paths. Some end up at the harbour, but not the one I'm following. A tram goes by, with no one in it. A bit further on, the supermarket sign glistens orange. The air inside smells faintly of detergent. The light is bright, near-white. Some customers pass down the aisles. They carry red shopping baskets with black handles, identical to the one I take from the stack inside the entrance. At the frozen pizzas stands a woman with a freckled face, her lips are slightly parted. Her basket hangs from one hand, the other curls around her upper arm. She's wearing a white cotton blouse and a pair of faded blue jeans. Seeing her is a shock. I'm attracted to her like I've never been attracted to anyone else ever before. She does not look at me, in fact she seems not to notice me at all. She picks up a pizza and scrutinises it, puts it back, then picks up another. I can't just stand and stare, and so I carry on down the aisle. I put some cheese and some bread rolls and a carton of juice in my basket. At the checkout, she stands behind me. Her nearness aches. I know I'll never see her again, and steal a final glance, turning my head to look at her. She senses my gaze and meets it. Fleetingly, her eyes register me, like a grazing sheep momentarily looking up before grazing on. She has blue eyes. Outside, I'm standing back against the wall with my carrier bag when she comes out and starts walking away down the street. A tram trundles up the hill, a luminous worm. I have no way of finding her again, and if I did there would be nothing I could do, for the huge attraction I feel is not reciprocated by any part of her. I start walking again. JUST COVERING ALL BASES. The rain pours and the words reverberate, I see the glow of the supermarket sign further along the road. I go up the three steps and inside, grip one of the red shopping baskets with the black handles, scan the shelves as I walk down the aisles. I detect a faint smell of soap and bread. At the frozen food a woman stands with her basket in one hand surveying the stacks of pizzas. Her other hand is clutching her opposite arm. She's wearing blue jeans and a white blouse. She's perhaps thirty years old. She's incredibly attractive. But it's not her face, her clothes, her body. It's her presence. Like an animal I stand looking at her before collecting myself and moving on to another part of the supermarket, my heart fluttering in my chest. The yearning I feel for this woman I know nothing about and will never see again causes my hands to tremble almost imperceptibly as I pluck my items from the shelves and place them in my basket. Cheese, juice, bread rolls. At the checkout she stands behind me in the queue. I feel her nearness with all my being. I won't ever see her again, and turn to look at her one last time. Her face is freckled, her skin is pale, her eyes are blue. She meets my gaze but reflects nothing back, I'm nobody, one of thousands that have stood and will stand in front of her at the supermarket checkout. In the street outside I am dizzy with emptiness. HE'S NOT THERE, a voice says, and Pappa picks up the sack of cement with both hands, shifts it under his arm and clamps it against his body, bends down to pick up the other, clamps it likewise, to his opposite flank. Pappa is as strong as an ox, and I'm not the only one to say so. My eyes follow him as he waddles away to what is to become our new house. Dust puffs into the air as he dumps the sacks onto the ground in front of me. He wipes his brow with the back of his hand and smiles, crouches down before me.

'Aren't you going to give me a hand, you little rascal?' he says.

I nod and he gets to his feet again. I wonder if Mamma is here, and if there's anything I can help him with. NOT CERTAIN? I recognise the voice, but when I look around not a single face is familiar, and no one appears to have said anything to me either. The faces modulate differently to those I know from home, as if they belong to a different piece of music by the same composer. Darker hair, different chins and noses. They reflect back from the windows as the train tears into a tunnel. Mine too. Commanding features, if I say so myself. Greying beard, a nice new haircut that morning, narrow glasses, a warmth about the eyes. A corpulent man in a suit and a backpack, they've never seen the like! When the train glides into the splendid underground station that resembles a ballroom, I follow the flow to the escalator, where I stand, upright as the sheerest fell, and allow myself to be transported upwards, out into the light of a spring night. The stairway leading up to the entrance is majestic, if somewhat faux. The doorman wears a uniform and nods as I come towards him. I nod back, then take the gilded elevator up to the room, where Live lies asleep in the bed with all her clothes on. She sits up as I close the door behind me.

'He's lying here dying,' she says. 'How can you say you're not certain?'

I stare at her.

Something's not right.

What is it?

I put my pack down carefully so as not to wake her and step quite as carefully into the bathroom. It feels like something terrible has happened. I turn both taps on to fill the bath. As the water tumbles down, I go back inside the room. She opens her eyes as I bend forward to kiss her forehead.

'You're back,' she says, and smiles that mild smile of hers. 'Has it been a good day?'

Eggs splutter in the frying pan where she stands. The kettle rumbles as the water comes to the boil, then abruptly switches itself off with a click. She fills the yellow teapot that has been waiting ready on the worktop with its three tea bags. The children are upstairs and have already eaten. I feel something pressing inside my head. The space becomes smaller. It doesn't hurt at first. But then it does hurt. Then pain is all there is. I make to get up, to get away. It's as if someone hammered a chisel into my brain. 'Jan,' Live says. 'Jan, what is it?'

People wearing surgical masks, leaning over me.

THE PATIENT'S AWAKE! reverberates around the fells. Leo barks and Pappa stands with his hands on his hips, looking down on the sheep as they trail along the path below us. Ragged and grubby they trudge, almost in single file. The new-fallen snow on the peaks across the fjord makes them look like they've moved closer in the night. Or else it's the crisp, clear autumn air that does it.

'This must be one of the finest spots there is, don't you think?' says Pappa. I nod and look down on the milking place, the sheds so weathered and grey they look like a part of the landscape. I get halfway to my feet, overturning the chair. 'Jan, what is it?' Live says. In the bathroom, the bath is filling up. I go in, turn off the taps, test the water with my hand.

SYVERT

I woke up when the captain's voice came over the tannoy and told us we'd started our descent into Gardermoen. Apart from a desperate thirst, I felt a lot better than when we'd taken off. Fortunately there was no one I recognised on board. Not that I cared much what people thought, but there was no getting around the fact that at my age parading a hangover in public wasn't a good look.

It was as if everything in my body was crying out for liquid. My head thumped in time to my pulse, a fuzzy, pendulating ache. The fasten seat belts sign hadn't come on yet, so I pressed the call button for assistance.

It gave a soft ping, and a flight attendant at the front turned round and scanned the rows. I put my hand in the air.

'Yes?' she said when moments later she towered at my seat.

'Do you think I could have some water? I'm afraid I must have been asleep when you came past with the trolley.'

'Of course,' she said, and went away to get some.

I turned and looked at the landscape below. So rich and green compared to the arid Russian plains. Norway's natural beauty was surely unsurpassed. And so varied too. Here were forests and rivers; where we lived, skerries and smooth rock from which to sunbathe and swim; the Vestland had its high mountains and fjords. Mum always used to say there was no sense in going abroad for your holidays when everything was so much better here. She had a point, even if she did miss out the big cities – we had none.

How good it had been for her to go on that coastal cruise before she was too old!

I could pop over and look in on her tomorrow night. Tell her about Alevtina and probe a bit, see if I could find out how much she actually knew at the time.

Or was it better not to mention it?

It was hard to know how she would react. My guess was that she wouldn't talk about it, or at least would play it down. But inwardly she'd be knocked off balance, it would upset her. And what good would that do?

On the other hand, Alevtina was a part of our lives now. It was a new situation for us. And Mum needed to be as much a part of life as possible, not removed from it.

The flight attendant came back with a small-sized bottle of water in her hand. As she gave it to me, there was another ping and the fasten seat belts sign came on.

'Thanks,' I said. She gave me a fleeting smile and strode back to the little cubby area they had at the front.

Did they really believe in all that safety nonsense? If we crashed, we'd die with our seat belts on, that was the only difference they made.

I drained the minuscule bottle in a couple of gulps, slipped it into the pocket of the seat in front, got my phone out and switched it on. That was another load of nonsense – mobile phone signals disrupting the aircraft's guidance systems. One could only wonder why they insisted. Presumably it was a way of making people sit still. Take away personal initiative and people were easier to control. The same thing with drunk passengers on board. It was so completely over the top, making emergency landings and sending police task forces in just because it was on a plane. But air travel was holy, you could do only as the high priests said.

There was no coverage yet anyway.

I slipped it back into my pocket and looked down on a river running blue through all the green, through fields and woodland, past white-painted houses and red barns.

Unsurpassed.

Then the pinging noises were coming from my phone. Ping, ping, ping, ping. I reached into my pocket and hurriedly muted the sound. The family across the aisle all turned to look at me, and the man in front of me twisted round.

I smiled apologetically and returned the device to my pocket without checking it.

Back to the fold, Løyning.

Outside, the landing gear was lowered.

You are a man who shies away from consequences, Alevtina had said. It was fair enough, she was being honest and said what she meant. Not everyone did. But was it true? No, it wasn't. I'd never shirked responsibility, no matter how far I thought back. Joar. Lisa. The kids. Work. The house. I'd even slogged away at the garden the first few years.

It looked like it was the ground looming up to greet us as we landed. No one clapped this time.

I could put it to Lisa. Ask for a straight answer. Was Alevtina right?

It wasn't a bad idea. Lisa enjoyed that kind of discussion. I could just see her, drawing her legs up underneath her on the sofa, talking about how things *actually* hung together, what the people we knew were *actually* like, what motives they had for saying what they said and doing what they did.

I had a feeling they'd be wary of each other. Both of them were smart. Lisa more open. But she'd be careful with Alevtina and would protect herself. She'd be all nice and polite, no one would ever guess she was keeping her guard up.

We could spend a whole evening having dinner with people we didn't know that well and Lisa would take an active interest in everything they said, as friendly as you like, and appear to be having the grandest of times, only to say afterwards that she couldn't stand them. I'd say I thought they were all right, because it was generally what I thought. But didn't you notice the way she was treating him, she would say then, or didn't you hear what he said after that? More bluntly she could declare that they were plain snobbish.

I got my phone out again. Jarle had been calling, Lisa had been calling, and then there was a number not in my contacts that had tried to get through a couple of times as well. Texts from Astrid, Joar, Dag, Jarle and Gjert – and one from Alevtina!

I opened hers first. She'd written in Norwegian!

Thank you for our meeting, my brother. It is very nice to know you at last. Let us stay in touch.

I smiled to myself. It was a bit like reading one of those scam emails from Nigeria.

I replied straight away.

Thanks to you too! Fantastic meeting you at last. Looking forward to you coming over so you can meet the rest of our family!

I replied to Astrid who was asking if I was home yet and if I'd had a good time seeing my sister, and to Dag who wanted us to go fishing together, and to Gjert who wanted us to go out drinking. I texted Lisa to say I'd just got in and would phone her shortly. I ignored Jarle's messages at first, deciding it was better to talk to him from the car. Joar too, whose text simply said *Call me*, could wait.

As people jumped to their feet to get their luggage from the overhead lockers I looked up the number of the unknown caller, only there was no info listed. Most likely just someone preferring to call me directly rather than go through the office.

All I wanted now was some more water.

What they hadn't got right at Gardermoen was the distance between the furthest gates and the arrivals hall itself. They should have gone with some kind of circular construction instead of stretching everything out along an axis. It was a good kilometre's walk to the baggage reclaim with nowhere to buy a bottle of water along the way.

Still, maybe the walk would do me good, get the last of the alcohol out through the pores. I had a five-hour drive ahead of me.

Standing in the queue at passport control I suddenly thought about that Russian policeman. Probably because he was the one who'd handed me my passport back. No matter how hard I tried, I couldn't recall his face. He'd been so anonymous, so drab that it was as if he hadn't been there. As if I'd dreamt him. How could such an indistinct man have risen so far in the police hierarchy?

I presented my passport with the photo page open as the signs instructed and was nodded through without further ado.

I could hardly believe that only the day before I'd seen a woman bleeding to death in front of my eyes on a shop floor.

Oh God, it was terrible.

But there was no need to think about it any more. Both the injured people had survived, if I was to believe what the policeman had told me.

But maybe it was to save me from anguish.

In the arrivals hall itself I went into the Narvesen shop and bought myself a couple of sweet buns, a Farris mineral water and a Pepsi Max. As I made my way to the parking facility my phone rang. The display showed the same unknown number as before. I had a carrier bag in one hand, my suitcase in the other, so I let it ring. I could always call back, and it was good to have something to do in the car as well if I got bored.

When Alevtina came I'd pick her up in a Tesla, I thought as the car boot opened. It would be a bit flash, I'd be giving in to something inside me and it wouldn't be like me at all, not the way I knew myself. But I'd never really liked the Audi that much. In fact, choosing a suitable car was a difficult business. Volvo: teachers and other lefties of comfortable means. BMW: immigrants with plenty of loose cash. Mercedes: traditional well-heeled segment. Audi? Self-employed business people with a good wad in the bank, maybe. And then there were all the other makes for those of more modest means: Toyota, Kia, Honda, Peugeot, Mazda. Hardly anyone drove a Ford any more. Opel had gone from the roads completely.

If I'd worked for Opel, I'd have gone in for putting out an Opel Lepo, I thought as I got in behind the wheel. The world's first motorised palindrome. That would get the sales going.

I guzzled half the Pepsi and devoured a bun before rolling slowly out of the multi-storey, through the barrier and out onto the motorway. It was impossible not to be struck by how organised everything was here compared to Russia. New tarmac, shiny new road markings, new cars, petrol stations like small, well-assorted shopping centres.

Even so, there were surely as many moaners here as there were over there.

I clicked the phone into the holder and was just about to ring Lisa when the unknown caller came through again. This time I answered.

'Hello?'

'Hello, am I speaking to Syvert Løyning?'

'You are, yes.'

'I hope you don't mind me asking, but would you by any chance have had a father by the same name?'

'I did, yes,' I said, immediately speculating as to where on earth he might be heading. Could it be an inheritance of some sort?

'And you have a brother called Joar, is that right?'

'That's right. Can I ask what this is about?'

'Yes, of course. My name is Helge Bråthen. I was wondering if perhaps we could meet? It's a rather sensitive matter, so I'd prefer not to talk about it over the phone.'

'I'd have to know a little more than that. I'm sure you can appreciate I can't agree to meet everyone who phones me up. If it's about a funeral, I'll have to direct you to our office. You'll find the number on our website. Or of course you're welcome to send us an email.'

'No, it's not a funeral. This is a personal matter.'

'Is it to do with money?'

'No, not at all. Would you have time tomorrow?'

'I can't say just at the moment. But if it's important, I'm sure I'll be able to accommodate.'

'It's important.'

'OK, I'll take your word for it. Are you in town?'

'I'll catch a flight first thing. Perhaps we could have lunch. At a restaurant of your preference, of course.'

'Fiskehallen is good. I'll book us a table there for one o'clock.'

'Appreciated. Will you be able to bring Joar along too?'

'He's in Oslo.'

'Ah, I see. Well, thank you very much indeed, and I'll look forward to seeing you.'

I picked the phone up and googled his name. There weren't that many called Helge Bråthen. The well-known architect, a psychologist, a photographer, a bank employee and another architect were the first who appeared.

I should have asked him what line of work he was in.

It could have been the psychologist. Something to do with Joar, maybe? Had he had a breakdown and been admitted to hospital and given my name as his person to contact?

No, it couldn't be that – he'd asked if Joar could come with me tomorrow.

I passed a sign to Jessheim where that furniture dealer was from. He'd be long dead by now. What was his name again?

Arnfinn Nesset.

No, that was the serial killer.

It was on the tip of my tongue.

Arnfinn Engen!

If it wasn't Joar, and had nothing to do with money or a funeral, what could it be?

There was no traffic ahead, so I sent him a quick text: *Need to know what it's about and who you are.*

He replied straight away. Very efficient.

It concerns your father. More tomorrow.

Stonewaller too.

I put the phone back in the holder and rang Jarle.

'Hello there,' he said. 'Just got in?'

'Yes, I'm on the E6. What's going on?'

'Nothing.'

'Still the same?'

'Yes, it's really weird. Not a single death in three days.'

'I did a bit of checking after we spoke last time. It's the same in Oslo.'

'I don't get it. How can it be?'

'Your guess is as good as mine. But it's got to be down to a massive coincidence, with all sorts of different factors involved. I'll ask my brother, he knows about probability calculus and all that. We'll be run off our feet tomorrow, you'll see. Probably more than ever before.'

'Will you be coming in?'

'Yes, of course. Thanks for holding the fort while I've been away.'

'Nothing to thank me for.'

'No, you're right there. Your watch and we're out of business all of a sudden.'

'Ha ha.'

'Catch you later.'

'Yes, see you.'

I put *Fair Warning* on Spotify, turned up the volume and pulled out into the fast lane.

Sang along to 'Mean Street'.

I didn't care much for this part of the trip, the landscape was a bit monotonous and boring, but the roads were good, so I usually put my foot down. Things got much better coming into Telemark. Sørlandsporten had never been the gateway for me, to my mind it had always been the Brevikbrua suspension bridge. Crossing that meant coming home. So when they led the E18 over a new bridge, the Grenlandsbrua, I continued to go by the old road even if it took a bit longer, just to give it the right mood.

After Drammen I gave Joar a ring.

'Our Russian explorer,' he said. 'How was it?'

'Good,' I said. 'A lovely sister we've got too.'

'Alevtina Løyning?'

'She does look a bit like Dad. It was really strange.'

'As long as she doesn't look like you, she'll be all right.'

'Very funny. Anyway, I can see you've been trying to call me.'

'I have, yes. Have you been having any unusual dreams of late?'

'What?'

'Dreams. You know, those weird films at night while you're asleep. Have you had any unusual ones recently?'

'Not that I can think of. But I can work out you have. We're not twins, though, so why should I have the same dreams as you?'

'I remember you having dreams about Dad, a long time ago now. When Mum had cancer. You said it was as if he was actually *there*. That it wasn't like a dream at all.'

'I haven't thought about that for years. But yes, you're right. Have you been dreaming about him too?'

'Not about Dad, no. About someone else. I don't know who it is. It's not like I can see him either. It's more like I *am* him.'

'Sounds like a nightmare.'

'That's exactly what it is.'

'Well, I've dreamt nothing of that sort. Anyway, when I had those dreams about Dad I was seeing him from the outside. He'd be sitting on the sofa in the living room, for example. Another time he came into the laundry room downstairs.

'Hm.'

'Anyway, it's not like you to be unsettled by dreams.'

'Maybe not. The thing is, it's not just me.'

A combine harvester was moving slowly over a field in the distance. It was bright red and the dust it whirled into the air glittered like a halo in the light of the low-hanging sun.

'You talk to others about your dreams?'

'Haven't you heard of dream banks?'

'No.'

'You can find them on the internet. People report the dreams they've been having and post them online. I think it started out as a research project and just went on from there. They've got tens of thousands of dreams collected there. Hundreds of thousands now, probably.'

'And you actually *read* them? Other people's dreams?'

'Of course. It's like a window on what's going on in the world. The subconscious picks up on everything and articulates it. So if there's anything at all you want to know about human beings and what's in flux, that's where you need to go.'

I laughed.

'I barely recognise you, Joar, you're like a different person. Yesterday you were saying the new star was a miracle and now you're into dreams. Are you going through some sort of life crisis or something?'

'The point is that the dreams coming into those dream banks have been notably different these last few days. It's very conspicuous. And not only that, they're all remarkably similar to the ones I've been having. That's why I'm asking if you've been having unusual dreams of late.'

'I'm usually asleep when I dream.'

'I'm being serious, Syvert.'

'I know, I can tell.'

'You've never been able to separate what's important from what isn't.'

'Unlike you, you mean?'

'Yes.'

I laughed again and sensed him smile at the other end.

'You're probably right,' I said. 'I'll give you that. But why is this important?'

'The first of these dreams were posted the night the new star appeared. I'm wondering if there's a connection.'

'Come on, you don't meant that seriously, surely?'

'Yes, I do.'

'It doesn't sound very scientific, if you ask me.'

'To hell with science.'

'What? Did you just say what I think you said?'

'Listen,' he said, 'give me a ring if you have one of these dreams, OK? Or if you hear of anyone else who does.'

With that he hung up, and a moment later I went back to my music.

It was completely dark by the time I pulled up at the house. The door was locked and my key was in my case, so I rang the bell. Footsteps sounded on the stairs and then her figure loomed through the door's frosted pane.

'A good thing you kept it locked,' I said when she let me in. 'The radio said twenty inmates escaped from the prison tonight.'

'Ha ha,' she said. I kissed her on the mouth.

'Are you hungry?'

'I had a couple of sickly buns in the car. Something savoury would be nice, though. Have you eaten?'

'I was waiting for you.'

She'd set the table with the posh place mats and the best china, cloth napkins and candles.

'Are we celebrating something? I didn't forget your birthday, did I?'

She went towards the kitchen and I sat down.

'Only joking, I know when it is,' I said. 'I've brought you back a Toblerone. Limited edition.'

'Good to have you home again,' she said, then opened the oven and with a pair of tea towels for oven gloves took out a steaming hot dish she immediately brought over and put down on the table.

'It's just a fish gratin,' she said. 'Do you want some wine to go with it?'

I nodded.

'You come and sit down. Let me.'

I took a Chablis from the fridge, pressed the point of the spiral into the soft cork and made a few squeaking turns.

'Anyway, there's no such thing as *just* a fish gratin,' I said as I pulled out the cork with a soft and satisfying thwop. I took the bottle over to the table and poured two glasses. The colour reminded me of my piss when I'd drunk sufficient fluids and the weather wasn't too hot, but I kept that to myself. Lisa was used to me airing a lot of my thoughts, but it didn't take more than a couple of weeks after I'd got to know her to realise that not every thought I had would be appreciated, and I quickly learned to identify the ones that wouldn't.

'Did you have a nice time with Sølvi here?'

I spooned a big dollop of the gratin onto my plate, then took some salad for the sake of appearances.

'Yes, it was nice, I suppose.'

'You suppose?'

'Well, she can be a bit demanding as you know.'

'Not so bad this time, though?'

I started eating. The gratin was so hot I couldn't taste anything. I opened my mouth and blew in and out a few times while it lay there burning on my tongue.

'No, it was nice. Drink some water, man!'

I did as she said, and washed the food down with a cooling couple of gulps. I looked at her and smiled. Her fine white sensitive skin had taken on a tinge of red and when she met my gaze and smiled back she looked like she was glowing. For some reason she'd always reminded me a bit of the fox's widow in that Ivo Caprino film, especially when she smiled. She'd called me perverse when I told her I'd actually fancied the fox's widow when I was a kid. It didn't help that several of my friends at the time admitted they had too.

'What ailments has she got now?' I said, and took a sip of the wine. It was delightfully chilled and refreshing.

'Back trouble. Money problems. And her love life, or lack of one.'

'How on earth she could grow up to be so weak when you're so strong is beyond me.'

'I'm not strong. Anyway, we haven't got the same father.'

'True. And you've got different men, too!'

'That's what I would have said, if it needed saying.'

'This gratin's delicious.'

'Yes, it's not bad. But tell me about Russia now. Or about your sister, anyway.'

I finished my mouthful while wondering what to say.

'She's very good-looking. She's very smart. I think she's got a bit of money, too. At least that's how she came across.'

'But what was she *like*? Mild? Abrasive? Deep? Superficial? Did you get on all right?'

'Deep, definitely. Her mother was a doctor. Her father, or stepfather, was a violinist. But I found her a bit, well, hard-hearted. I don't know really, I can't really describe it any other way.'

'Did you like her? If you're being honest?'

'Not to begin with, no. But thinking about her now, I think I do. You'll have to judge for yourself next summer.'

'How did she react to the letters?'

'She was a bit shocked, I think.'

'That's hardly surprising.'

'No. But she said something about me.'

'Oh?'

'Yes, she said I was a man who shied away from consequences.'

'I like her already.'

'It was those oil company shares of mine that did it, I reckon. They really pissed her off.'

I looked at her earnestly.

'Do you think she's right? Not about the shares, but about me?'

'Of course she's right. You pretend problems don't exist. You've always been like that.'

I felt my face grow warm. Why was she criticising me all of a sudden?

'No, I haven't.'

She just sat there with a smile on her face.

'It's nothing to be offended about!'

'I'm *not* offended.'

'Annoyed, then.'

Couldn't she just stop now?

'The first night we ever spent together, do you remember what happened?'

'Nothing.'

'Exactly. You'd invited me round, we were on our own, you could have done whatever you wanted with me. Almost, anyway. But you didn't do anything. You put your head in the sand and pretended I wasn't there. If that's not shying away from consequences, I don't know what is. And that's right from the word go.'

'I was twenty years old. I was so infatuated with you I didn't know what to do.'

'If you say so.'

'Anyway, I don't think that was what she meant.'

'Don't you?' she said, her eyes fixing me like she was egging me on.

'Besides, it turned out all right in the end. That's what counts.'

'I can't believe you're so offended.'

'I am *not* offended. Now give it a rest.'

We sat in silence for a minute. Now and then she glanced up at me. I pretended not to notice and looked at my plate, my glass, the bottle when I decided to pour myself some more. It wasn't a problem for me to talk about something else and move on, but I wanted her to do it. After all, she was the one who'd started.

'Do you want some dessert?' she said at last, getting to her feet and picking up her empty plate.

'What is there?'

'Fruit salad with whipped cream or ice cream, whichever you prefer.'

'Sounds good. Ice cream, I think.'

She took my plate too and went into the kitchen, leaving me to lean back in my chair, a bit light-headed after guzzling my wine.

'Do you think I should tell Mum about Alevtina?' I said, raising my voice sufficiently for her to hear, and craned to see her reaction.

'Why would you do that?'

'Well, she's a part of our life now.'

'Yes, but what good would it do her? You'd just be digging up the past.'

'Do you think so?'

'Don't say anything to her about it. Let her have her peace while she's still here.'

'The old bird could be around for years yet.'

Lisa took a tub of ice cream out of the freezer and a bowl of fruit salad from the fridge. She wasn't at all the domestic type, never had been, so whenever she had to do anything in the kitchen her movements were as if constrained by a kind of resistance. For whatever reason, I enjoyed watching her in those situations.

I wondered if it was because they made it so plain that here was something she wasn't that good at.

Before going to bed, I went up into the loft to see if there were any signs of whatever it was Lisa had said she'd heard that first night I was away. I found nothing, not even mouse droppings. I was sure it was just a squirrel, maybe a couple. If they found their way into one of those narrow spaces, it would definitely make a racket.

I went over to the little west-facing window and looked out. The new star stood majestically in the sky. Its light was so powerful that the stars around it couldn't be seen. It lit up the black water and shone on the treetops of the islet.

'Have you found anything?' Lisa called from below.

'No, nothing.'

I went back down, stowed the ladder and closed the hatch.

'Are you going to have a shower?' she said when I went into the bedroom.

'Why, do I smell?'

'You've been travelling all day. You'll need one.'

'I was going to, as it happens. As long as you don't fall asleep in the meantime.'

'Why not?' she said with a cheeky smile.

I went over, bent down and kissed her on the neck.

'I was really horny in Moscow.'

'I bet you were.'

'Won't be long.'

I couldn't find my shampoo. There hadn't been much left, so Lisa must have thrown it out, which was annoying, because you could always get more out of a bottle of shampoo, even if you thought it was empty, all you had to do was fill it up with water and you'd get a really good lather. The only thing I could do now was to use one of Lisa's, but they all smelled like they were for women. While the water cascaded down on me I sniffed the options, eventually choosing one that supposedly smelled of watermelon. It was the least fragrant of them.

She was lying with her glasses on reading some documents when I went back in. I lay down beside her.

'What are you reading?' I said.

'Work.'

'I can see that. What's it about?'

'Minutes from a meeting.'

'Weren't you there?'

'Yes, I was there.'

'Then why are you reading the minutes?'

'You were in the shower.'

'But why are you reading the minutes when you already know what was said?'

She put the papers down on the bedside table, folded her glasses and put them on top.

'We were discussing a whistleblowing case. I just wanted to look at the arguments again. It's a delicate matter, and I've got to make a decision tomorrow.'

'Are you going in tomorrow?'

She nodded.

'It was either tomorrow or Sunday.'

She switched off her lamp.

'I hope you don't mind me smelling of watermelon,' I said, and wriggled closer to her, then sat up on my knees.

'I like watermelon,' she said, gripping my cock in her hand and wanking me before taking it in her mouth.

'And I like you,' I whispered, a pulsating lust now taking control of my body. 'I like everything about you. Your tits. Your lips. Your pussy.'

I pulled out, she turned over, so pale and white there in the dark, and I slid into her from behind. Within moments she began to moan, it sounded like some enormous grief that soon would cause her to burst into tears. As if everything had been taken away from her. I thrust and thrust again, approaching climax, sensing it wane, clutching her breasts in both my hands as she reached back to feel me, and then, a moment later, I came.

We flopped down and lay there a short while without speaking, my arms around her, a leg on top of hers.

'That was good,' I said.

'Yes, it was,' she said.

'I've missed you.'

'I don't believe you. Not after three days.'

'I wouldn't say it if it wasn't true.'

I rolled over onto my back.

'Something of a weird situation at work while I've been away,' I said.

'Oh?'

'Yes. Not a single corpse in three days.'

'Has that never happened before?'

'No, never.'

'I'm sure I remember something like it. A couple of years ago. I remember you talking about it.'

'You're thinking of when the website was down. That was something else. This time it looks like there hasn't been a single death in three days. I phoned Oslo, it's the same there.'

'There must be a natural explanation.'

'That's what I said. It's just so strange. And then I was talking to Joar.'

'How's he coping with being a new media darling?'

'You know Joar. He's not bothered. But he said he's been having weird dreams. Not only that, he told me he's been reading other people's dreams in what he called a dream bank. It's something online, apparently. He said there were hundreds of thousands of them and the last three days they've gone all funny. He thought it had to do with the new star.'

'Joar said that?'

'Yes, that's what I thought. It's a bit mad, really.'

'So now you're thinking that no one dying has something to do with the new star as well?'

'How did you guess?'

I turned towards her. She gave a jaunty little shake of her head and raised her eyebrows at me.

'I can put two and two together, you know,' she said with a laugh. 'You said no one had died for three days, and then you said Joar thought his dreams had to do with the new star. It's not like I'd need to be a genius.'

'Well, I *don't* think it has.'

'Perhaps there's been some breakdown in the registration systems. Or some other glitch that's sending them all to other providers.'

'God knows. I'll have to look into it tomorrow. Let me know if you dream something weird, won't you?'

'I will. Sleep tight.'

'Sleep tight,' I said.

I laid my head on my arm, closed my eyes and was away in a moment.

With my suit jacket hanging by the collar loop from the hook by the rear door and the air conditioning on full, I headed into town early the next morning. The fjord beneath the bridge lay like a millpond, the sky above was bright blue and without a cloud in sight, sunlight flooding over the forest on the other side. I listened to the news programme on the radio for a while, but there wasn't a word about people not dying, so I could only suppose it was a mystery already solved and put some music on instead: Pantera's *Vulgar Display of Power*, it had absolutely floored me when it came out and it was still perfect for driving.

I'd forgotten to bring up the matter of the sailing boat the night before as I'd been intending, just to make sure she was still in favour. If I'd had it now, we could have gone sailing this afternoon, enjoyed an evening swim off one of the islets. Life didn't get much better than that.

As usual, I was the first one into work. After making some coffee I rolled up my shirtsleeves, sat down at the computer and went through everything that had piled up before I went away, and then everything that had come in since.

After a while, I heard Elin's key unlock the front of the premises and I went to say good morning when she came in. With her white cotton dress, her tanned face and blonde hair she looked like summer itself. I probably wouldn't be able to keep hold of her much longer, I thought. But then I'd been thinking that for two years now and she was still here.

'Morning, Elin,' I said. 'Nice to see you. Everything all right?'

'Yes, fine,' she said, hanging her shoulder bag on the peg. 'But I suppose you've heard we haven't had any in for the last few days?'

'Yes, I'm about to look into it now as a matter of fact.'

She sat down behind the desk, then stood up again and got her phone out of her bag.

'What was Moscow like?'

'Hot.'

'Same as here, then.'

'I'm going to pop over to Kongsro in a minute, and then I'll be out for lunch. Back around two o'clock, I should think.'

'OK.'

'Phone if anything happens.'

'Will do.'

I went out and opened the gate, got in the car and reversed out slowly. It was impossible to see if anyone was coming along the pavement before I was halfway out. An elderly man wearing a white cap stood back waiting. I put my foot on the brake and stopped, waved him by, then reversed the last bit into the street and pulled away in the direction of the river. I followed its course until coming to the bridge, turning a few minutes later onto the E18 only to immediately leave it again after a few hundred metres and make a left. When still a young man I'd put it to my boss that we build our own mortuary, our own refrigerated facility with viewing rooms, facilities for staff, storage and garage space. He'd dismissed the idea out of hand, I was getting rather too far ahead of myself, he said, but here it was, twenty years old already, discreet yet spacious, fine and functional.

I parked and went in. The lads had all arrived, they were in the staff kitchen, Jarle and Sander sitting at the table, Vidar standing back against the wall with a can of Coke in his hand. Jarle straightened up almost imperceptibly when I stepped in. I smiled to myself.

'Well?'

'Nothing,' said Jarle.

'Still?'

All three shook their heads.

'OK,' I said. 'What do we do now? Any suggestions?'

'Go out and kill someone?' said Sander.

'Sign on the dole?' said Vidar.

'Good suggestions,' I said. 'But before we do either, perhaps we should try and find out what's actually going on.'

'How do we do that?' said Vidar.

'You've checked the website and the phones, I take it? Made sure they're working?'

Jarle nodded.

'Do that again, Jarle, please, if you would. After that we each take a town where we're represented. Phone the hospitals, phone the care homes, and not least the hospices.'

'What do we say to them?' said Jarle.

'You ask if they've had any deaths during the last four days, of course. I'll take the town here, you divide the others up between you. OK?'

They nodded and I disappeared into my office, starting with the central hospital, phoning Kenneth, our contact there.

'Syvert Løyning here, from Remembrance Funeral Homes.'

'Oh, hello there.'

'Quick question for you.'

'Fire away.'

'How many deaths have you had in the last four days?'

'Wait a second and I'll check.'

I heard his fingers tapping at a keyboard.

'None, by the looks of it.'

'Wouldn't you say that's a bit unusual?'

'Not really. It happens occasionally – we've got good medical staff here, you know!'

'I'll bear that in mind. All right, thanks for your time.'

'Hang on a minute. Why do you want to know?'

'Someone gave us the wrong hospital, I'm having to ring round and check.'

'Ah, that makes sense. Well, speak to you again soon.'

An hour later I'd phoned every institution I could think of. They were all saying the same thing: no deaths, but it happened every now and then. That would be why there'd been no mention of anything in the media yet. No one had coordinated the data.

I got up and went over to the window, opened the blinds and looked over in the direction of the church, whose steeple was just about visible above the treetops.

I didn't know what to believe.

The clergy wouldn't have noticed anything, they'd still have people to bury for a few days yet.

I sat down again and called Joar.

'Syvert,' he said. 'Have you been dreaming?'

'No. Have you?'

'Yes.'

'Listen, there's something else I need to ask you about. It has to do with probability calculus.'

'Yes?'

'What's the likelihood of no one dying for four days?'

'Where?'

'In this country.'

'I mean where in this country, you idiot. In a small village it's normal, obviously. The probability decreases the bigger the locality and the more people we're talking about.'

'How about a city of about 90,000 people?'

'Aha! Work dried up, has it?'

'You could say, yes.'

'Let me just check.'

He was quiet for a minute.

'Well, it doesn't look like they keep statistics over individual towns or villages, which is a bit odd. But there's something here at the county level. It seems the norm for August as a whole is around 180, 190. The county has a population of about 300,000. Which means that where you are the town should be seeing about two or three deaths a day in August, if that sounds right. The numbers are small, so it's not unlikely there can be the odd period without any at all.'

'I've never known it before.'

'No, life and death tick on like a clock, don't they? But you could have worked this out yourself.'

'What if we include Oslo?'

'Then we'd be talking about a serious anomaly.'

'But it's not impossible?'

'I doubt it's ever happened, but it's not *impossible*. Statistical probability, probability theory, is maths. I can calculate the statistical probability of a phenomenon like this occurring, but the only thing it would tell us would be that it's unlikely. So maths isn't enough, what we're dealing with is biology, not some abstract regular system. Statistics is like the tip of the iceberg – it can tell us that in Agder 178 out of 300,000 people died in August, but if there aren't any dead your stats go out the window. And where do we look for the reason? In the 300,000 living. How much data do you think they conceal? How do we break the biology down into figures? You're not saying no one's died in Oslo either, are you?'

'No, not at all. It was just an example.'

'An example of what?'

'I'm just trying to understand what's going on here. Not that you're much help, as usual.'

'You have a nice day, too,' he said, and hung up.

I should have rung round and checked with the major hospitals in Oslo, but when the lads told me not a single death had been registered in the other towns where we had offices, I simply hadn't the heart. What would I do if it turned out to be the same story in Oslo?

Instead I drove back into town, parked in the yard and looked in on Elin on the off chance that something had come in while I'd been away. But nothing had, she was sitting staring at her phone when I came through the door. She was good at what she did, but never did anything off her own bat. Had it been me in that situation and I'd been twenty-two, I'd have started washing the floors or something, updated the records, anything at all but sit there doing nothing.

But none of that sort of thing was in her job description, a fact she without doubt would bring to my attention the moment I made any suggestion, so I left her alone and ambled off towards the restaurant. I could always have a beer before he came. I deserved one.

A minute later I stopped in my tracks. I should have got changed into something else for lunch. I couldn't go out in formal black trousers and white shirt in this heat. I looked like a funeral myself.

I turned, indecisive. Could I be bothered?

Maybe it looked like I was heading for an important lunch meeting? I decided it would have to do and carried on walking. It didn't feel good, what Joar had referred to as work drying up. I tried not to think about it, but it wasn't my thoughts that troubled me, it was the way it felt, it was like something dark that lingered underneath my thoughts.

I'd already spoken to someone in Oslo. I knew the same thing was happening there.

What if it wasn't a coincidence?

It had to be.

I emerged onto the pedestrian street, into teeming throngs of people, all lightly clad, all seemingly in high spirits. There was ice cream, there were prawns, there was bread and mayonnaise, there was beer and delightfully chilled white wine. No reason at all to hang my head and brood.

But if no one ever died, what would happen then?

Enough now, Løyning.

I got my phone out and gave Lisa a ring. I'd completely forgotten to tell her about my mysterious lunch appointment. It would be too late afterwards, she'd think I'd been keeping things from her. Lisa believed that everything happened for a purpose. There's a reason for everything, whether you can see it or not, she always said. Like the time we were going on holiday and I couldn't find the car key. The suitcases were packed, the kids were sitting waiting in the car and I was tearing about looking for the bloody key. It never got mislaid, I always knew where it was. Only not then. Have you looked in the bin? Astrid said. Why on earth would I look in the bin? I said. But I was so desperate, so stressed out, that I went and looked. And sure enough, there it was. We were going away for a whole week, so I'd gone out with the rubbish bag just before, apparently with the car key in my hand, and somehow I'd let go of it.

Lisa was in a sulk all the way to the airport, she thought it meant I didn't really want to go on holiday at all, it didn't help that I kept on telling her I did and that I'd been looking forward to it for ages. Misplacing the key had nothing to do with going on holiday. But she gave me a sarcastic look. She thought she'd worked out that the colleague of hers we were going on holiday with was someone I didn't care for and that I didn't like her family much either. But holidays were holidays, beaches were beaches, it didn't matter who you were with.

'Hi,' she said now. 'How's it going?'

'Good.'

'Did you find an explanation? I mean for no jobs coming in?'

'No, but I've done a bit of checking and it's all within the bounds of what's normal apparently. What are you up to?'

'Sitting here sweating in the office. Can we go for a swim this evening?'

'Good idea.'

'How about you, what are you doing?'

'On my way to lunch with some mysterious bloke. He phoned yesterday and asked for a meeting. Wouldn't say what it was about, apart from it having something to do with my dad.'

'Something too sensitive to talk about over the phone.'

'That's exactly what he said. I wonder what it can be.'

'If it's about your dad, my guess would be something to do with what he was actually up to in the Soviet Union in the seventies.'

'What, you mean spying?'

'Your mysterious bloke could be a journalist.'

'I never thought of that.'

I came to the end of the pedestrian street and saw the Fiskehallen restaurant further ahead at the waterside, its glass glittering in the sunlight.

'You don't think he could have more children, do you?' she said.

'Oh please, don't make me wonder.'

'Sorry. Just thinking out loud, that's all. Anyway, give me a ring afterwards, if you can. You've got me all curious now.'

'I will,' I said, and hung up.

It would mean Lisa and I would live for ever too. Astrid, Pål and Tor would be coming round to visit us for all eternity. Mum would be sitting in the care home looking down on the cemetery for thousands of years to come.

It was so stupid I could have laughed.

I walked a bit faster now, feeling out of sorts in my good trousers and shirt as I went past the beach that was packed with people in bathing costumes, kids shrieking and squealing.

Couldn't it be a good thing too, though? Did it have to be so weird?

Only when I came to the entrance to the terrace outside the restaurant, did it occur to me that I didn't know what he looked like. And that he surely didn't know what I looked like either.

'I've booked a table for one o'clock,' I said to the head waiter. 'Name of Løyning.'

'This way, sir,' he said. 'Your guest's already arrived.'

I followed him as he threaded a path between the tables to one at the far end, where a tall, slender man my own age got to his feet as soon as he saw us. I recognised him straight away, the thick white mane, the deep furrows in his long, equine face couldn't be mistaken. It was *the* Helge Bråthen. The famous architect.

'I hadn't realised it was you,' I said, caught off my guard.

'Helge,' he said by way of presentation, and held out a hand in greeting. 'Nice to meet you, Syvert.'

We sat down.

'Could I have a beer?' I said to the head waiter, then looked enquiringly at the architect. 'How about you? I thought I might be early enough to have one before you came, and now I've been thinking about it all the way here.'

'A beer sounds good,' he said.

'Make that two,' I said.

The head waiter gave a measured nod and looked rather offended, the way head waiters often do.

'You flew down this morning, then?'

The architect nodded.

'Flight got in at ten.'

'You won't have seen the sights yet?'

'Some. But I know the place. Rather well, in fact. I grew up not that far from here. When I was a teenager, this was my town, you could say.'

'That's right, you're from the Sørland yourself. I'd forgotten. Not much of your accent left, though.'

'I moved away when I was eighteen. I thought I'd retained rather a lot of the accent, actually.'

'It's not enough to just roll your r's, you know,' I said with a laugh. 'No offence meant. Accents can be a very sensitive matter.'

'None taken.'

A waitress came out through the opening in the glass wall, a tray with two pints on it balanced on one hand.

'They look like they've got our names on them,' I said.

He nodded. His elbows were propped on the table, his hands folded in front of him. They were large hands, though his arms weren't at all thick. He was wearing a pair of those long, baggy shorts with lots of pockets in them, beige in colour, and a white T-shirt. If the casual observer knew no better, they would perhaps think I was an employer, while he was a potential employee I'd invited out to lunch, or so I thought. Providing they didn't know who he was, of course. Which they probably did. I'd already noticed a few glances in our direction in the short time we'd been at the table.

The waitress put the beers down in front of us. I took a long mouthful and wiped the froth from my lips.

'You'll be wondering why I asked to meet you,' he said.

'Yes, I am,' I said. 'You said it was something to do with my father?'

'That's correct, yes. His name was Syvert Løyning too, as I understand it?'

I nodded.

'Did you know him?' I said. 'No, I don't suppose you could have done.'

'No, I didn't know him,' he said, now looking straight at me. 'I'm not sure how to say this. I've never told anyone about it before. Not a living soul. It feels right that you should be the first person to know, though it is very difficult for me to put into words.'

Lisa was right. He's my half-brother. The thought ricocheted through my mind. That's why he wanted Joar to be here too.

He was silent for a moment, and stared at the table. When he lifted his gaze again he was looking at me very intently.

'I was there when your father died. I think I could have saved him. But I didn't. I was just a boy.'

'What are you saying? You saw what happened?'

Just then, the waitress appeared again at the table.

'Have you had time to look at the menu?' she said.

'Not yet,' I said. 'Could you give us another few minutes, please?'

'Of course,' she said.

The architect rubbed his hands nervously while staring out at the harbour.

'Down the road from the house where I grew up, there's an inlet with a small marina. The road leads over a narrow bridge. It was winter.

A dark night in winter. The roads were slippery with slush. I was going down to the pontoons there. I saw a light shining in the water. It was a car. It must have crashed off the bridge only shortly before.'

'My father . . .'

'I ran back to tell someone. Only I didn't. I said nothing. I went upstairs to bed. They found the car the next morning and winched it up. I saw that too. Of course, he was dead by then.'

He looked at me with tears in his eyes.

'That was what I wanted to say to you. You, his son. If I'd raised the alarm that night, he could still be alive now. But I didn't.'

There was a lull in which neither of us spoke. I didn't know what to say.

'Can you forgive me?'

I shook my head.

'There's nothing to forgive here. You were a child. And you had nothing to do with him driving off the bridge.'

'But he must have been alive.'

'We've no way of knowing that.'

'It's very gracious of you to take it so well.'

'I can't really see any other way I can take it,' I said. 'Shall we have some lunch? We can talk while we're eating. Though not with our mouths full, of course.'

He looked down at the menu in front of him.

'Fish is the thing here,' I said. 'Do you care for fish?'

He nodded.

'I usually go with the cod. They do it with ginger and soy. Honey, actually, as well. It might not sound that appealing, but it's very good. I grew up on cod and potatoes with lashings of butter. But then so did you, I imagine.'

'It sounds familiar.'

'A lot's happened on the culinary front since then, of course. I was a cook when I was in the military and food's interested me ever since. I like to experiment in the kitchen. Very often, I'll give it an Asian twist. What do you reckon, do you want to try the cod?'

'Cod sounds good,' he said.

I swivelled round and waved the waitress over. That old feeling of being two different people had come over me again. One of us was up in the light, taking care of whatever was going on in the here and now, the other was scrabbling around in the darkness below, weighed down with heavy emotions, wordless, formless.

'We'll both have the cod, please,' I said. 'And two glasses of a good white wine, whatever you think goes best. Is that OK?' I glanced back at the architect, who nodded his approval.

She took the menus and went off to the kitchen with our order.

'You'll appreciate why I didn't want to talk about this over the phone.'

'Of course, and thanks for coming all this way to tell me. It can't have been an easy decision for you.'

He ran a hand through his thick white hair.

'I should have done so years ago. Only I hadn't the courage.'

'It wouldn't have changed anything as far as I'm concerned. What happened happened. Talking about it won't make it any different. I'm glad you chose to do so, don't get me wrong. But nothing's changed by it.'

'I'm not so sure.'

'Really?'

'The past exists to us, but it doesn't exist in itself. What's important is the way we relate to it. And the way we relate to things is something we can change.'

It had never even occurred to me that Dad could have been alive while still down there in those waters. But if he was, he'd have been able to get out. So if he was alive, he must have been unconscious.

'I get what you mean,' I said. 'And what you're saying is right, certainly. But in another way it's completely wrong. I haven't told you what line of work I'm in, but I'm an undertaker, I put people in their graves. And if there's one thing I've learned, it's that there are no two ways around it. Death, that is. My father died, and nothing can change that.'

He nodded.

'It must have been very hard for you to have lost him at such an early age.'

'It was what it was.'

He produced one of those e-cigarette things and held it up enquiringly for a second.

'You don't mind, do you?'

'No, go ahead.'

'I'd imagined you might have been angry with me for telling you about it. Or at least upset.'

'Why should I be?'

'But then you turned out to be a Stoic.'

He put the device between his lips and sucked on it, then blew out an electronic cloud of something or other.

'It's been a terrible secret to carry around. I really must thank you for agreeing to see me. And for the way you've taken it.'

'You're welcome. Listen, I just need to pop to the loo a minute. Start without me if the food comes, won't you?'

I stood up and went inside, through the restaurant interior, down the stairs to the toilets, where fortunately I still had coverage on my phone, even in the cubicle. No emails or messages of note, so I looked up *Stoic*, and while I pissed began to read what Wikipedia had to say about it. Stoicism, it said, was a school of Greek philosophy, and as far as I could glean it was all about keeping the mind separate from emotions. I balanced the phone on the edge of the sink when I was finished, washed my hands, tore off some toilet roll and dabbed them dry, flushed everything away and carried on reading a bit. *The ideal Stoic is unaffected by adversity and characterised by level-headedness and strength of mind*, it said, claiming then that a wise man or a person of *moral and intellectual perfection* would not suffer from destructive feelings.

So it wasn't an insult, I decided. Anyway, what reason would he have to insult me?

When I returned, the food was on the table. I realised he'd been waiting for me, and sat down.

'The portions aren't big, not by any means,' I said. 'But generally the food's so good it doesn't matter.'

He didn't say anything and I got the distinct impression that our meeting was over. That there was nothing more to talk about. In which case we'd just have to tread water for the next half-hour.

'What do you think?' I said. 'Does the honey work for you?'

'Mm,' he said with a nod.

'Have you ever been to Asia?'

'A number of times, yes.'

'I've been to Thailand a couple of times. Have you been there?'

'Not to Thailand, no.'

'Where have you been, then?'

'Hong Kong. Singapore. Vietnam. Japan, of course. China.'

'Business?'

'Mainly, yes.'

'You've been rather successful, is that right?'

'I can't complain.'

Again, a stillness ensued, during which I managed to sneak my phone out under the table, then glance at it to see if anything had happened.

'Your brother, Joar,' he said after rather a long silence. 'Is he an astronomer by any chance?'

'Yes, he is.'

'I thought that would be him. Will you speak to him about what I've told you? Or should I arrange to meet him too?'

'There's really no need. I'll talk to him. Besides, Joar was so little at the time that he has no memory of our father.'

Again, a lull. I'd never been so glad of the small portions here as I was now. A couple more forkfuls and he'd be finished. It didn't matter that a dessert would round off the meal very nicely indeed.

'What made you say I was a Stoic, exactly?'

'You gave me the impression that you relate to things you can do something about, and ignore those that you can't. Which is the Stoic in a nutshell, I'd say. Not knowing you, of course, I can't be sure it's true. But that was the impression I got.'

'What would you say was the opposite of a Stoic?'

'An hysteric, perhaps!' he said, and laughed for the first time since I'd sat down to join him.

On my way back to the office I phoned Lisa to tell her about the lunch. She was impressed that he'd asked to meet me after all those years, he didn't have to, she said. I was feeling a bit down about the whole thing, so I didn't tell her what I was thinking – that the only reason he'd done so was for his own sake. He'd been wanting to get it off his chest so he could feel better about it. Lump the whole thing onto me.

I decided not to tell Joar straight away, not really feeling up to going through it all again just at the minute. I didn't fancy work much either, so after checking in to hear if there'd been any developments, I sat down in my office and looked at sailing boats for sale online. It didn't have to be that big – I reckoned a thirty-footer would be about right – and it certainly didn't need to be expensive either, we'd only be jaunting around in the archipelago. There were a lot of nice ones going for around 200,000 kroner. But there was one in particular I kept going back to. It was an all-wooden forty-footer, and cost a bomb. Berths for six, meaning the whole lot of us. It was old, but looked extremely well kept. Mahogany cockpit, mahogany interior. Built at the Grimsøykilen boatyard in 1952. Stylish as hell. But – and it was a big but: it cost close on a million.

I had the money. But Lisa was never going to agree. She'd think about inheritance and the kids' futures, and that we needed a buffer in case anything happened.

On the other hand, I thought as I stepped over to the sink and then filled a glass from the tap, I could sell some of my shares. Take the money out of oil and invest it in sails. Alevtina would certainly approve.

Lisa wouldn't actually need to know how much it cost.

I put the glass down in the sink and rang the owner before I changed my mind.

The boat was still for sale. It was out in Høvåg, I could drive over and look at it now, if I wanted.

I put my head round the door to Elin and told her I'd be out for the rest of the day. Leaving town, I gave Jarle a ring, but there was nothing new to report, so I put good old Metallica on the stereo, the first live album, and realised I'd cheered up a bit.

The owner was standing waiting for me in the car park by the woods. A small, dishevelled-looking bloke with a harsh gaze and a wisp of thin hair about his skull. The first thing he said after we introduced ourselves was that he'd never be selling if he didn't have to. The boat was his life's work.

I followed him along a narrow, gritty path that led through the trees. After about a hundred metres, an inlet opened out in front of us and there, moored at the jetty, was his boat.

She was a beauty. A dream.

'I'll take it,' I said.

He spun round and stared at me.

'You should have a proper look first.'

'I've already seen enough. Unless there's anything major wrong with her, it's a deal.'

Out on the jetty he drew her in and we stepped aboard. Everything looked as good as new. He told me at length about all the work that had been done on her, while I nodded and smiled, asked a question here and there for the sake of politeness, but I'd made up my mind. She was my boat now.

'It'll probably take a couple of days for the transfer to come through,' I said as we stood back on the jetty again. 'Promise me you won't sell her to anyone else in the meantime.'

'I won't.'

'Promise or sell?' I said with a laugh.

'I promise I won't sell her to anyone else, was what I meant,' he said, the humour lost on him completely. 'As soon as the money's in my account, she's yours.'

'Excellent,' I said. 'I think she's the finest sailing boat I've ever seen. I can assure you she'll be in good hands.'

We shook on it and I walked back to the car while he went the other way, over the rocks towards a house that looked down from the bank.

I texted Lisa to say I was going to look in on Mum before I'd be home, but that I was still on for our evening swim. Nothing about the boat. I wouldn't let on about that until it was moored at our own jetty.

On my way back towards town I remembered a visit we'd had once from Mum's brother-in-law Oliver, he'd been in the area to buy, of all things, a sailing boat, and had yet to tell his wife, Jorunn.

Well, it couldn't be genetic, he'd only married into the family.

He'd been a bit too smarmy for my liking, had Oliver.

Jorunn must have liked him though, and Mum had always had a soft spot for him. She cried at his funeral. Quite unlike her. I'd wondered at the time if there'd been something going on between them at some point. But Mum and her sister were close, it was only natural she'd cried, it was a huge loss for Jorunn. Maybe Dad's death had come up in her too.

Our old house was on the way to the care home from Høvåg and I pulled in to sit and look at it for a moment, it had been ages since I'd been that way last. The people who had it now had tacked on a big extension that made the original house look more like a wing of the new one, and the entrance was now on the north side. They'd pulled the barn down as well, built a new garage and put down a lawn at the front.

Enterprising folk, I'd give them that.

There was a paddling pool in the middle of the lawn. A ball floated around in it. Two racquets made of yellow plastic lay on the grass, where a tricycle stood too, and various garishly coloured toys lay strewn about.

Oddly, it was Dad I thought about. I'd lived here longer without him than with him. But what came back to me was cautiously riding around the yard on the old moped with him standing watching in his wooden clogs and brown trousers, and the hours spent in the garage with him.

A woman in white shorts and a white top came out. She was wearing sunglasses too, and her feet were in sandals. After a moment, a bare-bottomed toddler emerged and toddled after her. The woman fetched a sunbed from the shadow of the house and unfolded it next to the paddling pool. I put the car into gear and drove on to the shop, bought a box of chocolates and a half-litre bottle of Coke, and continued through the valley. The care home was situated where the flatland began, a yellow-and-white single-storey building that stretched its way through grounds dotted with deciduous trees. Apart from the traffic that passed along the road outside, it was a quiet and peaceful place. Behind, the terrain sloped away towards the bed of the valley, where the river was at its widest and the church stood too.

Inside, I bumped into Margrethe who ran the shop there.

'She's sitting out on the patio,' she said.

'How's she getting on?'

'Fine.'

'Good!' I said, and turned down the corridor to the sitting room, where the patio door stood open.

Mum was sitting smoking at a table in the corner, in the shade of a parasol. Jørgen, an old stick of a man with a prominent nose and blue, moisture-covered lips, was sitting there too. His head shook slightly, a faint tremble that made him seem confused even though the rest of him gave an impression of composure.

'Hello there,' I said, putting the chocolates down on the table and pulling up a chair. 'This all looks very pleasant.'

Jørgen eyed me with suspicion, though he'd seen me plenty of times before.

'I'm Syvert,' I said. 'Evelyn's eldest.'

'Ah!' he said. 'Jørgen Kristoffersen, pleased to meet you.'

We shook hands.

Mum barely batted an eyelid. Still, I knew she was glad I'd come. She couldn't *not* be, surely?

'What do you do with yourself, then?' Jørgen said.

'Oh, this and that.'

'I'm a gardener. I've a big nursery not far from here.'

'You don't say.'

'But I'll leave the two of you alone. I'm sure you've lots to talk about.'

He got up and went inside, surprisingly light on his feet.

'I've brought you some chocolates. Do you want one? The box might be a bit hard to open, let me see,' I said, picking it up and discovering it was, I had to tear the plastic wrapper open with my teeth before I could remove it. I put the box down in front of her again with the lid open.

'Those ones with the coconut are nice,' I said, indicating one. 'How are you doing, anyway?'

'All right, thank you,' she said. 'What about you?'

'Fine. The kids are all right too, as far as I know. And Lisa's just Lisa.'

She reached forward and clawed out a chocolate she then devoured within seconds. She took another, and another after that, then lit the end of the cigarette she'd put out in the ashtray and puffed on it.

She could drop off to sleep all of a sudden in the middle of a conversation or a meal, and she couldn't walk without support, but apart from that there wasn't really anything wrong with her. Once it became apparent she couldn't look after herself properly any more, I suggested she move in with us. But she wouldn't hear of it – what would she do there? I arranged for some home care from the local authority, which worked out for a while, but then it got to a point where she needed more help than the scheme allowed for. Lisa and I looked in on her as often as we could, but eventually we had to concede that it wasn't practical, and secured her a place in the care home.

She seemed happy enough with that. For our part it had been a relief. She was my mother and I owed her a lot, but she'd become increasingly difficult and took it for granted that we'd come and attend to her needs. Only when Joar showed up, once in a blue moon, did she become radiant, full of gratitude that he was paying a visit.

It was easy to think that her mental faculties were diminished, often she would seem to be absent, as if she'd retreated to a place far inside herself and was too feeble to haul herself back into the world the rest of us inhabited. But then all of a sudden she could deliver a sharp-witted comment that revealed she'd been keenly following everything we'd been saying. She could be heavy going at times, if I had a little dig at her, for instance, and there was no response, but other times she'd have a go at me in return, sometimes she'd even laugh.

'I came back from Moscow yesterday,' I said.

Her eyes darted a glance at me.

'You never told me you were going.'

'It was only a couple of days.'

'Aha.'

She picked up the pouch in front of her and took out a pinch of tobacco, drawing the strands into the compartment of her little cigarette-making machine with quick, practised movements.

'You've not considered vaping in your dotage, have you? I'll get you the gear if you like.'

She attached an empty cigarette tube to the tip of the machine, put the lid down and pushed the slide back and forth in a single, hard motion. Then she removed the cigarette and tapped the filter end a couple of times against the tabletop before putting it in her mouth and lighting it.

'You've not lost the knack of that, anyway,' I said. 'Do you want a refill?'

She shook her head.

'I'll have a cup myself, then.'

I went into the sitting room where the big Thermos was and pumped some coffee into a cup. I stood at the window a moment on the way back and looked across at the white church. For some reason, I thought about the way I'd stood shaking in the shower. The blood on my hands that the water washed away.

It was like remembering a dream I'd had, or something that had happened a long time ago.

'You were never in Moscow, were you?' I said when I came back out.

She snorted.

'You know I was never in Moscow,' she said.

'Well, Dad was there, wasn't he? Only no one ever told me about that. I just thought maybe you might have been there with him at some point.'

'He was never in Moscow.'

She rested her cigarette on the ashtray and gazed out over the river valley, then seemed suddenly to notice the chocolates, took one and popped it into her mouth.

'These are nice,' she said. 'Thanks for bringing them.'

'I think he was,' I said. 'There was a Soviet visa stamped in his passport.'

'What were you doing looking in his passport?'

Her eyes flashed with anger.

I gave a shrug.

'It was in his things. Everything's upstairs in our loft now. You know that.'

She said nothing, but stubbed out her cigarette and took another chocolate.

'See if you can find someone to help me back to my room, will you?' she said without looking at me.

'I can help you back to your room.'

'No, you won't.'

'Why, because you don't want to talk about what happened in the Soviet Union back then?'

She didn't answer.

'Do you know who I met in Moscow?' I said.

She looked at me with eyes that were immediately so frantic and filled with anguish that all I could do was look away. I sat for a second, then went inside and found one of the carers, Karianne her name was, and asked if she could help my mother back to her room, she wanted to rest. Of course, she said, and I followed her back outside. Mum was eating another chocolate and looked up as if nothing had happened.

'I'll be off, then,' I said. 'Look after yourself and I'll see you again soon. Lisa sends her love. I imagine she'll come too next time.'

'You can save yourselves the bother,' Mum said.

'What?'

She put her elbow out like a wing and looked up at Karianne, who straight away took her by the arm and helped her up.

'What's that supposed to mean?'

She made no reply, but began slowly to walk, supported by her carer.

Lisa was in the garden when I got home, bending towards the tap at which her hand lingered as water gushed into the green watering can underneath. She had on a white bucket hat and a white shirt with long sleeves.

'Fishcakes, all right?' I called out to her from the open door.

She nodded and gave me a thumbs up, turned off the tap and picked up the watering can.

Through the window next to the cooker I watched absently as she watered first the big pots on the patio, then the rows of vegetables in the vegetable patch. The fishcakes swelled slowly in a frying pan while chopped onions sizzled in another and baby potatoes tumbled about in a saucepan of bubbling water. I chopped tomatoes, cucumber, red peppers and spring onions for the salad, all the while rehearsing various conversations with her in my mind. One about my meeting with the architect, the idea that Dad could have been saved, another about Mum, who perhaps didn't want to see us any more, still another about what it could mean if no one had died for four days. The issue with Mum probably wasn't worth bothering about. For one thing, I didn't think her anger would last – most likely everything would be back to normal again next time we went. For another, I'd been thoughtless with her and didn't need Lisa to tell me so. It had just been so incredibly aggravating of her to deny something she knew very well was true. I recognised the feeling from when the kids were younger, they could get me seething when they denied stuff, and I could say things then that I knew would hurt them. The nastier the better.

It was the same now with Mum.

But what good would come of closing her eyes to the matter just because it was hard to face? Dad hadn't just wanted a divorce from her, he'd fathered someone else's child. These were hard facts, of course they were. But it was nearly fifty years ago, for goodness' sake!

Why couldn't she say, OK, so it happened, but I've got my own life here in the present, with two lovely kids and three lovely grandkids, and a son who bends over backwards for me?

I transferred the fishcakes onto a dish, tipped the onions on top and the potatoes into a bowl and put the whole lot on the table together with the salad over which I drizzled some lemon and a bit of olive oil.

'Dinner's ready!' I shouted, filled a jug with water and put the plates, glasses and cutlery out.

Lisa came in with her face flushed and glistening.

'How was Evelyn?' she said as she sat down.

'Same as usual. It's hard to say really.'

'You didn't say anything about Alevtina, did you?'

'No, of course not. I mentioned I'd been to Moscow, that's all.'

'What did she say to that?'

'She wondered why I hadn't told her I was going.'

She lowered her gaze and began to eat. I studied her for a moment. She looked tired out.

There'd been something important about her day, I suddenly remembered, I just couldn't for the life of me remember what it was.

I cut off a piece of fishcake, nudged it towards the fried onion and piled some on top, lifted it on my fork and popped it into my mouth.

'I always think fishcakes are better cold, don't you?' I said. 'They're so porous and fluffy when they've just been fried, it's like there's nothing there to bite into.'

'That's an interesting take.'

'It is, isn't it? Meatballs and beefburgers are different altogether. They have a nice crust to them when they're straight from the pan. But when *they're* cold, they're just limp and chewy.'

She smiled faintly without saying anything.

'How was your day, anyway?' I said. Immediately, I remembered what it was she'd been working so hard on. A whistleblowing case. 'Did you get on all right with that whistleblowing case you mentioned yesterday?' I added.

She nodded.

'I think it's going to be OK.'

'Was it sexual harassment? Or something else?'

'No, it was to do with what some would call a robust leadership style. Others would call it abusive.'

'Anyone I know?'

'No.'

'It doesn't sound nice.'

'It wasn't.'

'An evening swim sounds better.'

'Much better.'

The light was dwindling when we came down to the jetty. The air was still, with the intermittent sounds of outboards, an occasional cry. Lisa dropped her towel and climbed down the ladder, let go and launched herself gently into the water. I was more hesitant – anything below 26, 27 degrees felt cold to me as I'd got older, and so I remained standing at the edge for a bit and watched her take a few strokes in the dark blue water. After a minute she swivelled and looked back at me.

'Aren't you coming in?'

I took the plunge, feet first, and felt the icy shock. But the sudden immersion, the cold water against my skin, the immediate taste of salt, was exhilarating. I was as free as a fish. It still took some beating.

She'd turned onto her back a bit further away and lay staring up at the new star when I surfaced. I swam over to her. Droplets trickled down her cheeks. When she flipped upright, I realised they were tears.

'What's the matter?' I said.

'I don't know,' she said. 'Come, let's just swim.'

After only a few strokes she began to sob.

'What is it, Lisa? Why are you crying?'

But she shook her head, her face contorting.

I smoothed a hand up and down her back, though it felt rather useless underwater. Her sobbing was uncontrollable now, her shoulders were shaking.

'Come on, let's go in,' I said. 'Can you manage to swim back?'

On the jetty I draped her towel over her and tried to catch her gaze, but it was as if all she wanted was to hide.

'What's wrong, Lisa?'

She breathed deeply a few times. Her shaking subsided.

'There,' I said. 'Let's get you home.'

I followed her up the path. I didn't know what to think. Nothing like it had ever happened before.

'Is it work?'

She didn't reply.

'Something to do with me?'

'No.'

We went through into the garden and she disappeared into the bathroom next to our bedroom and had a shower. I used the one downstairs, and when I went back up she was sitting at the table in the garden.

'Do you want a drink?' I said.

'That would be nice.'

I mixed two gin and tonics and took them out.

'Thanks,' she said.

'Are you feeling a bit better?'

'Yes.'

'What was the matter?'

'I don't know.'

We sat for a while without speaking. The light from the kitchen window shed a rectangle of illumination on the flagstones and as usual I found myself wondering how it could be so big when the window was so much smaller.

'I felt frightened all of a sudden,' she said.

'Of what?'

'I don't know.'

'You felt frightened for no reason?'

'It was something to do with the star. I can't explain it. Everything was just so dreadful all of a sudden. So very dreadful.'

She fell silent.

'Can you explain that a bit more? I'm not sure I know what you mean.'

She shook her head.

'Let's just forget about it.'

'You're sure it can't have been anything else? Perhaps you've been overstretched at work?'

She didn't answer. I sipped my drink in silence. It wasn't like her at all to be so removed. I hoped she wasn't heading for a breakdown.

I couldn't see the star from where we were sitting, only the light that shone down from it. A person would have to be pretty highly strung to start crying on that account and put all sorts of meaning into what was surely a perfectly explainable phenomenon.

I could understand how Lisa might, though. She was a sensitive soul. Unlike Joar. He was perhaps the most insensitive person I knew. Rational thought trumped everything in his book. But the idea that people's dreams could change because of the star wasn't rational thought at all.

At the same time, it was a fact that no one in the town where we lived had died since the star appeared in the sky. It was coincidence, of course. But how many coincidences did it take for something to no longer be coincidence?

It was *impossible* to believe.

Impossible.

Lisa might believe it. Joar too, apparently. But I couldn't.

It was impossible.

'What are you thinking?' Lisa said.

'I'm thinking about what you said. Trying to understand how a person can be frightened by a star.'

'It's nothing to make fun of.'

'I'm not making fun. Why would I?'

'You make it sound so stupid. *Frightened by a star*.'

Because it *is* stupid, I wanted to say, but didn't.

'It was what you said. And since I don't feel that way, I'm trying to understand how you can.'

'I shouldn't have said anything.'

'Yes, you should! I'm glad you told me.'

She sighed.

Was it about *us* now?

All this was driving me mad. Couldn't people just relate to facts? Mum knew Dad was having an affair in the Soviet Union before he died. Why couldn't she just recognise it as part of her life and make things less complicated for the rest of us? And now there was a new star. It couldn't be explained yet, but why did it have to be the end of the world all of a sudden? And why did the fact that I didn't believe it was the end of the world have to cause such tension between us?

'I'll go up and read for a bit,' she said, and went back inside with her glass in her hand.

TOVE

Meaning is inside. Outside there is none. I knew that. What I didn't know was how to remain inside when the outside forces exerted their pull. They didn't come storming – if they did, you could batten down the hatches and seek shelter until it all blew over. No, they came in disguise, as something inside, impossible then to discover. They wriggled in everywhere, separating you bit by bit, until all of a sudden everything near was distant, and everything distant was near. By then it was too late and you could no longer get back in.

I was on holiday with my family and there was a glass wall between me and my children. I saw my husband as if through the wrong end of a telescope. Whatever he did, it didn't concern me. I was on my way out.

What's difficult, no, *impossible* to understand when you're in that place, is that all this, all these forces, exist *within* you. Nothing happens on the outside, nothing changes there. It all goes on inside.

The countering forces are sleep and grief. They keep you grounded inside yourself. The problem with grief is that it hurts, yes, it hurts like hell, and is without hope. What door do you open then? The one that opens into meaning without hope, where everything hurts, or the one that opens into hope without meaning, where you're invulnerable?

Not that you can choose. Something always chooses for you.

I was on my way out, meaninglessness was beginning to prevail, but I wasn't yet in the place where elation filled the void, and I was drawn back in, first by sleep, then by grief.

A car pulled up outside and I opened my eyes and looked at the time. Almost half twelve. Who would be coming here now?

Although I'd long since used up what sleep I could muster, I closed my eyes again.

The voices of the twins a moment later, glad, boisterous.

Arne's low-pitched rumble.

Then Liv, his mother, and I remembered he'd said she was coming.

What would they say to her? Mum's still asleep. And Arne, an aside to her alone: Tove's not so good, you know how it is . . .

I thought I was sitting up in bed, and so vivid was the notion that I was disappointed when I realised I was still lying under the duvet with my eyes closed.

I couldn't just jump into yesterday's clothes and go down to say hello. I'd have to have a shower first and get ready.

Smile.

Chat.

I opened my eyes.

Even the thought was heavy.

And it was better for them I wasn't there. They could enjoy their grandmother's visit then, without having to worry about me. Without having to feel ashamed.

I heard Arne come up the stairs.

A moment later, he stood in the doorway.

'It's half past twelve, for God's sake. My mother's here. Do you think you could get up?'

'I'm not sure I can manage.'

'What? Why are you whispering like that?'

'Can't you just all get on without me?'

'Listen, Tove. My mother's come to see us. It's not like she has the chance that often. You can't just stay in bed, you can see that, surely?'

'I'm not feeling well.'

'I know that. But you can still get up. Sit in the garden with us a while. I'll help you if you want. Do you want some help? Shall I fetch you some clothes?'

'Arne, I can't.'

He looked at me, and his face became angrier the more he looked. Eventually, he turned away and went back down.

I knew he was right, and so I sat up slowly, put my feet to the floor. Leaned forward, head in my hands.

I needed to get myself together.

Couldn't manage a shower.

I'd just have to put my clothes on.

The T-shirt I'd been wearing was on the floor. My shorts too.

No bra. Needed a bra.

I lay back on the bed and pulled the duvet over me again, even though the room was boiling hot.

It was better not to show myself. Better for them.

I was useless.

I could hear their voices drifting from the garden.

The important thing was for them to feel good in themselves.

They were better off without me.

I closed my eyes.

Someone on the stairs. They came along the landing, knocked on the half-open door. I opened my eyes. It was Liv.

'Hi, Tove,' she said. 'Not doing so good, eh?'

She sat down on the edge of the bed and ran her hand over my hair.

'You'll be all right again, you'll see.'

'No.'

'Yes, you will. You'll be fine. You're such a lovely person, you know? There aren't many like you.'

Tears ran down my cheeks as I looked at her.

'Do you want me to take you in to the hospital, so you can rest there?'

'No.'

She nodded, and smiled faintly.

'I thought not. But listen, I'm going to help you get up now, and then we'll go outside and get some sunshine and some fresh air. The children are missing you, they want you.'

'No. I can't.'

'Why not?'

'They mustn't see me like this.'

'Don't be silly. You're in a place now where you're feeling very sad. But they know that. And you'll feel better once you're out. Trust me, Tove.'

'I haven't got a bra,' I said, and started crying again.

'That's all right, I'll find you one,' she said, stood up and went over to the drawers. A moment later she held one up for me to see.

'Here we are. Now, you sit up and put this on.'

I did as she said. Put my shorts and T-shirt on too.

She handed me a hairbrush and I tidied my hair.

'Right, all ready now,' she said buoyantly. 'See how easy it was?'

I followed her over the landing, down the stairs. I squinted in the sunlight.

The twins were filling the paddling pool with water. Ingvild was sitting at the table under the parasol, looking at her phone.

'How about some coffee?' said Liv.

I nodded.

I sat down slowly at the other side of the table. All my movements were slow now. It was as if they began somewhere in the darkness inside me and had to blindly feel their way before eventually taking shape in the light.

My thoughts too were slow and dark.

Arne was nowhere to be seen.

'Where's Daddy?'

'He cycled down to the shop.'

Liv came out with a cup of coffee for me.

'It's a gorgeous day!' she said, putting it on the table in front of me before sitting down next to Ingvild. 'Ingvild was just saying she'd like to come back and stay with me. Isn't that right, Ingvild?'

'Yes.'

'I'm looking forward to it already. You won't mind me borrowing her for a few days, will you?'

'No,' I said.

But I had to say more than that. Something positive.

'That'll be nice, Ingvild.'

'Yes, it will,' she said, and smiled.

'Do you remember Stian?' said Liv. 'Stian, who you used to play with?'

'Of course I do.'

'Well, he still lives in the same place. He's got a summer job working for the local council. I see him coming home in his workman's safety wear in the afternoons. A grand lad, he is.'

'I'm not ready for romance, if that's what you're getting at, Gran.'

Liv laughed. I lifted the cup to my lips and sipped some coffee.

She could take care of the kids, I could sit here and watch.

'Have you had any breakfast, Tove?'

'No.'

'Do you want me to do you an egg? A piece of toast?'

'No, thanks. I'm not hungry.'

'You'll need something inside you,' she said.

The next minute she was on her way to the kitchen again.

'She means well,' said Ingvild. 'Whatever you think.'

I looked at her. Had she seen through me?

She was only sixteen.

Over Ingvild's shoulder Arne came into view on his bike. A carrier bag of shopping hung from each side of the handlebars. They chinked as he put them down on the ground before leaning the bike up against the wall.

'Nice to see you up!' he said as he came into the garden. Behind me, the twins suddenly raised their volume. I realised they were now in the paddling pool, and twisted round to see.

'It's freeeeezing!' Heming shrieked, hanging over the side with his legs stretched out and submerged behind him.

I tried to smile, and gave a little wave.

When I turned round again, Ingvild wasn't there and I only just saw the back of her as she went inside.

Then Asle was standing in front of me, dripping wet, guzzling Solo straight from the bottle.

I felt obliged to say something to him. Something nice.

But I didn't know what, and before I thought of anything he was gone.

They were as quick as flies.

Liv and Arne came out together. Liv carrying a plate and a glass, Arne with a bottle of beer in his hand.

'Try and eat some of this,' she said. There were two eggs on toast on the plate, milk in the glass. 'You'll feel so much better for it. Sunlight and fresh air. Food and drink.'

'Thanks.'

'We could do a lot worse than this, couldn't we?' said Arne.

I nodded.

'When I was growing up, I wasn't allowed to be inside when the weather was nice. Do you remember?' he said to his mother. 'There were no excuses.'

'A good thing too,' she said.

'In some ways, perhaps. But I'd often want to read. And I'm not sure all your sun worshipping was as healthy as made out to be either. I'd be over the moon if our kids would sit inside and read all day. No matter how good the weather. Wouldn't you, Tove?'

I didn't know what to say and looked at him blankly. He raised his eyebrows as if to prompt me. But then he lost interest and took a swig of his beer while looking out across the garden.

Ingvild was now lying face down on a rug, sunbathing a bit further away.

Where were the twins?

I looked around. They weren't in the paddling pool.

Liv smiled at me.

'Aren't you going to have some?'

I'd completely forgotten about the food. The egg yolks had already stiffened a bit. I was sitting rather too far from the table, so I tried to move my chair closer while still sitting on it, but couldn't. I had to get up. I'd already done so in my mind, just not in the real world. It made it twice as hard.

'Drink some milk, at least!'

'That idea of milk being healthy isn't valid any more,' Arne said. 'Kids don't drink milk these days. That was in the seventies and eighties. Even then it was a vestige from the thirties, at least, when kids actually starved and butter and milk fattened them up. You're not even meant to eat bread any more. That's Norway's entire culinary heritage gone in the space of a generation.'

'It's all just a fad,' she said. 'Milk and bread are as good for you now as they always have been.'

I stood up and dragged my chair closer to the table, lowered myself down onto it again, then lifted the glass to my lips and swallowed a mouthful before putting it back down.

'Did you know the Neanderthals needed twice as much nutrition as us? They crushed bones and slurped up the marrow. Brains too. They ate so much fat they almost had it coming out of their ears. It was probably because they ignored the Health Directorate's dietary guidelines that they became extinct, don't you think?'

He laughed.

'Where have you got that from?' said Liv.

'I'm reading a book about them at the moment. Fascinating stuff. They've discovered signs of cannibalism among them. So they ate each other too. It's a fact. Though clearly not the most nutritional parts. There's a theory that says they ate their dead as a way of healing their grief over them.'

Liv shook her head and glanced across at me with an apologetic smile.

'You never did pay much attention to context,' she said. 'You just follow your thoughts and interests wherever they take you.'

'Why shouldn't we be able to talk about that now? When would it be appropriate to talk about the Neanderthals, in your opinion?'

'Perhaps not when people are eating.'

'You're not hungry, are you?' he said, turning his attention to me.

'No.'

'Has anyone seen Sheba today?' Ingvild suddenly said, rolling onto her side to face us.

'I haven't, no,' said Arne.

'She's probably having her kittens somewhere.'

'It'd be about time, if she was.'

Ingvild got to her feet.

'I'm sure she'd rather be left on her own, Ingvild,' said Arne.

'I know,' said Ingvild. 'I just want to find out where she is.'

I picked an egg-on-toast up off my plate and took a bite. The bread was dry and somehow didn't moisten in my mouth, even though I chewed it for some time. I took a mouthful of milk and swallowed.

The longing to just disappear into darkness was consuming me whole.

'Thanks for taking the trouble with the eggs,' I said, lifting myself up with one hand on the table, the other gripping the back of the chair. The table tipped slightly as I got up, and coffee sloshed from my cup.

'Careful!' said Arne.

His mother looked at me questioningly.

I couldn't speak.

'Are you going inside?' she said.

I nodded.

'I'll pop up and look in on you before I go,' she said with a wink.

That night, I had a terrible dream. We were out at the lighthouse. Arne, the kids and me. While the others swam and took in the sun, I lay sleeping, covered by a towel. The sun beat down, the sky was blue and empty, the sea stretched away and glittered. Some moored boats with Norwegian flags on their sterns dabbed at the water. Sails on the horizon. Nothing out of the ordinary there. The terrible thing was that it was someone else observing us. That I was dreaming what someone else was seeing. From a distance at first, while we were one family among others. Then zooming in on Heming and Asle, their eyes narrowed against the sun, Heming's then wide with glee; Arne had said something, suddenly he was standing with wet hair and wet trunks on the rocks next to them. Then my head, turning to the side in sleep. Ingvild, bobbing on the swell, trying to clamber up, falling back, trying again. Suddenly a close-up on her, the way she threw back her head, blood running down her thigh. Black blood. And then myself in the bath, blood running black from my nostrils, black over my lips, black as it dripped into the bathwater. My hand black with blood.

Nobody else had been there. What I saw was the product of my own imagination. Yet I'd sensed a will behind it all. A coveting of Heming and Asle, Ingvild, Arne and myself. While I'd been dreaming, it had been my will too, but it hadn't been me.

Only after I'd woken, when I lay with eyes wide open, staring at the ceiling, did I realise it had all turned around. The darkness had left me while I'd been asleep. I was frightened by the dream, but not of the day that lay ahead.

I breathed in deeply and purely, light and unburdened in all my being.

I'd never known it before. Normally the transitions were so slow as to be unnoticeable.

Was everything all right now?

I looked at Arne, who lay on his back beside me, expelling little bursts of air. The light of morning fell on him through the window, rendering him completely bare to me. I saw him exactly as he was, and leaned over and kissed him lightly on the brow. He turned his head to the side and slept on.

I got up as quietly as I could, found clean clothes in the drawers, took them with me to the bathroom and had a lovely, long shower. The clock above the door in the kitchen said nearly six o'clock. Outside, it was cloudy, and as I sat eating cornflakes at the kitchen table it began ever so gently to rain.

I was ravenous and devoured two large portions. Once I'd eaten, I took a cup of coffee with me over to the annexe, sat down on the sofa there and lit a cigarette. I felt the urge to start work right away, but it was always a good thing to hold out a bit at first. Rev the engine with the handbrake still on. Not thinking of what I was going to do, allowing my thoughts to flit about.

But it was no good. They flocked towards the pictures, the way bats flocked to the cave.

A woman naked, sitting upright in a bath. Whether blood was to be running, and whether that blood should be red or black, was something I would decide later on. But pale, vacant colours, yellow-white.

Jesus and the Virgin Mother, five canvases, various points of intimacy.

The family at the lighthouse, seen from a distance. Menace in the light.

No, I needed to get started. I had two, maybe three hours before they got up. Had to stick to my promise not to work. Albeit with a slight modification: not to work when they were awake.

A man asleep in his bed, unclad by the light of morning?

That too. No menace there, just innocence. Pristine, wide open.

With a sweep of my arm, I shoved away the clutter on the desk to make room for the canvas. I tore off a sheet of greaseproof onto which I squeezed out some of the colours I wanted to start with.

A faint, almost inaudible peeping sound came from somewhere close by. I put down the brush I'd picked up and opened the door of the adjoining room to look in.

'Are you in here, Sheba?'

All was quiet again. But the door of the cupboard up against the wall was slightly ajar. I went over and opened it. There she was. Sheba, outstretched and looking up at me as a writhing litter of tiny kittens crawled about blindly in search of a teat to latch on to.

She was purring and I crouched down to scratch behind her ear.

'So this is where you're hiding. How many have you had? One, two, three, four! Oh, aren't they lovely! Can I hold one?'

I cupped my hands around a kitten, and it gave an anguished peep as I picked it up, lifting its little head with unseeing eyes, peeping and peeping, warm in my palm and still rather moist and sticky.

'How fine you are. How very, very fine.'

I held the kitten to my chest and stroked its tiny head with the tip of my forefinger.

Sheba watched me calmly, trusting me.

I put the little one down at our Queen of Sheba's tufty tummy and took in the little nativity for a moment more before I went back into the studio, closed the door behind me and began to paint.

Shortly before nine o'clock I tidied up and returned to the kitchen, where I decided to surprise them with breakfast. It wasn't exactly where my talents lay, but I managed to heat up some bread rolls, boil some eggs, make some tea and put out the cheese, ham and marmalade along with some juice, all while looking forward to seeing their reactions. I wasn't just back on my feet, I was myself again.

'Breakfast's ready!' I called out. 'Come and get it!'

Arne got up almost immediately, wondering no doubt what had happened. I went and knocked on Ingvild's door, and when there was no answer I opened it.

The bed was empty.

Was she up already?

I went back to the kitchen and looked out into the garden. She wasn't there either.

Arne came down the stairs with slept-on hair, bleary eyes, grey stubble against his tanned skin.

'What's this?' he said.

'I've made the breakfast.'

'Are you better again?'

'Yes!'

'But you could hardly walk yesterday!'

'I know. I was really in a bad place. But then when I woke up everything was good again.'

'You are taking your medicine, aren't you?'

'Yes, Arne. I'm taking my medicine. You've no need to be concerned. I'm not manic or anything.'

'OK,' he said, and sat down. 'Are Heming and Asle awake?'

'I haven't seen them, so they're probably still in their room. Ingvild wasn't in hers, though.'

'She went back with my mother.'

'Oh, that's right! I forgot.'

I went up the stairs and opened the door of the twins' room. They were lying in bed with their iPads.

'Breakfast's ready, you two.'

They didn't seem the slightest bit surprised that I was back, but slid out of bed and wriggled into their shorts and T-shirts, as synchronised as ever.

'First rainy day today,' Arne said as we sat at the table. 'What are we going to do?'

'We could go into town,' I said. 'I haven't been since we got here. We could buy the boys a present each.'

Both Heming and Asle nodded.

'What price range are we talking about?' said Heming.

'Price range!' said Arne. 'Where did you learn to start talking like that?'

Heming shrugged.

'How about a hundred kroner each?' I said, pouring some milk into a cup without looking up to see Arne's reaction.

But it wasn't a problem. At any rate, he let it pass without comment.

When the boys had gone back up to get ready and we started to clear the table, I smoothed a hand over Arne's back, expecting a kiss, though none was forthcoming. He was obviously still annoyed at me for having been so poorly. Everything fell to him when I was like that.

'I could take the boys, if you'd like some time on your own?' I said.

'I wouldn't mind.'

'It'll be nice for me too, spending some time with just the two of them.'

'It will, definitely.'

I smoked a cigarette under the little porch canopy before going up and telling them to put long trousers and clean T-shirts on.

'Are *you* going to drive?' Heming said as we went over to the car.

'I can, you know. Even if I don't very often.'

'Isn't Daddy coming?'

'No, just us.'

I got in. Heming opened the door on the passenger side. Asle grabbed his arm and jerked him back.

'Ow!' he yelled. 'Mum! Asle's hitting me!'

'No I'm not! And it's my turn to sit in front!' Asle shouted.

'Settle down, the pair of you! There's a journey back too, you know. Heming can sit in front on the way there, and you can sit in front on the way back, Asle.'

'Why does he always get first go?' said Asle.

'All right. Heming, you can sit in front on the way back.'

'But you just said I could sit in front on the way there! You *said*!'

'Asle first, then you.'

'No!'

Heming jumped in. Asle tried to haul him back out.

'Mum!' they cried in unison.

I turned the key in the ignition.

'OK,' I said. 'Heming, you sit in front then. Asle, you can sit in front on the way back.'

'NO!' Asle shouted. 'You SAID! Heming ALWAYS gets to go first!'

He was right. But Heming was as stubborn as a donkey, he wouldn't be budged.

Arne appeared.

'What's going on? Haven't you gone yet?'

'Daddy, Mum said I could sit in the front,' said Asle.

'She did NOT!' Heming yelled. 'She said *I* could.'

Arne looked at me.

'They're both right,' I said.

'Heming always gets to go first!' said Asle with tears in his eyes.

'Just settle down, both of you,' said Arne. 'It's no big deal, is it? Heming, you can sit in front on the way home, can't you? You'll have something to look forward to then.'

'No,' said Heming.

'I beg your pardon?'

'Mum said I was sitting in front.'

'OK, in that case I suggest both of you sit in the back. Is that the way you want it, Heming?'

'Yes.'

'Get in the back, then.'

Heming got out. He glared at his brother.

'You sit in the front,' he said.

'All right, now get in, both of you,' I said.

Heming climbed into the back, and Asle slipped into the front.

'That's better,' said Arne. 'Now, I want no more arguing while your mum's driving. Is that understood?'

They both nodded. Arne lifted his hand in a wave and went back inside as I reversed out onto the road. The boys sat mutely as we made our way. We crossed the little bridge at Gjerstad and drops of rain now spattered the windscreen. They looked like wriggling little creatures. So vivid was the image that at first I wouldn't switch the wipers on for fear of sweeping them into oblivion.

'Aren't you going to switch the windscreen wipers on?' said Heming, leaning forward from the back seat.

'Yes,' I said, and that was that, short shrift. 'What shops do you want to go in?'

'The shopping centre,' said Heming. 'They've got everything there.'

'Good idea. Especially if it's still raining. What do you want to buy, Asle?'

He shrugged.

'A game, maybe, if I've got enough.'

'I want to go to a sports shop,' said Heming.

'What are you going to look at there?'

'Don't know. Just see what they've got.'

We drove over the big bridge that arced across the strait. Grey and almost devoid of boats, the water stretched away on both sides.

The joy of being with the boys swelled inside me.

'Do you know what's really impressive about you two?' I said. 'It's how *little* you actually fight. Most of the time you agree. Don't you think?'

Asle nodded.

'I always wished I had a sister or brother when I was little,' I said. 'You're both lucky there.'

'Didn't Nana want any more?' said Asle.

'She had enough on her plate with Mum!' said Heming.

I froze, and glanced at him in the mirror.

He was smiling. Clearly, he didn't mean anything by it.

The road followed the strait, which kept coming in and out of view between houses and trees, hillocks and knolls, outcrops of rock. It stopped raining, and when we came to the town, the sky above the mouth of the fjord had cleared up a bit. I pulled into the underground car park they'd blasted out of the rock, and from there we took the lift up into the shopping centre itself. The game Asle wanted cost two hundred, which I said was OK. Heming found a football kit that cost a hundred more, prompting Asle to protest until I told him it meant he had a hundred kroner owing.

Outside, the sun was shining through the clouds. The streets were teeming with people. I felt pride in the boys, one on each side of me as we walked towards the harbour in search of ice cream.

I caught sight of Egil sitting at one of the outdoor cafes there. My first reaction was to pretend I hadn't seen him and lead the boys over in the direction of one of the other places. I was so ashamed of myself for what had happened that I could hardly bear to think about it.

But shame was part of the problem. I knew that.

I didn't look in his direction as we went past, and I didn't know if he'd seen me or not. I bought the boys their ice creams and we went and sat on the harbour steps.

'Egil's over there,' I said. 'Are you all right sitting here if I go over and say hello?'

They nodded, licking away at their cornets of soft-serve.

I took the bull by the horns and went over.

'Hi, Egil,' I said. 'Mind if I sit here a minute?'

He smiled. His gaze darted from me to the street, to the table next to his, then back to me.

'Not at all. Of course not.'

If he was angry with me, he was keeping it well hidden.

There was a small suitcase on the chair next to his, which he removed and put down on the ground at his feet.

'It's just that I saw you sitting here and thought I owed you an apology. I wasn't myself the other day. I don't know what got into me.'

'That's all right. It's forgotten. Think no more of it.'

'Are you sure? You're not offended?'

'Yes, I'm sure. And no offence taken. I could tell you weren't quite yourself. It can happen to the best of us.'

'Thanks ever so much.'

'No need to thank me. I mean it.'

It was strange seeing him away from the environments of our two houses. I didn't think I ever had before. He seemed less at ease, a flutter of small movements, his hands, his eyes, his head, he even flexed his arm a couple of times.

He was well dressed in a pale blue short-sleeved shirt and khaki-coloured chinos, brown shoes, a brown belt. But his shirt was creased and spotted by a couple of small dark stains down the front, and his trousers looked a bit crumpled too. His shoes couldn't have been polished in ages.

'Are you going somewhere?' I said with a nod at his suitcase.

'Didn't Arne say? You're meant to be looking after my cat!'

He laughed.

'But yes. Just cross-country though. Train to Oslo first, then the sleeper.'

Heming craned his neck in our direction and I waved. He waved back.

'Well, I'd better be going,' I said. 'I've got the twins over there.'

He nodded.

'I know a bit about what you're going through actually,' he said. 'Had a bad period myself a long time ago, when I was young. I was in hospital for more than six months.'

'I had no idea.'

'It's not exactly something I tend to talk about.'

'Does Arne know?'

'I don't think he does.'

'He knows he's to look after your cat, though, which is more than I did!'

I laughed, and he smiled without looking at me.

'Well, have a nice trip!' I said, then negotiated the tables back to the pavement. Heming and Asle got to their feet as I came over.

'What were you talking about?' said Heming.

'Egil's going away,' I said. 'And we're supposed to be looking after his cat.'

Oddly, the mention of Egil's cat did not prompt me to think of our own. I'd actually been looking forward to seeing the children's reactions when I told them over breakfast. How could I have forgotten? It wasn't until we turned onto the gravel track and I saw the roof of the annexe that I remembered. I was about to say I had a surprise for them when we got home, but then it struck me that they would wonder why I hadn't told them earlier when clearly I must have known the whole time we'd been out. I'd have to pretend to discover them now, then go and fetch them so they could come and see!

But when I parked and we came into the garden, Arne was standing at the open door of the annexe.

'I've found Sheba,' he said, 'and she's got kittens! Come and see!'

Heming and Asle ran. I followed them. When I came in they were already kneeling down in front of the cupboard along with their dad, who now lifted out two lovely little kittens and handed them one each while instructing them to be careful.

It was a lovely scene.

A strong sense of joy filled me.

'We'll have to leave them in peace for a while now,' said Arne as he got to his feet.

'Why?' said Heming.

'They need to be on their own with their mother as much as possible the first few days.'

He came over to me. The twins put the kittens back and sat down to watch them crawl about.

'I thought you said you weren't going to do any work,' he said.

'While they're asleep I can, surely?'

Asle glanced over his shoulder at us.

'Come on, lads,' said Arne. 'Leave the door open behind you, so Sheba can get in and out.'

He paused on his way out.

'It's not *when* that worries me,' he said. 'It's what it does to you.'

'I'm fine now.'

'Well, I hope you're right. Are you taking your medicine?'

'Yes, Arne. I'm taking my medicine.'

'Good,' he said and went back into the house. The boys went after him. I looked in on the kittens again, took a photo on my phone and sent it to Ingvild.

Aaaah! Aren't they cute! she wrote back over a row of hearts.

Since the others had gone off to do their own things, I decided to look at what I'd started that morning. It wasn't bad, but it was a long way off what I wanted. Maybe oils weren't the right medium. Oils pointed to the motif in a way, asking that it be worked and reworked. It was almost the case that each stroke required another, at least that was my experience. I didn't want the motif to stand out or be as sharply defined as that. Watercolour had something of what I was after, but the problem with watercolour was that everything came out exactly as expected. A clouded, watery figure in a clouded, watery space.

Luc Tuymans did all his oil canvases in a single sitting with no subsequent work at all – if he couldn't get an aspect done in one day, he'd just leave it undone. I'd heard him talk about it once. How he would store up his energy, circle about – and then attack.

Detail so easily drained a picture of its energy. Radical simplification so easily became a cliché, or else it was too easy to see the idea that was behind it. A picture wasn't good until its energy transcended its idea.

She was lying in the bath with her arms at her sides. It made her look vulnerable. Childlike, too. A girl-woman.

I took a sketchpad with me over to the sofa and sketched a bit. Now I had her lie in the bath with her elbows resting on the sides. Her knees slightly drawn up towards her, and parted. Her head tipped back. Blood under her nose and on her lips, then. Not soft and ambiguous, but crystal clear. White bath, faintly yellow water, white-tiled walls, red blood.

It would be fun to do something photorealistic again.

It was almost impossible to stop myself from making a proper start, the pull was enormous, but I resisted, closed the door behind me and went to see what the others were doing.

Arne managed his seasonal alcoholism rather well, I thought. He would have a few beers during the course of the day, though never enough for it to show, then a bottle of wine over dinner, which made him a bit gabby, though the boys never seemed to notice. Once they'd gone to bed, he would consume a second bottle, or else a few drinks, usually in the garden. I wasn't worried, I knew he'd pull himself together again as soon as the holidays were over, and it wasn't like he was hurting anyone. He could get quite sentimental at times towards the end of the day, but that was all right, I liked it when people let their feelings out. If he drank too much, it would make him amorous, but that didn't bother me either.

I supposed it all gave his days here meaning. When he woke up he would look forward earnestly to having his first beer sometime before lunch, and then the next, which shrewdly he would defer for a couple of hours. Alcohol was like an anchor to him, quite the opposite of what others thought, which was that it was something frivolous and transgressive.

I felt much the same way about my work. I would feel a very strong pull towards it that was hard to resist, and it lent meaning to my days. It was an anchor too: without my work I never really knew what to do with myself, but would simply float about untethered. Lying in the sun was boring, I was too restless to read, and in the kitchen I was a disaster. The boys had their own world, which Arne, unlike me, could enter at will, he could join in with them naturally in the things they enjoyed, like playing football or badminton, swimming, fishing, even occasionally playing computer games.

The restriction I'd imposed on myself, promising not to work while we were on holiday, was based on an ideal: a world in which I devoted myself to the children and had fun with them doing all the things they liked, then sat with a glass of wine with Arne at the end of the day. But reality was nothing like that at all, so sticking to my promise made absolutely no sense.

The problem was that for Arne work was a job, something he was obliged to do against his will. If he'd been able to do as he pleased, he'd have loafed his way through life drinking. Which was fair enough, but it meant that he simply didn't understand me. He thought art was a career, the same as university was for him.

The stupidest thing I could do was to steal an hour here, an hour there. It would irritate him madly, because we had an agreement. It wouldn't make any difference at all to his mind that I would only be doing it when everyone else was occupied doing things *they* enjoyed.

So I decided to bring the matter up. After the boys had gone to bed and we'd sat down with a glass of wine in the garden, I put it to him. It was the end of the day, he was relaxed and contented and had just talked at length about how different he was from his father. He'd always liked his father, he said, but had never understood him, there was nothing there to identify them with each other. And now he'd got it into his head that something similar was perhaps happening with his own children.

'But they don't have to be like us, surely?' I said.

'No, not at all. That's not what I meant.'

He said nothing further, but gazed out over the bay with all its little lights, and so I understood that it was exactly what he meant. He just didn't care for it rebounding on him in a way that made it seem less acceptable.

'I started on a canvas today that I think has a lot of promise,' I said after a long silence.

'Oh?'

'It feels like I'm in a good place at last. Those drawings I was doing during the winter never really worked.'

'No.'

'It's very important to me.'

'But you said quite clearly you weren't going to work while we were on holiday. Or did I get it wrong? You wanted us all to be together, wasn't that it?'

'That was what I said, yes.'

'Only now you don't want that any more.'

'Of course I do. But I'm thinking I can work in the mornings before you all get up. Perhaps a bit after lunch, too. Just to keep things turning over.'

'I know you, Tove. Two days and you'll be working round the clock. Give you a finger and you take the whole hand.'

'I'm not asking you, if that's what you think. I'm telling you it's what I'm going to do.'

'So you're going back on our agreement? Just like that?'

'Don't make it any harder than it has to be. I'm going to do a bit of work, that's all. Didn't you, when when we were in town today?'

'No.'

'So what did you do?'

'I lounged about.'

'Fair enough. But I'd rather spend my own time creatively than doing nothing. What's wrong with that?'

'We're on holiday. The five of us together, you made a point of it before we came down here. You've just spent nearly a week in bed, the kids have hardly seen you, they've been quite worried as it happens. So why can't you spend some time with them now instead of spending it on yourself? It's not too much to ask, is it? Or is it?'

I said nothing.

He'd just have to be in a mood for a few days, if that was what it took.

He wants to control you.

I nearly screamed with fright.

He's jealous of your art.

I jumped to my feet and dashed to the bathroom.

Please, leave me alone . . .

I stared at myself in the mirror. There was no one else there. Only me, looking back at me.

Don't be scared. You're not mad.

Go to hell.

You might as well accept me. I won't be going away just yet.

I doused my face with cold water, pressed the towel to my wet skin, and held it there.

Everything was still.

'Are you there?' I said out loud.

No answer.

Why had the voice come back now? Something must have triggered it. Not that disagreement with Arne?

Maybe working had somehow displaced my turmoil, without me feeling it at first.

I went back out into the garden. Arne looked at me quizzically.

'What's the matter? Have you got the runs?'

I nodded.

'It's nothing.'

'It wasn't the fish, was it? The fish was as fresh as could be.'

'Who knows,' I said. 'I'm all right.

'Could be bacterial, though. I hope the rest of us don't catch it. That's the last thing we need.'

I woke up just after four, crept out of bed and down the stairs, made myself a mug of instant and had a smoke at the table in the garden before getting started.

I couldn't remember what I'd dreamt, so it couldn't have been anything unusual.

And the voice seemed to have gone.

It definitely had something do with working. The first time the voices appeared, I'd been completely immersed in a project.

I needed to talk to someone about it. Start the therapy again.

Right now it was imperative to put it all away. To go in there without a thought in my head. To work as if in sleep, for as long as I could.

And it went like a dream too. Sometimes it feels like painting isn't a matter of applying, but of revealing something that's already there. A kind of archaeology. This was what it felt like now. Element after element became visible. The window: it was night outside, of course, black against the artificially lit white bath. The soft body and the hard enamel. And the blood, yes, which was impossible not to look at and be drawn by.

At some point, I went and looked in on the kittens, cuddled them all one by one while Sheba considered me with her wise, warm gaze. Apart from that, I worked non-stop until packing in at nine when I went back to the house to make breakfast for everyone.

They were a bit tetchy, all of them, but I took no notice. Arne suggested we go for a swim as soon as we'd eaten, and I didn't mind. We stopped by the shop first and bought biscuits, crisps, some fruit and soft drinks, as well as Arne's six-pack of Stella, then drove along the main road as far as the church. From there, a gravel track led to what had once been a shooting range, where we parked the car. On the smooth rocks below was *Daddy's special swimming spot* as the kids always called it, a place he'd been coming to ever since he was a boy.

It was joyful to see their little heads breaking the silvery surface, and I would have have spent all day with them there in the sun, but after half an hour that felt more like two, I went for a walk up to the church, thinking I would have a look at it in the daylight and investigate whether it would rouse the same feelings in me as on that wild night.

It did, and even stronger. Bathed in cascading sunlight, the sea stretching away, blue and endless, the church appeared utterly detached from the desert religion it was supposed to house. The ship, the seabed roof, the smell of saltwater – it was the sea god with his son the fisherman who had been worshipped here.

Fantastic.

But it was to Mary I had to go.

Mary's body. Mary's fuck-body. Lust's consummation in the flesh. Blood and life. Blood and death. The folded corpse of the god-son dumped in the sea. Everything open under God's heaven. A world without secrets. A world in which nothing was hidden.

That was where I would go, I told myself as I followed the path down towards the shore again and saw them in the distance, sitting on the rock.

They'd put their T-shirts back on. So they'd had enough for today.

Which suited me fine.

'Where have you been all this time?' said Arne. There was a harsh tone to his voice.

'I've been up at the church.'

'You've been away more than an hour. You could have said before just going off like that. We've been sitting here waiting for you for ages.'

'All right, all right,' I said. 'My fault as usual. Sorry, won't do it again.' And then, to the boys: 'Have you had a nice time? What was the water like? Was it warm enough? Good!'

When I got back, I stood the canvas of the woman in the bath up against the wall. It wasn't quite finished, but I liked its crude quality, I could see right away how good it was with some parts fully done, while others remained undeveloped. It *was* archaeology, I'd exposed something, it was there, uncovered on the canvas. Night outside, artificial light inside. We lived in a bubble. Night in the blood, too, this archaic substance we'd brought with us into the bubble, from which there was no getting away. But not black blood, that was a poor idea, too illustrative.

However, it was the series depicting Mary I felt desperate to discover. I went for a walk first, down to the rocks, up into the woods, which were green and warm, full of hovering insects, scuttling beetles, wriggling worms. A biological factory. No snails, though, not without rain. Where did they go when the sun was shining? I lifted fern leaves and peered under toppled trees, but found none. But I had to focus now: the body of Mary, the body of Christ.

And then all of a sudden I couldn't remember what I'd been thinking. Panic threatened to seize me. What *was* it I'd been wanting to do?

I hurried back. Arne was setting the table outside. Ingvild emerged from the house carrying a big bowl of pasta in tomato sauce with peas and prawns, it was Arne's go-to dish.

'Hi, Mum,' she said.

'Hi, Ingvild,' I said, and smiled. How gorgeous she was.

'There's food on the table now,' she said as I went past into the studio.

'I'll be right there.'

Arne came and knocked on the door to tell me the same thing. It wasn't a problem for me, I put down my brush and went and sat out with them. My family. My children. Their movements were unhurried, and I had all the time in the world to study each of them in turn before they noticed and returned my gaze. Little Asle waiting his turn, always that little bit unsure, the way people are when they have someone above them to whose power they are subject. He looked at the annexe, looked at the chestnut tree, looked at his own thighs, though without seeing, for these were simply stations for the eyes to rest. Our little one, at home in the role, anxious only when he found himself alone, or felt himself to be. Heming, that thin streak of ruthlessness in him, carefully tipping the bowl, heaping some pasta onto his plate with the big spaghetti spoon. Ingvild squinting down at her phone, thinking no one had noticed. Arne, petty-minded for all his posturing, holding the bottle over his glass as the beer glugged. No more than seconds had elapsed, and yet I had taken it all in. It happened sometimes, they moved as if in slow motion before me, but I knew of course that it wasn't the case, that it was my eyes that were seeing things faster, the nerve connections speeding up. I anticipated their thoughts, too, knew what they wanted to say even as they began to speak, and could only sit there patiently and wait for them to finish.

Ingvild! She was back!

'Did you have a pleasant time at Gran's, Ingvild?' I said.

'Yes, it was nice,' she said. 'In fact, I was thinking of going to see her again in a few days, if that's all right?'

'Of course,' I said.

The pasta was with Asle now. Then it would be Ingvild's turn, Arne's too before mine. The waiting was making me hungry.

Arne was on his guard, I sensed. It required me to say normal, everyday things, to put his mind at rest.

'We could go fishing this afternoon, if anyone's interested?'

His face lit up faintly for a second, as if the idea activated a little lamp inside him. Ingvild looked at me unkindly.

'Only those who want to,' I said. 'No pressure. But there are mackerel out there now, is that right?'

'Shoals of them,' said Arne. 'But we mustn't – '

'Take more than we can eat, I know,' I said. 'But we could give some to your mother, couldn't we? And maybe to your hermit in the woods?'

'Kristen?'

'Yes, why not? It would be a nice, neighbourly thing to do.'

Now, at last, the pasta reached me.

'What do you say, boys? Do you want to go fishing?' Arne said.

Asle, the poor underling, looked at Heming. Heming nodded, and then Asle nodded too.

'Right, we'll do that,' I said.

I wasn't the slightest bit hungry after all, but scooped a small portion onto my plate for the sake of appearances. When we'd finished, I helped clear the table, then sat for a while in the chair under the apple tree to hint at a headache, aware that I needed to be devious after having suggested the fishing trip. I went up to the bedroom, drew the curtains and lay down on the bed. Arne came and checked on me and I gave a thin smile, my hand flat on my brow, told him I was afraid I wouldn't be able to go with them, but hoped they would have a lovely time. He believed me, even fetched me the paracetamol and a glass of water before he and the boys started getting ready downstairs. I lifted the curtain and watched them go down the bank, Arne with the red petrol can almost luminescent in his hand, the twins each carrying a plastic tub, one orange, one blue. I waited a moment in case they'd forgotten something, then went quietly down the stairs, unsure whether Ingvild had sussed me, and crossed through the garden into the annexe, where I sat down in front of the woman in the bath and considered her while smoking a cigarette.

'Mum?'

It was Ingvild, standing behind me.

'Hey,' I said. 'What do you think?'

'About what?'

'The picture.'

'It's good, yes.'

I turned round to look at her.

'Was there something you wanted to ask me?'

'No. I just wanted to see if Sheba was all right and give the kittens a cuddle.'

'You cuddle away!' I said, getting to my feet. 'Only not for long. I want to work for a bit and it's disturbing if there's someone in the next room.'

I went out to give her time with the kittens, walked around the garden, stood with my hands against the trunk of the apple tree and looked up into its foliage that rustled in the sea breeze, a rising, falling wave of gentle sound. That our lungs resembled trees, and the rustle of leaves sounded like our breathing, was no coincidence.

Suddenly, I saw my squirrel. In the mornings, it darted this way and that, up and down the trunks of the trees, back and forth across the lawn. Now it was sitting on a branch right above my head, staring at me with its shiny black eyes.

'Hello, you,' I said.

I half expected it to answer, so intelligent and sensitive was its gaze. I reached out a finger, but its eyes did not move, the little creature seemed interested only in me. The woman in the garden. Who was she? What did she want?

I heard the door of the annexe bang shut behind me, and my enchantment was broken – the squirrel scurried along its branch, leapt down onto the wall behind it and was gone.

'Don't slam the door!' I shouted.

Ingvild disappeared into the house without reply. I went into the studio, but all my concentration had evaporated, so I drove down to the shop and bought myself an ice cream, and when I came back I climbed into bed and was asleep by the time Arne and the boys returned, quite in accord with my headache story, which was fortunate at least. Fortunate, too, that when I woke up in the early evening it was to a feeling of being filled to the brim with energy and will, so much so that I easily managed to endure the last idle hours until the boys were in bed and it was permitted to devote one's time to something else. Arne came in while I was working, he was on his way to bed and wondered if I was too. Soon, I told him, and gave him a kiss: 'I'll be there before you know it.'

I struggled, unable to find the right articulation, unable even to settle on a motif with which to begin. The exorcism of the demons? Mary with the ashes falling from her open mouth? The underwater mood of the church and its aquatic deity? I decided on Mary washing his feet. Because there had to be that level of intimacy, in all the pictures, that was almost the whole point.

Where, then?

In an ordinary room in an ordinary house?

Too contrived.

Outside? The forest?

No, that would be the same.

To hell with all these thoughts! It's complete idiocy! What am I standing here *thinking* for?

I began immediately to paint the church. The trees all around. The ground sloping away towards the smooth rocks at the shore, the sea. The blue sky, the blazing sun. The white walls, the coruscating white walls. And then I decided it should levitate, rise into the air and be suspended there, metres above the ground.

It was fantastic.

I could scarcely believe it. It shouldn't have worked at all. But it did. It was exactly right.

Outside, it was dark and stars were in the sky. I fetched one of Arne's beers, sat down at the table in the garden and lit a cigarette. It was nearly two o'clock. Another seven hours before they would surface. I could finish the whole painting in that time.

This was the series I'd spent my whole life waiting for.

There was no doubt in my mind. I felt it in the depths of me. The source was bottomless.

All I had to do was let it pour out.

I couldn't sit here!

I stubbed out my cigarette and went back inside. I loved these colours. The nuances of green, from the lightest to the darkest aspects of the woods, the nuances of blue in the sea and the sky, the nuances of white in the walls. Especially the white, what happened when I shaded the part of the wall that faced away from the sun was magical.

The door opened behind me.

'I'm coming, I'm coming,' I said.

Arne said nothing. He looked at me as if I'd killed someone.

'Arne? What is it?'

He was wearing a red cap. Arne never wore a cap. His clothes were different too.

His grave expression widened into a smile.

'Don't you recognise me?'

The voice. It was the voice.

In front of my eyes, the face changed. It rounded and softened. Now it resembled no other I'd seen. The mouth was almost lipless, the cheeks pockmarked with acne scars.

'Oh, that's right, you've never seen me before! But you recognise my voice, I'm sure!'

He laughed.

'Don't be afraid.'

His face altered again.

Now it was my father's face.

But my father was dead.

And Arne was asleep.

'You think you're seeing things,' he said. 'But I'm real. Look, you can touch me.'

He came up to me.

'Or I could touch you,' he said, and gripped my upper arm, so tightly it hurt.

'Feel it?'

He let go, stepped past me and went into the other room.

'Who do you feel most comfortable with? Arne or your old dad?' he said from inside. 'Or maybe your friend the squirrel?'

I jumped to the door, flung it open and ran outside. I didn't know where to go, only that I had to get away. I ran across the grass, down the bank to the shore.

But, Tove, you don't think you can run away from me, *do you?*

'You don't exist!' I screamed into the night, then halted abruptly just above the jetty, spinning to look behind me.

A white figure appeared at the top and came slowly towards me. Now he'd taken Ingvild's form. It filled me with a terror so great that I could think of nothing but to get away.

I ran across the rocks.

'Mum! Where are you going! Mum!'

I stopped.

Was it Ingvild?

'Is that you, Ingvild?' I shouted.

'Yes,' she shouted back. 'Don't run!'

My eyes watched her intently as she came closer.

'Mum, what's wrong? Why are you running?' she said.

'How old were you when you learned to swim?'

She looked at me with bewilderment.

'I was three. What's happening? Why are you asking me that?'

I laughed with relief and joy. It *was* Ingvild, it *was*!

'Mum, I saw you run off down the garden. What's happened? Why were you running? It's the middle of the night.'

'I don't know. I fell asleep on the sofa. I was dreaming. A terrible dream. I had to get away.'

'Come on, we'll go back up now. It's night, you need to sleep.'

'You must too, sweetheart!'

I wrapped my arm around her and we set off back up the slope.

'It's not good for you to stay up at nights, Mum. Can't you take a sleeping pill, if you can't sleep?'

'Yes, I will. But I *was* asleep, I told you. I slept this afternoon, and I was asleep just before.'

'I don't want you to be in hospital again.'

'There's no need for that, I promise. Everything's fine, sweetheart.'

Neither of us said anything more until we were back in the garden.

'Do you want to look in on the kittens before we go to bed?' I said.

'They'll be all right, I'm sure. Let's not disturb them.'

'No, they won't mind. Just a little look. It's such a lovely feeling inside you get from them, the little darlings.'

'OK,' she said.

She opened the door and went in, with me right behind her.

My desk was as I'd left it. I heard her cross the floorboards.

He couldn't possibly be here.

Only when I felt sure did I go after her.

She was kneeling as she reached out to stroke Sheba's bedraggled fur. The kittens snuggled at their mother's tummy.

When I got into bed and lay down next to Arne ten minutes later, I tried not to look at him at first, afraid that his face would transform before my eyes. But after a while I was unable to stop myself. I turned my head and looked.

The face I saw was Arne's, unmistakably the face I'd seen a million times before, and unaltering no matter how much I stared.

Arne was Arne.

Good old, dear old Arne.

But I couldn't sleep.

I was too scared to return to my work in case he came back. I couldn't go out either. I hadn't even the courage to sit downstairs on my own and watch a film. So I lay there in bed, alone with my thoughts until dawn, when I got up and showered, made myself some coffee and went across to the studio. The sun flooding in through the windows made the place feel so familiar and secure it seemed almost to be making a fool of me and my absurd figments.

Wayward Soul, I thought to myself, and wrote it down. Then, after a moment's reflection, I changed it to the plural: *Wayward Souls*.

A scene viewed from without was nothing. Fact. Even a scene as intimate as a woman washing a man's feet. But viewed from within was a different matter altogether! Space upon space, opening out. The soul wrenching itself from reason's embrace, moving freely through every space, inquisitive and expectant, and the beast, scenting life, now stirs: meaning converges from every direction, and all is good.

Jesus had that effect on people when he touched them. All that was crippled and deformed was then straightened and smoothed, everything became simple, graspable and good.

But to touch him? To straighten out all that was crippled and deformed in Jesus? All anger, all despair, to let goodness wash over it and wash it all away?

The gaze, hers upon his, his upon hers.

The door behind me opened, and it was Arne, the real Arne.

'Are you having breakfast with us? Or has work taken you from us now?'

'Of course. I'll be right there.'

Breakfasts seemed to be getting slower and slower. So slow eventually that I felt I could get to my feet as Arne picked up his glass of orange juice, go to the loo, pee, wipe myself dry, wash my hands and return to my seat, all before he put it down again. But there were colours there too, and colours were outside of time. The teapot, yellow as a sun, in the middle of the white table. The green plates. The white bowl with its red strawberry jam. Yellow juice. White milk tinged blue in its glass jug. Bread rolls, sand-coloured.

'Daddy?'

'Yes?'

'Are you going to dive for the knife today?'

'I suppose I'll have to, yes.'

'Can we help?'

'Of course you can'

He looked at me as he explained that he'd dropped his knife in the water when they'd been gutting fish on the jetty the evening before.

'I saw it glance off the rock and then it was gone. It should be easy enough to find, though.'

'I thought I might go into town with Ingvild today and go round the shops,' I said and winked at her. 'Didn't you say you were short on summer clothes? Dresses and skirts?'

'Yes, that would be great,' she said.

'As long as you don't spend too much money,' said Arne.

It was a comment I didn't think deserved an answer. I was as careful with our spending as he was.

Once we were on our way, I realised I felt rather good about myself, a mother taking her teenage daughter out shopping for clothes, and Ingvild was all for it too, not at all tetchy or mute, instead she was rather chatty, telling me all about what her girlfriends were doing in their holidays and what they were really like, the ones I mostly only knew by name: Thea and Lena, Ingeborg and Sandra.

But as we walked around town, I became scared. A man looked at me as he came out of a shop, and it could have been him. I hadn't even considered the possibility. He could look like anyone at all. Another man sitting on a bench looked at me too, and when I looked back his mouth widened in a smile, just as his had done. All of a sudden any man at all could be him: every face, every pair of eyes, every cap, every hand that reached out to grab had me petrified. And when I looked at them, they naturally looked at me, and terror ran through me at will.

'Is there something wrong, Mum?' Ingvild of course asked. She'd always been sensitive to my mood changes, and now suddenly I was distant, as if my mind had stiffened. But there was nothing *wrong*, because he didn't *exist*. And with that thought as my shield I managed to negotiate the shopping centre, where Ingvild for once let herself go and came out bulging with shopping bags.

We had a piece of cake each at the cafe where Egil had been sitting. And I had a latte, Ingvild an iced latte.

'I bought your dad a red cap while you were in Lindex,' I said.

I showed it to her.

'He can't wear *that*, Mum.'

'Why not? I think it's rather smart.'

'But it'll make him look like he's trying to be young.'

'He's not exactly *old*, you know.'

'No, but he's middle-aged. That means he can't wear shorts in town, or white trainers. Hoodies are out of the question. And baseball caps are a no-go.'

'I didn't realise. Do you think he knows?'

'No! And it's about time you told him, if you ask me.'

The man at the next table looked like he was listening. He was seated with his back to us but had angled his head and was sitting completely still as if in concentration.

When we stopped talking he twisted round and looked at us.

He was in his sixties and wearing glasses. The pores on his nose were visible, he had a mouth like a fish and a bald, freckled head. It could easily have been him. If it was, I'd soon find out. I certainly wasn't going to allow myself to be intimidated.

'What are you staring at?'

'Mum . . .' Ingvild whispered.

'You were listening in on our conversation. Do you think I didn't notice?'

He shook his head without reply and turned away.

'The bare-faced cheek,' I said in a voice loud enough to be heard by everyone in the immediate vicinity. 'Come on, Ingvild, we're not going to sit here.'

She followed me in silence and didn't speak to me again until we were on our way out of town.

'I was thinking of going out to Gran's this afternoon. I can take the bus, though. Is that OK?'

'Yes, of course.'

'Thanks.'

'But you were only just there.'

'Yes, but before that I hadn't stayed with her for a year.'

'You're right, I hadn't thought about that.'

She came into the studio before she left. Three packets of my medicine in one hand, a glass of water in the other.

'Oh, thanks,' I said. 'Just put them down over there.'

'Can't you take them now? Then I can take the packets back to the bathroom.'

I looked at her and smiled. She must think I was stupid.

'Yes, all right.'

I pressed a pill from three different blister packs, placed them all on my tongue and swallowed them at once with a couple of mouthfuls of water.

'There we are! You can leave the glass. And have a nice time at Gran's!'

Each night after everyone had gone to bed I locked the door of the annexe from the inside before starting work. No one tried to get in, no one rattled the handle as I'd feared, and the voice was gone completely. The kittens opened their eyes and began to crawl around the floor under their mother's lazy eye. Arne no longer cared whether I worked or not, and my contact with the twins when I saw them, and with Ingvild on the phone, was fine. She sent me smileys and heart emojis and would ask me how I was several times a day. I worked on more than one canvas at a time, until after a while the whole series was in progress. Now and then I would stop to go for a walk along the shore, for there was something good about the darkness and the water, the stars and the woods together. Everything was open and closed at the same time, all I had to do was paint, everything would be good, everything was important. I had no need to eat, no need to sleep, my energy came from the darkness and those who slept in it.

I knew he would come back. Nothing ever shows itself once. Not people, not animals, not occurrences. I kept thinking I would not close myself off and run, but remain open and listening. There was a pull in the world, which the eyes could not see. There were forces at work, unknown by thought. When I sat and gazed at my two beloved boys, in the everyday that the eye revealed, with all its many banalities, that was what I thought: that there was a pull in them that connected them with the flooding darkness, out of sight, even for them, and yet there.

I had painted Jesus and Mary surrounded by darkness, their figures, Jesus seated, Mary kneeling before him, but no furniture, no ceiling or walls, just the two figures as if suspended in blackness. Mary had now my mother's, now my own features, while the face of Jesus remained my father's throughout, albeit eventually I decided I didn't care for that and painted it over. Then I found myself thinking about the eye of the monkey and its human scream in Moreau's watercolour, and so I gave Jesus a monkey's face while retaining the human body. I stood the canvas up against the wall and considered it for some time. It had changed everything. Now Mary needed something of the same treatment. I thought of the squirrel. But that would be too cute, it would drag the whole thing over towards parody. A badger, then? No, same effect. A monkey's face and a human body for her too? There'd be nothing cute about that, nothing graceful, nothing in any way comical. It would be real. The human confined.

Someone tried the door handle.

I wheeled round as it was rattled several times with force.

My heart pounded as if in a nightmare.

'Who is it?'

'It's me,' said the voice outside.

'Who are you?'

'I am who you want me to be.'

I unlocked the door. He stood swaying on the threshold. His face was craggy, his hands were big, and his eyes were white.

I stepped back into the room and steadied myself with my hands on the table.

He wasn't human.

And then he was. His face soft and round, the skin of his cheeks scarred, his eyes suddenly blue, bloodshot in the whites.

He smiled.

'I'll sit over there,' he said. 'Come to me when you're ready.'

'What do you want?'

'Only to talk.'

He sat down on the sofa. I stood against the wall. His head then jerked back and he gaped three times in quick succession.

It was Heming's tic.

It was Heming sitting there, blond and lean and delicate.

But the voice that spoke was not Heming's.

'You've lost your grip, Tove.'

I was so frightened by the sound of such a voice coming from Heming that I began to tremble.

The tic again. As if he was snapping for air.

'But I can't help you with that,' he said.

I closed my eyes.

When I opened them again he was crossing the room, as if by degrees, as if his frame were soft and stiff at the same time. He bent down to pick up a sleeping kitten.

'What do you want with me?'

He turned his big, cumbersome head. His face was raw and unfinished.

And he drew himself up like a beast.

'In two days a star will rise in the sky. The gates of death's kingdom will open. You will see what no one else can see. That is our gift to you.'

He stood beside me now, the kitten in the palm of his outstretched hand.

'Take it,' he said. 'And be good to it, for tomorrow you will kill it.'

I was alone in the room with the little creature clasped to my chest.

Heming was asleep. His face was smooth and untouched by the world. Asle was asleep beside him, a wayward leg on top of the duvet. Arne too was asleep, unmoving on his back.

It was as if they had nothing to do with me.

If I told them what had happened, they would dismiss it as they dismissed everything that was mine.

Perhaps it didn't matter.

It was a gift, he'd said. I was to see what no one else could see.

I already had.

I had seen him.

I painted him standing in the darkness under a shining star. Morning came. My wellies were wet with the dew as I went down the bank, and I saw snails again, the grass was alive with them. I followed the rocks along the shore and the sun came into the sky. I knocked on the door of Egil's place, but no one came, not even the cat. I continued on to the church, lay down in the grass in the churchyard and thought of all the dead bodies underneath me in the unfathomable soil. Would they return? It was impossible. They *were* soil. The soil was *them*. I walked home again, but everyone was still asleep and so I went the other way, down to the marina, where the shop had yet to open. I sat down on the quayside with my back against the wall as I gazed out across the harbour. Here and there, people emerged bleary-eyed from their boats. Gradually, voices could be heard, an occasional murmur, the hum of an outboard, and at last the shop opened. I didn't have my money with me, but took an ice cream nevertheless – no one noticed, and I made a mental note to pay for it next time. By the time I got home, they were awake. I tried to sit with the boys for a bit, but was unable to find rest for more than a few minutes. They were good, though, those brief moments together with them – my children as they sat eating, and my husband too, even if he possessed no more self-awareness than an ape and moreover was in a bad mood. Arne the apeman and his irritated *Aren't you going to sit with us?* to which I had no answer other than the obvious: *No, I'm not.* And then it was: *Why not?* And all I could say was: *I don't know, I just can't, can't, can't.*

In the studio I turned the canvases to face the wall. They were ridiculous. But I did not destroy them, I did not cut them into shreds, because then Arne would drive me to the hospital, I knew he would, because it would be aggression, a first warning of self-harm, and he didn't want any of that.

Art is simplification. Everything else is to pretend that something that isn't real is real. It's a deception. And what's known as creativity is no more than a children's game that has solidified into serious-mindedness. I would write a manifesto about it. Only not today. Today, I painted matchstick men and matchstick women dancing and fucking, and their boats. I gave them more body and cut them out on paper the way I suddenly remembered doing when I was a child making festoons of Christmas trees. It was like entering a tunnel. At one end I sat snipping away at the age of six, at the other I sat snipping away at the age of forty-two, it was almost as if I could wave to the person I was then, who I missed even though she was still there inside me somewhere and now had appeared before me.

They physically led me, took hold of my hand and led me over to the house when I emerged from the studio, not just the boys, but Arne too. Take things easy, spend some time with us, and of course I said I would, but whenever I sat down it was like nothing was happening and I would get to my feet again and go down to the shop or over to Egil's house or back to the studio in the annexe. Dusk came, and it was a relief, it meant no one would expect anything more of me. I stood quite still in the woods with my hand against the pitted bark of a tree and listened to the sounds that came and went. It was a bit like when your eyes adjust to the dark: I heard more and more the longer I stood there.

Something scuttled in the undergrowth. It was a crab, and it was followed by another, then another still. They made a ticking sound.

Arne didn't believe it. But I didn't give a shit what he believed, he saw nothing, understood nothing, and was forever standing in my way. He was envious of my talent, because he himself had none.

I cut away with my scissors, smoked, glued, and sang songs that made me feel good. I knew he wouldn't be coming back, he'd said what he had to say, but still I turned my head towards the door every now and again, in the hope that the other world would open itself to me. The night was dark, and when I stepped out to sit for a while at the table in the garden I discovered it was raining. I went back into the annexe and smoked on the sofa there instead. And then, when I got to my feet to go into the studio, I trod on something soft, something that let out a loud and high-pitched squeal.

It was a kitten, quite still now in a small pool of blood.

The dear little thing.

The poor, dear little thing.

Its body trembled, a paw twitching as if scraping at the floor.

He'd said so! I knew I shouldn't have been here!

I began to cry and ran through the door, to the house. Perhaps it wasn't too late.

'Arne!' I shouted. 'Arne, come quick!'

No response.

'Something's happened! Come quick!'

'Yes, I'm coming,' he called down from upstairs.

And then he was standing there looking at me.

'What's happened?'

The horror of what I'd done welled inside me and I was unable to speak.

'Tove, what's happened?'

I gestured for him to follow and we crossed over to the annexe where I pointed to the kitten lying in its blood on the floor.

'I didn't see it. I trod on it.'

I started crying again.

'I feel so terrible.'

He crouched down and stared in bewilderment at the kitten as if it were a car engine that had unexpectedly broken down.

'Can't you do something? Take it to the vet's in the morning?'

'We must put it out of its misery. I'll fetch a hammer or something.'

'Not a hammer, surely?' I said, and bit my lip so as not to burst out laughing. The handyman from hell. Hammering the life out of little kittens.

'There's nothing else we can do,' he said and went away.

The kitten twitched its paw. Now all I wanted was for it to die. Or at least to stop twitching.

Arne returned with a hammer in his hand. He stroked the kitten's head with the tip of a finger. It was completely still.

'Is it dead?'

'I think so.'

'What are we going to do with it? What are we going to tell the boys?'

'I'll bury it in the garden somewhere. We can tell them it's disappeared.'

Something hateful flashed in his eyes as he looked at me. As if I were the most despicable person on earth.

'I didn't see it. It just got under my feet all of a sudden.'

'It's OK. It's not your fault.'

He smiled without meaning it and turned towards the door.

'Where are you going?'

'To put some clothes on, then I'll go and bury it.'

'All right,' I said and went through into the studio. It wasn't where he wanted me to go. He wanted me to go to bed. As if it were even a possibility. No, I said. Yes, he said. Eventually he gave up and went out and I sat down at the desk with the scissors and carried on cutting out my figures.

Standing in the kitchen the next day I heard Arne talking to someone in the study. It could only be Egil. They were laughing as if they were having a nice time. After a while Arne came in. I was staring out of the window and didn't turn round, but listened to his familiar sounds.

'How are you feeling?' he said.

'Is that Egil you're talking to?'

'Yes.'

'Why didn't you come and get me? He's my friend too.'

He made a couple of feeble excuses. I turned and looked at him, feeling only scorn, then went into the study, where Egil looked up, and I smiled. He smiled back, then looked at the floor. I sat down in Arne's chair, demurely with my knees together and my hands gathered in my lap.

'Have you ever seen something no one else can see?' I said.

He looked at me with surprise. Or no, it was more than surprise, more like astonishment. His mouth fell open, his eyes questioning for a moment, before again he looked away, smoothing with one hand the fabric of his trousers against his thigh, then crossing his legs.

'It depends what you mean.'

'I think you know what I mean,' I said. I had no idea if it was true, but he didn't know that.

'Are you thinking of ghosts?' he said with a nervous chuckle.

'For example, yes. Or demons.'

'Demons? No, I haven't seen any of those. Do they exist?'

I didn't reply. He took a sip of whatever it was he was drinking, then let the glass rest in his palm, nestled between his fingers.

'I take it *you* have, though, since you're asking the question?' he said.

'Yes, I have.'

'Like what?'

I started to laugh. He looked at me, not quite knowing how to react.

'Arne, for instance,' I said. 'He woke up one morning and his dick had snapped. It was sticking out sideways at an angle about halfway up the shaft. What's more, it had shrunk!'

I laughed again.

'No one else saw that.'

Egil said nothing. His thumb turned the glass in his hand.

'They gave him some injections and he had to use a pump for a few months. So now his dick's almost as good as new. You didn't know that! He's a manipulator. I'm a magician. You didn't know that either, did you?'

He shook his head, his eyes staring at the floor in front of him. He jiggled his dangling foot, then after a moment put his glass down, lit a cigarette, picked up a dirty coffee cup from the table and looked at me to ask if it was OK to use for an ashtray.

I nodded.

'I was at a dinner party once,' I said. 'Everyone there was an artist.'

Arne came in with an ashtray in his hand.

'You know Erling Kihl?'

'Yes,' said Egil. 'Was he there?'

'It was his party. He was there with all his acolytes. I don't know why I was invited. Anyway, in comes his nemesis. No one had invited him. The whole table went silent.'

The thought of Egil now knowing Arne's most intimate secret, and that this was a fact to which Arne himself was oblivious, set me off laughing. Egil looked at me and smiled benignly. Arne pulled up the chair from his desk, wanting to take command and dominate.

'So Kihl found him a chair and asked him to sit down. Ha ha ha!'

Both were staring at me now.

'Ha ha ha! And this person sits down, only for the chair to collapse underneath him, leaving him flat on his arse on the floor. Ha ha ha!'

They laughed, albeit subduedly. Arne laughing without knowing what I was really laughing at only made it all the more comical.

'And then Kihl says: *Beware the spells I cast.*'

I doubled over laughing. I laughed and laughed and was unable to stop. Eventually, I managed to take a few deep breaths and compose myself, only to crack up again almost immediately, at which point I stood up and went to the bathroom, my whole body shaking with laughter. It wasn't funny any more, but it had me in its grip and was completely beyond my control. I splashed my face with cold water and after a moment it stopped. But as soon as I returned to the study and saw the two of them now engaged in deep and earnest conversation, I burst out laughing again. Realising I couldn't stop myself, I went out to the annexe where I let go completely, and my laughter was then like a blaze, its flames leaping and leaping again, though with longer spells in between, until at last it died out.

That afternoon, I found the perfect place in the woods. A sheer rock face fissuring into a narrow cleft at its foot. I took half a tub of red paint and an unopened one of white from the shed, various brushes and other paraphernalia, packed the whole lot into a rucksack and went back there. Inside the cleft, on the the rear wall, where the moss came away as easy as anything, I painted his life-sized image in profile, as red as blood. Around the entrance I painted an abundance of crawling crabs, birds and matchstick people, some on their knees in worship, some with erect, spear-like penises, one of which was bent in the middle, and of course I laughed out loud as I painted that one. When I had to return to the studio for a tube of yellow, I was waylaid by Arne, who wanted me to make dinner all of a sudden! I fobbed him off and went back to paint a yellow star above the red man in the cleft, and a yellow sun blazing down on the teeming crabs and other figures. I had no idea how long the paint would remain on the rock before being obliterated by the elements – perhaps a few weeks, perhaps a few months, perhaps a few years, I really didn't know – but my plan was to return and carve the work into the rock, a relatively uncomplicated job, but time-consuming even if the carvings didn't need to be that deep.

When the light faded, dissolving the red into grey and consuming all detail, I stashed the rucksack inside the cleft and set off for the church. It was tonight the new star would appear, and what better place to observe it than from the house of God?

I sat down with my back against the outside wall and looked out on the faint, faint shimmer of the sea in the final light, while stars appeared one by one in the sky above me. For some time, everything was quite still. Then a sudden commotion made me turn my head. From the woods, a flapping cloud of birds took to the air. More joined, and more still, and soon they flooded the sky, a great, restless curtain, shimmying first this way, then that, until seemingly they reached agreement and flew inwards over the land as one.

I stood up. An animal slunk across the gravel track, then another. Foxes. They vanished into the trees, and I sat down again.

Something was happening, there was no doubt.

Early that morning I had seen hundreds of crabs crawling all over themselves down at the inlet. Then there were the snails. And the crabs in the woods.

Perhaps I was the only person who knew what was coming.

Why me?

WHAT FUCKING DIFFERENCE DOES IT MAKE?!

I yelled at the top of my lungs.

And then the light changed. The darkness that hung above the woods paled, the sea began once more to glitter, and seconds later rays spilled over the trees.

A strange cry sounded across the landscape.

Kalikalikalikalik

From somewhere behind the church, it was answered:

Kalikalikalikalik

But my attention was drawn by the star. Round and heavy with light it rose up above the woods, shedding its thin and ghostly illumination, shining and burning as clearly as a sun.

Some gulls shrieked at the shore. Soon they were in the sky in numbers. Other birds gave voice to the woods.

I waited for more to happen.

Nothing.

The star was it.

A while longer I waited, before leaving the churchyard and setting out again along the narrow track. My mind filled with the palest faces, they stared at me from everywhere, but every time I tried to look there was no one there, only trees and bushes, and soon I saw the lights of the farms further down, the jumpy headlights of a car.

He'd said the gates of death's kingdom would open, that was why the faces were forming in my mind. But he clearly was no figment – the star he'd foretold was there above me.

I emerged onto the main road. A car full of young people went past. Not long afterwards, a man came walking in the opposite direction. As soon as he saw me, he spoke, though as yet we were twenty metres apart – it was impossible to make out what he said.

He crossed over and came towards me and I noticed now that he was limping.

'Have you got a phone I could use?' he said.

'I'm afraid not.'

He halted in front of me. Blood was trickling from his ear.

'Have you been in an accident?' I said. 'You're bleeding. There's blood coming from your ear.'

He lifted a hand to feel, then examined the blood on his fingertips.

'Damn,' he said.

He looked at me. His eyes were quite without warmth.

'I had a crash back there. Ran into another car. My head hurts like hell. I need to call an ambulance.'

'Ah,' I said. 'I didn't bring my phone. I'm not sure why.'

'Are there any houses around here?'

'There are some farms down there, further down the road after the bend.'

'Where do you live yourself?'

'It's quite far. The farms are much closer.'

He started walking again.

'Do you want me to go with you?' I said. 'Do you need help?'

'I'm OK. But the ones I crashed into aren't. They need an ambulance.'

'Further up the road, you say? I'll go and see if I can help.'

'Thank you,' he said. 'I'll get the ambulance. You do what you can back there.'

He'd crossed over again now, and all I saw was the back of him.

I set off at a trot, and ran through the bend, and the road was empty. I ran through the flat, open area where there were no trees, and the road was empty. I ran through the next bend, and the road was empty.

When I reached the shortcut, the path that led through the woods to the shore, I pulled up. There was nothing to be seen. If he'd been in a crash and it had only just happened, how come I hadn't heard anything? I wouldn't have done if it had been far enough away. But if it was any further than this, there were houses he would have passed before seeing me come towards him.

It didn't make sense.

Had he been a madman?

But there'd been blood running from his ear, so something must have happened to him.

Whatever it was, there was nothing I could do.

I turned onto the path under the tall pine trees and before long emerged onto the bare rock at the shore. I could see the jetty, our boat there, and behind it the bank leading up to the house, everything shimmering faintly under the great star.

That strange, moist call again:

Kalikalikalikalik

This time it was close by.

I looked up into the treetops. In one, the branches swayed as they might if some large animal were moving among them.

I headed for the house and started up the bank. When I entered the garden, one of the neighbours' Rottweilers was at the step in front of the annexe. It was gripping something in its mouth, shaking it this way and that while emitting low growls. Abruptly, it stopped and looked at me. Its eyes shone in the light of the star. It had taken Sheba. She hung limply from its jaws.

I stood transfixed.

Dropping its prey, the dog lumbered slowly towards me. From the depths of the garden, the other one appeared.

They lifted their heads and stared at me.

I didn't move a muscle.

For a moment they looked at each other, then turned and ran towards the road, where they disappeared from view.

I dashed forward to look at Sheba. Her head was almost torn from her shoulders and dangled as I picked her up. Her fur was soaked in blood.

I opened the door and put her down on the desk in the studio, then went and sat down on the sofa and lit a cigarette.

Had the car not been there?

I went back out to check.

No. It was gone.

Who was here, and who wasn't?

I went back round the side of the house, opened the door and nearly bumped into Ingvild who was on her way out.

'Where have you been?' she said. 'I was starting to get worried.'

I looked into her eyes. They were warm and lovely, not cold in the slightest.

She loved that cat more than anything.

'I'm really sorry,' I said.

'For what? What do you mean?'

'I don't know.'

Behind me now a terrible clamour broke out. I spun round.

'Mum, what is it?'

From somewhere in the distance, above the sea, there came a horrid laughter, howls and cries, and I bolted into the garden.

In they came at furious speed, a long, trailing procession, sweeping and swooping through the air, and I cried out in terror, for it was the dead who were coming, flapping and fluttering, shrieking and squawking, some winged, some on horseback, some clinging to each other's throats, hundreds of them, flying in over the shore.

'Ah, Tove!' a voice called out. 'We've heard about you! Come with us!'

'Mum! Mum! Where are you?'

They descended on the house and I ran for the annexe, the air alive with their hideous, chattering laughter.

'You can't hide from us! We see everything and everyone! Come with us! Tove! We want to fuck you! Fuck and fuck and fuck!'

I flung the door open, slammed it shut behind me and pressed back against it with all my weight. I could hear them outside, bickering and squabbling, wailing and howling, breathing and panting a moment, before their noises seemed to lift away into the air, to grow fainter, and fainter still, until at last they faded away into silence.

But a pounding remained. It went on and on.

'Mum! Open the door! Mum! Please! Open the door!

THIRD DAY

KATHRINE

I didn't always like the couples I married, but I'd felt a rapport with this one right from the start. She was the outgoing type with a zest for life, though she probably wouldn't have put it like that herself, I suppose to her it was just the way she was, while he, more reserved and a bit square, clearly gained from such uplifting company, it was exactly what he needed, to be drawn closer to life. Therese and Hugo were young, twenty-four and twenty-five years old respectively, and a lot would happen in their marriage, I thought to myself as I saw them standing there together outside the church, accepting the congratulations of family and friends, but if anyone stood to enjoy a long and happy life together, it was them.

When eventually they drove away after Therese had given me a lengthy hug and Hugo had thanked me for what he called an *exquisite* ceremony, I couldn't help but feel a stab of something akin to sorrow in my heart, for they had no place in my private life and the chances that I would ever see them again were small.

A part of me wished too that it could have been me embarking on such a new and happy life, I thought to myself, smiling at the father of the groom as he turned and waved goodbye, lifting my hand casually in reply, before going inside into the vestry to get changed. The rest of the day was set aside for paperwork. I'd promised Mum I'd drive over and look in on them when I was finished; Mikael was coming home from hospital today and I hadn't seen either of them since he'd had his stroke.

As I was leaving the church my phone rang. The display told me it was an unknown caller and I hesitated before answering.

'Kathrine Reinhardsen,' I said.

'Hello, this is Geir Jacobsen calling, I'm an investigator with the local police. I was wondering if you might have time to meet me for a brief chat. Preferably today, if that would work for you.'

'What's it about?'

'I'd rather not say over the phone. But it concerns an ongoing investigation into a criminal matter.'

'Does it involve someone I know?'

'No. No, it doesn't.'

There was a pause as I digested what he'd told me.

'Shall we say three o'clock?' he said.

'I'm afraid I can't.'

'How about earlier?'

'That's no good either, I'm busy all day.'

'Tomorrow morning, then?'

'That would be better for me, yes.'

'Shall we say nine?'

'Yes, that'll be fine. Where would you like to meet?'

'I'd prefer somewhere neutral.'

'Will my office be neutral enough?'

'Yes, absolutely. See you tomorrow, then!'

Karin was on the phone when I passed her door. She winked at me and I smiled back, went through into my office, switched the air conditioning on and lay down on the sofa. I needed to eat something, but I had no appetite for anything, and hadn't for some time.

My own phone vibrated. It was Gaute.

There's a surprise for you when you get home.

A surprise?

As long as he hadn't gone and done something stupid like buying a dog.

I sat up.

He couldn't have, could he? He wouldn't have texted me about it unless it was something out of the ordinary. But a dog? That would be something he'd need to prepare me for.

I knew he'd been talking about it with the kids.

No. He wouldn't have, surely?

If it was a dog, it was going straight back where it came from.

How exciting! I typed. *Can't wait!*

I went over and woke up my computer, mainly to take my mind off the false tone of my text. I went through my unopened emails one after another, leaving the most interesting-looking ones for later. It gave me something to look forward to. A few I sent on to Karin, among them one from the campsite where we took the confirmands in the autumn. I couldn't understand why it had been sent to me. I added some appointments to my schedule and skimmed through some official memos and the like, before curiosity got the better of me and I went back to those interesting-looking emails and opened the first in the pile. It was from Erlend and contained a new stretch of translation from the Book of Leviticus. I glanced quickly at the text before saving it for later.

There was a knock on the door.

'Yes?' I said, and spun round on my chair.

Karin poked her head inside.

'Have you seen *VG*'s online edition today by any chance?'

'No, why?'

'I suggest you have a look. It has to do with what we were talking about yesterday.'

I typed the beginning of the address into the search bar and went to *VG*'s website. Karin stood in the doorway behind me. I had no idea what she was talking about. It couldn't be the heatwave or the ongoing strike, and it certainly wasn't the attack they were reporting on a reality TV star.

Ah, there it was.

NO DEAD IN 6 DAYS

I clicked on the article.

The last six days have seen not a single death in Norway. No one knows why.

'The records show it's quite unprecedented,' says Heidi Larsen, researcher with Statistics Norway. While unwilling to speculate, she points to a

coincidence of factors as the most likely explanation. Director General Vidar Leknes of the Norwegian Institute of Public Health confirms to VG *that no incidence of death has been recorded anywhere in the country since Tuesday.*

'Clearly, it's very unusual, though of course we should keep in mind the distinction between deaths and reported deaths. We're checking our systems to make sure no breakdown of communications has taken place.'

'What do you make of it?' said Karin. 'Strange, don't you think?'

'Yes, it is,' I said, turning to her. Her expression was serious and I traced an unease in her gaze.

'So it's not just here.'

'No, it seems not.'

'What's the explanation, do you think?'

I smiled.

'I've no idea, Karin. Presumably it's like she says, a coincidence of factors.'

She nodded.

'I was thinking of having lunch now. Care to join me?'

'I'll pass, if you don't mind,' I said. 'I've a ton of emails I need to get out of the way. But thanks anyway.'

She closed the door behind her. I got up and went over to the window. The water from the sprinkler glittered in the sunshine and fell soundlessly to the yellow grass. It was good to look at. The water catching the light, the grass receiving the water.

A strange day in a strange summer.

First the man at the airport who was the spitting image of the man I buried the day after. Then the new star. And now no one dead in six days.

The policeman who phoned.

It could only be about someone I'd met. Someone I'd christened or married.

Or perhaps it was to do with that mysterious man. Kristian Hadeland. Perhaps he'd been involved in something before he died.

Half an hour later my correspondence was done and I could open the last of the emails I'd been saving, it was from the local university, an institution I'd never had dealings with before.

Dear Kathrine Reinhardsen,

As a professor of literature, I'm in the process of organising a series of lectures this autumn on the subject of the Epic Cycle. In that connection, I'll also be giving a course for postgraduate students concerning literary treatments of the underworld. We like to invite guest lecturers to contribute to such courses, which is the reason I'm getting in touch with you now. I wonder if you might like to join us and give a talk on the Church of Norway's views on life after death, based on some of the Church's core texts on the subject?

The course will extend through the autumn term, so we can be fairly flexible as to a date.

I hope very much this will be of interest to you!

Best wishes,

Arne Gjeving

I pushed away from the desk slightly on my chair while considering how to reply. The underlying premise, the suggestion between the lines, was that the Church of Norway had no views on the matter at all, and certainly no core texts. As such, there seemed to be an element of malicious pleasure in his invitation.

The best thing to do would be to write back and politely decline due to other commitments.

On the other hand, it was a challenge. If there was no official view, I could talk about the reasons why.

I drew my chair up to the desk again and typed a reply.

Dear Arne Gjeving

Thanks for your invitation. I'd be happy to talk to your students about the Church of Norway's views on death. I'll await your suggestions as to a date.

Best wishes,

Kathrine Reinhardsen

After I'd sent it, I opened Erlend's translation, Leviticus 14:33–57, and read through it carefully.

Infected Dwellings

The LORD spoke to Moses and Aaron: 'When you enter the land of Canaan that I'm about to give you as your own possession, and if I put a contagion in a house in the land that you possess, then the owner of the house is to approach the priest and tell him, "There appears to be a contagion in the house."

'The priest is to command that the house be cleared before he comes to examine the contagion so that not everything in the house becomes unclean. After this, the priest is to enter the house and examine it. He is to determine if the contagion is indeed on the walls of the house, with greenish or reddish streaks, and to determine if it appears to be deeper than the surface of the wall. The priest is to leave through the entrance to the house and seal the house for seven days. He is to return after seven days to examine it. If the contagion has spread to the walls of the house, then the priest is to command that they take out the contaminated stones and discard them in an unclean place outside the city.

'Now as for the house, they are to scrape off inside and outside the house and then discard the torn-out plaster in an unclean place outside the city. They are then to take other stones and bring them to replace those stones. Lastly, they are to replaster the house.

'If the contagion returns and spreads throughout the house after the stones have been removed, after the house has been scraped out, and after it has been re-coated, and the priest comes, undertakes an examination, and determines that the contagion has spread in the house, it's a chronic fungal infection in the house. It's unclean. He is to pull down the house, its stones, its lumber, and all the plaster on the house, and discard them in an unclean place outside the city. Moreover, whoever enters the house during the time it was isolated is to be considered unclean until the evening. Whoever has slept in the house is to wash his clothes, along with whoever has eaten in the house.

'But if the priest comes in to conduct an examination and determines that the contagion has not spread throughout the house after the house has been repaired, then the priest may declare the house clean, because the contagion has been cleansed. In order to cleanse the house, he is to take two birds, some cedar wood, two crimson threads, and some hyssop. Then he is to slaughter one bird on an earthen vessel over flowing water. He is to take

the cedar wood, the hyssop, the two crimson threads, and the live bird, and dip them in the blood of the slaughtered bird over flowing water. Then he is to sprinkle the house seven times. He is to clean the house with the blood of the bird over flowing water, including cleansing the live bird, the cedar wood, the hyssop, and the crimson thread. Then he is to send the bird away, outside the city, facing the fields, to make atonement for the house. Then it is to be considered clean.

'This is the law for every contagion of infectious skin disease and scabs, for fungal infections on clothing or in a house, and for swelling of the skin, scabs, and bright spots, to distinguish when it's unclean and clean. This is the law for infectious skin diseases.'

This was a notoriously cryptic passage, since the words the original used to describe what befell the house were *nega*, meaning contagion or touch, and *tsara'at*, which was universally used about leprosy and leprous bodies. Here, we were clearly dealing with something else, a greenish or reddish coating on the walls that was so unclean as to necessitate the whole house being pulled down if the initial measures failed.

In all likelihood this was about fungal infections, in which case the correct word would be *attack* rather than *contagion*. The whole passage then took on an air of rationality: in the case of your house being attacked by fungus, follow these measures. The use of *contagion* and *leprous*, though, the latter as in earlier versions, brought uncertainty to the fore, the mystery it must have been to them, that houses could become sick like people and had to be isolated in the same way.

However, considerations to clarity overrode whatever lay hidden in the shadows of ignorance, which Erlend of course knew just as well as I did, so I typed a brief, perhaps overly laudatory email to him in reply before switching off the computer, picking up my bag and going outside to the car, which was boiling hot despite having been parked in the shade of a tree.

No one came to the door when I rang the bell. I went round the back and found them sitting at a table in the garden. Mum in an airy white trouser suit, Mikael with a bandage around his head, contrasting with his smart casual wear: khaki shorts and a navy blue polo shirt. On the table were a bottle of wine, three glasses and two boxes of strawberries.

'Take that chair over there,' Mum said, indicating with a nod of her head a chair that stood oddly on its own under one of the old plum trees further down the garden.

'Good to see you, Mikael,' I said.

He nodded without smiling, his face as stiff as a mask, his mouth drooping at one corner, but his eyes gleamed with warmth.

I brought the chair over and sat down at the other side of the table.

'Well,' said Mum. 'Anything new?'

'No.'

'Everything all right with Peter and Marie? Gaute?'

I nodded.

'I think so, yes.'

Her back was as straight as a board. Her red hair hung loose about her neck.

'Would you like some wine?'

'No, thanks. I'm driving.'

'A glass won't hurt,' she said, already pouring me one.

Whatever I said, it had never meant anything to her.

She handed me the glass and I put it down on the table without drinking from it.

For a moment she looked at me.

She couldn't have guessed, surely?

No, it wasn't possible.

'How are you feeling, Mikael?'

He opened his mouth a couple of times without a sound coming out. Then he managed.

'N . . . not . . . t . . .' he stammered.

'Not too bad,' said Mum.

'. . . too . . . baaaaaad,' he said, as if the last word were running away from him.

'You're looking well!' I said.

'The rehab tends to give good results,' said Mum. 'Of course, they couldn't promise anything, but they were very upbeat.'

'The d-door . . .' he said.

I held his gaze.

'. . . is o-op . . .'

'He's saying the door's open,' said Mum. 'Yes, you've said so a number times already, Mikael, but I really haven't a clue what you're talking about!'

She gave a laugh and glanced at me.

Her cold eyes were full of unease.

'Have some strawberries, if you insist on not drinking our wine.'

I did as she said, pinching off the green stalk that I'd always thought looked like a starfish when I was little and popping the big red fruit into my mouth, sensing immediately the bitter-sweet taste as it tingled through my body.

'You must have been doing a lot of watering here,' I said. 'The grass at ours is completely scorched.'

'Oh, but I haven't,' she said. 'There's such a lot of shade here, that's probably why.'

'Yes, I suppose it is.'

The garden was more than a hundred years old and looked like a small park. With its many nooks and paths, divided in two by a row of fruit trees, it seemed bigger than it actually was. The house was an old Swiss-style villa, painted red with white sills and frames and filled with Viking-like art deco details. She and Mikael had bought it when they decided they were going to live together. The house in which I'd grown up had been sold. I understood why, but it still grieved me, especially because it meant that the few memories I still had of my father were no longer attached to any place that was mine.

'The crown of thorns is flowering again, did I mention it?' Mum said.

'No, you didn't.'

'Come on, I'll show you.'

She got to her feet. She would never normally take me to see something in the garden like that, so I realised she wanted to speak to me alone.

Sure enough, as soon as Mikael was out of sight on the other side of the fruit trees, she halted.

'He's not himself, I'm afraid.'

'Oh, I'm sorry to hear it.'

'He knows who I am. And clearly he knows who you are too. But when we came home earlier it was as if he'd never been here before. And then those bloody doors. The doors are open, he keeps telling me, over and over. The doors are open. I've no idea what he's on about.'

'It could be just a stage.'

'I suppose it could, yes. His brain has been exposed to trauma, so anything's possible. But as I said, the rehab tends to give results.'

'That's something.'

'Yes. But I don't like it. It's as if he's someone else.'

'But that's silly. He's still the same person.'

'I hope so. He was trying to tell me about Budapest just before. He's never been to Budapest, I know that for a fact.'

She looked at me with concern written all over her face. I almost felt glad that she was confiding in me.

'It's over here,' she said.

'What is?'

'My pride and joy. Look.'

She went over to a large shrub with puffy pink flowers. The stem was prickly with thorns and resembled a thin cactus.

'They're hard to cultivate this far north,' she said.

'It's beautiful.'

'How are things between you and Gaute?'

'Fine. We're talking properly again now.'

She nodded.

'Does he know you're pregnant?'

'Mum! Where did you get that from?'

'You are, aren't you?'

I felt a strong urge to say no. But I couldn't lie. Not about something like that.

So I nodded.

'And you're going to keep it?'

I nodded again.

'Very good, Kathrine. I'm pleased. A baby brother or sister will be good for both Peter and Marie.'

'How did you know?'

'I didn't. It was a guess.'

'But how come? I mean, it's not like it shows.'

She laughed.

'You were so despairing that night. And then when we met up the next day, that was when it occurred to me.'

'But I didn't even know then!'

'Something in you did. Why else would you feel thrown into such acute crisis when nothing had changed?'

No one could assume control of a situation like her. I had nothing to say. But I was filled with all sorts of conflicting feelings.

'Come on, let's get back to him,' she said.

The professor had already replied, I noted when I got into the car and checked my phone. He addressed me as Kathrine, even though I'd signed my email using my full name. He'd given me six dates to choose from and suggested we could meet for a chat about the talk and the general context.

I regretted having agreed to it. It was never good to follow one's first impulse. I should have left it alone for a while so as not to seem so eager. It could even have waited a couple of days, I thought as I dropped the phone onto the passenger seat before backing out onto the road.

As always after spending time with Mum, I felt a bit down. Perhaps the feeling was intensified by what she'd told me about Mikael being so diminished after his stroke. I liked him, and I liked Mum better when she was with him than on her own.

But that wasn't what was bothering me, if I was to be honest with myself. It was the stab of sorrow I'd felt as the newly-weds had driven away after the ceremony. The feelings that had been triggered by that and which now followed their own pathways inside me.

Why did it have to be so hard to know the right thing to do?

I had come to a decision. I was going to stay with Gaute. But my feelings weren't in it, and what then?

It was all about accepting the feelings I had, that they existed, *but not paying them any heed.*

About being big enough to contain both sides.

As I waited for some traffic lights to change, I speed-dialled Sigrid.

'Hey, hello!' she said. 'And thanks for a lovely time, by the way. Sorry

I didn't get round to phoning and saying so. It was a really nice evening all round.'

'Yes, it was,' I said, now following the stream of traffic towards the busy intersection. The next lights changed to red, but the car in front took a chance and sped across.

'And the world premiere was a delight!'

It took a moment before I realised she meant the play Peter had put on with the other kids.

'Yes, it was lovely.'

'Is something the matter?'

'No, not at all. What makes you think that?'

'You seem a bit quiet, that's all.'

'Mikael had a stroke the night you were at ours. He's just come home. Mum says he's not himself.'

'Oh no, how terrible.'

'It might not be that bad. She's probably just bracing for the worst case, getting herself more worked up than she needs to. I don't know.'

'No.'

'How are you, anyway?'

'All right, considering.'

'Still annoyed with Martin?'

'Oh, I gave up on Martin a long time ago,' she said with a laugh. 'No, seriously, that's all OK.'

As I went through the intersection the petrol light came on. I couldn't be bothered stopping to fill up, there was plenty left in the tank for me to do it in the morning.

'I've done a piece on doomsday visions through the ages,' Sigrid went on. 'It's in tomorrow's edition. It's been really fascinating. Come to think of it, it should be of interest to you as well!'

'What on earth prompted you to write about that? Oh, of course – the new star.'

'Yes, exactly. The angles on it so far have all been from astronomy, astrophysics and hardcore science. There's been nothing at all from a cultural perspective! So I spoke to a social anthropologist, a historian of religion and a psychologist.'

I didn't say anything and so there was a silence.

'Are you sure there's nothing the matter, Kathrine? I thought you'd be excited about this!'

'No, everything's fine, really. Maybe we could go out together and have a proper chat?'

'Yes, that would be nice. I've missed our nights out.'

'Me too. How about Friday?'

'Friday's good. Where do you want to go?'

'It would be nice to sit out somewhere. Bakgården, perhaps?'

'Good idea. I haven't been there for ages.'

'Text me if you can't come and we'll reschedule.'

'Why would I not come?'

'I don't know.'

'Kathrine, you realise you're sounding like a wet blanket now? You need a kick up the backside.'

She was right, I acknowledged after we'd hung up. I wasn't myself at all, but I'd known that already, before I'd even spoken to her.

I would have to pull myself together for Gaute and the children, not let anything show as long as I was at home.

Only then, halfway up the final hill, did I remember the surprise Gaute had mentioned. I was almost expecting a yapping dog to come running up to me when I opened the door.

Gaute was standing in the kitchen making dinner. Fried plaice by the looks of it, he liked that.

He came up and kissed me, his hands on my hips.

'Are you excited?'

I smiled an open smile.

'I've arranged a babysitter for tonight. And booked us a table at Sjølyst!'

'Have you really? How lovely!' I said, mustering as much enthusiasm as I was able.

'Really, yes!'

'That's marvellous! Thank you.'

I leaned in to kiss him back and ruffled his hair.

'Where are Peter and Marie?'

'Marie's on the veranda drawing. Peter's in his room.'

'In this weather?'

'I know. But their dinner's ready in a minute. I thought I'd let him have some time on his own.'

Marie appeared in the doorway. She had dark rings under her eyes.

'Hello, sweetie,' I said, crouching to receive a hug. 'Have you had a nice day?'

She nodded without saying anything.

'Marie had a nightmare last night,' Gaute said behind me.

'Did you? What was it about?'

She shook her head.

'I told Daddy. I'm not telling you.'

I got to my feet again.

'Mummy would like to know what you dreamt too, Marie,' Gaute said.

'No.'

I turned towards Gaute and sent him a discreet shake of my head.

'It's quite all right,' I told her. 'Do you want a glass of squash or something?'

She went back out onto the veranda without answering.

'It's not like her to behave like that,' said Gaute.

'No,' I said, taking a glass from the cupboard that I then filled with water from the tap before draining it in one long mouthful.

'How were things with Mikael?'

'Mum was worried. He's a bit muddled. Didn't know he was home, that sort of thing.'

'Did he recognise you?'

'Yes, right away. I don't think there's cause for too much concern, to be honest.'

I made a glass of squash and took it outside onto the veranda where I put it down on the table in front of Marie without saying anything. At first she pretended not to notice, but cast a sly glance while carrying on with her drawing. After a few moments, she looked up, then drew a few more lines before the urge got the better of her and she picked up the glass and drank greedily.

'That's a nice drawing. Do you want to show me?'

She pushed it towards me so I could see. Green grass, a green tree with a brown trunk and an enormous yellow-and-black bee, or was it a wasp?

'That's very good! Is it a bee or a wasp?'

'A bumblebee.'

'Yes, of course! How silly of me!'

I sat down.

'I can tell you now, if you want,' she said.

I nodded.

'I was in a cellar fetching potatoes and all of a sudden the floor was alive with rats. There were thousands of them, Mummy. I was frightened and ran up the stairs, but there were rats there as well and they were everywhere. I tried to run away, only I fell down and the rats were crawling on me. Then I woke up.'

'What a horrid dream.'

'Yes.'

'What did you want the potatoes for?' I said with a smile.

'To make the dinner.'

'Were *you* making the dinner?'

'Yes. I wasn't me.'

'What do you mean?'

'I wasn't me.'

'You mean you were someone else in the dream?'

She nodded, then concentrated on her drawing again.

'Where were you in the dream? We haven't got a cellar, and we don't keep potatoes in the basement.'

'In my house.'

'*Your* house?'

'Yes.'

'Dinner's ready!' Gaute called out from the kitchen.

'Will you go and fetch Peter and then wash your hands?'

She nodded and jumped to her feet. I filled a jug with water and smiled at Gaute as he looked at me, then put the jug on the table.

'Did she tell you what she dreamt?'

'Yes. A typical loss-of-control dream.'

I took a slice of cucumber from the chopping board and popped it in my mouth.

'Mm!' I said.

*

The last thing Gaute said to the babysitter before we went out was to keep her ears open even after the kids had gone to sleep, in case one of them woke up from a nightmare. To which she replied, a bit impatiently, that of course she would. I sensed she wanted us out of the house as soon as possible.

'Nice girl,' said Gaute after we got in the taxi. 'Don't you think?'

'She seems all right.'

'You don't sound convinced.'

'Yes, I am.'

'Yes, I am. No, you're not. Yes, I am.'

'What's that supposed to mean?'

'Nothing.'

'All right.'

I managed to stifle an exasperated sigh and looked out of my window. The sun was going down, its light dazzlingly low in the sky, the shadows long. I couldn't put it off any longer. I would have to tell Gaute tonight that I was pregnant. He would ask how long I'd known. Then why I'd kept it to myself until now. Because I needed to be certain, I would say. And it was true, I'd needed to be certain, and for a few days I hadn't been.

'You're quiet tonight,' he said. 'Is anything wrong?'

I looked at him and smiled.

'No, nothing's wrong. Quite the opposite, in fact!'

'What's on your mind, then?'

'Marie and Peter. Marie, mostly. I wonder if she's going through a phase at the moment. Moving on to a new stage in her development, perhaps. That dream she had.'

'Yes, I think you might be right.'

'How's that girl in your class getting on?'

'Gudrun?'

He tightened his lips and shook his head.

'Not so good. The mental health counsellor wants her admitted. The mother won't hear of it.'

'Admitted for what reason?'

'An eating disorder.'

'Nothing to do with the nightmares you told me she was having?'

'You're thinking about Marie now, aren't you?'

'That was what made me think about Gudrun, yes. Not that I think they've anything in common, of course.'

'And thank God for that. No, Gudrun may have to be sectioned. It's a terrible business.'

'You did the right thing, Gaute.'

'For once I think I probably did.'

The taxi took us into town. Brick facades were a warm red glow in the sunlight. Many of the streets were empty.

'Unbelievable to think it's September,' said Gaute. 'You wouldn't think so with the heat we've been having.'

'No,' I said.

'Just put us down here,' he said to the driver, then looked at me. 'A little walk will be nice before we sit down, don't you think?'

He paid while I stood waiting on the pavement. A slight breeze wafted from the harbour, thick with the smell of the sea. Two young men went past. One kicked an empty can absently and it rattled noisily across the paving stones. On the other side of the road, a seagull touched down with a cry.

'Right,' said Gaute as the taxi pulled away. 'On our own at last.'

We were given a table right at the edge of the jetty. The last rays of day dwindled as we sat waiting for the food. There was something watchful about Gaute tonight, he wasn't quite relaxed, despite trying to give the impression he was just that.

The new star shone, clear and brilliant in the darkness that now blanketed the islands to the west.

'Don't look now,' said Gaute, 'but Helge Bråthen's just walked in.'

'Really?' I said. I was drizzling some olive oil onto my side plate before dabbing a piece of bread in it.

'He turned sixty the other day.'

'Did he?'

I waited a moment before twisting on my chair to survey the room as if looking for a waiter. He was with a young woman. She had a baby carrier with a sleeping baby in it and put it down on the floor against the room divider.

When I turned round again, Gaute had draped an arm over the back of his chair and was gazing out over the dark waters of the harbour.

'A police investigator phoned me today and asked if he could come and see me,' I said.

'Oh? What did he want?'

'He wouldn't say over the phone. He's coming to the office in the morning.'

'What do you think it's about?'

'I've no idea.'

There was a pause during which neither of us spoke.

'This is so nice,' said Gaute then. 'The two of us alone together at last. When was the last time?'

'Far too long ago.'

'Yes, I agree.'

I should have told him then. But something held me back. Perhaps when the food came, so we wouldn't be interrupted.

'I'm glad we had that talk,' he said.

'Me too.'

'I'm still really sorry for not trusting you. You didn't deserve that.'

'We mustn't shut each other out.'

'No.'

'There's something I want to say.'

'Oh?'

'Yes. A big surprise.'

'You've got me excited now.'

'I'm pregnant.'

He stared at me without emotion. His eyes hardened, it was as if a wall went up inside him.

'With me?' he said.

'Yes, with you, Gaute. We're going to be parents again. Peter and Marie are going to have a baby sister or brother. Only if you want to, of course! You do want to, don't you? I know it wasn't planned. But I often think that's the best way, when it happens like that. It's more of a gift, in a way.'

He leaned back and folded his arms across his chest.

'How long have you known?'

'A few days, that's all.'

'Why didn't you tell me?'

'I wanted to be certain first. Now I am. I'm pregnant. There's a little baby inside me.'

He didn't say anything.

'Gaute. This is joyful news. What are you thinking? Tell me what you're thinking!'

He still didn't speak, but reached a hand out and fidgeted with the salt cellar.

'You said you trusted me. Do you?'

'Maybe.'

'Gaute, listen. For the last time, I've never been unfaithful to you. Never.'

'OK.'

'Something fantastic is happening in our life now. Please don't let anything come in the way of it.'

Just then, two waiters came to the table with our food. I straightened up on my chair to make room for them. Gaute looked out over the water again.

'Enjoy your meal,' a waiter said.

'Thank you,' I said. 'It looks lovely!'

After they'd gone, Gaute leaned forward.

'Do you swear?'

I felt like shouting. But I had to negotiate this. If I didn't, everything would just be impossible.

'I swear.'

'So I can take a DNA test after the birth and you won't have any problem with that?'

I scrutinised him.

It wasn't him, it was the jealousy inside him.

'Well?'

'If it's important to you, Gaute, I won't refuse.'

He nodded a couple of times.

'You have your guarantee,' I said. 'Can we focus on our baby now?'

'I *am* glad.'

'Good. Because I am too.'

'It's just all so sudden.'

'Isn't it always?'

'You know what I mean.'

He took a half of lobster and put it on his plate, then filled his glass with white wine.

We ate for a while in silence.

'Listen,' he said, 'I handled this really badly. I'm sorry.'

'That's all right.'

'It's fantastic news. I can hardly believe it. How far gone are you?'

'I don't know exactly. I thought we could go to the doctor's together.'

Behind us, the baby began to cry. I turned round to look. Bråthen's young wife stood bent over the baby carrier, unfastening the child as it waved its arms in the air.

'I'm not exactly young any more, so there's always a slight risk,' I said.

'Everything will be fine, I'm sure. You're healthy and in good shape. I wouldn't worry about it,' said Gaute.

On our way to the taxi rank, he put his arm around me.

'I love you, you know. I really do.'

I smiled and reached up to kiss him gently on the mouth.

'Can you forgive me?' he said.

'You're already forgiven.'

A car went past slowly. Gaute's eyes followed it for a moment.

'Remember I told you about that neighbour of Gudrun's who said he knew you?'

'Yes?'

'That was him in that car. I don't think he noticed us.'

'I've no idea who it might be.'

'Never mind. It would be nice to have a drink on the veranda when we get back. But you can't now, can you?'

'You can.'

'No, not if you can't.'

'Don't be silly. Of course you should have a drink. I'll keep you company.'

He put his hand on my knee in the taxi. I placed my hand on his as

I gazed out into the darkness. Another child meant there was no way back. Perhaps that was why I was pregnant?

The kids were asleep when we got home. We stood together in the doorway of their room and looked at them for a while after the babysitter had gone.

'I still can't grasp how they're a part of me,' Gaute whispered. 'Can you?'

'Yes.'

'But you carried them inside you. They were physically a part of you. So it's hardly surprising if we experience them differently.'

We went out onto the veranda. Gaute poured himself a cognac and handed me a glass of Farris mineral water, and we made a toast for our new baby. We sat for a while in the silent night, the garden below illuminated by the pale light of the star.

'Can I ask you one last thing?' Gaute said.

'Of course you can.'

'When I found that pregnancy test that night Sigrid and Martin were here . . .'

'Yes?'

'Didn't you say you'd tested negative? Only now you're pregnant. I just don't understand how the two things hang together.'

'I lied.'

'You lied?'

'I hadn't taken the test then.'

'Why would you lie about it?'

'I don't know. You were so angry. And if I'd just left it dangling between us like that . . .'

'What?'

'That I thought I might be pregnant but hadn't taken the test.'

He was quiet for a moment.

'Have you lied to me about anything else?'

I shook my head.

'Only what I told you. About the hotel.'

'Nothing else?'

'No.'

'Never?'

I sighed.

'OK, OK,' he said. 'I believe you. No more questions, I promise. And I *am* really happy, in case you're in doubt.'

Behind us, Marie appeared. She said nothing, just stared at us.

Gaute got to his feet.

'Have you been dreaming again?'

She nodded.

'So you're not sleepwalking?'

She shook her head.

'Come on, little one, we'll put you back to bed and I'll sing for you.'

He picked her up and she wrapped her arms and legs around him like a panda. Shortly afterwards I heard him sing for her upstairs, faintly, as if from a different house.

The next morning she remembered nothing of the night's intermezzo. She giggled with glee when I told her she'd come out onto the veranda. Not remembering meant she'd been sleepwalking, and the thought appealed to her.

We had breakfast together, all four of us. The sky was cloudy, but the air was as hot as it had been for days.

SEVEN DAYS WITHOUT A DEATH, ran *VG*'s first headline. I showed it to Gaute.

'I saw that yesterday,' he said. 'Very strange. Some expert or other was saying that three days would be a coincidence, perhaps four, but not five.'

'And now it's seven.'

'What are you talking about?' said Peter.

'There have been no deaths reported anywhere in the country now for seven days,' said Gaute. 'It's most unusual.'

'That was when the star appeared,' said Peter.

'What do you mean?'

'Seven days since the star appeared. Seven days since anyone died.'

Good God. It was true.

Gaute laughed.

'That's astrology, that is. The idea that the stars can affect our lives on earth. You don't believe that, do you?'

'No, of course I don't,' Peter said.

He glanced across at me after he spoke.

'Think of someone who's gravely ill,' said Gaute. 'They're expected to die any time soon, but they hang on, Monday, Tuesday, Wednesday, Thursday, until eventually they die on the Friday. That could be the case for any number of people at the same time. Or think of the motorist nodding off for a second behind the wheel, then looking up just in time to avoid that oncoming lorry. It probably happens more often than people crashing. Now think of the same thing happening to everyone for seven days. It's not likely, but it's possible. And that's what's happened now. The star has nothing to do with it.'

'But what if no one dies tomorrow either? How long can a coincidence like that go on?'

'You're a bright boy, Peter! I've always said so. But I think we'll put that question off until tomorrow!'

I went and fetched them an apple each when it was time for them to go. Peter was kneeling down to tie his shoes, Marie stood ready at the door with her little rucksack on her back.

'I believe in God a little bit as well,' said Peter without looking up.

'The important thing is to think for yourself. And to be faithful to what you believe,' I said.

I unzipped the top of Marie's pack and dropped her apple inside.

'Time you got going. See you this afternoon!'

I closed the door after they'd gone and went into my study. My intention was to do some work for an hour, there were some emails I had to attend to and a sermon to think about, and then drive down to the church where I was meeting some parents about a christening at eleven.

I wrote to the literature professor to say I was available on any of the dates he'd suggested, but that I was unsure if I'd properly understood the proposed theme for the talk – I didn't want to stand there going on about something no one was interested in.

He replied only a few minutes later and assured me my views would be interesting no matter what, and that he'd be happy to meet me for a chat if I felt the need for some more context.

I didn't quite know what to write back, so I put it to one side and attended to my other correspondence instead.

Just after nine o'clock my phone rang. As soon as I saw that it was an unknown caller, I remembered my appointment with the policeman. How could I have forgotten?

'I do apologise,' I said. 'It completely slipped my mind. I can be with you in twenty minutes, if you don't mind waiting?'

'No problem. Karin's made me a nice cup of coffee, so I'm not suffering.'

The petrol gauge lit up the moment I turned the key in the ignition. I'd forgotten that too. I'd have to fill up on the way, even if it meant I'd be delayed even further.

I stopped off at the Shell station and pulled in at the first pump, unlocked the little flap and unscrewed the petrol cap, and inserted the nozzle into the tank.

A dirty, dented old car came in and drew up on the other side of the pump island. I recognised the vehicle. It was the car I'd seen at the supermarket. It was. The same shabby old woman in the passenger seat, the same shabby old man who got out and started to fill up. Neither of them paid me any attention, even though, clearly, I was staring at them.

I put the nozzle back in place on the pump and hesitated a moment with the car key in my hand.

It made no sense to approach them.

They'd picked up a man I'd happened to encounter at the airport. It was hardly appropriate to point out to them now that he'd looked like someone whose funeral I'd conducted earlier the same day, but that would be my only reason to bother them at all.

'Excuse me!' I said boldly. He didn't react, though he must surely have heard me. He just stood there looking down as he held the nozzle, glancing up at the display on the pump.

I stepped closer onto the island.

'Excuse me,' I said again. 'I happened to see you a few days ago at the supermarket. There was a man I wanted to talk to who got into your car. I'm afraid I don't know his name, but I assume you must know him. Would you be able to help me get in touch with him?'

He ignored me completely. Didn't even look at me, just slotted the nozzle back into place on the pump, screwed the petrol cap back on, opened the car door and got in. The woman didn't look at me either, or at him, but stared out in front of her the whole time.

He started the car, drove slowly away to the exit, turned onto the road and was gone.

I got back in. Christ, what an unpleasant experience.

What was wrong with people?

By the time I parked outside the office a quarter of an hour later, it was already twenty-five to ten.

I was embarrassed to have wasted so much of his time. On the other hand, it was he who wanted something from me, not the other way round.

Unless I brought up the mystery of Kristian Hadeland and the shabby old couple who'd picked him up that day . . .

The thought made me smile as I crossed over the gravel to the door.

A heavily built, rather untidy-looking man in his mid-fifties, wearing jeans and a dark blue shirt with short sleeves, got to his feet when I came in.

'Kathrine, I take it?' he said, putting out his hand.

He had a tooth missing, which became apparent when he smiled. His handshake was firm, his gaze less so.

'Nice to meet you,' I said. 'Let's go into my office right away, shall we?'

'Good idea,' he said.

He picked up a leather briefcase I hadn't noticed and dropped his shoulder into the shoulder strap.

'I'm sorry for being so late.'

'Not to worry. Karin said it was most unlike you.'

'It is too!' she chipped in from her desk in the corner.

'Perhaps it is. I've really no idea how it could happen.'

I opened my door, turned on the air conditioning and dumped my bag on the sofa.

'Have a seat,' I said, indicating with a nod the two chairs in front of my desk.

He sat down on one, clutching his bag to his body, and crossed his legs.

'You'll have heard a confession or two here, I shouldn't wonder?'

'You could say,' I said.

'I've the greatest respect for your profession, let me say that right away. Being there for people in their deepest need, helping them find words for their sorrow and grief, making sure they don't lose their foothold. It's invaluable work.'

'Thank you,' I said.

He smiled, his gaze shifting to the dangling foot he then flexed a couple of times. There was something lackadaisical and rather evasive about the man that definitely didn't come across as policeman-like qualities. His smile made me think of a dosser – his teeth were stained yellow, and there was the gap for the missing one. At the same time, he possessed a confident air that seemed to emanate from deep within, as if to override those first impressions.

'So, how can I help you?'

'There's something I want to show you, if you don't mind?'

'Of course.'

He produced a laptop from his bag, then stood up and came round to my side of the desk where he opened it in front of me.

'This isn't something I'm supposed to show you,' he said. 'But put it this way: I trust you.'

'I'm bound by professional secrecy.'

He looked at me and smiled.

'So you never disclose anything of what you see or hear in this office to your husband? Your closest friends?'

'Nothing that could be connected to any identifiable person, no.'

'You must tell this to *no one*. Am I clear?'

When I nodded, he opened what I could see was a video file. The first frame, as yet frozen, showed a forest at night. He selected the full-screen option and then clicked on the play button.

Men in animal masks in a forest.

'Do you see what this is?'

'Devil worship?'

He nodded without taking his eyes off the screen.

The leader said something and the others repeated it in chorus.

Man is God.

We are men.

We are gods.

God is man.

'Who are they?' I said.

'I don't know. I have an idea, but I'm not certain.'

'Are they from here?'

He nodded.

'This has to do with those murders, hasn't it?'

He nodded again and paused the film.

'I'm not sure how I can help you, exactly,' I said. 'I've never engaged in devil worship. To be honest, I know nothing about it.'

'I wasn't expecting you to.'

'Perhaps you need to speak to someone from the university – the department of religion. Or a social anthropologist. If you're lucky, someone might have written about the devil-worshipping community.'

'I've already spoken to a religious scholar. He told me that what we've just seen is referred to as the *Tierdrama*, presumably taken from a book called *The Satanic Rituals* by one Anton Szandor LaVey. So we're on the right track. But something happens towards the end here. That's what I really want you to look at.'

He started the film again. The masks and the chanting voices were unsettling, but there was an element of play-acting about it all too, which made me think they weren't really committed, not properly. They were just kids trying to do something shocking.

'It's coming up now,' the policeman said, as if he could read my thoughts.

The figures with their animal heads stood now silent and motionless in a ring.

'There!' he said. 'Did you see that?'

'No, what?'

He rewound slightly.

'In the background, over by those trees. Something appears. Look at it again.'

I stared at the trees. This time I did see something move. Something dark.

Was that all?

I looked at him questioningly.

'It doesn't matter how slowly I run the clip, the movement remains just as quick. But it's there, isn't it? And then it's gone almost in the same instant. You saw it, didn't you?'

'I saw a shadow there, yes.'

'I sent a still off to the lab and asked them to focus on bringing out that shadow. Here's what they came up with.'

He opened a new file and an image came up on his screen. It was extremely grainy and unclear. But there was a figure there. Part of a body. An open mouth. Holes where the eyes should be.

'What do you make of it?' he said.

'An animal,' I said. 'Distorted by the enlargement.'

'That's what I thought. Only now I think it might be something else.'

He closed the laptop, dropped it back into his bag and sat down on the chair opposite me again.

'I still don't know what this has to do with me,' I said.

He fixed me in his gaze.

'Do you think there's a possibility that the Devil exists?'

Was he having me on?

I sensed him smiling, though he continued to look straight at me.

'You're a theologian and a member of the clergy. You've studied the Bible and the Church Fathers, and, perhaps more to the point, you've spoken to people who, for whatever reason, have found themselves in the deepest darkness. I'm not asking you what the Church of Norway believes, because I think I know the answer to that. I'm asking you personally.'

'You're asking me if the Devil exists?'

I felt a strong urge to laugh, but everything about him suggested he was being serious.

'That's right.'

'Well, no. I don't believe it.'

'So you think the Devil is merely a symbol, a rhetorical figure as it were, standing for all that's evil, is that it?'

'Something like that, yes.'

'What about all the historical accounts? People's encounters with the Devil through the ages – were they just seeing things?'

'It's not improbable.'

'And the consistency of those accounts – is that simply to do with the collective unconscious?'

'Listen, I'm a cleric, not a Jungian psychologist. But it could be something of the kind, yes.'

He nodded.

'Do you really think that what you saw in that video was the Devil himself?' I said, barely able to hide my incredulity. 'But it was just a shadow!'

'I know,' he said.

I shook my head in resignation, I couldn't help it.

'The thing is that right after that video sequence, a triple murder took place in the same vicinity, committed in a manner I'm unable to detail. That's the fact of the matter. I'm an investigator. It's my job to work out exactly what happened and ascertain with the greatest possible likelihood who was responsible. Are you with me?'

'It sounds reasonable.'

'And if we suppose that those three killings weren't carried out by any human being, that means they can only have been carried out by something that wasn't human. That follows, doesn't it?'

I said nothing. He gave a faint smile.

'I realise you probably think I'm raving mad. But consider it from my angle. We've got this ritual – devil worship. We've got three devil worshippers murdered. The killings have been carried out in such a way that no human being could possibly be responsible. This isn't in the public domain, but I can tell you now that the victims' heads had been wrenched back so violently that the faces of those young men were looking down their own backs. After I saw the image I've just shown you, which you must admit is mysterious to say the least, I set about doing a bit of research into the Devil as he appears in the literature. And because the killings were of such a ritual nature, I thought there was a good chance I might find some kind of precedent – an inspiration, if you like. Lo and behold, I came upon an account by one Philipp Melanchthon concerning the killing of the historical Faust. You know who Melanchthon was?'

'Of course.'

'I didn't. But do you know how Faust was killed?'

'No – but I can guess.'

'He was grievously mutilated – his head was wrenched so violently that his face was twisted against his back. It was the Devil who did it.'

I didn't know what to say. He actually believed it!

'You think whoever killed those three young men might have read the same thing?'

'It would be natural to assume so, yes. But then we have the image, we have the physical impossibility of the method. And in that light, another thought occurs, does it not?'

'And so you came to see a priest to find out if the Devil actually exists?'

'What I wanted to find out was how you viewed the possibility, yes. But I also wanted to talk to someone about it. Can you imagine what would happen if I put such a theory forward to my colleagues?'

I laughed.

'I'm sorry. I wish I could be of more help, but I'm afraid I can't. The Devil almost certainly does not exist in any concrete form.'

'I'll consider that,' he said, and got to his feet. 'I hope you understand. I'm not saying that the Devil does exist. Only that the possibility can't be entirely excluded.'

My meeting with the policeman seemed to me more and more absurd as the day wore on, to the point where I began to wonder if it had even taken place. Or had it been some deranged practical joke?

After the children had been put to bed, Gaute and I sat out on the veranda. He told me a little about his day, I told him a little about mine. After that, we sat without speaking for some time. I stole the occasional glance at him as he gazed out over the surrounding houses. He looked so mournful when he thought himself unobserved or when he wasn't engaged in conversation. The corners of his mouth drooped; it was age, but the sadness in his eyes was something else. I could only think that it was me.

'What did the police want with you, anyway?'

'It was nothing. A misunderstanding, that's all.'

'What had they misunderstood?'

'I can't talk about it. Professional secrecy. But it really was nothing.'

'Aha.'

I lay awake for a long time that night. My conversation with the policeman had unsettled me. I didn't believe in any devil, never had done, and didn't now. It was a bizarre notion, a primitive hangover from prehistoric times when the distinction between man and beast, flesh and spirit, was tenuous to the point of hardly existing at all. And yet it unsettled me. It was as if the mere thought, his entertaining of the idea that the Devil actually existed, made everything else seem trivial and stupid, and all that was human, the ordinary things we did and said, became cast in a doomful light. I couldn't quite grasp exactly what it was that I felt, or why, but it had to do with just that. And it had to do too with the little child that was now inside me. Because that child would be born into this same world. It deserved hope, joy, light, a future.

Quietly, I got out of bed, pulled on a T-shirt and crept downstairs. In the kitchen, I filled a glass with water and took it out onto the veranda with me.

Only You, God, can save us.

As soon as the words had come to me, I knew I did not believe in God.

We were all alone.

For some days I'd been telling myself that my appetite would return of its own accord, but the next morning when I looked at myself in the mirror I could see I was too thin and that I would have to make an effort to eat – it wasn't just my body that mattered now, I had a child to think about that needed nutrition.

Weren't eggs supposed to be one of the most nutritious foods there were?

I boiled four for my breakfast, but had barely eaten one before I felt sick. A glass of orange juice instead of water.

Gaute was cheerful and chatty, his thick mop of curls danced when he laughed or moved his head suddenly. The children of course loved him, probably more than they loved me. His students loved him too. All my friends thought he was wonderful.

I stroked my hand over his back when we kissed each other before he went off to work, then held his neck and kissed him again.

'I love you,' I whispered to him.

'What did you whisper to Daddy, Mummy?' said Marie.

'Never you mind, little Miss Curious!'

I finished my sermon before lunchtime. My thoughts of the night before felt so acute that I worked them into the text. The theme actually belonged to Easter, but I posited a division between ritual doubt and real doubt, calling it everyday doubt, the sort that suddenly imposes on everyday life, which it seems then to threaten from the inside. Doubt belonged to faith and was perhaps its most important component, since it was from the interface of those two states, the point where they came together, that the power sprang – the power of faith.

But I hadn't simply fallen into doubt that night. It was more than that – I had known. Had I not?

It could be argued that knowledge, bedrock-like certainty, came from God, and that uncertainty, doubt and ignorance were diabolical forces. It was an ancient notion, for when a person who knows suddenly doubts, it is as if something or someone has come between that person and the world, causing it to fall apart as a result. But the most fundamental doubt of all – was that not the doubt expressed by Jesus as he hung dying on the cross, maligned and tortured, and cried out that most gruesome of questions: *My God, my God, why hast Thou forsaken me?*

It happened in darkness. From the sixth hour there was darkness all over the land, the gospel said, unto the ninth hour. And about the ninth hour Jesus cried out – and was dead.

Eloi, Eloi, lama sabachthani?

Christianity was the religion of doubt. Jesus's question could be found too in the Old Testament, in the Book of Psalms, but the concept was not by any measure central to Judaism, the way it became to Christianity by virtue of those momentous final words on the cross. Oddly, doubt became ritualised there, in the message of Easter, and became both elevated and firm. But to Jesus, in that moment on the cross, it was anything but.

Doubt is alive. In doubt there is movement. God stands beyond doubt, but we do not. God does not seek, we do, and we seek not what we know, but what we know not.

I gained clarity when I wrote, and was able to accept the enormous comfort that lay in Christ's despair, and I ended my sermon with that insight. I read through it, decided I was satisfied, changed into a light cotton dress, put on my sandals, made sure I had everything with me in my bag, and went out. It was cloudy, though warm and humid. I decided to leave the car and instead took the bus into town and walked from the station and up the hill to the university.

I arrived in good time and sat down on a bench outside the library. I realised then that I should have told Gaute where I was going. Someone he knew might see me and mention it to him, he would wonder why I hadn't said anything – the university wasn't a place I frequented, so wouldn't it be natural for me to have told him I was going there? He would think I was hiding something. What was there to hide? I was meeting a professor, and he was a man.

No, it was too much consideration, I couldn't start thinking like that.

Anyway, it was too late now. It would be odd for me to phone only to tell him I was at the university. I could just hear him: Why didn't you say anything before?

I would tell him about the talk at some later point, there was no need to mention a preliminary meeting.

I texted Mum to see if everything was all right. I shouldn't have done, because she called me only a moment later.

'Kathrine,' she said, 'thanks for your concern.'

'No need for thanks, really.'

'There's something seriously wrong here. That's why I'm phoning you. It's too complicated for a text message.'

'Is it Mikael?'

'Yes. You know, yesterday he wanted white wine. You saw that, didn't you?'

'Yes?'

'He's always disliked white wine intensely. Always stuck to red.'

'Mum, that doesn't have to mean anything.'

'I know that, dear. But then he sat up all night in the study. He's never done that before. I know, I know, it doesn't have to mean anything. But then this morning, while he was asleep, I looked at his search history. He'd made searches for a lot of names. A great many, Kathrine. And all were Hungarian. I googled some of them myself. Most were a dead end, the rest led to people who had absolutely nothing in common, nothing at all to indicate why he was interested in them. They weren't writers or photographers or artists. They were ordinary people.'

'Perhaps he's working on some project he doesn't want to tell you about.'

'*And* – he's drinking milk at breakfast.'

I laughed.

'It's nothing to laugh about, Kathrine.'

'No, I'm sorry. But listen, it's nothing to worry about either. I saw him, and he was still himself. Perhaps he was in love with someone from Hungary when he was young, and never told you. And now the stroke has set him off.'

'Yes, that's exactly what I mean. He's changed, his personality has changed. How am I going to live with that?'

'Mum, he's the same person he's always been. Drinking milk and white wine all of a sudden isn't exactly devastating.'

'I'm not so sure. But thanks for listening, anyway.'

I got up and went over to where the department was located in a yellow-washed brick building with green ivy climbing up the walls. Students passed in and out of its doors, crossed the Museum square, sat on the benches of the gardens, and a feeling of nostalgia rose in me, I remembered so well what it had all been like, a time when everything had stood wide open to us without our knowing, because all we could do was be a part of it. A time when there was so much to be savoured, and yet we could not savour, for we were oblivious.

Gjeving's office was on the first floor. I knocked on the door. There was no answer and I looked at the time. I was on the dot.

I looked around. A lanky, long-limbed young man came loping along the corridor. Fair, shoulder-length hair, white shirt, beige trousers.

'Excuse me,' I said, 'do you know where I can find Arne Gjeving?'

'Arne? No, I'm sorry. Is he not in his office?'

'He isn't, no.'

'And you've got an appointment with him now?'

'Yes.'

'I can give him a ring if you like.'

'That would be good.'

He pulled his phone out of his pocket and scrolled until finding the number.

'Arne! There's a visitor waiting for you outside your door. Where are you?'

He listened.

'That's right. Yes, I'll tell her. OK. See you later!'

He slipped the phone back into his pocket.

'He's on his way. Five minutes, he said. And you're welcome to wait inside. I'm instructed to bring you anything you want. Coffee? Something cold, perhaps?'

'No, I'm fine, thanks.'

'OK,' he said. 'But shout out if you need anything. I'm only next door.'

With a wide smile he opened the door of his own office and went inside, while I went into Gjeving's, leaving the door open so as not to be caught unawares when he arrived.

The room was quite small. There was a desk by the window, a chair with an occasional table next to it up against one wall, and of course books everywhere. I scanned the titles on the shelves. He had several works by Scholem, I noticed – *Major Trends in Jewish Mysticism, Sabbatai Sevi, Origins of the Kabbalah*. Three thick volumes entitled *The Realm of the Dead: A World History*. A number of treatises on Greek drama. The complete Plato. Several editions of the *Iliad* and the *Odyssey*. The Nag Hammadi scriptures were there. A fair amount of German philosophy – Hegel, Nietzsche, Heidegger, Sloterdijk. Some French philosophers too – Bataille, Foucault, Derrida. Not that many novels, though he did have the collected works of both Bjørnson and Undset, some Ibsen and some Hamsun.

I sat down.

Five minutes could mean five minutes or twenty. It depended on what sort of person he was.

It wouldn't look good if I was staring at my phone when he turned up, so I got up again and looked for a book that could occupy me in the meantime. I picked out one of Bataille's entitled *The Sacred Conspiracy* and had just sat down with a random page when a tall figure appeared in the corridor outside. He was carrying a rather battered leather briefcase in one hand, a bicycle helmet in the other. His face opened into a smile, and he raised the briefcase in a form of greeting. I put the book down on the table and stood up.

'Hello!' he said. 'Very good of you to come! Sorry I'm a bit late. I had this stupid idea I'd cycle in today, of all days. It turns out I'm not quite as fit as I was the last time I tried, and that's putting it mildly.'

He put his bag down on the floor, the helmet on the desk, and extended a large hand to take mine in a firm handshake. But it was his eyes I noticed the most. They were unusually blue. Accentuated no doubt by his face being so tanned.

I hadn't expected a *handsome* professor.

'Thanks again for coming.'

'It's no trouble, really.'

'Did Henning get you some coffee?'

'He offered me some, yes.'

'But in this heat . . .'

'Indeed.'

'Please, do sit down,' he said, half leaning against, half sitting on the edge of his desk. He indicated the book I'd put down on the table. 'Ah, interesting choice! They had a kind of an Orphic sect going on back in the fifties, Bataille and his mates. Have you heard about it?'

'No, I haven't.'

'I'll spare you a lecture – an occupational hazard, I'm afraid.' He smiled. 'But you're welcome to borrow it, in case you're interested.'

'It's OK. Thanks all the same. It does look interesting, though.'

'Say the word, incidentally, if there's any literature you need for your talk, and I'll make sure you get it. But we can come to that later on. How about some lunch?'

I nodded and he led the way to the canteen at the other end of the building. I felt a bit like a student again standing in the queue with my tray. We sat down at a table over by the window. He acknowledged a few students and by the way they connected with him I could tell he was a popular lecturer.

I regretted I'd come. A meeting hadn't really been necessary and I didn't care much for being a foreign body, as I was here.

What had I been thinking?

That it would be good to remove myself a bit from the familiar.

'What was your thesis on when you did your theology degree?' he said.

'It was about sacrifice.'

'Really? Fascinating subject. Old or New Testament?'

'Both, actually. I relied a lot on Girard. Have you read him?'

'Indeed, and with great benefit. A long time ago now, though!'

'Same here.'

'Bataille makes good sense now. That society he formed, which I mentioned just before – it's what the book you picked off my shelf is about – seriously entertained carrying out human sacrifice. They never went through with it, but as I understand it they came pretty close.'

'Perhaps I should borrow it after all,' I said. 'I haven't given the subject much thought in twenty years.'

We began to eat. I had to force my salad down, while he seemed to encounter no such problems with his dish of sausage and chips, which he devoured with gusto.

'About the talk,' he said. 'It's completely up to you, of course. Any angle you like.'

'As long as it's about the Church's take on life after death?'

'Precisely,' he said. 'What *is* the Church's take?'

He wiped the corners of his mouth with his napkin and drank a mouthful of water before looking at me.

'That's in the Confession of Faith.'

'I believe in the Holy Spirit, the holy catholic Church, the communion of saints, the forgiveness of sins, the resurrection of the body, and the life everlasting?'

'You've done your homework,' I said, and smiled.

He smiled back.

'But do you *believe* in it?' he said. 'The resurrection of the body and the life everlasting?'

'That's the belief of the Church, yes.'

'What about you personally – do *you* believe in it?'

I met his gaze and didn't know what to say.

'What we're talking about is of course the crux of the faith,' I began. 'But the Church doesn't deal in literal theology any more. What I thought I might do – and this is actually one of the reasons I took you up on your invite – is to trace the faith back to its origins.'

'That sounds excellent. Perfect, in fact. You know, we read, it's what we do here. We read texts and put them into context. But promise me you won't put too much work into it. These things can easily become a case of pearls before swine.'

'No danger of that, I assure you,' I said with a laugh. He gazed at me, smiling.

'Are you sure you don't want to borrow that book? It does very much sound like you'd find it interesting.'

I knew I couldn't contain Bataille just at the moment, but to decline his offer again would come across a bit demonstrative. Besides, borrowing it didn't mean I actually had to read it. And if I did borrow it, I'd have to return it. Which would be a reason to come back to his office again.

It was a thought that would lead only to catastrophe. It had to be killed, NOW.

I popped the book into my bag, shook his hand again and went down into town to look in the shops for a short while before walking back to the church, strangely dispirited and elevated at the same time.

By the time I got home in the afternoon I was so tired I immediately went and had a lie-down. I set the alarm to ring after half an hour, only to sleep through and wake up in darkness in the middle of the night. Gaute was fast asleep beside me. I was desperately hungry, it was as if something were screaming inside me. I crept downstairs to find something I could eat. He'd kept some dinner for me on a plate he'd covered with tinfoil and put in the fridge. I took it out and my hands trembled as I removed the foil.

Lamb chops.

I didn't bother with the potatoes or the vegetables, but went straight for the meat, attacking first one then the other two chops. It was far from sufficient. In the fridge, I discovered another two and ate them as well. Ravenous, I searched for something more. Not bread or fruit or vegetables, it had to be meat. There – thank God – an unopened packet of salami. I pricked a hole in the plastic with a knife and made an incision along the length of the skin, tore it from the meat and went out onto the veranda with the thick, unclad sausage in my hand. The salty taste, the consistency were heavenly, the teeth sinking into the meat, the onrush of flavour.

The night was completely dark now and I went inside to switch on the outdoor lamp when suddenly it struck me that something wasn't right. The sky was cloudless, the veranda should have been illuminated by the light of the star. But it wasn't.

I looked up. There was no star.

In the same instant, the food came up again. I hadn't a chance to stop it and could only bend forward and sick it all onto the decking.

TOVE

'Are you normal now?' Heming asked. He looked at me from where he was standing, in the middle of the room, his arms limply at his sides.

I did the one thing I shouldn't – I started to cry, then reached out to him. He came to me, and I held his thin, reluctant body against mine.

'Come, Asle, you too,' I said.

Asle slipped from his father's side and joined us. Arne remained standing, watching our embrace. With my arms around the boys, I looked up and met his gaze. His eyes were cheerless.

'I'm very sorry about everything that happened,' I said to the boys. 'I wasn't myself. Can you understand?'

'Who were you, then?' said Heming.

'I was no one. I didn't know what I was saying or doing. But I'm well again now.'

'Completely well?' said Asle.

'Yes.'

I could tell by looking at Arne that he didn't want me making promises.

'So are you coming home now?' said Heming.

'I have to see the doctor tomorrow. If he says it's all right, which I'm certain he will, then I'll be coming home straight away.'

'Are we coming to fetch you?'

'I hope so,' I said, and looked at Arne, who nodded.

'Yes, we are,' he said.

After they'd gone, I lay down on the bed and tried to sleep. It was my only respite from the thoughts in my head. But sleep wouldn't come, and so I got up and went to the duty room to get my lighter, then stood in the glass smoking booth and smoked two cigarettes. The hyper little Serb came in while I was still standing there. He sucked so hard on his cigarette that his eyes bulged, and then spat on the floor. I didn't say anything and concentrated on avoiding his stare.

'Whore,' he said.

I stubbed out my smoke and handed the lighter back to the care assistant in the duty room. I went and sat down in front of the TV in the recreation room. There was some athletics on. People running as fast as they could in bright sunshine. The Serb came in and sat down next to me.

'Whore,' he said.

I should have gone to the care assistant and reported him for harrassing me, but I couldn't be bothered and decided to go back to my room. The young red-haired girl watched me from over by the window where she was standing. She had such a faraway look in her eyes, which occasionally would darken into anger. Ines, her name was, she was a law student. We'd talked to each other briefly that morning and since then it was as if she'd attached herself to me. She didn't say anything, just followed me with her eyes. It was often the way: the moment I was back on the level, I became aware of the needs of those around me, and I suppose it became apparent then too that I was a person capable of embracing others. In any case, they would come to me then. But not before.

I had screamed and hit someone. Here. In this corridor.

The shame I felt was so fierce it left no room for anything else. That burning shame was all I was.

From the room next to mine, the silent young man whose name was Jesper appeared. His uniformed police minder followed. I stood back against the wall to let them past.

He was shut inside himself, saw nothing, heard nothing, his face pale, near-white, without a flicker.

I stepped into my room as they went through into the toilets.

He hadn't said a word to anyone since he'd been admitted.

I lay down on the bed. The doctor would ask me tomorrow if I'd been having thoughts about suicide. I would tell him I hadn't. In one way it would be true. In another it wouldn't. When it hurt so much to be alive, why go on?

My children.

It wasn't for their sake. They'd be better off without me. It was for my sake. I couldn't bear the thought of losing them.

That meant I was well again.

I half expected to hear the voice cut in. It was an opportune moment.

But it didn't.

I *was* well. All that remained of my illness now was shame.

Something vaguely akin to joy tingled faintly in me and travelled through my chest. It reached my stomach and I trembled. Strings of anxiety vibrated inside me.

There was a knock on the door and I sat up. It was Aron, my contact person.

'Phone call for you,' he said.

'Who is it?'

'Arne.'

I went out to the phone at the end of the corridor. He'd only just been here. I suspected the only reason he was calling was to give the impression he was a good and caring partner. He knew they registered incoming calls. He didn't want people to think he was the sort who would let his wife down.

'How's things?' he said.

'Fine,' I said. 'I'm feeling a bit embarrassed about myself, but that's only to be expected.'

'Yes.'

'I feel terrible for the boys. I'm so afraid all this is harming them. Scared stiff, in fact. Heming's tics have got worse. Asle's retreating.'

'There's nothing wrong with them. They're as fine as can be.'

It was his way of saying he was a good and responsible father and that that was the main factor in their continued health, not that they had a mother who was mad.

'I hope you're right,' I said. 'Why didn't Ingvild come?'

'She was with friends. You'll see her tomorrow.'

'Yes.'

Neither of us spoke for a moment. An elderly man by the name of Einar shuffled past as if in a trance. He was from Stavanger.

'Are you angry with me, Arne?'

'No.'

'Are you sure?'

'Yes.'

Nothing about it not being my fault. Nothing about me having been ill.

'I think you are,' I said. 'And do you know what? I understand. I really do.'

'Nice to hear you're self-reflecting again.'

Another silence.

'I want you to know how much I appreciate everything you do for me and the kids,' I said.

'That's all right.'

'And how grateful I am that you got me transferred here. I haven't thanked you for that.'

'That was my mother.'

'Sorry?'

'My mother arranged for it.'

'I didn't think she liked me.'

'You're mother to her grandchildren.'

'That's true.'

Jesper came out into the corridor, his policeman behind him. This time he didn't look down. He looked at me.

I looked away – there was something so unsettling about him. It was impossible to tell what he might do if he felt he'd made contact with me.

'Tell me something.'

'How do you mean?'

'Something dull and ordinary. Like what you've been doing today.'

'I cycled in to work and came late for a meeting. The boys and I went down to the fjord for a swim after we'd been to see you.'

Jesper stopped in front of me. I turned away and faced the wall.

'Isn't it too cold to swim in the fjord now?'

I glanced to see the policeman steer him back towards his room.

'Not after the summer we've just had.'

'What else did you do?'

'That was all.'

'And term's in full swing now?'

'Yes. But listen, we can talk about all that tomorrow. I need to get the dinner ready now. Take care of yourself.'

'You too,' I said.

It would be dinner time where I was too before long. I wasn't hungry, but having something to do was better than having nothing. Talking to Arne had kept my worst thoughts at bay. As soon as we hung up they came flooding back. My feelings of shame and guilt were so overpowering it was as if all hope dissolved in them. I was destroying my children. I was destroying my marriage. I said and did the most terrible things.

I had offered myself to Egil with my children hardly more than a stone's throw away.

I went to the dining room. Three people were eating. I hadn't spoken to any of them. A sad-eyed bearded man in his thirties. A plump woman in her sixties who kept humming to herself. A woman my own age with a moonlike face and bulging eyes.

I sat down, buttered a piece of bread and laid a slice of cooked meat on top. None of the others even looked at me. I vividly remembered the demons and the dead I had seen, but the children were blanked out, even though they'd been there too. I remembered that Arne had been among the dead, and how terrible it had been when he forced me into the car. After that, everything was completely dark. But of course I knew what had happened. They'd filled me with drugs that had knocked me out completely, and kept on filling me with them until eventually I'd come to my senses on the ward here and emerged from the psychosis.

This was the true hell. Not what I'd seen. But this. Waking up to what I'd done.

The sad-eyed man met my gaze and smiled. The humming woman expelled a groan.

I ate my bread, then went into the recreation room. One or two patients were watching TV, a couple more moved restlessly about, another stood looking out of the window with his hands behind his back. There was an uneasiness in the air. Or perhaps it was just me, I thought, and went back to my room. All I wanted was to lie down on my bed and cry, to open the sluices of darkness. But inside I was dry and barren.

Everything had come to a halt. Not only time, which stood quite as still as I now lay, but life itself.

What kept life moving if not hope? Without hope, there was no future. Without a future, there was no momentum. Without momentum, there was no life.

Again I expected to hear the voice, interjecting with something ironic.

But the voice was quiet. I was well.

Despondent, but well.

Someone started shouting and screaming. Seconds later came the sound of running footsteps in the corridor, staff hurrying to the scene.

So much aggression was collected here. So much anger.

And the opposite too, an apathy almost without bounds, which no one could do a thing about.

I supposed it was a reaction.

I missed Ingvild dreadfully.

I couldn't lose her. I couldn't.

Should I phone?

No, I'd be seeing her tomorrow. Best not to burden her now.

I would see her on the outside, where everything was normal. Where I was normal, too.

I picked up the book Arne had brought me, made myself comfortable with a pillow in my back and tried to read a little – I'd be able to tell him that much, at least. It was a collection of Virginia Woolf's writings on the visual arts – *Oh, to Be a Painter!* it was called.

The consideration that lay in his gesture made me cry.

Perhaps not everything was destroyed.

I dried my eyes on the duvet and leafed through the book, finding a piece about Sickert, whom I loved, but I couldn't concentrate and soon put it down again.

Things had calmed down out there now. There wasn't a sound to be heard.

I closed my eyes and lay with my hands folded on my chest, but the corpse-like position perturbed me, and I turned onto my side instead.

Again I expected the voice.

But someone knocked.

'Tove?' they said softly, and knocked once more.

'Yes?' I said, and sat up as the door opened.

It was Jesper.

'You're *speaking*!'

'I've been instructed to bring you a final greeting.'

'A greeting? Who from?'

He jerked his head back and gaped like a fish. Three times in quick succession he gaped, then turned his face to me.

'He's leaving now, with the ones of his kind. He says goodbye, and that your task will be revealed to you.'

My heart raced in my chest.

'I don't know what you're talking about,' I said. 'You're insane.'

'Come,' he said. 'Come with me and you'll see.'

I followed him out into the corridor. All was quiet. Outside his door, the policeman sat sleeping on a chair, his head tipped back against the wall. Jesper smiled.

'Come with me and you'll see,' he said again.

And I went with him. Through the corridor, into the still and empty recreation room, to the window. Outside: the fell sloping steeply towards the fjord, the fjord, the fells across the water, the sky above, where the star was shining.

And then it shone no more.

Thanks to Kenneth Jan Hugdahl, Bjørnar Lia and Kristin Ørstavik for their careful readings and constructive suggestions – all remaining errors and shortcomings, failings and flaws are of course entirely my own. Thanks to Espen Stueland, Monika Fagerholm, Kjersti Instefjord, Greger Ulf Nilson, Yngve Knausgård, Bjørn Arild and Kari Ersland for their own insightful readings along the way. Thanks to Andrew Wylie and Charles Buchan, to everyone at Forlaget Oktober, and to Åsmund Forfang, Christian Heyerdahl and Sissel Sommer Steneby for their astute and discerning aid in matters of language. A special thank you to Mamma Andersson for her unique paintings. Last, but not least, thanks to the Norwegian editor of it all, Geir Gulliksen – without his help there would be no book.

While working on this novel I've made frequent use of Adrian Owen's *Into the Grey Zone* and *Sizing up Consciousness* by Marcello Massimini and Giulio Tononi. For all other literature I've enjoyed and benefited from during the writing, the reader is directed to the bibliography at www.themorningstar.no.

For the purposes of this English edition, Erlend's translation of the passage from Leviticus on pp. 452–3 has been taken from the International Standard Version (ISV).

THE LEOPARD

The leopard is one of Harvill's historic colophons and an imprimatur of the highest quality literature from around the world.

When The Harvill Press was founded in 1946 by former Foreign Office colleagues Manya Harari and Marjorie Villiers (hence Har-vill), it was with the express intention of rebuilding cultural bridges after the Second World War. As their first catalogue set out: 'The editors believe that by producing translations of important books they are helping to overcome the barriers, which at present are still big, to close interchange of ideas between people who are divided by frontiers.' The press went on to publish from many different languages, with highlights including Giuseppe Tomasi di Lampedusa's *The Leopard*, Boris Pasternak's *Doctor Zhivago*, José Saramago's *Blindness*, W. G. Sebald's *The Rings of Saturn*, Henning Mankell's *Faceless Killers* and Haruki Murakami's *Norwegian Wood*.

In 2005 The Harvill Press joined with Secker & Warburg, a publisher with its own illustrious history of publishing international writers. In 2020, Harvill Secker reintroduced the leopard to launch a new translated series celebrating some of the finest and most exciting voices of the twenty-first century.

Pedro Almodóvar: *The Last Dream*
trans. Frank Wynne
Laurent Binet: *Civilisations*
trans. Sam Taylor
Paolo Cognetti: *The Lovers*
trans. Stash Luczkiw
Paolo Cognetti: *Without Ever Reaching the Summit*
trans. Stash Luczkiw
Pauline Delabroy-Allard: *All About Sarah*
trans. Adriana Hunter

Álvaro Enrigue: *You Dreamed of Empires*
trans. Natasha Wimmer
Urs Faes: *Twelve Nights*
trans. Jamie Lee Searle
María Gainza: *Portrait of an Unknown Lady*
trans. Thomas Bunstead
Stefan Hertmans: *The Ascent*
trans. David McKay
Mayumi Inaba: *Mornings With My Cat Mii*
trans. Ginny Tapley Takemori
Ismail Kadare: *A Dictator Calls*
trans. John Hodgson
Ismail Kadare: *The Doll*
trans. John Hodgson
Jonas Hassen Khemiri: *The Family Clause*
trans. Alice Menzies
Karl Ove Knausgaard: *In the Land of the Cyclops: Essays*
trans. Martin Aitken
Karl Ove Knausgaard: *The Morning Star*
trans. Martin Aitken
Karl Ove Knausgaard: *The Wolves of Eternity*
trans. Martin Aitken
Karl Ove Knausgaard: *The Third Realm*
trans. Martin Aitken
Antoine Leiris: *Life, After*
trans. Sam Taylor
Édouard Louis: *A Woman's Battles and Transformations*
trans. Tash Aw
Édouard Louis: *Change: A Method*
trans. John Lambert
Geert Mak: *The Dream of Europe: Travels in the Twenty-First Century*
trans. Liz Waters
Layla Martínez: *Woodworm*
trans. Sophie Hughes & Annie McDermott
Haruki Murakami: *First Person Singular: Stories*
trans. Philip Gabriel

Haruki Murakami: *Murakami T: The T-Shirts I Love*
trans. Philip Gabriel
Haruki Murakami: *Novelist as a Vocation*
trans. Philip Gabriel & Ted Goossen
Ngũgĩ wa Thiong'o: *The Perfect Nine: The Epic of Gĩkũyũ and Mũmbi*
trans. the author
Kristín Ómarsdóttir: *Swanfolk*
trans. Vala Thorodds
Intan Paramaditha: *The Wandering*
trans. Stephen J. Epstein
Per Petterson: *Men in My Situation*
trans. Ingvild Burkey
Andrey Platonov: *Chevengur*
trans. Robert Chandler & Elizabeth Chandler
Mohamed Mbougar Sarr: *The Most Secret Memory of Men*
trans. Lara Vergnaud
Dima Wannous: *The Frightened Ones*
trans. Elisabeth Jaquette
Emi Yagi: *Diary of a Void*
trans. David Boyd & Lucy North

Karl Ove Knausgaard's My Struggle cycle has been heralded as a masterpiece all over the world. From *A Death in the Family* to *The End*, the novels move through childhood into adulthood and, together, form an enthralling portrait of human life. Knausgaard has been awarded the Norwegian Critics Prize for Literature, the Brage Prize and the Jerusalem Prize. His work, which also includes *Out of the World*, *A Time for Everything* and the Seasons Quartet, is published in thirty-five languages. His most recent, highly acclaimed Morning Star series includes the novels *The Morning Star*, *The Wolves of Eternity* and *The Third Realm*.

Martin Aitken's translations of Scandinavian literature number some thirty-five books. His work has appeared on the shortlists of the International Dublin Literary Award (2017) and the US National Book Awards (2018), as well as the 2021 International Booker Prize. He received the PEN America Translation Prize in 2019.